$\mathcal{V}$OICES OF THE $\mathcal{S}$OUTH

THE FINISHED MAN

Also by George Garrett

Fiction
King of the Mountain
In the Briar Patch
Which Ones Are the Enemy?
Cold Ground Was My Bed Last Night
Do, Lord, Remember Me
A Wreath for Garibaldi and Other Stories
Death of the Fox
The Magic Striptease
The Succession: A Novel of Elizabeth and James
Poison Pen
Entered from the Sun
The King of Babylon Shall Not Come Against You

Poetry
The Reverend Ghost
The Sleeping Gypsy and Other Poems
Abraham's Knife and Other Poems
Welcome to the Medicine Show
Luck's Shining Child
The Collected Poems of George Garrett
Days of Our Lives Lie in Fragments

Plays
Sir Slob and the Princess: A Play for Children
Enchanted Ground

Nonfiction
James Jones
Understanding Mary Lee Settle
The Sorrows of Fat City
Whistling in the Dark
My Silk Purse and Yours

THE FINISHED MAN

George Garrett

LOUISIANA STATE UNIVERSITY PRESS

Baton Rouge

Copyright © 1959 by George Garrett
Originally published by Charles Scribner's Sons
LSU Press edition published 2000 by arrangement with the author
All rights reserved
Manufactured in the United States of America

09 08 07 06 05 04 03 02 01 00
5 4 3 2 1

Lines from "A Dialogue of Self and Soul" are from the *Collected Poems* of William Butler Yeats, copyright © 1933 The Macmillan Company. They are used with the kind permission of The Macmillan Company, New York, Mrs. William Butler Yeats, and The Macmillan Company of Canada, Ltd.

Library of Congress Cataloging-in-Publication Data

Garrett, George P., 1929–
    The finished man / George Garrett.
      p. cm. — (Voices of the South)
    Originally published: Charles Scribner's Sons, 1959.
    ISBN 0-8071-2632-2 (paper)
    1. Florida—Fiction. I. Title. II. Series.

PS3557.A72F54 2000
813'.54—dc21

                                                      00-058170

The paper in this book meets the guidelines for permanence and durability of the Committee on Production Guidelines for Book Longevity of the Council on Library Resources. ∞

FOR SUSAN

A living man is blind and drinks his drop.
What matter if the ditches are impure?
What matter if I live it all once more;
Endure that toil of growing up;
The ignominy of boyhood; the distress
Of boyhood changing into man;
The unfinished man and his pain
Brought face to face with his own clumsiness;
The finished man among his enemies?

            YEATS—"A Dialogue of Self and Soul"

He usually continues in office until a worse can be found; but the very moment he is discarded, his successor, at the head of all the Yahoos *in the district, young and old, male and female, come in a body, and discharge their excrements upon him from head to foot. But how far this might be applicable to our courts, and favorites, and ministers of state, my master said I could best determine.*

            SWIFT—*Gulliver's Travels*

PROLOGUE

PROLOGUE

The Senator had just begun to speak. He bowed to the Mayor who had introduced him, and he stepped forward on the flag-draped platform, leaned, long-armed, smiling and relaxed on the speaker's podium, and he looked out into the clotted shirt-sleeves and summer dresses, the little field of faces, black and white, that were close-pressed and tilted up and toward him like wild flowers in a light breeze. He started with a joke. His voice crackled over the loudspeaker, and then he threw back his head to laugh with them, squinting under half-closed lids. As they laughed his face changed. His mouth tightened and turned down. The high angle of his cheekbones, the soft hound's eyes, the thicket of unruly hair, the ruddy, splotched complexion became no longer clownish, but, in a wink of time, the rude composite pieces of a tragic mask. Their laughter dwindled and the Senator moved closer to the nickel-bright microphones and their tangled web of dark wires and began to talk in a soft voice all of them knew.

It was at that moment that the loudspeaker whistled and clouded his words with static. The Mayor, a fat, fussy, grinning, kindly man, stepped up beside him to fiddle with the microphones, for a second shielding the Senator by his bulk. And it was precisely at that instant that the young Negro in the crowd raised a pistol and fired twice quickly before it was struck from his hand and fell, and those standing nearby scattered back and away from the listless weapon as if it were a live thing freed from a cage, as if somebody had turned a snake loose among them. Both shots struck the Mayor and he sat down hard, his soft full moon of a face wrinkled in pain and astonishment, shaking his head.

The Senator knelt beside him, and the young man, the Senator's man, came running from his chair at the back of the platform to kneel there too, shouting something which was lost in the surge of sound that came from the crowd now, a sound like rough surf.

Where they had recoiled, the crowd rushed forward again, as if poured into the tense void they had created, in the center of which the Negro stood, limp, his head bowed, like a man praying on his feet. They came with a fury of fists and feet, of flailing arms. And he collapsed under the sudden weight of them. But a policeman, a Lieutenant, a burly young man in a creased and tailored, immaculate blue uniform, black boots and belt glistening from care, charged into the ragged vortex. His whistle shrieked above their rage, and his shiny pistol winked in the light like a naked blade. They stepped back again. The Lieutenant seized the Negro, now sprawled in the tramped dirt, lax as a drowned man, hoisted his sagging body in the crook of one arm and dragged him clear, still blowing on his whistle, still waving his gun. He moved along slowly, dragging the man with him, across the park to a police car at the curb. The crowd fell back, silent, as he passed. Only when the car started, swirled away and out of reach in a wide u-turn with its siren screaming, only then did the fury of them find its voice again.

Then there was another siren, more distant, but coming toward them, the ambulance coming from the hospital.

The Mayor was still sitting up, hidden from sight by the podium with its microphones that still wheezed and coughed with static. His face was softened, a mask of pure dismay. His white shirt, taut over the slope of his belly, was soaked with blood. He shook his head and mumbled to himself. On one side of him knelt the Senator and on the other the young man, holding him in their arms. The siren coming toward them grew louder, came nearer, stopped suddenly, and they could hear the doors open and shut and a sound of running. They turned to look directly at each other, only their heads moving, their kneeling bodies, their posture remaining as rigid and stylized as a pair of bookends.

"I think that was meant for me," the Senator said.

"Maybe so."

"Why? Why would somebody do a thing like that?"

The young man was going to say something, but both of them were firmly eased aside by the ambulance driver and his assistant. The Mayor was placed on the stretcher. He lay back easy and closed his eyes. They picked up the stretcher and might even have run with it, but a doctor who had worked his way up from the crowd by that time grabbed the driver's arm.

"Take your time, boy," he said. "He's gone now."

I. BEGINNING: WITNESS

And when he came to himself, he said, How many hired servants of my father's have bread enough and to spare, and I perish with hunger!

LUKE 15:17

For Mike it had started a few months before in Oakland when he parked his car and came out of the hot Florida dance and glare of light and into the settled shade of the Osceola Hotel lobby. There for a moment, as he blinked his eyes, the world seemed flooded with shadows, under water. The same old-fashioned overhead fans, like listless oars, like tired wings, rippled the air, still coarse and rich with the ghostly odors of cigars, still somehow faintly warm and stale from already forgotten voices, the captured vibrancy of whispered secrets and the easy jokes of the dead. The potted palms were limp as old money. The heavy, uncomfortable, and always solid furniture had endured, loomed out of past decades like a platoon of uncles and grandfathers with gold watches, with vests, with stiff high collars. The sole glint of the day's brightness came from the brass spittoons, discretely placed. To come back now, after a long time, to open a glass door and walk into a room at once known and strange was as if, by drinking some magic potion, to shrink out of the flesh and blood of the grown man and become the child who had been knee-high and wide-eyed in the tall world.

Mike crossed the lobby and leaned on the counter and waited, staring at the desk clerk's thin inevitable back and the array of pigeonholes for keys, for all kinds of mail and messages. Then the clerk turned around, a young man about his own age, presenting the bland unruffled mask of his calling—like *croupiers*, Mike thought, like undertakers, like a high-class pimp.

"I'm here for Senator Parker," Mike said. "I just thought I'd check in and be sure that you're all set."

The clerk smiled briefly, tolerantly.

"We're all ready," the clerk said. "Any time he arrives. Will you be staying with the Senator's party?"

"I don't know yet. I may be."

"I see."

"How about giving me a ring when he gets here?"

The clerk pushed a tablet toward him and placed a crisply sharpened pencil alongside. Mike picked it up and started to write, then looked up and grinned at the clerk.

"Got a phone book?" he said. "I *live* here, but it's been a while. Isn't that something, forgetting your own phone number?"

"Memory does play tricks," the clerk said, handing him the phone book.

Mike flipped the pages, followed his index finger down the line of r's to Royle, and seeing his father's name and the familiar, forgotten number, he smiled to himself. We have our own magic of numbers these days, serial number, rifle number, laundry number, social security number, license number, but how in the world could you forget your own phone number? He wrote down c/o Judge J. F. Royle and the number, and he handed the tablet back to the clerk.

"*Your* name, sir?"

"My name's Royle, too. Mike Royle."

The clerk grinned as he wrote it down. "I didn't recognize you, Mr. Royle."

"I haven't been home in a while," Mike said. "I doubt if *anybody* recognizes me any more."

He turned away from the desk and walked across the lobby again, hearing the faint sound of the overhead fans and the clink and clack of china and silverware from the coffeeshop, then smelling the odor of fresh coffee. He decided to have a cup. No hurry, and he had been driving all night.

* * *

There had been a time when he would have been known in this place, when he had known it well. His father was the Judge then, not just a title, but flesh and blood, black-robed, powerful-shouldered, hunched forward on the high bench with his scarred bald head shiny in the filtered dust-thrilled light of the courtroom.—That's the face of Justice, someone had said, —in the Old Testament sense, a kind of a shaved, baldheaded prophet. And it was years before Mike had known what was implied by that remark: awe, true; admiration even. But not a mention of mercy. Power, but no sign of charity. He knew that power well. He had come many times as a boy with his father to this same place, the Osceola Hotel. He remembered feeling his own hand small, frail, slightboned as a bird, in that warm calloused grip. There had been times of celebration with bunting and flags and bright posters strangely garish in that heavy room, ice clinking in glasses and laughter and loud talking and thick columns of smoke rising and shimmying along the ceiling among the overburdened fans like blithe ghosts. And at other times he had come there with him too, to sit dutifully still on one of the stiff sofas while his father talked with someone or other in whispers, camouflaged by the forlorn potted palms. That was politics, he was told, and his father was going to be the governor some day.

But he was not the governor, not that time or the next time either when Mike was old enough to know, to go with his father and his brother Jojo, sometimes even being allowed to drive the car himself on the open road, to strange towns, to stand beside him on platforms and see him sweat and laugh, do everything but dance for the strangers, and at the very end of it to plead for their votes. And fail again. Afterwards his mother cried and his sister Mary Ann consoled her. His father sat in the study for some days with his whiskey and his law books and no one, no one except Charity, the colored maid, could go into that room and intrude on the privacy of his dark mood. Jojo laughed about it.

—It serves the old man right, Jojo said. He thinks he deserves it. Well, he ain't nothing but a bigmouthed cracker boy, and he don't deserve a thing, not a damn thing!

—You shut up, Mary Ann said. He's worth a dozen of you put together!

—*You!* Jojo yelled at her. You ought to be glad too. Maybe it will shake some sense in his head this time.

—Hush up, both of youall, Charity said. Don't you be talking about your daddy like that.

* * * * * * *

It hadn't been easy for Jojo. He was the eldest of the three children, almost ten years older than Mike. He had been a growing boy in the gnawing early years of the Depression. Oakland was a hard town then, a drab and bitter, hungry place. The Florida Coasts, East and West, with their rich palms and fine white sand beaches and the immaculate flash of the surf, were far away. Hot and shabby and hurt by the times, the town smouldered, glowed with a kind of heatless inner light like rotten wood in the dark. Those were the days of the Klan, and it was then and because of that and the times that his father became a judge, became much more than a cracker boy who had managed in some way to read the law and to marry a Singletree and, after a while, to bring her and their first child with him to live in that stark country town. They had lived in a small frame rented house, and all that she had to remind her of her inheritance was the Singletree silver, some good china, the piano that she played for solace or, perhaps, in a subtle way, as a gesture to humiliate her husband, to remind him of *his* background and inheritance. Then, too, there was her Episcopal Church which was, in Oakland, a chapel, almost a mission in a Baptist town. Jojo had known all of that, his father's still-youthful, caged vitality, his mother's restless disillusionment. And Jojo had seen, known, recorded the time when Joseph Royle became by a supreme effort of will and courage and even, for a brief moment, of heroism, Judge Royle. It was through Jojo, after all, that the story lived for them; for Mary Ann and Mike were too young to have seen or known much of it, though in the history of the blood to have seen really, to have been there as a witness in fact is finally irrelevant. We inherit wounds. We live with tribal scars.

* * *

For Jojo knowledge had started in the green park at Oakland. It was the Fourth of July, a hot, still, sticky day for a celebration. They went to the park, just the three of them, the little girl and the baby left with a neighbor. Joseph Royle was going to speak. He had said before in public that they were going to have law and order in the county and that the Klan had to be swept out of political office and authority. He had said they are few and we are many and we have the vote. So he went to say it again in a scheduled formal speech and they met him at the edge of the park and beat him nearly to death.

They beat the hell out of him. The band was playing to the crowd in the heatstricken park; so loud and near it blared that it drowned out the fury of white shirtsleeves around him. Nancy Royle screamed but he could only see her mouth open and her whole face and lips quiver tautly as if her flesh were elastic. He couldn't hear a sound of her anguish. Some of the women held her back, but nobody was holding Jojo. He saw his father go down amid that flailing of white like a man thrashing in surf and bobbing under. He came up gasping for air, scattering them every which way, his own shirt shredded and his crude, powerful body tense with heavy muscles, using his fists like hammers, his great bald head shining like a polished stone. He went down in the middle of them again, surged up bloody and terrible, roaring above the sound of the band. And, as if in a dance, they came in closer around him, forcing him to earth by the sheer weight of them. Then they kicked and beat him almost to death. When he had stopped moving, twitching, they stepped back again in a ragged circle and looked at him silently like a ring of hunters around a fallen beast. They scattered into the crowd again, and the band still played march music.

The women released his mother, and she ran and bent over his fallen father in the long bright curve of her summer dress, fanning him with one of those paper fans the undertakers put out for the ladies on public occasions, for advertising. She just bent over him fanning and nobody paid any attention. He was too big a man for her to move out of the sun by herself. After a little while a Negro came from across the street and together they dragged him under a shade tree. The Negro had a tin cup in his lunch pail and he got some water from an old stone horse trough at the edge of the park and sloshed it over Jojo's father. When the water hit him he shook his head and tried to sit up. He tried to say something through the bloody bubbles of his mouth, couldn't, laid his head back on the ground gently, slowly, like a man settling on the pillow to sleep. Then the woman saw her son. She called to the policeman who had been watching from a little distance.

—Take the boy home, Ernie, she said. At least you can do that.

The policeman took Jojo's hand in his own, as if the boy were a little child, and Jojo felt the strange sweaty chill of it, but clung to his hand, wouldn't turn loose. He clung to the policeman's hand and kept looking at his mother fanning the fallen man.

—You want a ice cream cone? the policeman said. Sure you do, boy. And I'm going to buy you one.

That sounded like a fine idea, and they turned and walked away from the park together hand in hand.

Those were bad times with so little money and people having to claw and wrestle each other for the little there was. It was the time of the Ku Klux Klan. Not the men in sheets, crackpot fanatics, to be joked about or piously deplored, but a ruthless political machine and a club for the lost and lonely, the embittered and the discontented. They had the county then and a lot of the state and they meant to keep what they had. They didn't hate Joseph Royle. Nothing personal when they beat him. They were afraid of him. They knew him. He was one of their own kind, a hard farm boy who had read the law and now was a lawyer and, being self-educated, having had to sweat into his learning, he believed in some things with an unsophisticated tenacity. So they met him at the edge of the park and crippled him. Always after that he had a limp and a cane and the hurt face of a prizefighter.

When he finally came home from the hospital, still bandaged, using his heavy cane, Jojo stood shy in the living room next to the upright, rented piano his mother sometimes played and watched his father move awkwardly among familiar objects like a stranger.

—What's this? his father hollered. He was bent over the desk, looking through the drawers.

—What is it? his mother said from the kitchen.

—I say what's this you've got in the desk drawer?

And he pulled out of the drawer a shiny pistol and held it

loosely in his hand like a dead thing. His mother came from the kitchen wiping her hands on her apron. As soon as she saw him standing there with the pistol in his hand she started to cry.

—They almost killed you, she said. They're liable to kill you next time.

He started to stamp out of the room past her, but she snatched at the gun. He pushed her away.

—It's mine, she said. Let the blame fall on me. I bought it with my own money. I have the right. They might try and do something to me or the boy.

—You know I don't allow no firearms, his father said. If it wasn't for the boy, I'd beat you with my cane.

She turned away, hiding her face in the crook of her arm and he heard his father stamping through the kitchen and, slowly, down the back steps, and he heard the banging lid of the garbage can. After that it was very quiet for a moment, so quiet the boy could hear a mockingbird in the backyard, probably in the pale mulberry tree, making a sound like a cat, and even behind that sound the hum, not much louder than the noise of a bumblebee, of the colored washwoman next door who always sang and hummed when she ironed. He heard his father then begin to mount the back stairs like a clumsy creature on three legs. When his father spoke in the kitchen his voice was so soft, controlled, he might have been the Episcopal minister.

—You don't have to worry, he said. I'm home now and you don't have to be afraid any more.

—It's too much to ask. I can't go through it again. Those women held me and I could have scratched my eyes out of my head rather than to watch any more. I could have torn out my heart and shredded it to pieces.

—And what am I supposed to do? What am I supposed to be? God knows I'm not a little boy any more.

—They hurt you, she said. My God, how they hurt you.

—They only *confirmed* me, he said. You could call it the laying on of hands.

—We can go, she said. Let's move to Jacksonville. You

can practice there. We can live with Daddy. You can make a good living in Jacksonville and we'll be safe there. You have the children to think about.

—We're not going anywhere, he said. I'm going upstairs and lie down a few days and get a hold of myself. Then I'm going back out on the street and hold up my head again.

—I believe in you, she said. I know you have the strength. But it's so futile, like Samson pulling the roof down on the Philistines.

—If I have to I'll pull the house down on their heads, he answered, laughing the big outdoor laugh that sounded like a wild animal in the dark.

—Whoever heard, he went on, still laughing, whoever heard of a baldheaded Samson.

After his father went up to the bedroom, climbed the flight of stairs painfully, his mother came in from the kitchen and sat down at the piano. She played a couple of little waltz tunes. He knew them, but he liked "The Washington and Lee March" better. She was in the mood for little waltz tunes. She had never liked it in this raw town, Jojo knew that. She was a lady and her people were different. They had been to Jacksonville to visit, and he remembered his grandfather, a kind man with a soft voice who always smelled warmly of whiskey and cigars. He stayed in the house now, padding about, lightfooted as a cat in his bedroom slippers, and he had opened his leather-bound history books and showed, in fluttering disorder, the pictures of the world's history to Jojo. He knew how ashamed his mother must feel in this town, thinking about the big house and the people there, especially his grandfather.

—All right, he remembered his father shouting at her one night after they had returned, a long hot drive, from a visit. Make a hero out of him! A true and regular knight in armor. Just remember this. They would all be in the poorhouse if it wasn't for me. There wouldn't be any big house for you to go and visit and show off to the boy. Oh, he's a fine old gentleman and I love him, but bear in mind when he's sitting in the armchair by the fire and talking so well behind the smoke of a twenty-five cent cigar, so gracefully, that it's *my* cigar he's smoking. He's a fine gentleman by grace of *me*.

—What's the matter, honey? his mother said, looking away from the bright slick piano keys, stopping in the middle of a tune. You look so sad, honey boy. Don't you be sad. Everything's going to be all right.

Then she lay her face on the piano keys and started to cry, noiselessly, only her body shaking as if she had fever and chills, and the tears rolling down her cheeks. The boy went outside in the backyard and picked up a stone to make that mockingbird be quiet, but the mockingbird was gone. He climbed up into the mulberry tree and looked all around, as high and proud and lonely as the king of the mountain, and nobody, nobody would dare to come and pull him from his perch.

They had a little dog in those days, a Boston bull, as cute as he was ugly, and smart. He could do all the ordinary tricks like begging, rolling over, and playing dead, but they had taught him a very special one. In the afternoon they'd turn him loose and he'd run all the way downtown to the post office. The clerk would put the mail in his mouth and he'd run straight home to stand at the screen door scratching with his paw until somebody let him in. He never messed up one of the letters. It was called a mighty fine trick and the people around town knew all about it and talked about it.

It hadn't been long after Joseph Royle came home from the hospital, on a Friday afternoon, when Jojo noticed that the dog didn't come back from the post office. He took it for a sign and kept quiet about it. Around supper time the clerk from the post office brought the mail to the house. His father limped out on the front porch and took it from him.

—Thanks for the special delivery, he said. Did you happen to see my little old dog today?

—No, sir, the clerk said. It's the first time I can remember that dog didn't show up.

—That's a remarkable thing, his father said. How would you account for it?

Jojo stood just inside the front door, his face pressed against the screen, watching. He could see that the clerk was embarrassed. He wanted to do right but he was scared. And Jojo could tell also that his father knew this and he would get the truth out of the man easy. He would have the truth even if the man went down on his knees and begged.

—I don't know, sir. I don't have any idea. Maybe he run away.

—Ha! Ha! His father laughed like a big gust of wind in the man's face. Oh! Ho! That's funny. After five years all of a sudden the dog gets sick and tired and runs off.

—Well, the man said, it *could* have happened.

Jojo watched the bulked muscles in his father's body tighten under his shirt and saw him jut his neck forward, thrust his bald battered head so close to the man's face they could have kissed. When he spoke now, Jojo knew, he would be staring into the depths of the man's eyes, so deep the man would feel naked. And when he spoke it would be hardly more than a whisper, but with the tone of a growl in it, like a dog guarding a bone.

—Now you listen to me, he said. I know what happened to my little dog. They done killed him. I know that much. Now what I want out of you is the truth. That's what I'm going to get. I'll have the truth from you if I have to gut you like a catfish from your jaw to your crotch. You understand me?

—Yes, sir, the man said. They killed him all right. Chief of Police shot him right outside the post office.

—They had a big laugh? That produced a great big laugh?

—Yes, sir. Chief of Police said he don't allow no mad dogs running loose in this town . . .

—He's a real good shot? He's a marksman with that pistol?

—Yes, sir.

—Will they give him the distinguished dog-killing medal? Will he cut a big notch in the barrel of that thirty-eight and strut his fat ass up and down the sidewalk like a bad man?

—I don't know, sir. I really don't know what he's going to do.

30

All of a sudden his father broke into a wide bright smile and slapped the clerk on the back. The clerk jumped like he thought he was going to be struck down, but when he felt the hand soft on his back and the arm around his shoulders, he relaxed. He leaned back on that arm and let it hold him up, like a girl in a man's arm.

—Well, his father said, you done right to come here and tell me. It took some doing what with people waving pistols around and shooting dogs and things. Come on in the house and have a cup of coffee. You want a cup of coffee, don't you?

—Yes, sir, the clerk said. I'd be much obliged.

In the morning, Saturday morning, Joseph Royle was up early, singing in the bathroom while he shaved. It had been a long time since he had been singing in the morning. Jojo went into the bathroom and stood beside his naked father watching him shave. Keeping his eyes on the mirror, he popped a white lather beard on Jojo's chin with his shaving brush. He laughed while Jojo wiped his chin with the back of his hand.

—You better watch. You better study me, he said. One of these days you'll have a beard to shave. You want to know how to do it right.

—How come you still got hair growing on your face and none on top of your head?

—That, boy, is a mystery, his father said, tipping himself a wink in the mirror. If I knew the answer to that question I'd be a millionaire.

—Would you like to be a millionaire?

—Well, I don't know. I don't have an idea what it's like to be a millionaire. You might just as well ask me if I'd like to be a jaybird.

—I know what it's like to be a jaybird.

—You got to be mean to be a jaybird.

—You do?

—But maybe a jaybird don't think he's mean. Maybe he don't know what mean is.

—I never thought of that, Jojo said. A jaybird is smart, though.

—Oh, you can be smart, real smart, and you still can't tell

31

how you're doing something. You can tell most of the time what you're doing, you can't always tell *how* you're doing it or why.

—I always know why I'm doing something.

—You're lucky, his father said.

—It's not so lucky, Jojo said. Sometimes it worries me so much I don't feel like doing a thing.

His father laughed and splashed himself with water, rubbed his face hard with a towel until it flushed all over, and then patted some sweet-smelling lotion on his cheeks.

—Looka here, boy, he said. I'm as pink as a new baby.

Jojo went with him into the bedroom to watch him dress. He dressed as if he were going to the courthouse or the church, the Episcopal church of his mother where the people dressed better and walked softer than in the Baptist church, the church of his father's family. His father put on a dark suit and a white shirt and a necktie. He wore his best shoes, black ones, shined up like patent leather. When he had finished and inspected himself in the mirror, the two of them went downstairs to breakfast.

—Where in the world are you going? Nancy Royle said.

—I thought Jojo and I would take a stroll down to the post office and pick up the mail.

His mother stood by the table like a statue of a woman with a coffee pot in her hand.

—Don't take the boy, she said. You don't want to do that.

—We're just going to stroll downtown.

—You know what I mean, she said. Keep Jojo out of it.

—No, I don't know what you mean. I just got an idea I'd like to go down and get the mail.

—He doesn't have to go along. If you have to go downtown, just looking for trouble, let him stay here.

—Ask the boy. Ask him if he wants to go or not. You want to go with me?

Jojo though about it before he said yes. His mother looked angry, but she must have known there was nothing to say, so she poured the coffee and sat down. When they had finished, Joseph Royle rose from the table and picked up his cane and hat.

—It might be a waste of time, his mother said at the door. There might not be any mail.

—We'll see about that.

Saturday was the day for the country people to come to town, the farmers, the ranchers, the citrus growers, the hired hands and the negroes from the sawmills and turpentine camps. They came, clogging the highway with trucks and wagons, on foot, the women to pass their time window-shopping and gossiping, the men to lounge in knots and clusters at public places. They leaned against the walls and posts, squatted on their heels, smoked and chewed and spat and studied each other, friends and enemies. Saturday had always been a strutting day, but now there wasn't much to buy in town and no money to buy it with anyway. Joseph Royle could not have been more conspicuous that day, his shaved face shining in the light, his Sunday clothes vividly crisp.

They had started to mount the stairs to the post office.

—Hey, lawyer!

His father stopped and turned slowly, glanced along the line of farmers who were sitting on the fence by the walk until he found the face that went with the voice, a tall thin long-legged farmer, his clean khaki trousers flapping loosely above high-top mailorder shoes, his eyes keen and uncommitted.

—What are you going to do now?

—Nothing, Joseph Royle said. It's up to them. They got to think up something else to do. They tried to kill me with their hands and they couldn't. The best they could do was to cripple me up a little bit.

He let his voice rise as the man swung down from his perch and came forward to the edge of the steps. Others came, one by one, from the fence and the curb and the sidewalk and grouped close to listen. Jojo stood in his father's shadow and listened, noticing how he assumed the old pattern of the country speech, the rhythm and tone of it.

—Why, a whole army of them jumped me and tried to kill me, but they couldn't. Know why? They forgot something you and I both know. They forgot I was a man, a dirt farmer's boy raised up in this state, a real cracker. They thought maybe reading a law book had changed my flesh and blood to something soft. You can't kill a man that easy. You can stomp him and beat him and make a cripple out of him. You can cut and shred him in little pieces and scatter the parts of him like chaff in the wind, but when you turn your back and wipe your hands, all those parts come together and he's standing there again ready for a fight.

—Tell them about it! somebody yelled. Tell them about it!

—That's what I'm doing. I'm telling all about it. Those boys forgot that a man in the truth has got nine lives like a cat. I got about eight more coming to me. Oh my! Oh my! They found out though. Oh my! didn't they find out.

—Didn't they?

—They know now I got blood like hot turpentine in my veins and two big fists like knotty pine, like cypress knees, and I got a head like a cannon ball. Oh, they found out. They know about it now. And what do you think they done? They was so mad I wouldn't just lay down and curl up and die for them. They was mad, as all around frustrated as the preacher comes for Sunday dinner and don't get nothing on his plate but the tough old neck of the chicken. They wanted breast and soft meat.

—Keep talking. Tell 'em about it!

—Why, they just didn't know what to do with theirselves. They didn't know whether to shit or get off the pot. And then, and then, and then an idea come to one of them. They got a plan. Down come the Chief of Po-lice and hid hisself behind that tree over there, laying for my dog. There he is trying to hide his fat ass behind a tree and along comes my little old bulldog to pick up the mail. And out pops the Chief of Po-lice. A bang! bang! Shooting a little old dog. It made him feel good. It made him feel so much better. Oh yes, none of them could kill a man, but they was brave enough to rise up in righteous indignation and shoot down a puppy dog. Well now, my friends, I'll tell you the honest truth, when I got over being mad about it, I was glad they done it. It showed them up for what they are. What do you think a dog is?

He levelled his cane and jabbed out with it at the crowd.

—Know what that dog was? He wasn't nothing but a poor

little old son of a bitch and any man that would shoot a dog is lower than a son of a bitch. He's lower than anything in all of God's whole wide creation except maybe a diamond-back rattler. And I got my doubts about that. I'll let a rattler come a-wiggling on his belly in the dust of my backyard before I'll let their Chief of Po-lice come a-hanging around.

Jojo stood tense beside his father, looking out into the crowd of faces. It was a big crowd now, out into the street, and his father was shouting out to them. They were bunched together and they swayed with his voice, were moved by the rhythm of his waving cane, as if they were dancing to a tune.

—Man back here says we're blocking the street, a voice called from the street.

—Tell the man to go and get a policeman. I'm going to stay right here. I'm disturbing the peace and I'm going to keep right on disturbing the peace.

Joseph Royle flung off his hat. It sailed in a wild arc, fell in a flutter like a wounded bird into the crowd. He tore the coat off his shoulders and his white shirt shone in the sunlight when he spread his arms wide.

—I'm bigger than a dog, he yelled. Ask the policeman can he hit me from the street. Let them kill me now if they're going to because if they don't they must reckon with me. I'll come on and I'll be tearing flesh off of bones and I'll be scattering brains and innards from here to kingdom come.

—Tell 'em! Tell 'em about it!

—Ain't nobody going to shoot at you. Keep talking.

—I'm going to tell you all about your Ku Klux Klan. Oh, they're a brave bunch, they are, a noble order of dog-shooters. They come out by night, dressed in white sheets like children on Halloween, and they spend their time harassing the poor niggers and the poor folks. Poor folks . . . That's all of us ain't it?

—Amen. Amen.

—Oh, they're waxing fat and sassy on taxes, and who's paying them? Your sweat, brothers, and mine put every new hole in the Chief of Po-lice's belt. And, brothers, that's a mighty big piece of leathergoods.

(Laughter)

—You could rope a calf with it!
(Laughter)
—You could hang a man with it.
—Let him be careful he don't trip up and hang hisself, a voice hollered.
—Now, when they go out by night in their fancy costumes, they burn the fiery cross. Burn it! That's what they do with the holy cross of our Almighty Lord and Saviour, Jesus Christ!
—Amen! Amen!
—Let them take heed! Let them heed my words. We're not going to pluck them out and run them out of town. We ain't going to run them out of the state or the United States of America. Let them take heed lest we purge the last trace of them off the face of the earth. They can't hurt us. We ain't afraid. We ain't dogs, by God!

Joseph Royle kept talking, shouting at them, and Jojo saw that he was leading the crowd now like a bandmaster. When he wanted to he had them growling and snarling like animals in the zoo. He put his arm around Jojo and leaned over close to his ear.

—Let's quiet them down a little, he said. It's time to quiet them down.

Then he began to talk softly, so soft they had to strain to hear him. He told them what the law was, and he told them what he had been planning to say on the Fourth of July about the vote and the elections in the fall. They yelled at him to run for office until at last he held his hands wide apart and they got quiet. He told them if that's what they wanted he guessed he would have to do it and if he lived to take office he would throw the whole bunch of public enemies in the jail and throw the key away.

—Now I've said my piece, he said. I'm going across the street and celebrate our victory in advance, going to buy my boy a bottle of soda pop and smoke myself a rich man's tencent cigar.

The crowd fell back in front of them, making a path. They walked all the way across the street through the dense Saturday crowd, his father dripping sweat now, smiling at everyone and calling out to the people he knew. Afterwards as they strolled home, people, friends and strangers, stepped up and shook his father's hand and looked into his eyes. And now Jojo knew for the first time how close is violence to love, how one may trigger the other in a flash of time. If you rubbed the lamp and said the right words you could call up a giant.

When they entered the house his mother was playing the piano.

—Was there any mail? she asked. Did you get a letter?

—Isn't that remarkable? Joseph Royle said. I got to talking to some fellows and forgot all about the mail.

After that the conclusion was foregone; everything was quiet. His father went back to work at the law office, the summer ended and Jojo started school again. It might never have happened. He might have dreamed it all in the long, breathless heat-humming days of mid-July, except that there was a car parked right across the street from the house night and day, and always a man in it, sitting in the front seat with a high-powered deer rifle sticking out of the window.

In November they held elections, and one midnight the telephone rang and they woke Jojo and the two little children. As they walked to the courthouse the band was playing in the street and there were fireworks and men fired rifles and pistols in the air. They climbed the flight of steps in front of the courthouse and stood there while the people cheered and hollered, Joseph Royle, now Judge Royle, laughing, tears of joy running down his cheeks, shaking his big cane at the people while they cheered him. Nancy Singletree Royle smiled and smiled, looking right through the swirl of faces, smiling and not seeing any of them, like a queen from another country.

* * *

It was no wonder, then, that after his second try for the governor's high chair and public mansion and his second failure Judge Royle, who in that last bitter campaign, like some classic general, had hopefully bared all his wounds, retired into his study and stayed there, locked for a few days with his books and his whiskey and his black thoughts. Jojo, tormented, torn in two as he was by his confused allegiances, began by cursing his father for an upstart, an ignorant cracker with boundless ambition, a martyr complex, and a compulsive urge to demagoguery (and all done, paradoxically, in the language of a cracker), and he finished, half-drunk himself, in tears at the injustice of it, tears and self-contempt, finished by packing a suitcase and leaving. They heard from him a few years later when the war began. He had been working in a bank in New York, and when the war started he enlisted immediately. He was a fighter pilot and a good one it was said. That, at least, must have been some pleasure and consolation to Judge Royle, though his wife wept again and again for all the wasted years of her firstborn.

Who but Jojo could have believed that anything in this world changes cleanly, quickly, and irrevocably? Only for Jojo the romantic theatrical gesture of packing a bag and slamming a door, vanishing, believing himself free at last, to reappear later in a new guise, but in truth still webbed, still tightly tied to all his past.

After the war Jojo had drifted, tried his hand at one job and another, starting in the North, but always heading South. He began as an airline pilot in New York. Fired for drinking on the job. A construction job in Camden, New Jersey, an air-taxi service in Raleigh, N.C., bought a half interest in a shrimp boat out of McClellanville, S.C., where he had Singletree cousins, drove a taxi in Savannah, Ga., and now he was working as a disk jockey on an all night show in a little radio station barely two hours' drive from Oakland. But he would not come home. He had come home once when the war in Korea broke out. He couldn't pass the physical to fly again and he wanted his father to use his influence and see what he could do. Judge Royle laughed at him.

—You had your time up in the clouds, boy, he said. Now let's see if you're man enough to stand on your two feet on the ground.

And Jojo cursed him again and left.

* * *

The others were left to act out their parts, and yet in so doing each of them changed. Nancy Singletree Royle ever so slowly began to withdraw into a kind of walled garden of her own making, an interior place strictly bounded by her flower garden, a few books, her music, and, more and more, her migraines. Mary Ann, on the other hand, was transformed from her awkward role as the unmarried daughter, seemed to flourish for the first time. As her mother retired, by fits and starts, Mary Ann became gradually the mistress of the house, its hostess and caretaker, and finally the almost wifely custodian of her father's whims and energies.

And Judge Royle emerged blinking, unshaven and a little pale from his siege in the study and returned to his duties on the bench. For a time he continued as before, the scarred and now more saddened face of Justice, leaning forward in the dim light of the county courthouse to listen to the long, winding and often tedious argument of the law in practice, a skein, a tangled spool of words in which somewhere was threaded a clue to truth, to right, to justice. He listened, groped for meaning and translated. When his term ended he did not run for office again, and he declined a chair on the State Supreme Court. He retired to private practice, made money, which must have pleased him for a while at least, and then, after a stroke, retired altogether. Mike had news of him from time to time in the long, carefully penned letters, so careful they seemed copied from other drafts, that Mary Ann wrote to him. He was going to write a book. First it was to be a textbook for lawyers, and, later, it appeared to be a kind of personal history, memoirs of his years on the bench. Next it was growing fancy vegetables (Mike heard nothing more about the books) and, most recently, raising fine pigs.

—He seems to be in the best of spirits, Mary Ann had written, —leaning over the fence and watching his pigs. Lord knows they smell to high heaven, but he's happy and, I suppose, that's all that matters.

* * * * * * *

"Would you like some more coffee?"

Mike shook his head and put a dime on the counter. He went outside into the abrupt dazzle of midmorning sunlight and stood for a minute on the sidewalk watching the people, all of them strangers now, pass him like dark shadows. He got in his car and started it, nosed into the shiny herd of traffic that crawled along the main street, prosperous now, with shiny new store windows, crammed with their carnival of things, new offices, and, he saw, a brand new picture show.

Maybe he should have called to let them know he was in town. But what can you say on a phone to sum up years?

The house was at the edge of town, or what had been the edge of town once, for now there were camplike subdivisions, motels and filling stations and used car lots and shopping centers far beyond it. It was a frame house, large, rambling and high-ceilinged, an old-fashioned Florida house, coolly shaded by liveoaks, much like the one Nancy Singletree had grown up in. The lawn was trim, the paint seemed fresh enough, and the border of azalea bushes along the front porch was well watered, well cared for. As he parked the car Mike could hear, then saw a sprinkler on the far side of the lawn turning its silver whirls of water round and round in a steady whisper. The smell of the grass was sweet. The pigs must have been far in back; he couldn't smell them. He could hear a scrabbling of squirrels in the limbs of the liveoaks, and a mockingbird flashed a gray and white diagonal across his view.

He mounted the steps, and as he stood at the front door, pressing his face against the screen he saw Charity coming from the kitchen down the dark hall, wiping her hands on her apron.

"Are you home for good, honey?" she said, unhooking the door for him.

"I don't know," Mike said. "I'm home anyway."

And he stepped inside.

* * * * * *

"I don't know *what* I am, son," Senator Parker said. "Cracker? Sure enough. But what else? A little Indian somewhere or other. A little French, a little Spanish. Maybe even a drop or two of nigger mixed in—don't quote me. Who knows? God knows what all I am."

He was standing in front of the mirror fingering his face, rude, raw, homely and unforgettable. He had just finished shaving and glowed from hot water and lotion, and he stood now at the mirror in a starched shirt, the cuffs rolled back at the wrists. He was a tall, powerfully built man, and except for the face which could have belonged to no one else in creation, he had the body, the feet, the great carved hands that without a heavy tool in them seem slack and ineffectual, all the parts of the archetypal farm boy.

"I'm the man with a hoe," he said. "Hand me those cufflinks on the table, will you?"

Mike rose from the unmade bed where he was sitting and fumbled among coins and keys on the bedside table. He glanced at the cufflinks as he gave them to the Senator, saw that they were expensive handmade silver, that each was a mask, one the mask of comedy, the other of tragedy, the classic grimace, classic grin.

"Alice gave them to me," Parker said. "She used to be a thespian in her school days. Now, don't let the opposition get ahold of *that* item. I'll have to spend half the campaign explaining what it means and defending her honor out in the provinces."

The Senator fitted them neatly in place without assistance and bent toward the mirror to adjust his necktie.

"Couple of out-of-town newspaper men down in the lobby," Mike said. "Bird-dogging."

"Who?"

"A man named Atkins from Jacksonville and somebody from Atlanta."

"Don't tell them a thing. They'll find out soon enough."

"Atkins looks pretty shrewd," Mike said. "He knows there's a story."

"Let him keep on guessing."

"He wants to look at a copy of the speech."

"My God, its extempor*aneous*," the Senator said, throwing up his hand in a grandiose gesture of mock dismay, grinning at himself in the mirror. Then he turned around and faced Mike, slouched back against the dressing table, his bright smile slowly vanishing.

"I know that Atkins of old," he said. "Of old. We don't owe him or his paper a thing, not a damn thing. Let him sit in the sun and sweat with the rest and wait and see what happens."

When he wasn't smiling, Allen Parker wore an expression of ineffable sadness, not likely to be misinterpreted as self-pity, but more as a kind of universal compassion, as the kilned finish of an intelligent, lonely man who has had a hard life and endured, not so much in triumph as in tragedy. He looked, then, as if he'd seen firsthand most of the common woes of this world and even, maybe, one of the rare keyhole glimpses of hell. It was a face not unlike that of Lincoln's in the later portraits. It was a great political asset, he often said, to be as ugly as sin.

He opened the closet and took his coat off of a hanger.

"Well, it's going to be a hot one," he said. "Phone downstairs and say we're coming on down as soon as Alice is ready."

Mike picked up the phone and listened and waited for the desk to answer.

* * *

Allen Parker was something of a mystery and a legend in the state. Like Joseph Royle he had managed the agile leap from obscurity to a kind of prominence in the early days of the Depression, the end of the crazy Florida Boom. He may have been right when he said that he didn't know what he was, and he was, as likely as not, a curious compounding of all the blood and dust of the State—the Indian, the English, the Spanish, French, the Negro, and, as he sometimes said in public, "one part pirate and one part gator." He didn't know who his father had been, or at least he cheerfully said that he didn't. His mother was a rawboned country woman who had been a schoolteacher in West Florida. Lonely, except for her fatherless child, she worked and saved and sweated, as Allen Parker had to work and sweat and save as soon as he was able, just beyond toddling, so that he could have an education. And somehow he did. He went to Harvard and to the law school there, and then, inexplicably, he returned to his poor county, a harsh country of thin cotton, scraggly tobacco and a few sawmills and turpentine camps, no money and small future and grim past, to open an office and practice law, the owner of an expensive diploma, a good dark suit, and a diction and an accent unfamiliar enough to be labelled affectation by his neighbors. His return, *that* must have been a bitter disappointment to the woman whose motives, whatever else they may have included and consisted of, surely were fanned and fired by the overwhelming wish to see some part of her, her flesh and blood, escape the sweaty boundaries of the dirtpoor, hard country. Still she kept on working for him, continued as before to sweat and save, to deprive herself with joyless rigor, so that, in spite of what she must have thought of as the folly of his choice, he could keep an office open with its rows of costly leatherbound lawbooks, its polished desk, and his name etched splendidly on the frosted glass of the door.

The beginning of Allen Parker in politics was ringed with enigma for Mike. The facts were clear enough, the truth strangely illusive. He had run for the legislature, stumped the county, from the back of wagons and trucks, at the foot of Confederate monuments or next to the quaint and already rusty cannons of the First World War, standing on the steps of public buildings or on green park benches, and talked himself into an elected office. There was the mystery of it. From Joseph Royle to Judge Royle was a metamorphosis Mike could reasonably understand, deriving, as it did, from the forces of the man's vitality, his courage and, as one could see now, inexhaustible ambition. Royle was a cracker and spoke the cracker's language. But how to explain the bastard son of a lonely, proud, tight-lipped, tightfisted, country schoolteacher, a man who had gone away to the North, like one of the rich, for the kind of education none of them could afford and come back then to sit with his huge feet on his polished desk waiting for clients who seldom came or came with the timeless trivial problems of land and animals and small estates and petty crimes to be served and, maybe, to pay? How could he reasonably understand the way in which, during those troubled times, Parker captured first the imagination, then the votes of the strangers he wished to represent? Mike could picture him, standing up before the rough rednecks in their faded overalls and faded workshirts and the thin, weary wives in cheap dresses, with all of their natural reticence, all of their shrewd contempt and closelipped pride, and Allen Parker in his already fraying and shiny dark suit and the high separate collar of those days, speaking to them in what was, for all purposes, a foreign accent and almost a foreign tongue, never talking down, but speaking in those days (Mike was told this, and even today there was some truth in it) more like a university professor on a lecture platform talking of high matters to young and ignorant students. He had tossed the garnered coins of a classic education out to a troubled, hostile, skeptical crowd. He had intelligence, honesty, which was as yet untested by luxury or excess of temptation, a love of the country (else why was he there?) and a kind of passionate and painstaking rationality to offer. He offered, too, youth, great inexperience in the affairs of the world, an awkward strong body and an ugly memorable face.

Mike admired, respected, and now worked for the man. It was easy to do now. It was the *then* that worried him. Lost himself, Mike stirred the ashes of old campfires, studied the outdated maps of pioneers, eagerly read yellow messages in bottles.

Maybe it had been the strangeness of Allen Parker, the original absurdity of him as a politician. Wasn't it a time in the world for absurdity? Wasn't Hitler, for example, blessed with an unmistakable Austrian accent and a corporal's rank at just the time when no German of distinction would do, could be believed in? Perhaps it was that they saw in Allen Parker at once an image of themselves and all their aspirations: the grotesque farmer's body, the college man's mind, the expensive suit that though already well worn was still more than most of them ever expected to own, the face that was clownishly homely, yet seemed scarred with their own wounds. His politics? Not drastically different for those times. Like those of many others, they seemed then radical, now moderately liberal. His views, seen in the perspective of a later time, were, indeed, representative of the prevailing opinions of the South. In domestic affairs he was a New Dealer, before that name was coined. In foreign affairs he was an internationalist, against any form of isolation and/or appeasement from the beginning, willing and eager on the occasions of Manchuria, China, Ethiopia, the Spanish Revolution for the United States to play a part in the world commensurate with its power. Still, in local affairs, the world of the South, of the state, county and town, he had displayed the traditional Southern conservative attitudes. Parker had never been wholly exempt from the curious tension created by his regional tradition: the inevitable tension between the strong ideals of a democratic society and the ingrained dream of a natural aristocracy. There was nothing extraordinary in any of this. But whatever it was that possessed him and so managed to convince the voters, he found himself in the legislature and not too long after that in the Senate of the United States.

* * *

"Senator Parker will be coming down now," Mike told the desk clerk. "Will you have the car out front."

"Alice?" Parker knocked on the door of the adjoining room. "Are you ready?"

The door opened and she entered smiling and, as always, a little breathless, in her light, gay, expensive summer dress looking like a young girl off to a party.

"Do I look all right?"

"Don't ask me," Parker said. "Mike, does she look all right to you? You should know all about clothes and things."

"I'm afraid I'm no expert on fashion," Mike said. "My guess is that you'll have more people admiring you than listening to the Senator."

She smiled and seemed pleased. Alice Parker, childless, still possessing the figure of a young woman and the mind of a girl, seemed easily, endlessly pleased.

"Let's go," the Senator said.

They rode down in the elevator and, when it opened, faced the brisk lightning of one or two local flashcameras; then, with the Senator setting the pace they moved quickly across the lobby. Atkins was waiting at the front door, a small, lean, graying newsman with a tired, knowing look that might on another, in the right place, under the right circumstances, have been called insolent.

"How about it, Senator? I've been hanging around here half the morning."

Senator Parker paused, smiled at Atkins and put out his hand. To Mike's surprise Atkins, as if briefly hypnotized, straightened and shook hands.

"Glad to see you, Mr. Atkins. How are things?" (Then to

45

Mike and the others bunched at the door) "I hesitate to ask Atkins a question like that. Mr. Atkins is a good reporter, but he's one of those writers with an everlasting apocalyptic point of view. It makes for good, exciting copy, but it can be bad for the digestion at the breakfast table."

Even Atkins grinned.

"What are you going to say?" he asked.

"I have the first sentence in mind," Senator Parker said, stepping past. "After that I'm in the hands of God."

"Are you going to run again?"

But the Senator was already out the door and halfway across the sidewalk. A State Trooper stiffened, clicked his heels together and opened the back door of the car with a flourish.

* * * * * * *

It was not intended as an important occasion. In the city park of Oakland, a patch of tended green with its moss-bearded oaks and carefully arranged palms, they were going to unveil a monument, an expensive, imported marble obelisk. On it in gold letters were listed all the known names of those from the county who had been killed in the wars, or, as the monument's ineffaceable gold rhetoric put in, "had fallen, in this land and in far foreign fields, in the nation's service." The first name was that of a soldier named Reese, probably a straggler, maybe a deserter, from Andrew Jackson's forces in West Florida, who had apparently been killed by Indians and his body buried there and marked by some early, forgotten settlers. The most recent was a Corporal J. T. Winston, a Negro who had been with the First Cavalry and had been killed in the last rugged chaotic mountainous days of the war in Korea. His name was the last on the side of the obelisk devoted to the colored dead. The marble base bore a heavy burden of the county's names, but there was space, smooth naked rock, for more.

Originally the affair was intended to be local. None of the more prominent public figures of the state had been invited or had asked to attend. But then the Democratic Party had intervened on behalf of John Batten, Attorney at Law, ex-Marine, and the party's recently announced candidate to succeed Allen

Parker. Some time previously Parker had announced his intention to retire and to support Batten in the Democratic primary. Batten was scheduled to speak. As if to demonstrate his double intention, the Senator had later suggested that he would be willing to fly down from Washington to attend the ceremony and, perhaps, to say a few words.

In spite of the heat of the day there was a goodsize crowd at the park, clustered in a half moon of chairs around the veiled monument. As the car glided to a formal stop at its appointed place and a motorcycle policeman, deft, whitegloved, leapt for the door, Mike noticed that most of the men still had their coats on and most of the women were wearing hats. He fell in step just behind the Senator and Alice Parker as, smiling, they began to walk toward the rostrum, just to one side of the monument. The front rows of the chairs were reserved for mothers and widows and for those veterans who had been crippled by their wounds. In wheel-chairs, legless, with empty sleeves, they sat waiting patiently in a partial shade. A National Guard band played martial music, and an honor guard from the American Legion Post, fat and solemn, though wearing like a badge the embarrassment of men long out of ranks and uniform, stood at parade rest in front of the rostrum.

They mounted the steps, the Senator and his wife taking a place on the front row and Mike moving to the back to find a chair next to a man who introduced himself as the County Health Officer. Mike didn't know him, didn't catch his name, and reproached himself for it, now that politics was his game. The band continued to play, and, after a few minutes, he heard the sirens of motorcycle policemen, then saw the black, rented limousine smoothly park at the curb, disgorging, with some of the comedy of the packed clowns' car in the circus, a cramped group of local officials and among them, tall, handsome, grinning, John Batten, a face he knew from the papers. The honor guard rumbled into a stiff present arms, and there was some applause as Batten mounted the steps and took his place.

The unveiling ceremony was brief. The Mayor, whose name Mike remembered was Beardsley, read from a sheet of paper the statement drafted by a committee outlining in Victorian language the intent and the meaning of the monument. Then a rabbi, a priest and a Protestant minister prayed briefly and somewhat differently. The County Health Officer nudged Mike as they bowed.

"We tried to find us one of those A-rabs that hollers from a tower too," he whispered in a warm, bourboned breath. "Just to be sure."

After the prayers the Post Commander of the American Legion and his wife, both of them wearing the shiny overseas caps of the organization, stepped forward. After some tugging on a reluctant length of rope—"I voted for just breaking a bottle over it," the Health Officer giggled—the veil slid aside like a falling shawl revealing the fresh marble. The honor guard fired a ragged volley of blanks in the air, a burst of smoke, and then two buglers blew taps, one from the white Legion Post, the other, so far as Harper could see, the only member of the Negro Legion participating.

"We had to have the night-fighters represented too," the Health Officer said.

The Mayor introduced "our distinguished guest," John Batten, who stood up to deliver the day's address. He was young, he was healthy, he was goodlooking. He had a pleasant voice and the mildly boyish manner of the successful young man who had, without doubt, read a prize essay to the PTA or the UDC, delivered a high school valedictorian address, captained a college debating team. He wore his success like his health. It shone. This, then, was the enemy.

John Batten talked a while. He mentioned Jefferson and the Tree of Liberty and those who had nourished its roots. He spoke modestly of his own part in the Second World War. He saluted those known and unknown who had fallen, on both sides, he said, because in the long tangled perspectives of history we find that friends and enemies change as the times change, and we must not be crippled by old hatreds. And there are good men and patriots everywhere. This led him to speak of the threatening cloud of nuclear oblivion and the necessity of winning the peace as we had won the wars of the past.

John Batten paused, patted his brow adroitly with a crisp,

folded handkerchief and, by a light and airy logical leap, a muted progression through the need for more dedicated public servants to his own desire to serve, spoke of his candidacy for the Senate. He spoke of the legacy of leaders like Senator Parker, "here today among us," and he humbly hoped that he would be able to carry on those fine traditions. His talk was well received. Here and there men in the audience stood to clap for him when he returned to his seat.

Allen Parker was introduced, stood up to speak. He said he wasn't going to say much, and that since the formal part of the ceremony was over, he hoped nobody minded if he took off his coat. Which he did. And there was a sputter of applause as the men in the audience began to take off their coats.

Mike smiled to himself and watched the alert profile of John Batten.

Allen Parker complimented the townspeople for "the simple dignity" of their memorial, and he complimented John Batten for his address and his desire to serve by entering public life.

"Nearly thirty years ago," he said, "I was a young lawyer like John Batten, and the same infernal demon breathed in my ear and moved me to take myself seriously enough to think that the taxpayers of my county ought to support me."

Laughter. An almost imperceptible tightening at the corners of John Batten's smile.

"I'm not sure that it was a wise demon or a wise decision—if decision it was and not sheer self-hypnotism. But it was done, made, there was a fork in the road passed, with always the promise and never the possibility of coming back to make amends. If I were a really good man, I'd warn John Batten to step back one pace and think it over again, however *dedicated* he may be. If I were a wise man, I'd hand him the sputtering torch and say, 'Take it, brother, it's all yours. You can *have* it.' If I were a brave man, I'd confess before you all a record of failure, of heartbreak, of frustration and foolishness, of all the things done and left undone by me at your expense. But I'm none of these things. I'm a politician and my virtues are on my shirtsleeves. I'm just a politician who sometimes fancies himself to be a 'public servant.'"

49

There was some laughter. Puzzled, the audience leaned forward to listen more closely. John Batten's jaw moved as he whispered behind his hand to the man sitting next to him. Mike saw Atkins moving steadily through the fringes of the standing crowd in back, not waiting any longer.

Senator Parker smiled at the crowd and said that much as he'd like to step aside for young John Batten, he felt better than ever. He said that he hoped John Batten would stand for election as announced because he hadn't had a real, rowdy, rousing campaign in years, and he knew John Batten would be a hard man to beat. With that he turned and stepped across the rostrum to shake the hand of the amazed Batten who half rose from his chair to take the Senator's hand as a flash camera winked a blinding light. The crowd applauded.

Mike saw Atkins going across the street toward the drug store and its telephone at a dead run. Senator Parker sat down. The Mayor declared the ceremony concluded, and the band began to play.

"That's what I'd call a double cross," the County Health Officer said. "You might call it a regular crucifixion."

* * *

"I don't quite understand," Alice Parker said, as they drove back to the hotel. "Are you going to run *again*, Allen?"

"Tell her, Mike."

"Well, *is* he?"

"Yes Ma'am, I'm afraid so."

"Lord, why didn't you tell me?" she said, perfectly serious. "I would've had my hair done."

* * *

As soon as they were back in the hotel room, the telephone began to ring. Parker sat on the edge of the bed, his shirt opened across his chest, and chatted easily with a series of callers. He smoked and talked along affably, but Mike could see nothing in his face but weariness. His voice, disengaged, spent across the tense rigging of wires, must have seemed, sounded relaxed, pleasant, even amused. Still talking, he motioned with a pouring gesture, and Mike went downstairs to order ice and whiskey.

When he came back with the bellboy, the bottle and the ice, the Senator had managed, one-handed, still listening and speaking on the telephone, to strip down to his undershorts. Sweat glistened on his hard body. Mike poured them both a drink. He could hear Alice Parker splashing in the tub, humming a tune to herself. Parker finished a call and left the phone off the hook.

"Son," he said, "there's going to be some hell to pay for a while."

"I guess some folks are going to get pretty upset."

"You better believe it," Parker said. "There's going to be confusion in the ranks."

Then, sipping his drink, he shook his head and laughed.

"The thing is, the main thing, we can tell friends from enemies."

"Don't you know that already?"

"You can always guess, you can *suppose*. But you can never know without some kind of a test. The unexpected is as good a test as any. Right now we're liable to find out who a few of them are. Take a few calls, will you?"

Allen Parker stretched out on the bed, tinkled the ice cubes in his drink and stared at the cracks in the plaster of the ceiling. Mike knew what he had to say. It was, quite simply, at this time, that Senator Parker—who was unavailable at the moment—felt in good health and that he had decided not to retire from politics. For those who expressed some measure of interest or of support or commitment, he was to say that the Senator appreciated it very much and would be in touch with them soon. There was a pad next to the phone ready to take down their names.

* * *

The truth of the matter was more complex. In January, Mike, depressed by the gray winter in New York, depressed by the routine of his job, deeply troubled by his recent divorce, had written to Parker asking about some kind of a job. It had been just a whim, but Parker's reply had been cordial, interested and not promising.

"Your father was a great friend of mine at a time when friends were few," Parker wrote. "And, of course, I'm sorry to hear that you're unhappy with your present job. I think, perhaps, you are wise to consider going back home, and it may be that you would find public life stimulating. (It's certain to be exasperating!) I wish I could help you and I may be able to in some way. But you should know that this is my last term. I'm planning to retire and have some kind of a life of my own. Let me know if there's anything specific I can do for you, though. I'd be glad to talk to you any time."

Mike had gone back to work at the law firm, for the next weeks performing his duties with the slow, gray, steady gestures of a somnambulist, thinking now and then of South America, of Indonesia, of the Middle East, of any place far enough from himself, his troubles and the strict pattern of his life. During his lunch hour he liked to wander on Fifth or Madison and look through the windows of the travel agencies, of airlines, railroads and shipping companies. Behind shiny windows the bright maps of the world glittered with a surplus of promise. And then he received a second note from Senator Parker.

"Certain things have developed which have changed my plans. Would you be interested in coming down to Washington for a talk?"

It fell like a lucky coin at his feet and he snatched at the chance.

The thing that had happened was quite simple as Parker explained it. John Batten was the Party's bright young man. *He* had worked for the Senator once and had seemed to Parker in every way a fine prospect to succeed him. He had made a mistake with Batten, though. He had been wrong. He had *assumed* Batten's politics. He had assumed that Batten's allegiances, alliances, loyalties, friends and enemies, would be his own. He had erred in imagining a kind of reincarnation of himself (the original sin of fathers), that this man, trained and cultivated, educated for the job, would follow the way that he had gone. In the weeks between the first letter and the second it had become apparent to Parker that this wasn't so. Batten's handful of speeches—still ostensibly without specific political motive—had troubled Parker. Then came the news—if you could call it that, the gossip, the grapevine, the reliable rumor that must pass for communication in that world—of Batten's financial allegiances. His campaign was to be paid for, not by those who had supported Parker through the years, but by those who had fought him in every election, those who were his enemies.

Unsaid, but explicit, was Senator Parker's bafflement, not so much at the behavior of his protégé, for he was wise enough to know that in politics the rule rather than the exception is turn and counterturn, cross and double cross, as a sense that he (Parker) was out of touch, that maybe in some way John Batten was more representative of the State and the weather of the times than he was. His old enemies, the major national corporations, the railroads, the power company, the big citrus growers, once the enemies of the people as well, might have subtly transformed themselves into friends. Maybe with the change in the times power and wealth weren't necessarily to be equated with danger. That they should unite against him wasn't surprising. That they would find it easy to support his own man and that John Batten could without embarrassment accept their support was a wound. It must have made him feel very old.

—I'm tired, Parker had told him. I'm worn out with the whole business. I'd like to say the hell with it and let it all go. I'd like to find somebody else to fight for me, but there isn't anybody else. Just me.

And so he had asked Mike Royle to do a little work for him during the coming campaign.

—There won't be any money in it, he said. But there's an education of sorts, or at least the *chance* that you'll learn something. And once we get going, you'll be busy, you'll be outside of yourself in a crazy world of crucial smiles and handshakes. It might even be a cheap kind of therapy if that's what you're looking for. You won't have much time to worry about yourself. Once you start living in politics, which is entirely a world of appearances, of two tight little dimensions, your life's like a game of cards.

* * *

Mike thought about it a while, agreed, and here he was talking on the phone for Parker in a hotel room in Oakland, with the Senator stretched out on the bed beside him and in the bathroom the splashing and humming of Alice Parker, happy as a child in the cool bathtub. On the other end of the line, humming in his ear, were the voices of strangers, at first the people from around town (most of whom knew his name), then newspapers beginning to call in, and, as the afternoon went on, there were calls from the capital and all over the state. Soon his own voice took on its task mechanically, by rote, and he felt strangely other than himself, hearing all those voices, each with its bodiless color and character, each with its guarded secrets and, too, its own kind of nakedness, and his own voice sounding like someone else talking (is that *me?* is that *really* me?) answering what soon appeared to be the same questions, diverting the same demands, repeating an identical formula of gratitude and interest.

"Leave the phone off the hook a while," Parker said finally. "If you do too much politicking at one time you feel like you've been drinking out of a spittoon."

Parker stood up and looked at the list of names on the pad.

"Well," he said, "it could be worse."

"How do you think the papers will treat it?"

"I expect they'll roast me alive," Parker said.

They sat for a moment. There was a knock at the door and Mike went to answer it. He opened it and looked into the solemn face of John Batten. Batten stood there with his hat in his hand and stared at Mike.

"I'd like to see Allen if I can," he said.

"Come on in, Johnny," Parker called. "Walk right in. This is Mike Royle, the Judge's boy."

Batten shook his hand and walked into the room. Senator Parker sat, long-legged, on the edge of the bed, smiling, and Batten stood, turning his hat in his hands, shifting his weight from one foot to the other, then sat down in a chair.

"Allen," he said. "I don't pretend to understand all this."

"What don't you understand?"

"I don't see what you, what any of us has to gain by you running again."

"That's not the point, Johnny," Parker said. "The point is what have I got to *lose?*"

"One thing you can lose, sir, is the election."

"Well, we'll have to wait and see . . ."

"I don't want to fight *you*. I don't want to have to run against *you*," Batten said. "That's not the idea at all."

"Johnny, I'm afraid you're going to have to. There isn't anybody else."

"You're really firm about it?"

"My mind's made up."

"I won't say I'm not disappointed. I *am*," Batten said. "But what hurts most is that it has to be you."

"You have to run against somebody. You've always got to run against somebody."

"Well," Batten said, standing up again, "I'm just sorry, that's all. I wanted you to know about that."

"I know you are," Parker said. "And I'm glad you came to see me."

"It's going to be a rough one, Allen. We aren't going to be easy about it. We want it pretty bad."

"Sure you do. So do I."

The two men shook hands, then Batten turned to leave. He stopped and offered his hand to Mike.

"Be careful," he said. "This is a contagious disease."

Parker whooped with laughter behind them and Batten left, shutting the door softly behind him. When the door clicked shut Allen Parker's face softened and saddened.

"I never would've guessed that he'd come up here to see me," he said. "That took some doing."

"What happens next?"

"What happens next is it's my turn in the tub. See if somebody's trying to get me on the phone."

* * * * * *

The three men—Senator Parker, Judge Royle and Mike—were standing along the fence looking at the Judge's hobby. Fat, pink-snouted, dirty, his fine pigs were thriving from good corn and care. Mike looked at them and wondered at his father's pleasure in them, his animation. The Judge, pointing his cane proudly like a general's swagger stick, named each one of

55

them, described their quirks and characteristics, and was clearly delighted, pleased with himself.

"We had pigs when I was a boy," he said. "Nothing fancy like this pen. They just ran loose in the yard around the house. Sometimes *in* the house too. I remember one time we had a terrible thunderstorm. One of those wild, cloudy, late afternoon storms, and a pig got in the house. Went wild, what with all that lightning and thunder and rain pounding on the roof, ran all over the damn house with all of us chasing it. My daddy would get both arms around that pig, but every time he did, the pig would squiggle loose again and leave Daddy holding an armful of air. Well, Daddy was mad as a doused rooster and hollering and cussing and knocking the furniture, such as it was. He even got down on his hands and knees to chase that pig. And all of a sudden everybody, Daddy too, commenced to laughing at the same time. What I mean is we rolled on the floor and laughed and just let the pig go. It kept on lightning and thundering and the pig kept on running around and squealing. And we just laid there on the floor laughing. It took a while to get everything straightened up afterwards. And, you know, when it came time, my daddy didn't have the heart to butcher that pig. He said it was like cutting up a member of the family."

"A good chance to laugh like that didn't come along too often," the Senator said.

"You're right, you're so right. But when one *did* come along, when we had the chance to just rear back and laugh or lay down and laugh our guts out, we did I'll tell you."

"I remember one time seeing a whole pen full of drunk pigs," Parker said. "Some old fellow ran a still out in the woods—on a calm day you could see his smoke about five miles—and this farmer nearby bought a lot of his old mash and fed it to the pigs. I mean to tell you those pigs got cock-eyed drunk. Their legs bowed and they all got wall-eyed and cross-eyed and they squealed and carried on like something to behold. I was about ten, I guess, and I swore off corn whiskey then and there, right on the spot. I took a solemn vow. Course, I haven't quite kept to it."

"Kind of hard to stay sober in this day and age," the Judge

said. "Did you ever see a drunk bear? Now, I'll tell you one time . . ."

* * *

Mike knew very little, really, about his father's early life. He had never seen his Royle grandparents, who died before he was old enough to remember them. There were cousins, but he didn't know them or what had become of them. Joseph Royle had, it seemed, cut all the ties with his family and his past before Mike was born. There had been one time, though. He must have been fourteen or fifteen and about to be sent away to the military school in Tennessee. His father had wakened him in the early morning, the still, slow, gray summer dawn with only a few birds stirring in the leaves and here and there the sound of a rooster crowing.

—Get up, boy, his father said. When I was your age I'd been up an hour or so by this time.

And he rubbed the sleep out of his eyes and got out of bed to put on his clothes.

—Where are we going? he said.

—We're going for a ride in the car.

And they drove off, just the two of them, not even stopping for coffee, in that early morning, leaving the still-sleeping town behind them, the tires singing on the open road as his father drove fast and the sun came up, glanced off the windshield and the polished fenders, poured like molten gold among the tall pines. Soon in the open country they saw the farmers already working their fields, the women already hanging up wash and the little children playing in the dusty yards. And they passed, Mike remembered, a truckload of prisoners from a State Road Camp, in stripes still in those days, packed tightly in a truck, their black and white, white-eyed faces staring at the road behind them, and the guard in the ringmount next to the cab, a hard, angular country face, shaded by a widebrimmed hat, cradling the shotgun, whose barrel glistened in the light like a black snake.

—Some of my victims, I guess, the Judge said chuckling, as they passed the truck and left it far behind.

Judge Royle drove all morning long with a kind of fury, seventy, eighty miles an hour, leaving the roadside farms, the crossroads stores and filling stations, the brief, shady towns, in a swift glazed blur behind them. Finally they turned off the paved roads altogether, drove on rutted and washboard dirt trails into the silent heart of the country. There were a few ranches, an occasional farm, and once they passed by a sawmill, heard the great blade whining and saw two men scampering like crazed shadows, struggling with a heavy log, sweaty, shirtless, dust- and chip-covered. Then at last they came to the place, a lopsided, paintless shack, a crude brick chimney leaning away from it, a fallen porch, a rusty pump without a handle in the sandy yard, a single feathery pecan tree for shade. His father parked the car by the ditch at the side of the road and looked at the house for a while.

—All right, get out, he said. Walk up there and look around. Take a good look.

Mike climbed out of the car and walked slowly over the uneven rain-gouged clay and sand, past the pump, stepped on the rotten boards of the porch and into the close, hot air of the house. The bright sun winked through chinks and holes in the tin roof. There were things, still. There are always things: the head of a cheap doll, its two sightless button eyes staring at nothing, a rusty kitchen pot, riddled with holes, a calendar picture, all of its dates stripped away, showing wistfully, incongruously, the snow-capped Rockies seen from the blue and cool perfection of a mountain lake. A striped lizard poised on the warped floorboards, stared at him, tested the air with a quick tongue like a little flame, then scuttled away, leaving behind him barely perceptible tracks in the dust. Looking down, Mike saw the prints of other animals, some dogs, and one large pair of prints that might have belonged to a wildcat.

He wiped the sweat off of his brow and walked through, looked out of the sagging rectangle of the back door on the small field all given over to weeds now, but poor soil for weeds even, it seemed, and beyond that the green dense wall of pines and cypresses that marked the edge of low country, maybe a swamp. Far off, above the trees, a lone buzzard circled, tossed on the shimmering, thermal air like a burnt scrap of paper.

—Did you take a good look around? his father said when he came back to the car. Did you get a feel of it?

—Yes, sir.

—That's what I came from. That's *my* home. Your roots, boy. Kind of different from the Singletree place. Well, ain't it?

—Yes, sir.

It was, indeed, different from the big fine house overlooking the St. Johns River, rich with shade, its wide lawn mowed, its sense of space and air, its tended flowers.

—I came from that place. I walked four miles to a one-room schoolhouse, when I could go, to learn to read. And I read myself right out of that place. I had to do my reading at sunset and at noontime and on a Sunday because my daddy wouldn't waste valuable kerosene on my reading habits. Do you know how far the nearest free library was? Nine miles. I used to go down there in the middle of the night, walk the whole way, and be there in time for it to open. As soon as it opened, I'd turn in all the old ones and grab me ten, twenty pounds of books—just any books, I was so crazy to read—and I'd throw them in a croker sack and walk back home. And when I got back I had to make up all the time I'd lost. I probably read more books in those years than you will in a whole lifetime.

—Yes, sir.

—You see that patch of ground? Well, it's as near worthless as any piece of ground I know of. My daddy squeezed the last drop of his sweat and my mother's too into that ground. And it didn't do them a lick of good. Both of them are buried in that same sand. And you know something? Even the cemeteries don't grow green around here.

He turned the car around and drove back as fast as he had come, and silently.

* * *

Now, years later, he could stand at the gate of his pig pen, which he called his "courthouse," and joke with Allen Parker about those days, swapping the invariable country yarns, laughing over old wounds, as if he'd never been crippled by them.

"You take a pig, now," he was saying. "A pig, he's got one nature. Very uncomplicated. He don't care to be nothing but a pig. He's dirty. He stinks to high heaven and he spends his life wallowing in dung and mud waiting for a butcher. But he's just what he is and that's all there is to it. I think God must have loved pigs when he made them.

"Now a man, a man walks on two legs, and it says in the Bible that he's in the image of God. He shaves every day and he takes a bath every now and then. This side of the jungle we don't eat each other up any more. And for all of that a man is dirtier, and wallows in more shit and mire than any pig ever dreamed of. The stink of man—once you get your nose trained to detect it—is the foulest thing in creation."

"It depends on the way you look at it," Parker said.

"That's *my* point of view. I've got twenty years on the bench to back it up," Judge Royle said. "That's why I love pigs."

They turned away and began to walk up the long sloping lawn to the house.

"Judge," Parker said. "You spoke for me years ago when I first ran for the Senate, and I haven't forgotten it."

Judge Royle laughed.

"Well, I meant what I said. I said you were, or seemed to be, an honest man in a time when crooks were as thick as flies on flypaper. I said you had a good education and knew what being hungry was, when most of our office holders here were fat-bottomed petty politicians who got their training in the saloons and the county jailhouses. I said I thought you were the best man for the job. I meant it, and I reckon I'd say it again."

"You might just *have* to this time."

"Well, I'll do what I can for you, Allen. Things have changed, though."

"How do you mean?"

"The times have changed and the people have changed. You and I, Allen, were leftovers in this society. The world's gone along awhile. Our wars are over and done with, and children who never heard of them are wondering what all the tumult was about. We're as quaint and out-of-date as a couple of knights in armor."

"Speak for yourself," Parker said, laughing. "I never felt better, and there are plenty of dragons out on the roads these days."

"And windmills," Royle said. "See how you feel later. Still, if you need it, if you think it will help you any, I'll come out and stand on a stump and do a little hollering for you."

They had reached the house, turned at the foot of the steps to look back down the lawn to the stolid clump of oaks where the pig pen was concealed from sight. Then the two of them stood aside while the Judge, using his cane, mounted the steps.

* * *

The women—Alice Parker, Nancy Royle and Mary Ann— were sitting on the wide porch waiting for them. They sipped iced tea, and Alice and Nancy, friends from a time when the moneyed and respectable families of the state—the landowners, the noted lawyers, the Episcopal ministers and bishops, the high-priced doctors—could be named and numbered in a kind of free hierarchy like branches of a single family, talked gaily of those days, those lost happy days. Against the last flagrant colors of the twilight, and that light softened as it fell over them by the trees and the green of the azalea bushes, the oleanders with their pink flowers like something spun out of sugar, the poinsettias and hibiscus, and the vines along the sides, honeysuckle and morning glory, the light itself somehow partaking of the faint sweetness of green, of earth, of blossoming in the air, and the two women in bright summer dresses, against and in that light they seemed to Mike identically and strangely young. Alice Parker and his mother were sitting, seemed to float, on the white porch swing. They were buoyed by the light, the air; fragile and, in the deceptive moments while the day consumed itself in flames, beautiful and wholly unreal like something painted by Fragonard or Watteau.

Mary Ann seemed, if anything, older, juxtaposed against the two. Suntanned, firmly in a straight-backed wicker chair, wearing a plain cotton dress and her hair pulled back tight and smooth in a knot, without the least glint of jewelry, she seemed more of earth than light and air. Though the same light touched, blessed her too, there was no magic in it to transform her. She looked up when she heard them coming around the corner of the porch. She rose to greet them.

"Why, here are the gentlemen now," Nancy said, giving the swing a little push. The two women soared high and free, kicking their feet, and Alice Parker's laughter fell like a shower of coins.

"Would you like some iced tea?" Mary Ann said. "I'll call Charity."

"*Iced tea?*" the Judge said, sitting down heavily in a rocking chair. "Tell Charity to bring the whiskey and the ice. We've been down looking at my pigs."

"Oh, *Daddy!*" Mary Ann said.

"They're goodlooking animals," Parker said. "I'd show them off myself if I had them."

"Do you have time for a drink?" Mike said.

"I'd love to," Parker said, "but we've got a plane to catch. Let me see if I can collect Alice from that flying swing."

* * *

Mike drove them to the airport. Parker sat quiet, spent it seemed, and listened to his wife chatter about the times she had visited the Singletrees in Jacksonville, and all the fun they had in those days, the days when the Army camp was there and the Singletree house was filled with guests and officers, gay cotton dresses and starched khaki. Nancy used to play the piano for them and they all danced. She knew *all* the latest tunes. Later, they would walk by the river and watch the ships pass, coming and going, their little constellations of lights blinking and the whole river laved in a cold lunar glow. It was the saddest, gayest time in the world, she said, and she had the prettiest clothes.

The Senator closed his eyes and nodded and listened and made no reply.

While they were waiting for the plane, he talked to Mike

about his plans. Mike was to stay on in Oakland and run things in that county and that part of the state for the time being. There would be many details, but there were other experienced people around the state who would be able to help him. Parker himself would be coming down a few times before the campaign really got going. In the meantime Mike was to get things ready in the area, to line up some good steady workers, to separate the sheep from the goats among the oldtime Party workers, to study the direction of the local newspapers, to write some letters and make some phone calls, and not to promise anything.

"It's going to be a fairly slack time for a little while, but it's important," he said. "Use it. Get to know the place and the people again. Since you've been away, you've got a kind of an edge, an advantage of rediscovery."

The flight was announced and they went outside to the mesh fence to watch the plane land, huge and silver, with its lights pulsing against the gradual dark. It taxied to the loading spot.

"I was serious about all that," Parker said. "I really hope the Judge will stir himself and speak for me."

"I expect he will. You never know about him, but if he says he will, I expect he will."

"It's going to be rough. We'll need all the help we can get."

They walked to the edge of the ramp where, framed in the light of the open door, a young stewardess waited, smiling the vague inviting smile of her trade. Alice Parker pressed Mike's hand and boarded the plane, but Parker tarried, took Mike's shoulders in his hands.

"Do *you* think I did wrong, boy?"

"About what?" Mike said, surprised.

"About John Batten. How do you feel about it?"

"You're the boss," Mike said. "I work for you. I don't know Batten from Adam."

Parker shook his great head and laughed, slapped Mike on the back.

"Boy, you *will*," he said, still laughing as he went up the stairs. "Before this is over and done with you will know him well."

Mike remained at the fence to watch them take off, stood looking after the plane as it rose and diminished until its lights were lost among the wide-flung stars.

* * *

Mike drove home slowly, letting the warm night air bathe over him, hearing the electric rise and fall of insect noises in the dark. For a moment he pictured the whole state, the fabulous peninsula singing to itself in that dark, on the map just an absurd appendage to the nation, covered now by the darkness that had been coming on so long, so steady, a vast and gradual shadow from the East. On the coasts, East and West, with their bright beaches and palm trees, and the ephemeral wink and glitter of neon like an enormous pinball machine belling the squandered coinage of thousands of wishes, on the coasts the tides, rising or falling under the strict moon, chewed at the edges of the shore, cast drifts of snowy foam with each breaking wave. By now the last of the seabirds and scavengers, who had hovered and hunted in the twilight, slept. Even the pelicans (a happy memory for him, clowns on earth, perched on the docks and pilings like foolish newel posts, but, once in the proper element of air, great oarsmen, soarers, windswimmers) were still. He let his mind move inland into the fringe of the palmetto jungle, there where the Spaniards had clanked in expensive and useless armor and claimed a world, *the* new world once, searched for dreamed-of treasure and longed-for youth and the never-never land they never found. And they left behind them a few imposing forts, a sprinkling of missions, now ruined, overgrown, to be found only on lost winding dirt trails amid the green heat and hush of that jungle. Beyond that into good farm country, the rich, black-bottom soil where truck farmers had just to tickle the ground to yield two or three fine crops a year. At last to the center of the state, where he was driving now, with its wide sparse ranches, its farms, its even military rows of citrus trees, its towns with lakes and liveoaks.

The towns. There are old towns in West Florida, plantation towns from the ante-bellum days, left behind like curious sea creatures tossed up, then relinquished by a retreating tide, quietly enduring with their histories and their scars. There are the old Spanish settlements, now tourist attractions under their glowering forts, like Pensacola and St. Augustine. There are the port cities, Jacksonville and Tampa. There are industrious new towns, little cities like Orlando. And there are the fantastic, unabashedly vulgar, blaring tourist cities ringing the coasts, outposts with all the glare and gilt of carnivals, adolescent daydreams of *luxuria*, calling most for the shrewd satiric lines of a Steinberg, the quick shy inquisitive eye of, say, Cartier-Bresson. These are the cities of *this* century, its wildest dreams of ersatz opulence, sad diminished ninevehs shining among studio jungles with, sometimes, studio flamingoes and studio Seminoles, too, to add to the local color. Cities reclaimed, at least temporarily, from the unpredictable tides, from the persistent mosquitoes. And farther inland the towns like Oakland where, save for his vision of the coast, he might as well have been a thousand miles from the unlikely ocean.

But all of it was whole in the hot dark summer air, breathing a history, ghosted.

An almost seasonless land, yet with a year of subtle changes from the time when the frail orange blossoms cast a too-sweet odor over acres of the land to the time when, ripe and rich, the oranges burden the trees like baubles among the waxy leaves.

With the dark a hush settled over the land. Then the insects made crisp music, and he thought, if he listened very carefully, he could imagine, if not hear, as if captured in a seashell, the whispers and long sigh of the tide.

* * * * * *

Though it was still early when he got home, Mike noticed that most of the lights were already out. He went into the living room and found Mary Ann reading a magazine in the lonely yellow stain of a single lamp, the rest of the room given over to shadows. He could hear, vaguely, the muffled sounds and rhythm of his mother's hifi set from upstairs, playing in the dark, he assumed, for he hadn't seen any lights on upstairs. Mary Ann looked up and motioned him to go back toward the study.

Judge Royle's study bulged with books, its walls gaudy with their varied and disordered dust jackets and bindings. His desk was a wasteland of odds and ends, ink bottles, pens and pencils, paperclips, wire baskets wildly stacked with leaning towers of old mail, and a yellow desert of scribbled-on legal paper. Mike stood in the open door and watched his father writing. Judge Royle looked up at him.

"Come on in, boy," he said. "Find a place to sit down if there is one."

Mike moved a pile of books, paperback detective novels he noticed, from a chair and sat down facing the desk. The Judge fiddled with his fountain pen. Mike hadn't been in this room often, except furtively when he was a child, intrigued by the odor and the mystery of its privacy. Then it had seemed a kind of magician's chamber. Once, he remembered, he had been thoroughly spanked with the back of a hairbrush when he had been caught prowling there. It was a forbidden place, a cave ever after tinged in his consciousness with a dim sense of guilt, and it had never occurred to him to enter the room again unless he was asked to.

"I'll admit the place is a mess," the Judge said. "But that's life. When I first went on the bench I used to marvel at all the judges around and about who could keep their desks so clean and neat all the time. Their lives seemed so neat and uncluttered. They were great stackers and filers and organizers. Your grandfather Singletree was that way, and I was very impressed. That's the trouble with analogy, boy. It took me years of hard experience to find out that all those orderly people were just trying to hide the clutter and mess inside. These days I just let it all hang out."

Mike grinned. He had lately been given to making inventories of things, to compiling lists and stacks of cards, to making memos to himself. *That*, it seemed, was the whole fruit, crop, of his father's experience, reduced to its lowest common denominator, its simplest factor, the knowledge, that every thoughtful child carries in his head like a gyroscope, that the whole world is double, that there is one that we look at and that looks back at us, and neither is true and both are alien.

castled, like snails, in enigma. There must have been, he thought, something remarkably innocent about the young Judge Royle at the beginning of his career, for all his apparent knowledge of men and their ways, his nearly surgical ability to lay bare with glittering precision the hidden motives of others like twitching and exposed nerve ends. Otherwise how to explain his deep hurt when he was gored on the horns of appearance and reality? Otherwise what cause for the biblical ferocity, real or merely reputed, of his justice?

"I must've inherited the trait," Mike said. "I have a hell of a time keeping my things in shape."

Judge Royle stood up and poured Mike a drink of whiskey.

"I'm glad you decided to come on home," he said. "It must prove something or other. But I can't say I understand it yet."

"I'm not sure I understand it myself," Mike said.

"You're a mystery to me, all of you. What do you expect to find? For instance, what in the world does Jojo expect to find for himself?"

"I'll tell you the truth," Mike said. "I wouldn't know about Jojo."

* * *

His children, and especially Jojo, must have been, of all Judge Royle's diet of disappointments, the most forlornly absurd, the bitterest taste in his mouth. Early he must have known, learned anyway, that all he could expect from his marriage to Nancy Singletree was the children. And, perhaps, the gratification of his developing sense of irony. He, who would have been turned away by the Negro help at the Singletree's back door once, sent away for being the whitetrash he obviously was, had by sheer will and sweat and a little luck prospered just enough and just at the same time when Anthony Singletree's fortunes had waned or, at least, at just the same time when the true state of Anthony Singletree's fortunes was becoming known. And Joseph Royle, a young lawyer, married the daughter and went on to support the rest of them in the manner they were accustomed to and had long since, practically speaking, lost any claim to but the habit of gentility. Had he tried? Mike wondered. Had he tried to love Nancy Singletree, and had she stiffened, remained always a kind of hostage and a sacrifice to her father's good name and bad luck? Mike knew that he would never know. Who's to blame? Since his own marriage had failed, he was baffled beyond judging another's. The Church was right about that, at least, he thought. All marriages are mysteries, as secret, tenuous, as ever near and likely to disaster as the analogous wedding of spirit and flesh in a man. Only God could know when the serpent intrudes and whispers in his soft voice. Only God knows who's to blame.

It was natural then, he supposed, perfectly ordinary and to be expected, that Judge Royle should have turned his hopes to his children. First on the eldest, Jojo, he heaped the burden of his hopes and fears; it was a kind of wedding of father and son which, in turn, failed as it was bound to, with Jojo finishing by defiantly and maybe foolishly rebelling against all his heritage. Judge Royle's Adam in whom he was well pleased thumbed his nose in the face of his creator. Then there was Mary Ann. A fat, unhappy child, and now an attractive woman, though she seemed at pains to disguise it, she was intended to be raised as a grand lady in the archaic manner or, more accurately, in a manner that never was, that was dreamed of and conjured up out of the ten or twenty pounds of mixed books in a croker sack Joseph Royle had lugged home and labored over. She was to be, become what Nancy Singletree should have been. She, of course, hated it from the beginning, wept while practicing the grand piano he bought her, and she never had much talent for it, though she had enough to please him. She was the despair of her expensive dancing teacher, and eventually came home from a year in Paris with a grim little to say about it except that it was gray and cold a lot of the time. And *there* was another irony for the Judge to ponder on. She stayed on at home, displayed no interest in the available young men, eligible or otherwise, and became in the end precisely what he had wanted her to, yet with such a difference. She renounced all her freedom and freely chose to remain here and care for him and, in a curious way, to triumph over her mother. And now there was Mike, the youngest, who in his way must have been a disappointment, coming home now to rake up the bones of his inheritance.

* * *

"I'll never understand Jojo," the Judge was saying. "I gave up trying long ago. But what I *am* curious about, amused too I guess, is what *you're* up to."

"Right now I'm just doing a little work for Allen Parker."

Judge Royle waved a brusque hand, brushing away the idea like an annoying fly.

"What I'm wondering is what you expect it to give you."

"I don't know," Mike said. "I really don't know yet."

"My God!" Judge Royle said. "I can tell you from my own experience. You don't have to give up a pretty good job and come down here and dabble in politics."

"Maybe it runs in the family."

"Politics has always been a great game in this country, a grandiose hobby. And in the South it's a *disease*, believe me. It wastes us away. It's always with us like pellagra and hookworm. It's violent, usually stupid, and it burns up the energies of some of our best men. It has ruined more good men than liquor and sex combined. If you want to fool around with this kind of thing, this kind of vice, why don't you settle for a little of the rational gangsterism of New York City or even the pompous dog-eat-dog of Washington? Lord, boy, it strikes me as crazy as hell."

"I wanted to come home, and this seemed like a good thing."

"You'll learn *something* all right. I just hope you learn it quick before you make yourself over into a complete fool. If you're on the winning side, you're the child of fortune. You'll start to believe in the essential falsehood of the world. You'll end up thinking the earth trembles when you visit the barbershop or get your picture in a newspaper. You'll imagine that stars and stones weep when you make an enemy. You'll start living more and more in your mirror, and you'll believe what you see there. That's pure vanity, vanity pure and simple. That's all you'll get from success.

"Now, let's suppose you lose out. You've stood up there for

the world to see bucknaked and danced your little hootcheekootchee. Then you wait, breathless as a bride, for the world's answer. Thumbs down! So you go on home and gnaw the sour bone and chew the marrow of your own pride, like a mean old dog, and you say to yourself either the whole thing is rotten to its slimy, nasty core, or that you yourself are the rotten thing and got just what you deserved. And that, boy, is pride turned upside down, pure vanity again. So either way, you're apt to exchange whatever snivelling modest little virtues you may have possessed for a stinking stew of vanity."

"I guess I'll have to see for myself," Mike said.

"It's a pity, a shame," Judge Royle said, "we can't educate our children. What's the point of human history, anyway?"

The question, Mike was happy to see, was rhetorical. His father bent over his papers again, chuckled to himself, and started to write on a yellow pad. Mike finished his drink, rose, and started to walk softly out of the room.

"Just a moment," the Judge said behind him. "Just tell me in a few words what it is you see in Allen Parker."

Mike turned and looked at him.

"Well, I think he's a good man, and," Mike added, "he certainly has been successful."

Judge Royle squinted fiercely at him, his scarred bald head catching the reflected light of the desk lamp like bronze. The two men, father and son, stared at each other.

"Shut the door behind you," the Judge said, lowering his head to write.

* * *

"It's such a shame!" Mary Ann cried, tossing her magazine in a crumpled flutter across the room. "The stories in the magazines these days bore me to tears."

Mike smiled at her.

"What's wrong with them?"

"For one thing I've read them all already. I used to be able to enjoy the *New Yorker* stories, but even they've started to sound like each other."

"What is it they always say?" he said, vaguely, not really

interested in the state of modern fiction one way or the other. "There are only a dozen or so plots anyway."

"It must be the truth," she said. "I *know* I've read this story before several times. With different names, of course."

Mike lit a cigarette for her and sprawled on the couch across from her chair. Sunbrowned, thin, severe, she still had something of a young girl's softness about her. It showed sometimes in an awkward grace, quick moods, the way she was curled now in her chair like a cat.

"I'm just looking for something to read in the evenings," she said. "Daddy's wild about detective stories these days. There must be a thousand of them lying around the house—all with the most lurid and intriguing covers."

"Why don't you try one?"

"I have. They bore me too," she said. "Besides, who cares who's guilty?"

"Some people make a good living out of caring."

"It's just that it doesn't seem very important to me, that's all."

"Why not?"

Petulantly Mary Ann stubbed out her fresh cigarette in the ash tray and stood up. She stretched slowly toward the high ceiling until she stood on her toes, poised and taut as a diver.

"Because I guess we're all guilty," she said in a voice so soft, so impassive that he wasn't sure she had said it at all.

"You haven't had any supper," she said then. "There's some cold chicken in the ice box."

"Have you had anything?"

"I'll have some coffee with you," she said.

* * *

They sat together on high stools at the kitchen table, he toying with cold chicken and Mary Ann sipping black steamy coffee. The kitchen was still, as he had remembered it, neat and clean and bright, like a kind of little shrine. Charity, who swept up their dirt, picked up their discarded clothes and shoes behind them, made their beds, cleaned their bathrooms and prepared their meals, always left the kitchen in shining order when she went home at night. When he was a boy, Mike thought that the kitchen at night with its scrubbed and mopped floors, its gleaming fixtures, its clean hanging pots and pans, its icy-white, wiped porcelain, was the happiest place in the house to be. There was a sense in that room, Charity's signature of things, that though chaos and old night might be ranging the whole world outside like wild beasts, still some small corner of order was possible. But it was more than that, his boy's feeling that he could never then and only partly now put into words. It was that you knew that it had been used all day long and now there was a sense of completion, the proof positive that something, after all, could be finished for a time.

"Mike, are you all through with the law?"

"I don't know yet," he said. "I don't think I'd ever make much of a lawyer."

"How can you tell when you've just started?"

"I've had a sufficient dose of it," he said. "The main thing, I guess, is that everything has changed. It just isn't what it used to be, or, anyway, it isn't what I thought I wanted."

* * *

He wondered, as he answered her, what he had really expected the law to be. He knew what it had been for his father, and he knew, too, what it had been the generation before that for Anthony Singletree. Those were the fine wild days of it, Mike imagined, the end of the last century up to about the time of the First World War that everyone had named the Last War for such a short, unlikely time. With the Reconstruction ended, the great lawyers, the ones who counted, who in the whole state might easily have been numbered on the fingers of both hands, pursued their craft with a now extinct, colorful, curious excitement. They were more actors than agents, and their stage, their arena, was the courtroom. In those days they rode the circuits around the state, a half a dozen distinguished lawyers and a judge, and they tried all the cases. It was a sort of fantastic game, a masquerade of rational wrestling, or, better, of fencing, as brilliant and abstract as the stage duels, steel and verbal, of Restoration rakes. Each wore his own costume and had an assumed manner, his known and familiar gestures as rigidly exact as if he'd been a character created by some antique psychology like the theory of the humors. Anthony Singletree had always appeared in court in striped pants and a morning coat. He spoke in soft-voiced classic periods, playing out his rhetoric, his eloquence and logic, with the dexterity and abandon of a cowboy's lariat. Another always wore a white linen suit and a string tie, bellowed like a great bull, sweated and shouted in a choleric passion for justice. Still another, a famous one older than the others, wore his Confederate officer's uniform, all the insignia cut away, brass buttons replaced by bone. The judges themselves cut fine figures in their black immaculate robes, and it was said that some of them, fittingly for those times, insisted on bailiffs in livery. In brick and frame county courthouse, in stores and schoolhouses, even churches, converted for that purpose, they duelled each other with equal intensity and fervor over the ownership of a cow or a murder, rape or a stolen sack of flour. And in those days the people came from miles around to watch them perform. Many the fly-ridden, heatstruck, dusty room that rang with their rhetoric, was dazzled by a logic as deft as a magician's sleight of hand. In the evenings the great men, olympians they must have seemed, withdrew to themselves, to whatever boarding house or hotel they were staying in, ate together, played cards with each other and the judge, drank and laughed together, matched stories of horses and hunting and women and never once mentioned, wouldn't have dreamed of discussing the crude reality of the spent day or the day ahead. It was, of course, high comedy, though, since it was Southern, the dark angel of the grotesque hovered over it all. It was also, Mike thought, urgently irresponsible. They had only themselves and the code of their kind, for better or worse, to believe in.

Then there was the other generation, his father's, when the whole world, and the South and of it this single state, saw at last without deception its own cruel image in a true mirror. The fairy tale looking-glass was shattered once and for all. A beast glared back at the world, and who knew whether to laugh or cry? That was real war, then. Its field was still the courtroom, its action still the single theatrical moment of passionate performance, but now it had become a thing of close combat, as far in those few years from the earlier way as, say, a bayonet charge in the mud from the handful of splendid knights prancing on the sward of Agincourt. The old men threw up their hands in dismay, washed them, died, or, like Anthony Singletree retired to live in the fiction of memory and specious splendor, to pad about his house in soft bedroom slippers, breath warmly smelling of whiskey and cigars, a perfect gentleman, a kindly softspoken man with all the time in the world on his hands to show his small grandsons the pictures in his leatherbound volumes of the world's history, to worry about the state of his lawn, the health and welfare of his flowers, and to sit in the evening and in his old mannered voice to tell again the tall tales of the old times. How Joseph Royle, who was daily encountering real dragons, creatures of the primal slime who breathed real fire, must have suffered, listening patiently to all that! But he, too, had his code, his form of reticence. He would have listened all night long to the old man with a perfect impassive attention, like the Spartan boy with a wolf under his shirt.

For Mike the law was something else again. His concerns were contracts and loans and taxes. Numbers danced before his eyes like so many veiled Salomes. Words were shifty, not to be trusted, but to be patiently stalked like game birds. He had not been in a courtroom since he left law school. All his battles were fought with insistent, unseen, watchful enemies who were all around him like the many gods of a primitive people.

* * *

"The thing is," he said to Mary Ann, trying to sum it up, "I just don't think I'm cut out for it."

"I imagine Daddy's disappointed."

Mike stood up and took his empty plate and the cups and saucers over to the sink to rinse them in hot water.

"I guess so," he said. "It won't be the first time."

"Why don't you just leave those things for Charity? She'll take care of them in the morning."

"Oh, I don't know," he said. "I just feel like cleaning up behind myself for a change."

* * *

When he came out of the kitchen, flicking the light off behind him, he found Mary Ann on her hands and knees, fumbling among the books at the bottom of the bookshelf.

"Want some more light?" he said. "I don't see how you can even read the titles."

"Oh, I can see fine. I'm used to it," she said. Then, half-turning: "What do you suppose he ever saw in her?"

"Who?"

"Allen Parker. Why would a man like that marry a woman like her?"

"Beats me," he said. "It's a mystery."

He left her looking for something to read, and he climbed the darkened stairs. The music in his mother's room had stopped playing now, and the house was very quiet.

* * * * * *

Mike's room was almost unchanged. Or, rather, it was so changed by care and keeping, by the *permanence*, his mother's orders that it should stay "exactly as he left it" and Charity's hands could give it, that he felt like a stranger among the familiar things of his past. For *he* had changed, or thought he had, from the boy who made model airplanes out of balsa wood on rainy afternoons and strung them from the ceiling with thread, caught in the fierce angles and attitudes of dogfights. And still, turning a little in the breeze of the fan he had going, a pilotless Fokker dived for the floor and still the strutted (and a little lopsided to his eye now) Spad with its target insignia on the wings followed in hot pursuit.

He lay on his bed smoking, watching a fat-winged cockroach move across the ceiling, its twin delicate feelers like some kind of enormous waxed mustache. The windows were open and the electric fan hummed and performed its halfcircle, each time casting a tepid wave of air across the soles of his bare feet.

There was a gallery of photographs on his bureau, himself, or what had been himself, in progressing, ascending order, framed in good leather. There was the small boy in a sunsuit, curly-haired, running toward the camera. The legs were blurred by his movement, and behind him a swing hanging from an oak limb was blurred too, as if still swinging, just freed of his weight. There was a group picture, his mother, Jojo, Mary Ann and himself all in bathing suits on the beach, posed against the background of a dune whose seawheat was touseled and blurred by a seabreeze. They were squinting and grinning in the bright glare of the sun at the forgotten cameraman. Next he was standing with his father on the observation roof of the Empire State Building. Judge Royle with his straw hat in one hand like a tambourine seemed relaxed and amused. Mike was still in short pants and very solemn. His stiff pose gave an impression of resignation, as if he'd been seized and made to stand still for one wholly wasted moment between wild dashes around the roof in search of new and magical vistas. The wind seemed to be teasing both of them. Their clothes ballooned, and his father's necktie was loose and awry like a long lazy tongue. Then, taller, paler, grim, Mike appeared in the gray uniform of the military academy in Tennessee, posed against the gray granite of the rectangular barracks that looked like a prison and was named for an Episcopal bishop. Less elegant he was soon after still in the gray world, wearing fatigues and a steelpot, cradling an M-1 in a muddy field in Austria. There were others standing around behind him but he couldn't make out their faces and didn't remember their names now. There was a group picture from the University, a row of dark blazers and white shirts and identical club ties, and somewhere among them must be his own face grinning. The last snapshot was a wedding picture, enlarged. Elaine was just about to feed him the first piece of cake. Elaine was laughing. Nearby, just behind them, a waiter passing with a tray of champagne glasses winked. And there were others, friends and relatives in the background watching, most of them seized by empathy, their mouths opened too for that irretrievable instant when the sweet white cake is still untasted.

Himself like a hand of cards dealt out in a half-dozen frozen moments. But nothing, neither this room, arranged, he thought, like some ancient Egyptian's tomb, the clothes of all sizes in the closet, nor the deadly dogfight overhead, had really caught or kept anything. Time was the nervous cockroach on the ceiling with a comical mustache. It progressed by fits and starts and

proved that all those pictures of himself were so many ghosts.
—Catch me with your camera, Love, and I'll smile for you forever, he had written expansively on the back of a snapshot Elaine took on the honeymoon.
—Poetry too! she had written underneath. You're full of little surprises.
Neither the smile, nor the poetry, nor his store of surprises had been enough.
It wasn't that Mike was feeling sorry for himself. Self-pity could scarcely have been so passive as his mood. Nor was it the inevitable young man's dismay at mutability, though mutability may have been the occasion. It was more physical than mental, a great weariness, an overwhelming sense of sloth on the hot still summer evening. He was, he thought, too lazy even to think about those pictures, to take one of them and concentrate on it, on precisely the moment and the feel of it, with luck and memory and the five good senses to capture the essence of *that* time until it shadowed and eclipsed the inconsequential void which was called right now. Spun out, studied, arranged, either chronologically or in any other order, those pictures might have summed up a life. But he was willing to let them be. Glazed and framed and always two-dimensional, guiltless and uncommitted, they could simply be pictures on a bureau.
Mike looked at his wristwatch. It was only ten o'clock. It was going to be a long night of it, just lying here trying to think about nothing at all, trying to fall asleep. He sat up and put on his shoes. He changed his shirt, counted the bills in his wallet, combed his hair, and went back downstairs.
Mary Ann was still reading and did not look up. Farther back in the house a blade of light showed under the study door. He walked out of the house and breathed the night air. He heard a tom cat howling somewhere and from farther off a freight train whistle made its lonesome song. He got in his car, switched on the lights and drove off.

* * * * * * *

The Club El Tropitan is about twelve miles out of Oakland in the piney woods country. You follow the highway south for a while, past the filling stations and drive-ins and motels, the used-car lots still brightly lit and flourishing with bunting and flags and whirlygigs, and the rows of silent cars looking like sad wooden horses put out to graze. You go beyond the last of the allnight, roadside diners and the truck spots where the huge trailer trucks, like prehistoric beasts, cluster in casual disorder. You turn off the paved road onto a rutted dirt trail that winds into the woods. Set back deep in the woods, surrounded by an improbable golf course as shaggy as a bearskin, is the Club El Tropitan. Few, if any, the golfers who may ever have tried to play around in the kneehigh grass and among the torn and faded flags. The club was built of good stone in a pseudo-Spanish style, the golf course was laid out, during Prohibition. The fine romantic days of rum-runners slipping into the jungle inlets of the East Coast, passing their fragile cargo to be loaded into the black heavy lowslung cars with souped-up engines that sped away, often lightless over the back roads, are long gone. Gone too the original gangster owners who were said to fire their submachine guns only in the air and only on the Fourth of July, vanished like the last of the buffalo hunters. They've been replaced by modest businessmen. There's nothing illegal about the place now, except for a little gambling, some renting of bedrooms upstairs to casual transient couples and, once in a while, a stag-show which could hardly be said to represent the civic moral tone. It's just a nightclub now, and there are others, even in this county, nearer and more accessible.

 The significant thing is that it has survived. Maybe, Mike was thinking, because in Prohibition people just got in the habit of it. Over the years the surroundings, the lonesome drive in the woods to get there, the absurdity of the country club disguise, all these things became inseparable parts of a pattern of pleasure. Then again, there was something else he was aware of, knew in his bones. There's a little wince of guilt that is a requisite portion of any frowned-on pleasure, whatever it may be, from whoring to contract bridge. Mike remembered one time hiding with some other boys in the woods to watch a night church service of the holyrollers. For them tobacco, *especially* tobacco for some reason, was a mortal sin, chewed, smoked, or dipped.

While the preacher shouted fire and brimstone in a milewide voice, people crept out of the church and into the bushes to smoke. At times during that sermon the night air flared with matches like a cloud of fireflies. Properly damned by a puff or two, they'd return to that echoing arena of salvation, perhaps to be converted again, to roll on the floor and sweat and shout the good news in the Unknown Tongue. That was part of the explanation. Sin just couldn't be sinful unless you could feel *bad* about it. The Club El Tropitan was reached by a deviation from the straight and narrow (U.S. Highway 17), arrived at by a furtive gesture along a crooked way, had a secret and romantic history and, thus, could appeal at the same time that it appalled.

Still there was another aspect he was aware of, the peculiar Southern heritage. And this, he thought, must really be the basic difference between ourselves and our New England cousins. The reason we never burned witches or sewed on scarlet letters wasn't that we weren't concerned with depravity, natural or supernatural. We *expected* it. The Southerners had, in fact, a less exalted view of man than those stern moralists in black and white clothes from the harsh, rockstrewn country. A man was bound to sin, sure as the world. With this as a premise, it followed that the thing to do was to keep it out of sight, if not out of mind, never to confuse the realities of virtue and vice with personal and civic morality. Civilization, culture, must be as abstract and decorative as a snowstorm in a glass paperweight. So it would be that within the circle of Anthony Singletree lack of tact or poor horsemanship might be deadly, unforgivable sins. But, paradoxically, violation was necessary, just as a strong faith needs some blasphemy. Even Judge Royle, who had shared so little of either the joys or the despairs of the aristocratic society, had to have his pig pen nearby. And so it was that without even thinking about it the most vehement moralists, from the fistpounding, biblethumping fundamentalists to the last thin lines and farflung outposts of the Drys, might well have wept if the Club El Tropitan had burned, been struck by judicious lightning, or even fallen into disrepair. Where could the Devil go then?

* * *

"Don't I know you from somewheres, boy?"

Mike swivelled halfway around on his bar stool and looked into the lean gray face of Atkins. His eyes were wetly bright, and, set in the pinched shrewd face, surrounded in contours of lines and deep crow's feet, they seemed the eyes of a hunting bird, gull or hawk. He felt, as before, a little uneasy with Atkins.

"I know I'm crocked, bombed, gassed, drunk," Atkins said, struggling onto the stool beside him. "I am a godamn cliché newspaperman. Which is precisely how come I'm a sneaky little newshound at my age instead of some kind of an editor with a big desk and a broad bottom. You know what kind of an editor I'd *like* to be? A f—ing society editor. Man, I could *write* that trash: 'Miss Periwinkle was a veritable vision of loveliness in different shades of shrimp.' How's that?"

"I don't believe a word of it," Mike said. "You don't look sorry for yourself to me."

Atkins shook his head and signalled the bartender for two drinks. The bartender, a crisp marionette in a white starched jacket, suntanned, impassive as a priest, tilted them a nod and spun like a dancer to his business with glasses and ice cubes and whiskey.

"*Look?* You don't know. You just don't know," Atkins said. "If there's one thing *I* know it's that everybody, every grinning man jack of them," (He waved his arm in a stiff circle to include everybody in the room. Mike had to duck the dramatic gesture as it came around.) "every manly jackass of them spends the greater part of his allotted time on this orb feeling sorry for himself and wishing he was anybody but him. Oh, why wasn't *I* born richer, handsomer, more powerful, immortal, *etcetera, etcetera, etcetera, ad nauseum?* Why ain't I God? I would be *so* nice. Their brains are all clogged up like a cesspool with self-pity. And your reporter is no exception, drunk or sober. You know what I'd rather be than me? Do you know?"

"No, sir, I don't have the slightest idea."

"I'd be happy if I could just be a big fat huge nigger washerwoman. I'd like to spend the rest of my days boiling the dirty clothes of the world in a black wash tub, stirring them with a peeled stick, singing the whole time, hanging them up to dry, letting the sun and air get to them. Starching and ironing and sending those clothes back as clean as a whistle. I tell you the most beautiful thing in the world is a stack of clean laundry. It looks good, it smells good. Hell, I imagine it *tastes* good too. And do you know what those sonofabitches done? Do you know?"

"No, sir."

"They came along and invented the automatic washer and the automatic dryer. The bastards!"

The bartender put the two highball glasses down in front of them. Atkins looked at his, stirred it with the swizzle stick thoughtfully, sipped it and made a sad face.

"What do they *put* in a drink nowadays, tarwater?"

Then he squinted and focused his eyes on Mike.

"Don't I know you? Did I ask you that before?"

"I'm the guy that was with Senator Parker this morning."

"I'll be damned," Atkins said. "Sure you are. I knew you when I saw you come in here. I know all about you. See what liquor can do to a perfectly good memory?"

He produced a crumpled pack of cigarettes and with grave dignity offered one to Mike, then took one himself, licked his lips, pinched the end of it, like a roll-your-own, bit it, wet it, turned it around in his lips. He made an effort to strike a match, failed, and Mike lit it for him. Atkins leaned way back, perilously on the stool, caught himself, recovered and puffed deeply.

"Yeah," he said. "I know all about you. I took the liberty. But I can't figure it out."

"What can't you figure?"

"The sense of it," Atkins said. "You proceed to throw up a perfectly good job working in New York—and don't tell me it wasn't a good job. Any job that pays you money is a good job. You throw up your job and come back down here to spend your time and energy for next to nothing working for The Lost Cause."

"What makes you say that?" Mike said, grinning. "It's a while yet before election day."

"Go ahead and grin at me. Go right ahead and laugh . . ."

"I wasn't . . ."

"Yes you were. You most certainly were. But no offense. You're just green enough, ignorant enough to have the right to grin."

"Everybody's been saying that all day to me. What do *you* mean?"

Atkins put his arm around Mike's shoulder and leaned on him like a wounded man.

"Look," he said. "Looka here. You won't believe this, but I respect, I *respect*, old Allen Parker. He's been a good man and he's a better man than I am. Maybe the best man this no-account state ever put in a national office. But, my boy, boy mine, he has already lost this election. He ain't got a Chinaman's chance. And I expect in his more, shall we say *lucid* moments, times when he's not even able to kid himself, he knows it."

"You must be right. I *must* be ignorant."

"Never mind the sarcasm. It's wasted," Atkins said. "So many things. The Party. They want Batten *nationally*. Parker's an old-time New Dealer. He's outlived his time and he's got all kinds of dangerous seniority. What they need is a stable of new bright young men, not some oldtimer, some old prima donna making a series of crack-voiced farewell tours. That's the first thing. Point two: *Money*. The big money, such as it is in this state, is behind Batten. They've invested in him. Now, what do you think that means?"

Atkins sighed and put out his cigarette.

"If this conversation keeps up I'm going to wind up sober, and then where will I be?" he said. "Here beginneth the first lesson. These men who are backing Batten are business men. Let's understand that. Business men, not gamblers. They are making an investment. Now, let's make the distinction between a business man and a gambler. A gambler, amateur or pro, honest or a cheat, stands a chance of losing his money. His element is risk. He takes that risk and when he loses, all he can do is throw up his hands and say that's the way she bounces. Now *these* boys, this money that scared Allen Parker into running again, these boys ain't gamblers. They are in business. They do not intend or foresee the losing of a dime. They aren't risking anything. Parker knows this. Batten don't know it yet because he's green too. But he will. You better believe he will."

"Parker is still the man he's got to beat."

"So it seems, after this morning. And my guess is that they're not exactly overjoyed about what happened. Like I said, they aren't going to take any chances. So you just watch what happens. I predict—Atkins predicts, how does *that* sound?—I predict certain things will follow inevitably, just like a little trail of horseshit behind a fat old draught horse. First, there will be a *third* candidate introduced onto the scene. Somebody to split up the cracker vote with Parker. Second, this campaign is going to be fought out on some surprising issues you haven't even thought of yet. And one of these issues, Atkins predicts, will be the happy little issue of the two races."

"Parker has never been a white-supremacy man. He's always had the Negro vote."

"Yes, indeedy. For what it's worth. But this is going to be a rough and dirty one. Before they get through with Allen Parker, they'll be making him holler 'Nigger, go back to Africa.' "

"Batten won't get mixed up in something like that."

"Batten will do whatever he's told to."

"I doubt it," Mike said. "That would be a shame."

"It would be a terrible stinking shame to see a man like Allen Parker get shit thrown all over him and have to go down on his knees and beg. It would be a godamn disgrace, even in this day and time of disgraces."

"I don't think it's likely."

"Wait and see, buddy boy," Atkins said. "You just wait and see."

They sat quiet for a moment sipping their drinks. Mike looked at himself and the gray little man beside him, captured in the swimming mirror behind the bar. And behind them was the big room, dark and cool as a cave, where waiters in white jackets moved among the tables, swift, decorous, attentive. He could hear the sound of voices as soft and murmurous as wings and the sudden fizz of laughter like sodawater. And then a colored band mounted the bandstand and began to play, drowning it all with sound.

"Listen," Atkins said, conspiratorial. "I got two pigs with me. *Two!* How about that? Like the bum at the cafe window, my appetite exceeds my ability."

Mike laughed. "What are you doing with them now?"

"I got them sitting at a table over there." He jerked his thumb. "They're eating the biggest steaks in the house."

"What do you want me to do?"

"Do whatever you want to," Atkins said. "I'm just going to get quietly plastered."

* * *

The two girls—Helen and Darlene—were picking over the ruins of their T-bone steaks. They could almost have been twins, short, stocky, square-jawed and -headed.

"I told you they were hungry," Atkins said. "I could tell they were hungry when I first looked at them."

The two heads raised from their plates simultaneously, like cows mildly disturbed while grazing. They saw Mike and grinned dutifully with very white teeth.

"Are you a gangster?" One of them (Helen? Darlene?) said.

"Not at the moment," Mike said, sitting down. "It's out of season."

"Popsie said this place is where all the gangsters were."

"Who's Popsie?"

"*Him*," the other one said, stabbing viciously with her fork in the direction of Atkins, who was waving both arms for a waiter.

"Oh," Mike said. "*You mean Popsie!* Well, he's right. Half the unemployed gangsters in the state are right here in this room."

"They don't look like gangsters to *me*. I mean *you* do, but you don't dress like one."

"Ever hear of a disguise?"

The waiter brought another round of drinks.

"Can't you see he's kidding you, Darlene?" the other one (Helen obviously) said.

"Oh, for Christ's sake," Darlene snapped. "I *know* it. I'm just trying to have a little fun. Do you *mind?*"

Helen bit her lip and turned away to look at the band.

"Do *you* mind?" Darlene said to Mike.

"No, it sounds like a bright idea to me," he said. "What shall we do? I'll tell you what. You get up and do a striptease to attract their attention and I'll stick the place up."

"Oh for God's sake," Helen said. "I'm ready to go back to the hotel."

"Go ahead then," Darlene said. "Nobody's *making* you stay."

They drank and the two girls glared at each other. Mike's legs were bruised by their swift signals under the table. Atkins gently lowered his head to the table, spilling his drink, and went to sleep.

"Do you have a friend?" Darlene said.

"I haven't got a friend in the world," Mike said. "Tell you what. Let's us dance and see if *we* can be friends."

The band was playing what seemed to be a rhumba. At least when they danced under the bandstand the grinning leader shook two rattling gourds at them.

"You dance so well," Darlene said.

"I won a contest," Mike said. "A lifetime subscription to Arthur Murray."

"What do you do?" she said. "I mean really, seriously."

"What do *you* do?"

"We're high school gym teachers," Darlene said. "We're on vacation."

"Isn't that a funny coincidence?"

"What?"

"I'm a high school gym teacher too."

"You slay me," she said. "You just slay me."

He tightened his grip on the small of her back, pulled her short square firm body tight to his, smelling the odor of sweat and powder, the cheap, inexpressive, everhopeful perfume, feeling the warm slight mound of her belly against his groin. One more drink and he'd think himself clever. Two more and Darlene would look like Ingrid Bergman.

"How's your friend?"

"Oh, she's all right. She doesn't mind."

"I mean is she as nice as you?"

"She'll do in a pinch," Darlene said, laughing.

And once again they danced by the bandstand. Apparently it

wasn't a rhumba any more. The band leader had exchanged his gourds for the gleaming curve of a saxophone.

* * *

Mike woke, fuzzyheaded, and glanced at the blue luminous dial on his wrist watch. Two-thirty. Someone beside him stirred, groaned and cuddled a pillow. It was female, quite naked and sound asleep. He noticed that her back was evenly tanned all over. (Now what beach would *that* be?) He slipped out of bed and started to hunt for his clothes in the dark. Their clothes were scattered around the room. It looked like a big wind had blown them off a washline. He dressed and put her things in a pile on a chair. He put five dollars on top for cab fare, or whatever, and tiptoed to the door. Just as he turned the handle and it clicked she sat bolt upright in the bed. She stared in the dark for a moment, then snatched the sheet to cover herself.

"What are you doing? Where are you going?"

"I've got to stand reveille," he said and shut the door behind him. He heard her starting to cry.

He went down the dark hall and down the stairs to the dining room of the club. The tables were hooded and the chairs were upside down. The dancers had all gone home. A colored man was mopping the floor near the front door, and at a lone table Atkins slept and snored. Next to him, a tangle of hair and rumpled clothes, Darlene snored too. (How did *that* happen?) He walked to the door.

"You want to wake 'em up?" the Negro said.

Mike handed him a folded dollar bill.

"No," he said. "Let them sleep it off. They'll be all right."

The moon was up, shone through the woods and gleamed on his car and the other, a convertible with an Indiana license plate, in the parking lot. He got in his car and drove away fast.

* * * * * * *

It was after five when Mike finally found the radio station, a small modern building of concrete and glass, and parked his car in front of it. The stars were gone, the sky was the gray of dirty water, and the sun was coming on. He could feel it. He heard a rooster crow. He went inside the building, past a desk by the door where an attendant was sleeping, and he looked into a glassed-in studio.

There sat Jojo, his sleeves rolled up past his elbows, talking into a microphone, his face animated, smiling, talking a stream of words that Mike couldn't hear. There were paper cups of coffee, a couple of ash trays heaped with mounds of cigarette butts and ashes, and scraps of paper littered the floor. Jojo was getting fat now and his hair was much thinner. He had let it grow long on the sides and back to hide his baldness. To Mike's surprise he saw that Jojo had a mustache now too. He leaned close to the microphone, his lips moving quickly, then leaned back and signalled to a booth just beyond the studio. Pressing his face to the cool glass, Mike could see the shape of the engineer in the control booth. He was reading a magazine, and without once lowering it from his eyes he started a record with his left hand. Jojo stood up and stretched tiredly. He lit a cigarette, looked around and saw Mike. His face wrinkled into a big smile and he waved. He came out of the studio.

"Mike, baby, what in the world are you doing here? How are you? How've you been?" he said, hugging him. "Look, I've got about ten minutes to go. You just wait here while I wrap up the show and we'll go out to my place and have some breakfast. It's great to see you."

Jojo went back into the studio, flipped a switch and the music blared out into the office. The man at the desk sat up, shook his head, rubbed his eyes, grinned at Harper, and looked at his watch. The music ended.

"Cats, we were off the wall on that one." Jojo's voice came, rich and insinuative, in the radio announcer's accent of no time and no place, and wholly unrelated to the slumped, weary body, the soft, round, saddened face. "Now fasten your seat belts and *no* smoking please! Your boy is going to have you buzzing the ceiling on this next one. Hold tight, we're going to rock. We're going to shake the glass out of the windows. We're going to wake up the chicks and the roosters too. Hold on to your hats and coats, here's nobody else but" (he waved to the engineer who put the arm of the record player on a spinning disc and the sound of a saxophone soared out, invisibly, on the air) "you guessed it. It's the late, great Charlie Parker! Go man, go! Go crazy!"

He looked at Mike and shrugged, picked up a piece of scrap paper and made a note on it. Mike went back outside to get some fresh air and to see the red dawn coming on.

* * *

They stopped at a roadside diner and had breakfast. Jojo, it turned out, lived in a motel. He had a hot plate to cook on, but it was broken.

"I sometimes wonder if a living soul is listening to my stuff. I sit there pooping my guts out and it gets lonely as hell. Every once in a while it dawns on me that maybe there's nobody, just nobody out there listening anywhere. I tell you that's a lonesome feeling. Know what I mean?"

"Sure," Mike said. "I got an idea."

"Of course, *some* people listen some of the time. I get phone calls and mail. But you never know at any given moment whether anybody's out there or not. It gives me the creeps."

"How do you like your job?"

"Oh, so-so. The station manager's been down on me. I got drunk and missed a couple of shows. He doesn't approve. But things are getting a little better. I may work into a good show one of these days. All it takes is a break. I wonder if the old man ever listens to me."

"Who knows?"

"You know something, Mike? I got a crazy idea this evening. I got to thinking I might go back into flying again, flying for the A-rabs."

"What gave you that idea?"

"Jack Teagarden singing 'The Sheik of Araby.' Don't laugh now. An idea can come from anywhere. Those A-rabs need flyers in the worst way. They've always got a war going somewhere."

"Come off it, Jojo. You're too old to fly."

"I could fly the hell out of their heaps. I checked out—unofficially—in a National Guard jet a couple of weekends ago. I showed those kids a thing or two. That's the one thing I can really do—fly. The A-rabs would probably make me a f—ing Colonel or something. They'd give me the works—a harem and double rations of shishkebab."

Mike laughed.

"*Now* what are you laughing at? Did you ever see one of those belly dancers? I mean a real, honest-to-God A-rab belly dancer?"

"Where would I see a belly dancer?"

"You literal-minded slob," Jojo said. "No wonder you don't understand. Haven't you got any *imagination?*"

"Same old Jojo," Mike said. "You haven't changed a bit."

Which was at once true and false. Physically Jojo had changed a great deal. As a boy, as a young man he had been extraordinarily handsome, almost beautiful. But (He would joke about it once in a while.—I'm just the opposite of Dorian Gray, he'd say. Every sin I've ever committed, even the sins of *omission,* is written on my flesh. I'm like a godamn tatooed lady. Even thinking about dissipation puts marks on me.) now he was like a comic caricature of himself, an image cast up by a distorting mirror in a carnival glass house. Facetiously, yet half in earnest, he wrote in an occasional long rambling letter, just as he'd been talking now, of one hairbrained scheme after another, all of them calling for movement, romance, the absurd, and none, or just as likely any of them would be his next gesture.—It's the damned Singletree blood in me, he used to say. (And some of their Singletree cousins *were* daft—Raymond, the tap dancer, Henry Lee, the poet, killed in Korea, Angus who survived the Army to come home and was now in the State Mental Hospital in Chattahoochee.) But, Mike thought, there was a difference. Those Singletrees never pictured themselves as crazy, unusual, different. It never even occurred to them that they weren't conforming to the way of the world. It took no conscious effort on their part simply to be themselves. Jojo, on the other hand, was deadly serious, seemed to dodge from prank to prank like an illusive *picaro* in an old tale, the difference being that all of the jokes were on himself. It was a curious form of loss, of waste and buffoonery. It was, strangely, a kind of vocation, as if in some utter humiliation, in some desert of himself, he might propitiate his wrathful gods and, reduced to the nudity of blessed foolishness, atone, be healed and whole again. Change was Jojo's element. He thrived in it. He burned in it again and again like the mythical phoenix.

Mike was torn between pity and envy. At least Jojo seemed to care enough to thumb his nose at everything.

The Tahiti Motel, where Jojo was staying, was an extravagant group of vaguely Southsea "huts," built around a lawn that was green and trim and clipped as a carpet. It was shaded at the four corners by shabby coconut palms. (It was too far north in the state for them to thrive.) In the center of the lawn was a gnarled, fat old orange tree on which had been grafted the limbs of other citrus trees so that in season it must have seemed like a fairytale tree, bearing like great lollipops its simultaneous weight of oranges and tangerines, grapefruit, lemons and limes. There were a few cars drawn up at the cabins. A bald man in dark glasses, wearing a shortsleeved sportshirt luridly depicting a confusion of surf-riders and hula dancers, palm trees and monkeys and alligators, came out of a cabin, looked at Mike and Jojo and began to load matched, imitation-leather luggage into the trunk of his car that yawned at him hugely like a slack-jawed hippo.

"I'm the complete modern man," Jojo said, unlocking the door of his cabin, "the complete dangler."

The chill vacuity of air-conditioning greeted them. Jojo stopped in the center of the room, breathed deeply like a swimmer coming up for air and waved his arm around the room.

"I live in an air-conditioned, hermetically sealed, homogenized, phony Southsea hut. There's a fancy thermostat here, and I can have any temperature I have a whim for, from hell's outskirts to Little America. I've got plenty to keep my mind occupied." (He pointed to stacks of Detective and Confession magazines.) "I have a portable radio to keep the lines of communication open with the big bad world outside. I've even got a record player and all the records I can swipe from the studio. I've got an icebox, plenty of cheap liquor, and—I've never tried it, but I know it's true—if I clap my hands three times a dusky figment of my adolescent daydreams will come in here awiggling her belly and say 'I am Tondelao!'"

Mike sat down in a canvas chair.

"And you mean to tell me you want to throw up all *this* for the sake of a bunch of A-rabs?"

"Did I say A-rabs?" Jojo said. "Excuse me. What I meant was *bedouins*, the no-mads, the ones that are always folding tents and stealing away. I mean real ones, of course. The folks who stop here are only pseudo-nomads. I guess I'm the only full-blooded bedouin, the only born transient in the place. And I *live* here."

* * *

Mike borrowed Jojo's shaving kit and stood in the bathroom, facing himself in the flattering deepsea blur of a tinted mirror. With some breakfast and a drink and now the pleasure of shaving he was feeling better, well enough to wonder what would ever become of the two plain, unhappy gym teachers from Indiana and the gray little newspaper man from Jacksonville. What would become of Allen Parker, waking at this moment amid the ponderous white piles of stone in Washington? Or Judge Royle, already up, in his study perhaps, or taking a first morning look at his pigs? Or Nancy Singletree Royle, still asleep? Charity who would already be in the kitchen fixing breakfast? Mary Ann? Elaine, what would she be doing now? He could picture her stumbling around the apartment (she always took a while to wake up) a tall, thin, pretty girl in her aquamarine nightgown who looked very good in the morning for some reason, banging the pots and pans and ending by making coffee while forgotten water trickled and steamed in the bathroom basin.

At this moment in the thin band of first light countless people, all of them God's children, were waking from dreams like deepsea divers surfacing. They had prowled and rooted among the shifty wrecks and bones of their desires, each searching for something (surely it was there), a treasure chest sparkling with appalling calm. And then you woke, you rubbed the sleep out of your eyes, and as the shadow of mortality fell across you, you retreated into the castle of your flesh. You washed it, shaved it; your bowels moved and you ate and drank and gradually dispelled the notion of the first blest moments of the light that all would be well, that all your enemies would turn into pumpkins, and before this day was done a bright miraculous stranger from a far land was going to touch your sleeve and whisper in your ear that all your wishes were granted.

It was so like Jojo to be finishing *his* day. The world awoke and Jojo went to bed.

* * *

"I would've thought you'd had enough," Jojo was saying.

"Enough what?"

Buttoning his shirt, tucking it in, Mike came out of the bathroom to find Jojo in skyblue silk pajamas, propped up by pillows on his bed.

"Politics."

"I never had *any*, unless you count the times the old man ran for governor," Mike said. "And I was too ignorant to know what was really going on."

Jojo grimaced. "I wasn't," he said. "I knew exactly what was going on the whole time. It made me sick at my stomach. I went around wanting to puke."

"That was different."

"How? How the hell was that any different?" Jojo said. "Where did he ever get a damnfool idea like that?"

Mike shrugged. He was sorry they had come at last to the subject. It embarrassed him to see Jojo, cap and bells cast aside, like a hurt little man.

"It's a pity," Jojo went on, "that it took a narrow-minded, petty demagogue with a wild desire to be a martyr to stand up for law and order at that time."

"Somebody had to do it," Mike said. "Your old families, your Singletrees, with their fine names and fine silver wouldn't lift a finger. Who was going to take the responsibility if he didn't?"

"You may be right," Jojo said. "But it's a pity. This isn't an age for heroes. Whenever we get a hero he's a caricature."

"Why do you hate him?"

"Wouldn't you?" he said quickly. "Wouldn't you, if you were me?"

"I don't know," Mike said.

"I'll tell you the truth," Jojo said, smiling. "I don't know either. I really don't know for sure whether I hate him or not."

Inexplicably, even before his grin faded completely, Jojo's eyes brimmed with tears.

"Pigs!" he said. "Can you beat that? Oh, Jesus Christ, pigs! Do you think I care? Do you think I give a damn?"

And then he began to sob, to choke with sobbing, and he turned away, buried his head in a pillow so Mike wouldn't see his face, his back heaving, his hands clutching and clawing at the sheets.

Mike picked up his coat. Gently he laid a sheet across Jojo's back, and he went outside where the hot early morning air was like an oven door in his face. Sweat popped out all over his body at once. The bald man with dark glasses and the fabulous shirt had gone toward whatever destination he was seeking.

Mike got in the car and started the drive home.

* * * * * * *

Charity fixed a pot of fresh coffee for him in the kitchen. Mike was very tired now. All the way back the raw light had shimmered off the asphalt road, waves of pure heat rising and dancing, and he had rubbed his eyes, nodded and nodded, and had nearly fallen asleep. Now he was sitting in the kitchen drinking hot strong coffee. With breakfast cooked and served, the beds made and the bedrooms cleaned, the kitchen spotless, Charity was reading her Bible. Thick-lensed glasses perched on her nose and her angular black face was wrinkled in concentration, her finger slowly marking her trail from word to word and her lips silently repeating the words to herself as if to taste and savor the shape and texture of them. Charity had learned to read when Mike did, had sat patiently while her tutor in short pants showed her some of the mysteries of the printed word he had learned in school, until she was able to read her own Bible. It gave her great joy and comfort, she said, to read it all by herself.

She had first come to work for them when Joseph Royle became a Judge. It was more fitting for a Judge to have help in his house, Nancy Royle had said. Judge Royle laughed and answered that he guessed she was weary enough of a hot stove and a long broomstick, and he wouldn't mind having a good experienced cook in the kitchen for a change. Nancy Royle laughed at that herself. They were still able to joke about their marriage then. And Charity came to work for them first in the rented house and then when they moved to this place, the house the Judge built, once the biggest in the town, an expensive reproduction of the houses Nancy had known as a girl, perhaps to try once more by a grandiose gesture to please his wife, perhaps to humble her, perhaps both at the same time. Charity had come seven days a week (with Thursday and Sunday afternoons off) for nearly thirty years and given most of her daylight hours to this family. Each of them felt differently about her. Nancy Royle retained an easy sentimentality toward Charity, said of her that she was a "good oldtimey nigra," and found by her presence in the house a satisfactory link to her childhood. She was reticently accepted by Judge Royle. He came from people who didn't have servants, who had sweated to earn their bread, had tilled the same earth as the Negro, and once made up the bulk of an army and the bulk of its devastating casualties in the war to defend the right of others to own, feed, clothe, care for or mistreat that race. He grew up, then, envying and despising the patronized domestic servants in big houses. Yet Judge Royle had read widely and knew too from experience what it was to work hard and long for small wages and what the knot and gnaw of being hungry was like, and somehow he had transcended his bitter inheritance. It was said that he was as fair and as fierce with a black man as a white man when he was on the bench. He didn't believe, could scarcely even have *known* of the myths Nancy Royle clung to of an ever-smiling, childlike, watermelon-gorging, trinket-loving, lazy, razor-wielding, oversexed race that God, in His ways mysterious, had darkened and humbled and made to serve. Still in his own way he was the sterner taskmaster. A servant was paid to serve, and he was demanding. Mary Ann had been, briefly, a champion of equality, a fiery debater whose passionate logic could reduce her mother to tears; but now she seemed indifferent except for being a little appalled at the nostalgic sentimentality of keeping a fulltime servant in this day and age. Jojo was, as always, flippant.

—You better be careful, he had said. If Mike really teaches

that nigger how to read she's liable to stumble on the news that Lincoln freed the slaves.

For Mike the relationship had been more subtle and difficult. Charity had raised him, and he knew more about her than the others. He remembered her mother, a frail tiny woman who wore a bright bandana like a turban and sometimes smoked a pipe. She had been born in slavery. He could remember when she used to come every day with Charity and sit on a stool in the corner of the kitchen, a tiny, leathery, birdboned, bright-eyed woman who could sit there all day long, perfectly straight and silent, even when she was sound asleep.—I just squnch up and don't take much room, she said. Sometimes she would tell him about the old days, about the big loud bell in the morning and how much cotton she could pick when she was going good and the house as big as a church building where the white-folks lived; and she sometimes talked, too, of the nighttime world, of root ladies and hexes, of ghosts, of the patrols in the deep woods and the sound of their fierce hounds belling. But it was all a vague memory for her, long gone, colored by the distorting effort of recovery and probably, except in her own mind, as false as the romantic fiction about the times with its magnolias and honeysuckle, its banjos and singing, loyal darkies, its brave tall forlorn riders in fine uniforms who rode to glory in a swirl of flags and dust.

The past is what we make of it, Mike thought, and we'll make it anything but true. We will do everything with it except be responsible for it.

Charity had grown up in another time, another generation, in poverty and without even the teasing notion of hope for a change. To live her life she sold most of it. To raise her own family of children, six of them, she lavished her care and attention on another family, and, thus divided, remained a partial stranger to them both. Her children had run half-wild and half-clothed in the savage and picturesque jungle of unpainted shacks in Black Bottom, across the railroad tracks. Somehow some of them had survived. She had outlived two husbands. One, a plumber's helper, was a good man and a good worker, bought his own house on his own patch of land, roofed the house to last a while, put in plumbing, fenced it and painted it and furnished it. He used to come to pick Charity up in the evenings in his own car. He died early. The other was a younger man, a handsome, swaggering worker on a railroad section gang, quick to laugh, quick to fight, hard drinking and careless. Another woman's husband shot him dead.

—Lord, child, Charity had told Mike once, I've had both kinds, the good and the bad, and it's hard to say which is the best. A good man keeps the roof over your head and plenty food on the table. But that bad man, he could make you laugh when your stomach was empty and the house was leaking like a sieve.

Two of her sons were dead. One was killed in a honky-tonk fight, and the other drowned in the Pacific in the War. His name was on the county's obelisk in the park, and one of these days, on a Thursday or a Sunday afternoon, she would walk all the way downtown to see it. Another boy went to Philadelphia and she never heard a word of him again. One daughter went to college and was a schoolteacher in Houston. Another, in and out of the county jail a dozen times before she was twenty, married and went North. She sometimes sent a postcard to Charity or one for Charity to read to her own daughter, born blind, who lived with Charity. Then there was Jay, the youngest, Mike's age. She had brought him with her every day she could, at first to play with Mike and later on to wash windows and move furniture around and work in the yard. Jay still lived in Oakland, drifting from one job to another—bellhop, waiter, fruitpicker, construction laborer—worked when he needed money, was in and out of trouble, and was always available to drive the Judge when he wanted to go somewhere.

We come pretty close to getting to know them for a while in childhood, Mike thought. But then we lose it, the knack of knowing anything, man or beast or flower, that's strangely other than ourselves. And we and they retire into ourselves, into two dimensions, and we pass among each other like shadows. They've lived on the same land, lived off it too, been buried in it, suffered and enjoyed the same seasons and weathers, but really shared so little, been deprived of so much. And both of us have been deprived of sharing whatever wisdom and foolishness the other may have garnered out of time.

He could remember exactly at this moment the times when

that mutual awareness had come. The time for Charity had been the first time she could no longer discipline him as she always had.—Don't you touch me! You can't tell me what to do, he had said to her, and he saw, before he even felt his palm sting, the neat print of his hand on her cheek and her eyes flare up in sudden anger and dismay. And then it was as if a light went right out of them, and ever after she looked at him with the wary, guarded, uncommitted gaze she reserved for the white adult world. And he was *Mister* Mike soon afterward. With Jay it had been different, but no less final. They had a gang in the neighborhood then, and Jay was in it too. One day there had been a fight with another gang, boys from another part of town, whitetrash, in the park. They fought with beebee guns and hard green dates from the date palms and finally at close range with fists and sticks, and they managed in bloody joy to drive their shabby barefooted enemy from the park. That same night some men, dressed in their best clothes, had come to see the Judge. They talked about it and seemed to him to threaten. He kept them standing at the foot of his front steps with their uneasy hats in their hands while he cursed them for threatening him and, in turn, threatened to have them all locked up. He told them he had come far enough along in the world for *his* children to play with whom they pleased wherever they pleased. He told them he knew their names and faces and they had better walk a chalk line in this county for a while. Mike stood in the shadows on the porch and watched their lean, troubled faces in the light as the Judge tongue-lashed them. Then the Judge gave them one minute to be off his land, and they put on their hats and walked, stiff-backed, down the lawn and out of sight. —Did you see them? the Judge said. That's *scum*, boy. Some of them had pistols in their pockets. I'd like to have seen one of them be man enough to touch one, just touch a pistol in front of me. And then his body relaxed and he laughed, left Mike standing on the porch and went into the house, laughing.

But, nevertheless, soon afterwards he talked to Charity and Jay didn't come again for a long while. And when he finally did come it was to work and not to play any more.

* * *

Mike finished his coffee and put the cup and saucer in the sink.
"What's Jay up to these days?" he said.
Charity looked up, took off her glasses and held them in her hands.
"Why, he's got a job working for the railroad. Part time," she said. "Jay, he's married now."
"You don't say? When did that happen?"
"It's been several years ago," she said. "He's got two children now—both boys."
"I'll be damn," Mike said. "Things sure do change."
"They do," she said. "They surely do."
He started to leave the kitchen.
"Have you seen Mr. Jojo yet?"
"Yes," he said. "I was with him this morning."
"How is that poor boy getting along?"
"Oh, about the same. About the same as ever."
He left the kitchen, and as the door swung to, he looked back and saw she had her glasses on again and was reading the good book.

• • •

"They're off and running," Mary Ann said, tossing the morning paper to him. "And where are *you?*"
"Where *was* I, you mean."
"All right, where was you?"
"I went out to see if the Tropitan is still there."
"Is it?"
"Don't ask me," he said. "My testimony wouldn't hold up in a court of law."
"There are times," Mary Ann said, "when I wouldn't mind being a man."
"I went up and saw Jojo early this morning."
Mary Ann stood up from the couch where she'd been sprawled reading the paper. She smoothed out the bathrobe, an old one of Mike's she was wearing and tightened the sash firmly around her waist.
"Read what your bossman says," she said, leaving. "You've got to memorize the party line."
He shouldn't have mentioned Jojo. He knew it as soon as he

said it. They had been so close once. When she was a girl, all her store of admiration was cast, worshipful, at Jojo's feet. But she had never been able to forgive him for leaving, for breaking away, maybe not so much for the act itself as for the freedom, the power of choice to stay, to come or go, she felt she didn't share. And, Mike guessed, she must be contemptuous of him now, of what he had let himself become. Mary Ann had been a fat unhappy little girl. That she was now an attractive, self-possessed woman was not only the result of her will and discipline. It seemed that those qualities were born in her when Jojo left, and fed and thrived, as it were, on his gradual decay. So that however you looked at it (and she in her chosen loneliness, with time on her hands, must have often seen the brute truth, if only in brief glimpses like a fugitive beast in a dream) she was as much tied to him as ever. It was curious how each of the people in this house, each in the furious invincible rigidity of his chosen humor and form of isolation, remained fixed in intricate dependence on the others, at once blessed and wounded. Love is wrestling with a strange angel, Mike thought, who wasn't sure, yet, if he had ever loved anybody or was able to.

* * *

Mike looked at the paper. There was a prominent interview with John Batten and, too, a formal statement which he'd issued. In the interview he admitted that Parker's reluctance to retire had disappointed him. He thought Parker had earned a rest. This had, of course, complicated the issues and his own plans. He said it was very clear that the campaign was going to be a fight, a sad one in a way because he had always admired much about the Senator, but he felt the people were ready for a change. He was confident of being elected. Parker had apparently been interviewed at the Washington airport. His tone was easy and confident. He said he had just changed his mind about retiring. He said he was sure the voters wanted a man with experience and seniority to represent them in the Senate in these troubled times. He said he planned to be back in Washington for another term. Alice Parker, asked to comment, had said whatever Allen did was fine by her.

The formal statement by Batten was a numbered series of a

dozen points, a kind of platform ranging from a pledge "to fight for a firm foreign policy in the face of the communist conspiracy," to a promise to do what he could to help encourage new industry to move to the state "where labor problems are at a minimum." Below this was a large, paid advertisement in which Batten listed a group of questions he planned to ask Parker during the campaign, and he urged the voters themselves to demand answers of Parker. Mike glanced down the list, smiled at a couple —"Where is your Florida Ship Canal now?" and "Whatever became of your old friend Henry Wallace?" Only one query in the long list referred to the issue of race: "What *do* you think about the forced integration of our public schools?" At this moment it all seemed rather comical, an ineffectual, expansive shotgun blast fired in the dark.

He turned to the editorial page and read a rather cautious attack on Parker, far more cautious than its headline, "A Great Doublecross?" indicated. A lively campaign was predicted, and a short one with the Primary coming this year in early September. The editor, at least, saw that the issues were clear, Parker representing the "oldline liberal view," Batten the "modern moderate position." He spoke respectfully of Parker as "a shrewd old campaigner," and he praised Batten's "youthful vigor, his industry and sincere dedication." All this was to be expected. Rab Stuart, who owned the paper, had never once backed Parker, but experience had taught him that he'd better maintain at least an appearance of objectivity.

Then there were the three photographs. One showed John Batten on the rostrum speaking. With his studied determination, firm-jawed, his thick, curly but well-barbered hair, slim and tall and broadshouldered, yet strangely nondescript, he might have been a young movie actor playing a part. Another had captured for posterity the moment when Allen Parker wheeled and crossed the platform, his hand extended to John Batten and Batten half-risen from his chair. In the picture it looked as if Parker had just given Batten a great shove back into his seat. The Senator's grin, in black and white, was villainous while Batten's expression was more of hurt than bafflement. The third picture showed the three of them—Parker and Alice and Mike Royle—emerging from the elevator in the hotel. Mike was amused to see that his expression conveyed (what he was *feeling* was complete surprise when the door slid open to the blinding flash of a camera) pale determination, youthful, thoughtful enthusiasm.

He folded the paper and started upstairs. He would take a nap, and after lunch he could settle down and get started working. As he closed the door of his room behind him he heard the telephone ringing downstairs. He threw off his shirt and lay down on the bed. Tired as he was, he thought he ought to be able to sleep now. Then he heard Charity's voice calling him from the foot of the stairs.

"Mr. Mike, come quick. Washington D.C. is on the line."

II. MIDDLE: VICTIM

Ye shall know them by their fruits. Do men gather grapes of thorns, or figs of thistles?

MATTHEW 7:16

ALLEN PARKER had already rented an office for Mike in Oakland. It wasn't an expensive one among the new buildings in the center of town or one of the small, air-conditioned, one-storey, concrete and glass offices which were scattered in residential areas and were lately favored by the successful lawyers and doctors and the representatives of large, national businesses. The budget prohibited that kind of extravagance.

—Things are going to get a whole lot better, Parker had told him. We'll get a hold of some money all right. But I'll be damned if I'll waste it on showplace offices. I never have before and I won't this time.

When Mike went downtown he found that his office, the new county headquarters, was a single room, a big one with two long windows looking onto a side street. It was a brick building, "The Professional Building," that had seen, even in the brief history of Oakland, its place and time and occasion for prosperity wither away. It had a transient character now. It was used by young men beginning, without money enough yet for anything better, and it was used by young, doubtful businesses. It was a refuge for older men, doctors and lawyers, a couple of dentists and a chiropractor, equally troubled by doubts and lack of money, the town's losers, clinging to a sweet flypaper of hope, snared in it, or caught at least in the pretense, the necessary illusion that success is always a possibility, that a change for the better is crouched like a mythical beast just a little farther down the path.

Then, too, there were others more furtive, the fly-by-night businesses, the get-rich-quick dreamers, the sad tents of clutchers and clawers whose fingers were gifted with no Midas touch, always one breathless step ahead of a yelping pack of creditors and the stern, inflexible grip of the County Sheriff.

They might, Mike thought as he entered the doorway, passed the board in the dim hallway with its rash of names promising a wealth of services and the brass mailbox where the names must shift and change in a perpetual game of musical chairs, and mounted the two flights of sour-smelling stairs, they might all as well in earned wisdom or at least some brief honest moment of self-scrutiny have forsaken the lean bitch-goddess of Success with her beguiling song and dance and settled for survival. Still, it pleased him to be working here. It was a far cry from the law firm with its shiny floors, its spongy carpets in offices, its muted efficiency, its perfectly ruthless, tiptoeing enterprise.

And he could look out of his windows on a street like Nostalgia. It was, after all, the oldest business street in town, and once—still in his boyhood—it had managed to maintain a dour solidity, a plain and homely facade. Directly across was the Royal Palms Hotel, once a great favorite with drummers when selling was still half-ritual and half of cards up sleeves and rabbits pulled out of hats. There used to be a hive of salesmen staying there. Mike could remember how they used to sit in tall-backed rocking chairs on the front porch, comfortable after a large supper, and they rocked and smoked and laughed and talked among themselves until at last the dark came and took them, swallowed them whole except for the lazy chorus of their vague voices and the small red inextinguishable moons of their Cuban cigars. And their voices rose and fell, their laughter was soft and easy in the dark, with lightning bugs flashing explosive heatless winks around them for punctuation.

He could remember them, too, in the hotel's barber shop where he used to go and get his hair cut when he was a boy. Big-bellied in the days when a man's girth was one measure of his prosperity, white- and curly-haired as rams was how he pictured them, with gay neckties and gold watch chains and Panama hats that always clustered on the hatracks like exotic fruit, and on their feet always the two-toned, pointed shoes, sleek as clipperships, that the shineboy sweated over. Wrapped in white cloths, attended by acolyte barbers in snowy, high-necked jackets, at once teased and treated by the manicurist on her little low stool (she sometimes acknowledging a leaned hoarse whisper with a quick whinny of laughter —what did they think of to say to make her laugh?), flanked by tall, multi-colored, many-scented bottles and lotions and powders, they seemed in the boy's eyes to be fabulous strangers, far voyagers, rich beyond all telling with the whispered secrets of the wide world.

Yet a man, boy no more, could be the victim of that kind of memory. He must have known even then it was a spurious dignity he had conferred on them.

He could just as easily call up another clear memory of that barber shop as well, now watching its striped pole turning below his office window. He could recall one time he went to get a haircut, and his father (who never went to that barber shop to have the edges of his baldness trimmed or for a shave) had come to pick him up. Mike was still in the barber chair, so Judge Royle sat down to wait for him and read the paper. One of those, a fat and white-haired salesman staying at the hotel (Maybe he was drunk, Mike realized now, picturing the high flush of the man's face, the pink-rimmed, bloodshot eyes.) had been kidding the shineboy. That was the usual thing. The shineboy was a little bit simpleminded. Everybody knew that. And no matter what they might say to him, he only looked up from his kneeling, sweating labor, sweat dripping from his black face, and grinned. Mike listened to the big man's chattering away at the shineboy, and then in the mirror he could see his father's face tightening in what he knew was anger, though he didn't know why yet. It might have just been something he was reading in the paper.

The shineboy finished up with a rhythmic flourish of the shoe-rag, a pop and a snap like a blank pistol going off. And he tapped the toes of the man's shoes in the ritual signal and backed away a little, still on his knees, looking up like a small dog begging.

—You call that a shine, boy?

—Yassuh.

—You mean to tell me that's a *shoe*shine?

The shineboy looked puzzled, eased back, wary, on his haunches.

—I asked you a question.

—Yassuh. I guess that's what I call a shine.

—You mean you're all finished?

—Yassuh.

—No you not, the salesman said. You forgot something.

Mike looked furtively, quickly past the turned, grinning barber beside him and saw Judge Royle beginning to stand up, his face drawn in fierce lines now. And he knew that trouble, some kind of trouble was coming.

—Nigger, you forgot to blow the lint off my toes.

The shineboy grinned and nodded his head and leaned forward, off balance, his lips puckered to blow the last dust and lint off the gleaming toes of the salesman's shoes. Just as he bent his head and blew the salesman gave a little kick, and the shineboy tipped over backwards on the floor, sat up and rubbed his chin, licked at a tiny fleck of blood on his lips.

The salesman and the barbers laughed.

Mike, trapped by mirrors on both sides of him, parcelled out and multiplied into an infinity of selves, watched the rest of it in the mirrors, his head rigidly fixed.

—I believe you're a stranger in town, Judge Royle began softly.

The salesman looked at the bald man with a cane standing in front of him and smiled.

—I don't believe I've had the pleasure, he said.

Judge Royle grabbed him with his free hand and jerked him out of the chair and onto his feet.

—What's the big idea? the salesman said. What seems to be the trouble?

—I don't like what you just did, Judge Royle said. I don't like your ways and I don't like you.

—Hell! the salesman said, fishing in his pocket, finding and tossing a fifty-cent piece that rang like a little bell on the stone floor beside the befuddled shineboy. —Hell, it was just a joke.

—Well, now the joke's on you. Get out!

—Wait a minute. Wait just a big minute . . .

The salesman must have given the Judge a slight push, touched him anyway, because down came the cane with a whistle and popped across the salesman's head. He howled, clutching at his head with both hands, staggered, and the Judge hit him again and knocked him to his knees. The big man knelt bloody-headed and groggy on the floor beside the shineboy. He shook his head and blubbered.

—Go get a policeman, the Judge shouted at a barber. You go

get a cop and you tell him Judge Royle said to take this scum across the county line. And when this thing here (he jabbed the kneeling salesman with the point of his cane, and the salesman moaned), when this yellow dog comes to hisself, you just tell him I said if he shows his face in Oakland again I'll put him on the road gang and sweat some of the lard off him.

He snatched Mike out of the barber chair, white cloth and all, hair half cut, and dragged him toward the door. At the door he stopped, let Mike free and shook his cane at them all.

—You! he said. All of you. If you ever let something like this happen in here again—and I hear about it—I'll close your godamn barber shop and put you all in jail. Understand me?

They nodded, silent and shocked.

He pointed to the shineboy who was standing up now.

—You, boy, clean up the mess.

Shamed and amazed, Mike had cried all the way home.

—Don't cry, his father said. What's the matter with you? He got what was coming to him.

Then Judge Royle laughed. He slapped his cane and laughed.

—This here's my *portable* courthouse. It's a wonder I didn't break the damn thing in two on his hard head.

Such a thing wouldn't be likely to happen now, Mike thought. But it is a part of the heritage, the inheritance. It shadows us still, the tremor of violence, the terrible swift sword. Anyhow, they were all gone from the Royal Palms Hotel now, the old-time salesmen, a vanished breed, except for one or two, doddering and feeble and lost, but still trying to sell, who might come there to wail at the wall of the past.

Now there was a sign nailed to a column on the front porch— "Cheap Rooms." And the police in their shiny black cars would often be parked there, day as well as night, going—sometimes running—in and out, sometimes returning with a catch, some protesting or resigned man or woman between two of them. It was a sadlooking place in need of paint and upkeep. But once in a while in the early evening when the first darkness covers the pitiless nakedness of things like a shawl, you might hear a wild burst of sourceless laughter like a ghost's or maybe the sound of music from somebody's radio.

And the street had decayed as well. It was riddled with cheap stores and fly-haunted groceries, pawnshops, a few bars, and beyond that the twin tracks of the Atlantic Coast Line Railroad. On the other side of the tracks was abruptly a Negro section, more cheap stores, groceries, pawn shops, bars, and the colored movie house. It was in many ways a mirror image of the street on this side of the tracks. But decay and poverty had broken down the finality of that barrier. On the street below Mike's office the two races mingled and overlapped like backwater when the tide is turning.

* * *

If he thought about the past enough, Mike knew, he might hit on some meaningful scene of truth like the brief incident in the barber shop. And then, having stumbled on this clue to the truth and himself, the thing to do was to muddle it, to crush and squeeze the essence out, until you *knew* what it was, a truth quite aside from the accidental event in time, or at least shielded by the brisk action of the event. Much was there for him to learn. There he was, the perennial spectator, uncommitted, but caught in the tricky, duplicating mirrors of his apprehension, wishing, perhaps, to be so fragmented, scattered beyond recognition or responsibility or action. There was the Judge, pure action, impulse, rage or joy, not stopping one gray instant to think, and in this case right, Mike guessed, very right, if grossly illegal. The thing about that kind of power was the brute and naked honesty of it. The truth of his own shrinking, wincing away from reality was the fundamental falseness of it, the ostrich's comic, buried head.

But even this kind of thinking—if you could call it thought, the flux and flow of images in the instructive disorder of a dream —even that was a kind of fleeing. Having stumbled upon truth naked, you found yourself running away as fast as you could with the hounds of your own consciousness yapping at your heels, belling for your blood. The Judge had said that politics was a disease of the region. Well, equally acute was the danger of infection from the past. If you were a Southerner, whether you liked it or not, you had to live in and with your past. You had to try to make sense out of it. The present was ghosted, shadowed.

Nothing you did, but you troubled the dust. Mike's solution, his whim, had been to run away again, to flee this time into the cardboard world of politics, to oversee another's worries. And the fact of the matter was, he guessed, that he couldn't care less what happened, who won or lost. He would throw himself into it with all the energy he could arouse, but whatever happened he would be perfectly safe. He was about as likely to bleed as a stone.

* * * * * *

Senator Allen Parker didn't seem worried about the prospect of a third Democratic candidate to contend with.

"Sure," he told Mike on the phone, "it's a possibility. I'll give Atkins that much. The thing is, though, who can they get? Who's around who can swing enough votes to make it worth the trouble? Even if there is somebody—let's assume for a minute that there's somebody I've completely overlooked—who'd be dumb enough, politically naïve enough to be taken in and fooled like that? Who would want to be used?"

"You don't think they could *buy* somebody?"

"Nobody who counts. Some oldtimer, maybe, just to muddy the water. But nobody who counts. You can't pay a good man to lose an election unless it's for President. No, sir, I doubt Mr. Atkins' notion. I doubt it very much."

In any case it would be tested soon. In ten days the candidates would have to qualify. The first significant date in an election campaign is the date of qualification. At that time all candidates for elective office in the state must pay a small fee and file with the Secretary of State. After that everything is official, a matter of public record.

With ten days left before that deadline Mike began to work. He put a large picture poster of the Senator in one of his windows, and he hired a part-time secretary, hoping that later on there'd be enough eager women volunteers to take care of the answering of telephones and typing of letters. He phoned the newspaper and let them know that he would be acting as Parker's chairman in the county. The next morning a brief story appeared in the section devoted to local news. There was an old picture from their files showing himself thin and young, hopelessly young in his OD Army uniform with the brass insignia of the Infantry on his lapels. They had managed a brief biographical sketch as well which, fortunately, spent most of its space on his family history and the career of his father. He had from Parker a list of his supporters in the county, ones who had contributed money in previous campaigns or helped out in one way or another. It was a very short list of names. There was a second, longer list of doubtful but possible allies. Using these, Mike started writing letters and making phone calls. Buttons and bumper strips, photographs and campaign booklets, all the paraphernalia, were on the way.

Mike lived at home and worked every day at the office.

He had only been working a few days when L. J. Benjamin, Parker's State Chairman, came to Oakland to check on his progress. He appeared one afternoon, unannounced and unexpected, a thin dry wisp of man (—Looks like a sick boll weevil, Parker had said) deeply suntanned, his face pinched and seamed and eroded in deep lines, his lips compressed as if he suffered from some kind of continual gnawing internal pain. His other expression was a look of pure nausea. He came in without prologue, his broomstick frame lost in the rumpled flowing of a seersucker suit, carrying in his hand an old-fashioned, wide-brimmed, sunbleached boater hat with a ribbon of indeterminate color around the crown. He shook Mike's hand and said who he was. He looked around the office and groaned.

"Where's the closest bar?"

"Right down the street," Mike said. "Just a couple of steps down the block."

"All right, sonny boy, let's go. This place depresses me."

L. J. Benjamin turned and left the room and Mike hurried after him.

They found a booth in the back and just sat there a while, silent, staring at each other. Mike was fighting a powerful urge to laugh out loud. Benjamin ordered a double bourbon, straight, without benefit of branch water or ice cube, and he sipped it like a dose of castor oil. Mike drank a beer.

Finally Benjamin sighed and pushed his straw hat far back on his head at a jaunty angle. He opened his mouth to say something, but at that moment the juke box in the corner, a squat Silenius wreathed in vines of multi-colored light, belched and shook and bellied forth a shattering surge of noise. Benjamin squared his hat, stood up and walked, stiff-backed as a cadet, to the offending corner. He unplugged the machine with a decisive yank. In the abrupt silence that followed he glared at everyone else in the bar, then with a strut like a fighting cock came back to the booth and sat down.

"We never carried this godamn county but once since the Depression anyway," he said. "So I guess you won't do us any harm."

"Thanks," Mike said, able to laugh at last. "Thanks a whole lot."

"Never mind. It's what I deserve for getting mixed up in all this in the first place."

"Why did you?"

"What's that?"

"Why *did* you get into politics?"

Benjamin's face crinkled and cracked. His grim mask crumpled into a multitude of jagged parts and loose ends like a china plate breaking. He laughed out loud.

"Hell!" he said. "It's the only thing in this world I'm any good at. What else would I do with myself? What a question!"

It was true that L. J. Benjamin was a tough and aging Party hack, a caricature of the cynical, arrogant, strangely dated breed. But he was, too, a man gifted with a bright, simplified and startling vision of reality. He had a squinty, close view of the truth like a jeweler studying facets and flaws, like a man at a microscope. Large issues interested him hardly at all and events only a little. Even though he had worked for Allen Parker in every campaign since the Thirties, he probably knew next to nothing about Parker's actual voting record in the Senate or the shiftings, bobbings and weavings of his political stance. Cared less. Benjamin was interested in people, not in people as individuals or in general, but simply people as voters, their habits and whims, their standards and eccentricities. What he knew and cared about with a kind of rigorous fury was the voting public of this state. It was possible to imagine, if not believe, that he knew by heart the funny-bone and secret itch of each one of an otherwise faceless mob scattered over the more than sixty counties. He would know who must be persuaded and how, who couldn't be, who must be bullied, battered, shamed or bought. If such a store of extraordinary knowledge had embittered him, inspired his natural contempt, it had as well taught him a nearly absolute discretion like a good priest's. His face revealed no secrets except that it is a bad world, getting worse. He was really all eyes and ears. (—Ben's as slick as a watersnake, Parker had said. But in the end he's got a wealth of tact. In politics that's a cardinal virtue.) Whatever it was that impelled him—not money certainly or he would have been a pure fool, not prestige, being always anonymous, always no more than a hoarse whisper in a great man's ear, and maybe at most the born misanthrope's bittersweet joy in the continual revelation that the world is peopled by fools and knaves—whatever it was he was supposed to be the best man for the job. In slack times, the dead space between political campaigns of all kinds and scope, he played with real estate (the official game of the State) and bet on horses and greyhounds. But in politics, he would have insisted, he was no gambler. He worked for winners.

Mike wasn't surprised, though, that he was far from happy about the forthcoming campaign.

"It's bound to be a rough, dirty fight, tooth and claw, from start to finish," Benjamin said. "It started with a naked doublecross. Of course, that's the Senator's privilege, but you can see it sets a tone for the whole show. It even gives us a little edge of surprise. But Batten's people have been thinking about this for a long time. They've had time to be ready for anything. We'll just have to wait and see. Don't *you* worry about it none. I do all the worrying."

He finished his drink, adjusted his hat and stood up.

"By the way," he said. "Just who in the hell is Vivian Blanch?"

"How would I know?" Mike said. "Am I supposed to?"

"Well, she seems to be another one of the Senator's godamn brainstorms. I thought maybe you'd know her."

"Never had the pleasure."

Benjamin shrugged. He walked to the corner and plugged in the jukebox again. It jumped, renewed, and flashed and blared into life. He turned and walked outside with Mike following behind him. On the sidewalk, in the midst of the quick flow of pedestrian traffic, he halted, donned a pair of dark glasses and offered his hand.

"Like I said, you'll do all right. You got a good name in this county, and that's better than nothing."

With that he spun around like a ballroom dancer and walked away toward the main part of town. Grinning, Mike stood and watched him go, broomstick-thin and stiff, until at last the battered straw boater disappeared around a corner.

* * * * * * *

The following morning, out of the puffed contents of a brown envelope which had come air-mail, special delivery, Vivian Blanch appeared. In name, anyway. Her delicate and feminine signature was stamped in blue ink at the bottom of pages of mimeographed material sent out to all of Senator Parker's workers. There were elaborate and inclusive forms to be filled out, charts to be kept, suggestions, directions, orders, and a pink blizzard of little square memo sheets, each of which bore an impressive VB stamped at the top. It was a little like the odds and ends, the remnants of a half-dozen jigsaw puzzles. Mike looked at some of it, then put in a call to the Senator.

"I know I should've called or at least written about this," Parker said. "But I've been pretty busy up here. Miss Blanch is going to work for us in public relations. She's supposed to be damned good. She has a reputation and a lot of experience. I think we're going to need somebody who's in touch with the latest methods.

"Besides," he went on, "women are going to count for a lot this time. We need a woman helping us."

Mike winced at this burst of persuasion. All right, so he wanted to hire this woman for some reason or other, but why did he have to begin on the defensive?

"Look," Mike said. "Excuse me for asking, but does Benjamin know about all this?"

"Ben? Sure, but not in any detail. I guess I better get in touch with him right away before he falls into a fit or something."

"What do you want us to do with all this *stuff?*"

"Tell you what. Don't fool with any of it yet. I'm going to fly down to that meeting in Miami on Friday. I'll bring Miss Blanch with me."

When the call was finished, Mike lit a cigarette and sighed. He had known that breed in New York, the type of bright young career woman, immaculately groomed, illimitably aggressive, a sweet fruit on the surface with a pith as hard as horseshoes, bastioned, fortified, well-protected by the social myth of her sex's inherent weakness and modesty. All their activity depended on the myth. They could be as ruthless and singleminded as birds of prey, but forced into some tight, difficult area, a space without retreat, they could by magic transform themselves into women again. In any battle they had the final alternative of retiring behind a smoke-screen of tears or drawing like a rabbit from a hat some miraculous *non sequitur*. Their highest god, it seemed, was a faithful and accessible *deus ex machina*.

He could picture Miss Vivian Blanch already, a grim fury in an expensive tailored suit, her mind replete and her language riddled with the slogans and semaphoric logic of Madison Avenue that has come to pass for the communication of knowledge and information. Well, anyway, this new addition to the strange crew was bound to create some comedy. Sooner or later there was bound to be a confrontation scene, a great unmasking. And the meeting of the Tiger, Benjamin, and this Lady was going to be something to see. Somebody was liable to lose shirt and skivvies, hide and hair, in that encounter. He hoped it wouldn't be L. J. Benjamin.

* * *

That same day Atkins called him from Jacksonville.

"Well, well, well," he said cheerfully. "I hear you've got the famous woman on your so-called team now."

"Who's that?"

"Vivian Blanch."

"Looks like it," Mike said. "Do you know her?"

"A bitch, boy! The archetype of all bitches. You can believe you've got your troubles now."

"What do you think got into Parker?"

"Senility maybe," Atkins said. "No, I'll take that back. Parker's still just a country boy at heart. This gal is the real, slick, big-city article. She used to have a TV show, a panel with all the windbags for guests. Didn't you ever see her in action?"

"I just watch the ball games and the fights. The rest of it is crap."

"That may be so, but you still missed something."

"What's that?"

"Sex," Atkins said. "S-E-X."

And his laughter coughed in the black receiver and crackled in Mike's ear.

* * * * * * *

On Friday the County Chairmen and the regular workers met in a hotel at Miami Beach. It had been planned merely as an organization meeting with Benjamin running the show. Now with the Senator and the public relations woman flying down from Washington it was going to be something else again.

Mike left Oakland early, before dawn, drove across to the East Coast and down the winter pilgrims' route of U.S. 1. He was planning, hoping anyway, to have a good time as a witness to this scene. Nothing that had happened to him yet had the threat or impact of reality. He might have been dreaming all of it. And the setting for the meeting suited his mood with perfect decorum. He knew about the hotel, a new and shiny place, in fact the newest and shiniest, latest of the long packed line of monstrous, fabulous hotels sprung like exotic hybrid plants from the weary imaginations of winter-bound Easterners, opulent daydreams of the tropics, rising out of the sand and scrub of what had been, only a generation or so before, a tidal bog humming with the song of mosquitoes. Nothing real, nothing dangerous could happen against such a background. No matter how serious the complexities which might arise, all things were bound to end with fanfare and a song and dance, a buck and wing. All of the East Coast beginning with the preserved Spanish town of Saint Augustine was like that, each town, each cluster of motels and tourist courts, designed to meet the need, the desire for something that never was and hadn't been there before. There were smaller and modest places to be passed through, like New Smyrna and Titusville; there were bustling and ambitious ones like Daytona and Fort Lauderdale. There was the unlikely Cocoa with its barbed wire and the huge guided missile base from which long-range and deadly missiles were fired by intense scientists into the vague oblivion of the South Atlantic Ocean. People would come from hundreds of miles to huddle all night in the sand dunes waiting and watching for the moment of the long dramatic countdown and then the flash of flame that signalled the departure of another missile or rocket. Pilgrims to the shrine of scientific advance and speculation. There was the ponderous solemnity of Palm Beach for the very rich. And then, long waited for, long prepared for, one might come at last to Miami Beach and its delectable mountains.

The hotel was a glittering thing of glass and concrete facing an ocean as calm as a bathtub. It was ornate inside with rich imported stones and spiralling carpeted stairways, with potted tropical plants and tanks of the imported fish swimming sad-eyed and decorative in the riskless world of elegant captivity. Winter, of course, is the true season, but still the lobby, as spacious as the nave of a great cathedral, was busy with tourists, speckled with their dark glasses, sweet with the odor of their suntan lotions. Mike was directed to the small dining room, where the meeting was to be held, by a bellboy as splendid as a general in light opera.

Mike was prepared for what he found there. He had imagined the group this way. All of these people seemed like type-cast actors in an old play. Or, they seemed to have been cut neatly out of cartoon strips, Benjamin's breath giving them such life as they possessed. Those from the larger and more prosperous communities were larger and more prosperous-looking, round and affable, glowing with good health and grooming. Those from the smaller, more rural counties fell into a pattern too, tended to be lanky and big-boned, leather-faced from sun and wind and open air. Still, within these two basic types there were pleasing variations. The men from the big resort areas were in tourist habits (one or two even carried cameras dangling from leather shoulder straps), wore sunglasses, appeared to be supple and insinuative.

The ones from old Florida, West Florida, betrayed all the conventional characteristics of the smalltown, smalltime, Deep South politician. They were open and easy going behind admirable paunches that often were crossed with gold watch chains. They were quick to repeat the old jokes, wore seersucker and palm beach suits. One man he met had affected the string tie. The cattlemen had fancy Western shirts and hats, expensive handmade boots and a mildly veiled contempt for everyone else who was there. The farmers, who were probably the most affluent of the group, wore outdated, ready-made, doublebreasted suits, were softspoken and stiffly reticent, but still grinned a good deal at everything and managed to keep to themselves. It seemed a kind of masquerade party.

Over all this circus or menagerie presided L. J. Benjamin. His role was as the classic lion tamer. From the moment he entered the crowded room, shaking hands with the alert and sourfaced Benjamin at the door and moving on to meet others, Mike had the feeling that if for one moment Benjamin should throw up his hands in pure disgust or dismay and then turn his back on them all, all order would at once go out of the precarious system. He imagined they would fall on each other in snarl and dust like a large, noisy dog fight. But at this point Mike Royle felt he was ready to be pleased by everything, by anything at all that happened. He had found, he surmised, a fine comedy in which he could play a minor, observing role, engrossed but not involved, amused without being committed to anything under the sun.

After letting the men move around and talk a while, Benjamin went slowly to a rostrum at one end of the room and banged with a gavel until everyone found a seat and the room was quiet. The meeting began with a few casual introductions and a little joke. The chairman from Tarpon Springs came late, entered the room with a kind of tiptoeing bewilderment and looked vaguely for a place to sit down.

"What the hell's the trouble with you, Cris?" Benjamin shouted at him. "Those Greeks down home driving you crazy?"

Cris Demopolous, a large Greek sponge fisherman, shook his head and flashed a gold-toothed smile, and everyone laughed.

Then Benjamin got down to work. He started off with a brisk

analysis of the situation facing them. He said he wanted to wipe out once and for all any little false hopes they may have been hiding.

"Let's be practical," he said. "Practically speaking we've got about as much pleasure ahead of us as a pig in a butcher shop."

He told them that it didn't look like there would be enough money to wage a really decent campaign against Batten. He pointed out that Batten's backers were much better organized, had considerable national party support and plenty of help from big businesses that wanted to move into the area.

"And let's face it," he said. "Allen Parker won't never win no youth and beauty prize. He ain't the bathing beauty type, but . . ."

And with that "but" he began to construct the frail, webbed structure of possibility. He began the gradual hypnosis of confidence. He dabbed at his lean sad face with a handkerchief, softened his hoarse voice and worked. Allen Parker had always been a winner. It was Parker, not young Johnny Batten, who had position and a public record. "They got to bring the fight to us," he said. And, best of all, they all knew that Allen Parker was a tireless and able campaigner. He would drag them all along by his coattails if he had to. He was as tough as an old rooster. He wasn't going to let any young banty come strutting around his hen yard.

"Anyway, we don't have to work and worry ourselves grayheaded. A whole lot of people are going to vote for Parker just out of the habit of it."

He let them chuckle, then went on, more loudly, banging his fist like a hammer on the table so that the invariable carafe and tray of water glasses jumped and rattled.

"I know damnwell we're going to win this one," he said. "If I didn't I wouldn't be standing up here now."

Senator Parker's entrance was perfectly timed. He appeared, unannounced, just at that moment, coming through a side door. The door burst open and he came in quickly, tall, ugly, brimming with energy and confidence; and without pausing once in his approach to the front of the room, someway he managed to shake a hand here, to pat a back there, to mumble a swift, monosyllabic greeting. By the time he reached the rostrum and was shaking hands with Benjamin, the men in the room were on their feet, clapping and cheering for him. He held both arms high in a V and grinned at them. Mike noticed that every movement he made, each of his gestures was a broad one as if he had been standing before a group of thousands. The effect was almost magical. It somehow communicated the sense of belonging to an enormous throng.

"I thank you. Thank you very much," he shouted into the uproar. "And thank *you*, Ben. I've got a few things—a very few—I'd like to talk to you about. But first it seems to me that as long as we're *here* in this fancy hotel, we might just as well take advantage of it and pleasure ourselves a little. On me."

As if in answer to a cue a squadron of uniformed waiters rushed into the room to take orders for drinks. During the moments of clamor and confusion Senator Parker and Benjamin talked together in close, intent whispers, their faces in impassive profile. Mike stared at them, saw Benjamin shake his head and look away in what might have been sudden anger. But he turned back, recovered, and relaxed into his thin familiar shrug. When at last all the men had been served and the noise began to diminish, Benjamin banged his gavel and Parker faced the group and began to speak to them in a soft voice.

His approach was quite different from Benjamin's. He seemed to assume great confidence, almost over-confidence on the part of his workers, and he mildly cautioned against this mood. It occurred to Mike at once that, of course, Allen Parker would know exactly the mood of his audience after that surprise and a round of drinks. Hand in glove. Parker urged them to work hard for every possible vote, and he promised them for his part an active personal campaign right up through election day.

"I know this for a fact," he said. "Johnny Batten may be a damnsight better looking than I am and a damnsight younger too. But . . ." (He held up for inspection his huge, limp, ungainly hands.) "I guarantee I can outshake that boy any day from dawn to dusk from now until September."

They laughed and there was some applause. Parker grinned and continued.

"You know, in a way I feel kind of sorry for young Johnny.

He doesn't know what he's got himself into. He just doesn't know yet. Well, I'm the man who can tell him. Win, lose, or draw, he's going to have one mighty sore, raw right hand."

When they laughed again, his face changed, drew into more serious lines as he spoke of all the problems of waging a modern campaign in an age of mass advertising and television.

"Things have changed more than a little since the days we remember. Those were the days when you put on your Sunday-go-to-meeting clothes and you went and stood up on a couple of planks laid across sawhorses and hollered your lungs out. And the one who could holler the loudest and longest got himself elected. The voting public is much more sophisticated now. They may not be any more *interested*, they may not be *as* interested as they used to be. But they sure are harder to please. A man couldn't get himself elected to the job of Public Washroom Custodian in the old ways anymore. There are new methods, new techniques and ways of reaching and appealing to the modern voting public.

"Now," he went on, "I'd be the last man here to throw away the tried and true in favor of the new-fangled and speculative. I'm too set in my ways at this stage. And old Ben here, I guess he's even more rigid than I am. But I think every one of us will agree that it would be nothing less than folly to sit idle on our be-hinds while the opposition takes advantage of all the latest developments. And it's for this reason that I've decided to get the services of someone with a wealth of experience in public relations. This lady—it's a lady—is going to work closely with Ben and myself and all of you to make our campaign up to date in every way, the very latest model. So, I'd like to introduce to you our new public relations assistant—Miss Vivian Blanch."

She came through the same side door through which Parker had entered, but with a great difference in style. Where he had come into the room quickly, as if propelled by an excess of vigor and overabundant energy, she simply strolled, like a cat on a leash. Mike's picture of what she would be like had been wrong. Astonishingly wrong. Wearing an expensive, stylish Italian dress, carrying in gloved hands like a chalice a champagne glass that sparkled in the light, bejeweled with pendant earrings, a jangle of gold bracelets and the wink and flash of a large diamond ring, heavily perfumed (In fact it was the sweet cloud of her perfume that jerked all heads around as if pulled on a string to look.), teetering on the thinnest and highest of heels, Miss Blanch smiled and walked slowly across the smoky roomful of staring men. She was smiling, not at any one of them or at the group as a whole, but with the ghostly smile of someone entirely abstracted, amused perhaps by some private memory or remembered joke. It was a provocative smile, in its own way ironic and at least condescending. Her eyes, accented savagely by thin quizzical eyebrows, by mascara and eye shadow, were bright with a vacant liquid glaze as if she were drugged. All that she needed, Mike decided, was a long cigarette holder and a casually draped fur piece. But still, he thought he detected beneath the fantastic armor, the lithe, hard, well-trained body of a woman with enormous self-control. She might have been a dancer or an athlete in disguise.

There was a gasp and a silence. Somebody in the back whistled slow and loud. A few snickers poised on the edge of laughter. Senator Parker scowled, but just then, always alert, always the tactful master of the present moment, Benjamin stepped up and began to applaud. The men straggled to their feet and clapped politely. Miss Blanch brightened, planted a quick kiss on Parker's cheek, offered a white-gloved hand to Benjamin, and, turning, raised her glass high and toasted them all.

She asked them to sit down and please to make themselves comfortable.

She began to speak to them in an indeterminate, indefinite accent of no place or time, a kind of *Pygmalion* English, spoken as if she had memorized the phrases from a book. She said she was happy to be part of Senator Parker's team. She mentioned, in passing, a bright cluster of names, a nosegay of the known, honored and notorious whom she had worked for in the past. She said she didn't want to interfere in any way with "the existing mechanism," but still she felt sure she'd be able to make a few practical suggestions. After all, she declared, it would be pointless to ignore the entire body of knowledge and experience gained over the years by the specialists in advertising and public relations.

As Miss Vivian Blanch saw this political situation it was clearly another version of the age-old conflict between youth and experience. Every effort would have to be made to create the association in the public mind of youth with inexperience, of youth and ignorance, innocence, and instability. Still, in counterattacks the health and vigor of Senator Parker would be stressed.

"We all know," she said, "that a great many of the voters in this election are older people who've come down here to retire. The point is that we mustn't allow ourselves to fall into the trap of *apologizing* for the Senator's maturity."

She went on to say that in a mood of enthusiasm she had mailed to each of the county chairmen a selective batch of forms and charts together with a number of suggestions. The forms should be filled out in detail and returned to her as soon as possible. The charts should be kept up to date. By means of information on these forms and charts, however irrelevant or inconsequential some of the items might seem, Parker's headquarters would be able to have "a grip on the pulse" of the voting public from day to day, even from hour to hour.

"We've been told the truth," she said, "that we aren't embarrassed by riches. Here's where a little advice from the feminine standpoint can be useful. All women know it's a fact that when you *feel* your best you *are* your best. The same thing applies to money. Whenever my bank account starts dwindling and everything seems to be going wrong, I run right out and buy myself an expensive hat or a new dress. Then everything seems to get better."

She urged them to avoid all appearance of penury and to make their county headquarters as attractive as possible.

"Get the women to help you."

She concluded with a prediction. Lately she's been studying the Senator's record and, of course, she'd been following the lines of argument in Batten's speeches and press releases. She was convinced that this particular election could very well hinge on the issue of foreign policy. She thought that Batten's basic lack of interest in or knowledge of the international situation might be his weakest point, "his Achilles heel." She couldn't urge them strongly enough to familiarize themselves with international affairs and the Senator's record on foreign relations.

She asked them if there were any questions.

"Miss Blanch?" A portly, red-faced man from West Florida, he of the black string tie, arose. "Miss Blanch, on one of these charts you mailed out I noticed it calls for a day-to-day record on the weather—the temperature, humidity, whether it was sunny or cloudy and so forth . . ."

"That's correct."

"Well now, please excuse my ignorance, but what kind of good is all that going to do Al Parker?"

Some people laughed, but she answered him quickly, unruffled.

"That's a good question," she said. "That's the kind of thing I wouldn't expect you to know. Let me tell you just *one* of the uses of that data. On the basis of those facts, just the simple facts of the day's weather, we can make a very accurate estimate of the percentage of voters in your community who will have read the daily paper. This balanced against the contents of the paper on that particular day, or covering a limited number of days, for example a week, can tell us whether or not we—or the opposition—have made our points, whether we have to worry about bad publicity, whether certain things will have to be re-emphasized in that area. And so forth. Is that clear?"

"Yes, m'am," he said. "But where I come from we ought to keep track of another fact along those lines."

"What's that?"

"Whether or not the fish is biting," he said. "When the fish is biting it don't matter what the weather's doing. Half the county's sitting out on the river bank with a cane pole. The only thing mentionable they'd be using *our* paper for is to swat flies."

In the face of the swelling laughter Benjamin banged with his gavel and ended the formal part of the meeting. He thanked and clapped for Miss Blanch, and once again the men managed to stand up and applaud. The squadron of waiters descended on them again, and from the side door a fat musician wearing a tuxedo entered and struck up "Happy Days Are Here Again" on his accordion.

* * *

In the Men's Room Mike found himself standing at the rank of urinals between Benjamin and the man with the string tie. Benjamin hawked and spat.

"The international situation!" he said. "I'll be a sonofabitch. What next?"

"I don't know about you, Ben old buddy," the portly man said. "But I'm fixing to run right out and buy myself a new hat. I'm feeling kind of poorly today."

* * * * * * *

"Why don't you take me to dinner?" Vivian Blanch said.

"Aren't you with the Senator?"

"Oh, he has to *politic* this evening. I just want a nice quiet digestible dinner."

"All right," Mike said. "But why me?"

"You're far and away the youngest man here."

"Fair enough. One condition, though."

"What would that be?"

"You slip away and put on flat shoes and something a little less conspicuous. I hate to be stared at and towered over."

"You're *not* towered over."

"You're the one who said it first. It isn't how things really are, it's how you *feel* that matters."

"I have to change anyway. I can't even sit down in this dress."

"Good," he said. "You run change. I hate to eat standing up. It reminds me of the Army."

Except for little groups of talkers and late drinkers the meeting had broken up. Most of the men were already on the way home. Parker and Benjamin were planning to have dinner with a few of the more important people in the Senator's suite, and Mike had planned to eat alone, maybe see a movie, then drive back home in the morning. He was tired now. His early mood of exuberant curiosity had faded. The idea of being selected as a dinner companion for Vivian Blanch was wearisome. Still, he thought he might as well muster his energy and try to enjoy himself. He probably would never have another chance in one lifetime to observe such a remarkable creature at such close range.

She met him in the lobby in a few minutes, entirely transformed, wearing at last the modest, yet expensive tailored suit of the good girl Friday and looking, he thought, a little older than she had at first, but better. As she walked toward him smiling, she seemed to have something about her of a young girl's hesitancy, a vague aura that made him think of a little girl in grownup clothes. But that little girl was of no more substance than a ghost, flashed across his consciousness like a wild child on rollerskates seen for an instant from a moving car or train. The woman herself was perfectly self-possessed.

"This is so much better," he said. "This is how I imagined you'd be in the first place."

"It's my official uniform. I thought you'd like it," she said.

"But I'm not sure I like that."

"What?"

"Being the way you imagined me. I don't believe it. Anyway, men don't imagine women *with clothes on*, do they?"

"Oh, I don't know," Mike said. "Sometimes the erotic machinery just breaks down."

"That's not the way I heard it," she said. "I wanted to make my grand entrance today baked in a cake, in the nude. But Parker is basically a Puritan. He would have none of it. So I compromised and came as Aunty Mame."

"I think you did very well. As Aunty Mame, I mean."

"Oh God, I was a mess. I was ghastly," she said. "Do you think men really are?"

"Really are what?"

"Puritans."

"Lord, how you like to generalize!"

Vivian Blanch laughed.

"Shall we go?"

"Let's."

* * *

Miss Blanch had decided that what they needed most was seafood. She had just the place in mind, a decor of fish nets and conch shells, mounted tarpon and sailfish, checked tables and candles in bottles, and the waiters wearing sailorsuits with bell-bottomed trousers.

"I know it's terribly bourgeois, but I just love atmosphere," she said.

"I'm glad you do," he said. "Because we're going to pay for it."

"When a woman passes thirty she has to invest in just the right place with just the right light. It isn't luxury, it's plain necessity."

"All right," he said. "But what about me? Maybe I'm not at my best in fishnets by candlelight."

She smiled at him and patted his hands on the table.

"You were picked out of all that seedy crowd for youth alone. Beauty is something else again. To my way of thinking the proper escort for an evening in public is just a kind of a shadow, a nice clean swagger at the lady's side."

"You've been reading too many fashion magazines," he said. "What about the proper company for an evening in private?"

"You'd be surprised," she said.

They had cocktails and studied the elaborate menu. She was in a mood for local delicacies, so they ate boiled Gulf shrimp, a *bisque* of periwinkle, pompano *en papillote*, a green salad with avocadoes, and they finished with a cornucopia of tropical fruit. Through the meal she talked along, aimless and brittle, with anecdotes of her work, of the people she had known, of Madison Avenue, its games and pleasures. They found, as people who have lived in New York, strangers in the city, always do, that they had a number of mutual acquaintances. They talked about the current books and plays and movies and public scandals. It was all easy and familiar ground, very safe territory. And, fortified by cocktails and white wine and brandy, Mike began to think that it was all, in fact, very pleasant. It was civilized to be able to melt out of the troubled and anxious three or more dimensions of the self and into a studied two, to be able to talk with idle intensity about nothing at all and all the while to deal out for brief inspection (and even *that* not for long) not any part of oneself, but instead a series of abstract, conventional images like a bright hand of cards. It was like a game of double solitaire.

When they finished and left the air-conditioned dining room for the warm darkness of the summer night, they strolled a while arm in arm along the sidewalk, came to a row of nightclubs, each with its small colored awning, its sly wink of neon, its yawning uniformed doorman, each with its tinted picture posters of half-nude entertainers, each tossing a blare of music into the street.

"This is supposed to be a wicked city," she said.

"It's sort of wide open, if that's what you mean."

"Shall we investigate?"

And they began the desultory round of the clubs, drinking a little too much, dancing sometimes, watching the floorshows, and talking, always talking. They heard the same jokes, all with the blurred professional nastiness that's like nothing so much as a dirty word scrawled on a wall and not quite rubbed off. They heard the same tunes, perennial and popular. They saw the same floorshows again and again. Vivian Blanch was flushed and talked avidly, but she seemed entirely in control of herself, able to match him drink for drink. The truth was, he thought, that in a contest he'd probably be carried away feet first long before she weakened. The interchangeable rooms swam around his head.

Vivian Blanch was fascinated by the striptease.

"I've never seen a real one," she said. "I mean like this where they take *everything* off."

"You'll get used to it. It gets old pretty fast."

"Oh, you're so damn *blasé*," she said, banging the table for emphasis so that the glasses jumped and sloshed. "So damn pompous and *blasé* about everything. You don't understand what I mean at all."

He lit cigarettes for both of them and tried to look earnest and interested. Her pretty face swam near and vague in front of him like a fish in a bowl.

"What *do* you mean?"

"I think—seriously—I think the striptease is the one great American contribution to civilization."

She paused to give her words time to circle about his scarecrow head. She sipped her drink sagely.

"See what I mean?"

"Not exactly," he said. "But go ahead. I'm all ears."

"Look," she said. "It's a *symbol*. It's *symbolic*."

"Oh."

"And we were the first ones to discover it."

"What about Salome and the seven veils?"

"That's different. That's *historical*, for God's sake. I'm talking about modern civilization."

"Okay."

"Nakedness is what I'm talking about. Nakedness is truth isn't it?"

"Sometimes."

"What do you mean *sometimes? The naked truth*, that's what we always say, isn't it?"

"That's right."

She seemed very serious now. Little beads of sweat had formed on her brow. Wisps of hair were awry.

"So what's the naked truth? I'll tell you. Nothing! Nothing at all. A naked woman is nothing but skin and meat and bones. If one of these women just walked out here naked and stood there, there wouldn't be anything to it. Just one more naked woman. But—don't you see?—you get colored lights, you have music, you put on a costume and you strip in a kind of dance. You take it off a little bit at a time. The style is everything. You *create* something. You create the naked truth while you're trying to find it. It wasn't there before, but now it is. It's magnificent. It's mystical."

"Well, here's to nirvana," Mike said, raising his glass.

"Here's to anarchy, nihilism, to zen, to yoga, to vegetarianism . . ."

"To nudism."

"Yes, yes, yes, to nudism, weightlifting, esperanto, fishnets and candlelight . . ."

"And politics."

"By all means. Here's to your old Southern politics."

She gulped at her drink, made a wry face and set it down hard, upsetting the bulging ash tray.

"I was serious, you know," she said. "I really envy and admire them."

"Who?"

"Artists! The stripteasers!"

"You ought to tell the girls about it. They look bored as hell," he said. "Besides they catch colds in the wintertime."

"Godamn you!" she said. "Godamn you anyway! I hate people like you. I loathe worldier-than-thou people."

"Sorry," he began . . .

"No," she said, seizing one of his hands and making a sandwich of it between her moist palms. "No, no, no! *I'm* sorry. I shouldn't talk like that. It's just I think it's so important. There aren't many *important* things."

She blinked and looked into his eyes, then shivered and averted her head.

"Excuse me," she said. "I think I'm going to be a little bit sick."

When she came back to the table, much paler, but walking all right, almost sedately, he paid the final check of the evening, and they went outside and walked in the direction of the water, hearing the soft sigh of the surf on the sand. She leaned against him and hummed a broken little tune.

"That's my husband's tune. He made it up. Like it?"

"It sounds all right."

"Maybe to *you*," she said. "Maybe it sounds all right to you. He used to hum it in the bathroom before he came to bed. I could always hear him humming it above the running water. He was one of those men who always run the water in the basin when they're in the bathroom. It was a kind of a signal. The tune, that is. It meant 'get ready, you bitch, you're in for a night of it.' He was a wild man. I mean he *is* one."

"I didn't know you were married."

"Oh, Lord," she cried. "Never again! I've had it all. The first one was brilliant and handsome and an adulterous bastard. Second was richer and sweeter and duller than dishwater. This last one, my boudoir jockstrap, he is the bitter end. Never again! I'm going to divorce him while I'm down here."

"Right in the middle of all this?"

"Killing two birds with one stone. Never leave a tern unstoned," she said. "That's my motto. What about you? What are you doing here?"

"I don't know."

"Oh, be *honest* with me!" she said. "I heard you were married. What about your wife? Tell me all about her."

Mike opened his mouth to say something about Elaine and his marriage that might seem clever to her, but, quite suddenly, he discovered he was wordless.

"Hah!" she said. "I knew it. Knew it the whole time. You're not really one of *us*. You're not really one of the chosen people—the spectators. You know what you are? You're just another godamn victim in disguise."

"Let's go home."

"By all means," she said. "It's way past my bed time."

He stepped off the curb into the street and put his fingers to his lips to whistle for a cab.

* * * * * *

Mike plunged his head into the basin, lifted it dripping and looked at himself in the mirror. He stared back at himself like a grotesque image in a hall of mirrors.

"Jesus, I'm tight," he heard himself saying. "I am so drunk."

The phone had been ringing since he entered his hotel room. It continued ringing. He thrust his head once again into the cold basin. In the back seat of the taxi she had cried. "I've made such a mess of today," she had said. "Poor Allen." He pulled his head out of the water and shook himself like a wet dog. He went to answer the phone. Found it finally, and after some confusing exchanges with a couple of operators he heard the voice of Atkins in his ear.

"What do you think, old buddy? What do you think now?"

"A *what?* What for?"

"Listen, is something wrong with this connection?"

"No, I'm just drunk. Just very, very drunk. Now slow down for me. What's all this?"

"You mean you don't *know* yet?"

"Quit picking on me, Atkins. I'm sick. Listen, you're all the time calling me up and giving me a hard time. Why don't you just leave me alone?"

"I'll give you the straight story. This evening your old man, the Judge Royle, announced that he's a third candidate for Parker's seat in the Senate. What do you think about *that?*"

"I don't know," Mike said, hanging up and speaking to the black, neatly cradled telephone. "I just don't know."

He tore his shirt off and reeled into the bathroom. He turned on the shower and the little room steamed. Then he bent over the swimming reflection of himself in the toilet bowl and shoved his finger down his throat.

* * * * * * *

When he turned into the driveway, even before he had a full view of the house, Mike could see that there were cars parked in front. The late morning sun danced off their shining chrome and made little mirrors among the leaves. Out of sight somebody was working on the wide lawn with a power mower. It ground out a rising and falling rhythm like a dentist's drill.

He pulled the car off the driveway and parked in the shade. He straightened his tie in the rearview mirror, noticing that his fingers shook a little. Then he got out and walked slowly toward the front door, his feet crunching the light gravel.

Mary Ann met him at the door. Her eyes were redrimmed and puffed from crying, shadowed from lack of sleep.

"Can't anybody in this family get a good night's sleep?"

"I'm glad you're here," she said. "Maybe *you* can talk to him."

"When did all this happen?"

"Some men came yesterday morning after you'd left. They talked to him all day long. After supper, about eight-thirty I guess, he said yes, and they called the newspapers."

"It's crazy," Mike said. "It's the craziest thing he's done yet."

"He isn't up to it," she said. "It's going to kill him for sure."

She turned her head away and started to cry. Mike put his arm around her shoulders.

"I'll see what I can do," he said. "I'll talk to him and see what I can do."

Judge Royle was in the dining room with a group of men. They were sitting at the round table with papers spread out around them, and in the center of the table there was a large, colored map of the state. Mike stood a moment in the doorway and watched them huddled together there, talking in low voices. A gold shaft of sunlight lanced from one of the windows. In the heart of it motes of dust broiled furiously. Judge Royle glanced up and saw Mike.

"This is my youngest," he said. "The one who's working for Allen Parker."

The men chuckled politely and Mike shook hands around the table. There was a banker, a business man from Orlando, a retired Army officer, Beardsley, the mayor of Oakland, and a young lawyer from Sanford, about his own age, deferential and bug-eyed behind thick and heavy-rimmed glasses.

"How does the great man feel this morning?"

"I haven't talked to him yet," Mike said. "My guess is he isn't exactly wild with joy at the turn of events."

"Poor Johnny Batten," Beardsley said. "His head must be swimming. One damn thing after another."

"Why would he care? What's he got to worry about?" Mike said. "This isn't going to hurt him a little bit."

There was a clumsy silence. Mike realized that he must have been yelling. He didn't want a scene. He didn't want to make it any more embarrassing than it already was. But, curiously, realizing that he felt that way made him even more angry. It *was* embarrassing. And not just for him. It was a spectacle of folly.

The banker sat down again and straightened a stack of legal-size paper.

"Well now, Judge, if we can just go on . . ."

"Daddy, I drove all the way here, straight through from Miami without a wink of sleep. I want to talk to you."

"We're doing a little work," the Judge said. "Maybe after lunch . . ."

"I want to talk to you right now."

Judge Royle smashed his heavy fist on the table. Its slight burden of papers twitched and rustled. His companions sat tautly.

"You're interrupting!"

Mike put both hands on the table and leaned across, his face so close to his father's that he could feel his warm, quickened breath. He looked into his father's fierce, clouded eyes, and he spoke as softly and as slowly as he could.

"I apologize for interrupting," he said. "I'm sorry. But I have to talk to you. Right now. I'm sure these gentlemen will be kind enough to excuse us for a few minutes."

"By all means," the retired Army officer said, starting to stand up.

"Sit down," Judge Royle told him. "We'll go in the study."

Mike followed his father out of the dining room and into the back of the house. The Judge shut the study door behind them and flicked on the electric fan. It stirred the warm close air and rippled the papers on the desk. He sat down in his swivel chair and glared at his son.

"Where in the hell are your manners?"

"I'm sorry," Mike said. "But I have to talk to you."

"What on earth *about?*"

Mike was angry and confused. He hated this, having to stand up in front of his father's desk like a disobedient boy in short pants waiting to be punished. The strength of his past memories rose up to grapple with him. He felt very tired. He was sweating. He mopped his face with a handkerchief.

"Don't you *know* what's going on, Daddy? Don't you understand?"

"If you're going to stand there and talk riddles . . ."

"All right, I'll talk plain," Mike said. "I'll make it very clear."

All in a rush Mike told him that he was merely being used by Batten's people to split Parker's vote a little, that he was simply being conned, victimized.

Judge Royle laughed. He tilted back in his chair and laughed.

"How long you been in politics, boy? Couple of weeks? Ten days?" he said. "And you lose sleep to drive a couple of hundred miles to come and tell me some long song and dance you've dreamed up."

"Who *are* these people?" Mike said. "Except for Beardsley, did any one of them ever do anything for you? Did they raise money for you and stump for you and vote for you when you ran for governor?"

"That was different. Things were very different then."

"How was it any different?"

"These people argue a very interesting case. They figure— and I'm inclined to think plausibly—they figure that your man Parker and this young man Batten are just about deadlocked. They seem to feel that a darkhorse with some strength and a little reputation stands a good chance to slip in at the end and win that seat. They seem to be of the opinion that I'm the man to do it."

"Are you crazy? Talk about a long song and dance!"

"Watch your tongue! This is still my house and don't you forget it."

"I'm trying to remember that," Mike said. "I am trying to remember that you are my father and I'm your son. I'm trying to think about you. I want to tell you that you're an old man now, that you're too old for this nonsense. You haven't got a chance of being elected."

Judge Royle looked down at his hands on the desk. He studied them, opening and closing his fingers like folding and unfolding a fan. He cleared his throat.

"Suppose," he said in a whisper, "suppose I said I knew all that. Suppose I agreed with the logic of everything you said. Then what?"

"I'd advise you to withdraw your name and forget about it. I'd urge you for your own sake to quit right now."

"Now, let's suppose I knew everything you've been saying was right and reasonable, but anyway I wanted to go ahead and do it. Suppose, in full knowledge of the truth and the consequences, I went ahead anyway because I wanted to."

"There wouldn't be anything I could do," Mike said. "Except to pray for you."

Judge Royle sat up straight and smiled at him.

"But of course I *don't* believe you," he said. "I think I have a good and gracious chance of being elected a United States Senator."

"If you live until election day."

"I don't want to discuss it any more," Judge Royle said.

He rose and switched off the fan. Mike started to open the door.

"What about you, son? How does it affect you? That's one subject you haven't brought up."

Mike answered him without looking back.

"You know as well as I do," he said. "It makes a damn fool out of me."

* * * * * * *

Half an hour later Mike had packed his things, and he came running down the stairs, stumbling, passed Mary Ann and Charity in the hall without a word and snatched a brief, blurred glimpse of the dining room and the men in their shirtsleeves now, standing up in a circle around the map on the table. He ran across the drive and threw his luggage into the back seat of his car. He backed the car around. Out of the corner of his eye he saw his father's car back smoothly out of the garage and stop. Then in the rearview mirror he saw Jay get out and raise the hood. He stopped. He would have to speak to Jay, to say hello at least, after all this time.

Jay shook hands with him and grinned. He asked about Jay's wife and his children, said yes, he was glad to be back home again, remarked that it looked like Jay was putting on weight, and then there was nothing left for them to do but to stand and grin across wide blank years at each other.

"Well, looks like I'm going to be back to driving the Judge again," Jay said finally. "I like that. The Judge, he always say, 'Jay, put your big foot on the gas pedal and let her roll.' We roll, too. Don't no cops ever stop us. And I can park it any place I please. Don't nobody ever say a word."

"He's a lot older now."

"He's not as spry as he used to be, but he's still got the fire in him. Likes to go. Know what I mean?"

"Look after him, Jay. Don't let him run himself to death."

"Oh, I look out for him," he said. "But the trouble is, the Judge don't like to feel *looked after* too much."

They smiled again, shook hands, and Mike left him tinkering with the engine. It was gone for good. He and Jay would never be more than strangers now. Mike sat behind the wheel and drove away, feeling bad.

* * * * * * *

Mike took a room at the Osceola Hotel. After he had shaved and had some coffee, he drove up to see Jojo. It seemed to be the next thing that had to be done. At least with Jojo he could talk about it and straighten it out in his mind. Jojo's losses and his folly had given him one kind of honesty, an ability to witness the actions of others without the distorting process of envy, empathy without false sympathy. Jojo seemed unlikely to bear false witness against his neighbor, whatever else his sins might be.

It was the middle of the afternoon before Mike got there, parked in the motel courtyard and, finding the door to Jojo's cabin unlocked, went in. The blinds were drawn and the air conditioner purred as it tried to create an arctic atmosphere. Jojo lay sleeping like a large, soiled teddy bear, but when Mike touched him, he sat up quickly, blinked, got up and went into the bathroom to splash cold water on his face. He returned and sat on the edge of the bed, dangling his bare feet, smoking, ready to talk.

"You just don't know him like I do," Jojo said. "I'm years and years ahead of you. I knew all along he was going to do something like this."

"He can't *believe* in it. He knows what he's doing."

"Sure he does. Bullshit doesn't fool him a little bit. He knows it isn't peanut butter. He knows better than anyone else that he hasn't got a prayer. That's why he's doing it. It's just another gesture."

"But why?" Mike exclaimed. "It seems so senseless. That's what bothers me. I can make some sense out of everything else he's done."

"Can you?" Jojo said. "Maybe you think you can. What would you say if I told you he knew, knew even before he started out that he never had the slightest chance of being elected governor? Not the first time or the second either. He knew it and he did it anyway, heart and soul, pooped his guts out, all the time knowing that it was a complete waste of time and energy, not to mention little incidental things like money and health and his family."

"But he was hurt. He was really hurt then."

"He acted hurt when he lost out. He acted so hurt I guess it really *did* hurt."

"It's this time that I'm worried about," Mike said.

"I know what you're thinking," Jojo said. "You've got an idea buzzing around like a fly in your head that maybe he's doing this because of you. You've got the idea that in some way you've offended him and this is his punishment or revenge or whatever you want to call it."

"It's occurred to me."

"That's what he wants you to think," Jojo said. "There may even be something to it. Give him that much credit. But it isn't enough to matter. Don't flatter yourself and feel guilty. If it hadn't been this thing, it would've been something else. He's been getting ripe for something for quite a while. This idea was dropped in his lap and it struck him as just crazy enough to be interesting. All you had to do with it was to give him the chance to convince himself that he was doing something to teach you a lesson. The truth is he's always trying to teach *himself* a lesson. That's the secret of it."

"I don't know. I don't think I see it that way."

"That's just the half of it," Jojo said. "Let's don't talk about it. I'm sick to death of the subject. It's his funeral."

Jojo went into the kitchenette. Mike sat listening to the air conditioner purr and to the sound of Jojo getting ice cubes and glasses. Jojo came back in a moment with two tall drinks.

"That's what I came up here for," Mike said. "To talk about it."

"What good is it going to do you?"

"The one thing, the one thing I wanted was not to get involved in anything."

Jojo laughed out loud.

"You're as crazy as the rest of us," he said. "You're crazy as hell."

"Maybe," Mike said. "But I still want to try and work it out."

"Okay," Jojo said. "I'll try and be simple. It's pretty simple anyway. If you think about a subject long enough and hard enough, live with it, marry it and sleep with it, it gradually gets real simple. He is in love with lost causes. All of us are, but in his case the lost causes serve to confirm his original opinion that this is the worst of all possible worlds. If there were any windmills around, he'd ride for miles to have a tilt with them. If there were fair damsels in distress, he'd work himself to death trying to rescue them whether they wanted to be rescued or not. He likes to see himself as Saint George out hunting for the Dragon. But the truth is, and he damnwell knows it, *he's* the only dragon he'll ever know. It's the basic premise of our bloodline—incurable, congenital romanticism. We commit horrible crimes in the name of it. We're in love with ruins, and if there aren't any around, why, we'll just pull everything to pieces and make some.

"Okay, that's part of the trouble. Now add to it the notion that in the midst of all this he really wants, *desires* whatsoever things are good and true and beautiful and right. He wants people to love each other, just to love each other and to be just and honorable and brave and so forth. Naturally none of them are. Few of them even want to be. So the constant shock of this little fact about the nature of man, *homo insapiens*, that most folks simply take for granted, turns him into a crazy, brutal old cynic. He becomes destructive. He's just a godamn sentimentalist, don't you see?

"But wait. That's not all. Not quite. There's the other thing. There's the cult of the gesture, preferably the absurd gesture. And this is more than a blood disease. It's a regional characteristic. It's the South, old buddy, yours and mine. We start out laughing and scratching. Bands play and pretty girls wave and blow kisses, and it's all a big joke. And—bango!—before you can say Rumpelstiltskin the joke's turned inside out and we're chewing on marrow bones and wearing sackcloth and ashes. The trouble is we can never have anything pure and simple. Start with comedy and all of a sudden the stage is littered with corpses. Get going in the high tragic style and halfway through the first act the old king will slip on a banana peel. The rest is slapstick."

"Except nobody laughs. I'm not laughing now."

"Who the hell is?" Jojo said. He shook his head and took a long drink. "Trouble with me is I get going and I talk too much. Don't ever come here again and wake me up and ask a simple question."

"The thing is, I really believe he means well."

"Don't we all? Christ, don't we all?" Jojo said. "Listen, Mike, you look pretty beat to me. You better get some rest."

"Sure," Mike said. "I'll get some rest one of these days."

When he left, Jojo put on a bathrobe and followed him out, barefooted, looking like a fat mendicant, to the car.

"I'll tell you something you don't already know," Jojo said. "Last night I was down at the studio when the news came in. As soon as I heard about it, I got on the phone. I begged him to let me work for him. I told him I'd do anything—drive for him, sharpen pencils, empty wastebaskets, clean latrines, anything at all."

"What did he say?"

"What do you think? He told me to go straight to hell."

* * * * * * *

Senator Parker was not happy. Publicly he followed the lead of John Batten and for the newspapers released a statement welcoming "the distinguished Judge" to the race. Privately it was another matter. Mike found him late that night in a hotel room in Orlando where he had gone to make an evening address at a convention of county sheriffs. Benjamin was there in his inevitable seersucker suit, tapping on the crown of his hat with nervous fingers. Vivian Blanch, cool and composed, was sitting at the desk typing something on her portable typewriter. A colored bellboy was standing by the bureau with ice and glasses and water and a bottle of bourbon. Senator Parker, weary after a long day and his speech, was dressed in a bathrobe, his gaunt, hairy legs thrust out limply in front of the arm chair he was sunk in, his feet bare. He looked tired and troubled. The room was smoky with the ghosts of cigarettes, and the phone kept ringing. And Benjamin kept answering it and putting off the callers with brusque monosyllables.

"Tell the operator downstairs to quit putting those calls through," Parker said. "That phone is going to drive us all crazy."

The bellboy handed Mike a highball. Benjamin talked in a soft, hoarse voice to the operator. Vivian Blanch continued to pick away with two fingers at her typewriter making a noise like lazy crickets. Senator Parker stared at his huge bare feet and wiggled his toes.

"I'll say this, Mike," he said finally. "I never expected this to happen."

"Neither did I."

"You *didn't?* You didn't have any idea?"

"No, sir," he said.

"That seems hard to believe."

"Look," Mike said. "I don't care how it *seems*. It's a fact. It's the truth. That's all there is to it."

The Senator flushed and his face wrinkled with anger, but Benjamin hung up the phone and spoke between them.

"He's right, Allen," he said. "It's just a fact now. No use worrying about anything but what to do about it."

Senator Parker stood up, stretched and smiled. He walked to the window. There was a view of a large lake from the window and in the center the iridescent pulse of an illuminated fountain.

"They used to have white swans in that lake years ago," he said. "I wonder what became of them."

"Naturally I'll resign," Mike said. "It would be kind of awkward for you now."

Vivian Blanch stopped typing and turned around.

"If anybody is interested in my opinion," she said, "I think if Mike stays with us it might undercut the Judge's strength a little. Maybe a lot. If his own son is working against him . . ."

"What do *you* want?" Parker said, leaning back against the windowsill, looking at Mike with the bright peak of the fountain leaping behind him. "Do you want to quit?"

"I think I'd like to finish what I started."

Parker looked puzzled.

"You don't mind working against your own father?"

"He's working against me, isn't he?"

Parker grinned and shook his head. "That's one way of looking at it, I guess."

"All right," Benjamin said. "I'll go along with the idea. If Mike wants to stay, it might even help. But as far as the county's concerned, we've got to put somebody else in there. We don't need no family feuds in Oakland."

"Why?" Vivian Blanch said.

Benjamin gave her his purest look of nausea. "You just take my word for it, m'am."

"Ben's right," Parker said. "Find somebody else in Oakland. If we've got to lose the county, at least we can lose it gracefully. Mike here can work with us. I need somebody with young legs. And, Vivian, you make what you can out of it for the press."

"Have you talked to your daddy yet, boy?" Benjamin said.
"I saw him this morning."
"Well, there's still one thing more you can do."
"What's that?"
"Go and talk to John Batten tomorrow."
"All right," Mike said. "I'll do that."

Mike finished his drink and started to leave. Parker was looking out of the window again, brooding on the agile pyrotechnics of the municipal fountain. Vivian Blanch was typing. The bellboy was marvelously discreet. He might as well have been made of ebony or smoke for all the evidence he gave of having heard a word or being aware of anything besides his bottle, his glasses, and his ice cubes.

"Godamn it!" Parker said, banging his fist against the wall. "Godamn it! Judge Royle stood right there and looked me in the eyes and wished me luck and lied in my face."

Benjamin burst into laughter. He whooped, his thin body bent and doubled over with laughter.

"Allen, you're a sight," he said. "You're a perfect sketch!"

Parker looked at him furiously.

"What's so funny to you, Ben?"

"Go on and get off your high horse," Benjamin said. "After what you done to John Batten, you ain't got the first cause to complain."

Parker's face relaxed into a slow smile, like a mischievous boy's, and he tipped a nod to Mike as Mike shut the door behind him.

* * *

Mike pushed the button and waited for the elevator to come. As he stood there, he noticed a sweet odor of perfume in the air, and he turned to see Vivian Blanch standing behind him in the hall. She took his hand and squeezed it. She seemed brightened, perhaps by all the excitement of the last hours, quickened by the speed and confusion of events, thriving on chaos.

"I'm sorry about last night," she said. "I got pretty drunk."
"Think nothing of it," Mike said. "So did I."

* * * * * * *

John Batten's campaign headquarters in Miami was a busy place, neat and shiny. Until recently it had been a large travel bureau, and even now with the familiar counter and partitioned inner offices put to new uses, the posters of Iceland and Togoland replaced by smiling large-scale photographs of John Batten, it was possessed by at least a shadow of its former self, a little of the richness of possibility, the fabulous freedom of "where do we go from here?" It troubled Mike, evoking his last winter in New York, his wintry breath against the window panes of other travel bureaus, his heart restless for movement and activity. But still, this was different in an ironic way. The quiet, irrepressible voice of self-transcendent irony told him: "You see, here we are, right back where we started from."

Telephones jangled. Typewriters and business machines clacked and chittered. Pretty young secretaries came and went with the easy glide of their vocation, as if sailing along on roller skates. A man's voice flared in exclamation or anger in a room out of sight—"But I don't give a damn what he told you . . ."—and dwindled away vaguely to form only another melodic line lost in the counterpoint of office noise.

Mike gave his name to a receptionist, sat down in a metal and canvas contour chair, guarded by green potted plants on either side, and waited. He didn't have to wait for long.

John Batten came out to greet him, in shirtsleeves with his sleeves rolled up to the elbows and his collar open, his tie pulled down. He shook hands with Mike and led him into the sanctuary of his office. Obviously he had interrupted something to see Mike. Several cigarettes were quietly burning in an ash tray. Batten seemed at the moment taller, younger, more robust than he had before, but Mike was tired and trying to keep his head. He was beyond being angry with Batten he thought, and he guessed, as he took a chair and Batten sat on the desk facing him swinging his legs, that his only genuine emotion, the only thing he was really feeling was curiosity. He simply wondered what Batten would say and how he would say it.

Whatever Mike might have expected or wished for, it was apparent that Batten had nothing to say, no apology or explanation to make. He just listened attentively to Mike, heard his story out. More than anything else he seemed amused. He refused to acknowledge any responsibility, direct or indirect, for Judge Royle's decision."

"Oh, I suppose I'll have to admit that it doesn't look like it can *hurt* my chances, not now anyway," he said. "But I'm afraid it isn't any of my business one way or the other. Somebody has been misleading you. I'm sorry to hear that your daddy's health is bad, but if he wants to run for office, that's his affair, isn't it?"

"You're telling me you had nothing to do with it."

"That's what I'm trying to say," Batten said. "I can assure you that's a fact. Think about it. It's too crazy. We're too busy ourselves to get mixed up in schemes like that."

"I'd like to be able to believe you," Mike said.

Batten frowned. "Have it your own way," he said. "I want to win this election, but I don't want blood on my hands, so to speak. If I win, I want to win in my own right, on my own ticket."

* * *

Mike left puzzled. Repetition of success had sanded away the rough edges of John Batten. He was smooth as a polished stone, but it was precisely because of his blurred uniformity, the lack of jaggedness, the healthy unscarred wholeness of him, the absence of any subtle or obvious defects that might have goaded another man like a buzzing, insistent fly, that it was hard for Mike to picture him capable of performing a crime of any importance, just as it would be hard to imagine him possessed by any great, single, consuming virtue. John Batten's type wasn't regional; rather, since uniformity defined it, he was a man to be found most anywhere in the country today like the popular, attractively packaged foods available in supermarkets from Taos, New Mexico to the windblown coast of Maine. To Mike the type seemed to be the final product of our culture, our education and our ideals. He had been molded as neatly as a lead soldier. The only difference between a John Batten in Detroit and a John Batten in Tallahassee (and *that* difference, too, would be weakened now by the ever-spinning lathe of standardization) would be the special manners of the particular place. For such a character, after all, manners elbowed the old verities.

Mike had known and disliked the type long before he had ever heard of John Batten. That last winter in the city he had come on a book of Brady's photographs, and he had seen with awe and sadness at once the faces of the great men of that time, of the generals and of the politicians, of Daniel Webster and John C. Calhoun, of Lincoln, each face etched with memorable, unique qualities. Singularity seemed to be the one thing those men shared. Even noses and ears seemed to be different then, on a grander scale, and he thought from this later vantage point in time that maybe their crude psychology *had* applied for them, worked, that a man's true character *could* be read in his face, in his eyes, in the jut of his jaw and the shape of his mouth. And what of the public figures now? he had thought. Those raw strong faces looking at him from Brady's photographs with the direct impact of primitive sculpture had startled and inspired him. Recessed, filed away in consciousness, those pictures and his indivisible feelings about them may have had much to do with his sudden whim to leave his job and to come home and work for Allen Parker.

That Mike should have envied and disliked John Batten at sight wasn't surprising to him; for in many ways he could sense that Batten was a mirror image of things he distrusted, feared and was ashamed of in himself. But he couldn't believe Batten had the gift and power of duplicity to hear him out and to smile and quietly and firmly to lie in his face. He left the interview and walked away down the sidewalk in a daze, a little fever of self-doubt.

* * *

He came to a drugstore, and he went inside into a phone booth and put in a call to Atkins in Jacksonville.

"I don't give a shit what *he* told you," Atkins said. "His people and his money are behind the whole thing. You went home yesterday to see for yourself. Who else was there?"

Mike told him the names of the men he had seen at his father's house.

"All right now," Atkins said. "Beardsley's out. He's just window dressing and so's the old Colonel. But for Christ's sake! The rest of them have been working for Batten all along. I always used to think the Judge was a pretty smart man, but he's being taken for a royal ride. Don't he *know?*"

"I'm afraid maybe he does," Mike said.

Realizing he had been duped, fooled as much by himself and his preconceptions as by Batten, Mike began to feel a surge of hate for the man. He began to hate and fear the man and to doubt himself more than ever.

He telephoned Benjamin. Benjamin brushed his anger aside impatiently.

"Batten probably don't know the first thing about it," he said. "Forget it. It was worth a try and that's that."

* * * * * * *

After the names of the candidates have been filed with the Secretary of State, a political campaign of importance in the state has a way of beginning with a certain ceremony, a certain formidable dignity. It is apt to begin like one of the great naval battles of a half century or more ago, with lines of dreadnoughts steaming in solemn formation toward the dubious horizon. Crisp, bold signals are winked, wigwagged and sent upward into the sky in bouquets and clusters of pure color like rockets or flags. A line of battle is formed. Highranking officers peer for the thin feather of smoke that will betray the enemy's presence. Finally the Admiral, turning to an aide with a casual, eminently quotable remark, gives the order to open fire. Simultaneously two powerful flotillas commence firing. Huge projectiles are hurled in high arcs toward an enemy known to be there, but unseen, distant by some remote and estimated range. Then, as in the logic of a dream, just so swiftly and without plausible transition, time reverses and the scene changes. Suddenly we are under sail, blown or calmed by the fickle winds. We are at short range. There is a great deal of smoke, confusion, and clamor. The element of ponderous dignity is forgotten, and the work is close and cruel with knives and wild oaths.

In his opening speeches following qualification Senator Allen Parker spoke gravely and at length and with a dignity befitting his office. He spoke with the lucidity of knowledge and long experience about national, local and world problems. He discussed and debated the issues of foreign policy, labor problems, the plight of small business, the vices of the Republican Party, the farmer's troubles, tariffs and high taxation. He spoke of his own record dispassionately, though, of course, he tried like any good salesman to call attention to his more successful ventures, to remind his hearers of his more popular gestures. He campaigned in his best professional manner. He was able to do as he had done in the past—to stand on the pedestal of position.

This couldn't last for long, and he knew it.

There is still in the South a notion that politics, like poetry, must delight as it instructs. But the fact is that instruction, high sentence, is often allotted only the briefest of prologues. Follows behind the serious chorus, who bows and leaves the stage, a roaring, roistering procession of days, like the ghosts of a thousand brass bands, torchlight parades, laughing, cursing, sweating, shaking fists. In a blink of the eye a political campaign can become an enterprise of tense moment to moment, all tunes played by ear, of sheer exuberant improvisation in dead earnest. Great issues struggle out, protesting, like children at nap time; and in their place the morning's headlines—a pulsing tremor in the stockmarket, a revolution in Central America, a threat in the Middle East, something or other fired by somebody hopefully into vacant space, aimed at the Moon or Mars—become for the span of a day vitally significant, to be forgotten with the arrival of the next day's morning paper. Problems unique to the state, to counties, to particular towns, loom at every crossroads like hairy giants. But most of all a campaign, begun in good humor or at least the appearance of it, as a kind of fencing match of native wit, with occasional barbs fired without malice into the Opposition's vulnerable breast, most of all an important campaign becomes a battle of personalities. A more primitive form of combat replaces the early stage. Half-naked, without armor or shining weapons, the men running for one of the most distinguished offices in the land end by wrestling with each other, throwing clods of dung and dirt, cursing in monosyllabic gasps and damning each other's souls to endless perdition. All metaphorically of course.

In the campaign of Allen Parker, John Batten, and Judge Joseph Royle for the United States Senate this likely metamorphosis was much feared. The Governor wrote an open letter to all three candidates, complimenting them and urging them "in all fairness to the Party, the State, to each other and themselves to maintain an exemplary decorum and to let the public decide for itself by thoughtful scrutiny." A Leading Figure in the Democratic Party was quoted by the press as saying "I hope those birds have enough sense to keep it clean." An influential Editor in the state delivered himself of a rhetorical editorial in which he said, sadly, that all of the candidates were good men for the job, and that whoever won, the State was bound to lose. He looked for a dignified and serious campaign.

L. J. Benjamin read this editorial when Mike showed it to him. He read it, bit off the end of a cigar and lit it with a flourish.

"Somebody better tell the old boy not to bet on it," he said. "It's just about as likely as a heavy snowfall in Key West."

* * * * * * *

By the first week in July the direction of this campaign was evident to the most casual observer. Already, venerable American institution, the newspaper cartoons had begun to sprout like pimples. Allen Parker as doddering Father Time. Allen Parker as a barefooted L'il Abner, posed against the solemn dome of the Capitol. John Batten in short pants as Lord Fauntleroy with a lollipop.

By the Fourth of July, the traditional day of fireworks and barbecues and displays of oratory and invective, the two principal candidates had already assumed their roles.

* * *

"It's high time to wake up old Rip Van Winkle," John Batten cried. "He's been sound asleep for twenty years in Washington. He's had a good long rest at the taxpayers' expense."

"Where, O where, is Little Boy Blue?" Allen Parker demanded. "Where is this child who wants to look after the sheep? I'll tell you where he is. He's under the haystack of Privilege, of Special Interest, of Big Business, fast asleep."

* * *

"I hate to think," John Batten said, "it *pains* me to imagine my worthy opponent in his declining years, the twilight of a long life, standing up there in the hot Florida sun and trying to sell the public a tired old product of twenty years ago. He doesn't know the times have changed. Let's do him a big favor. Let's get behind the old Senator and give him the well-earned rest he deserves."

"I would just as soon send out a little waggle-tail puppy dog to guard against the wolves," Allen Parker said, "as I would permit my interests, my *state's* interests to be placed in the youthful and inexperienced hands of my Opponent. It would be sheer folly to send him up among the grown men of Washington. Let us unite to save him if he will not save himself."

* * *

"I'm reminded of the ancient Greek philosopher Diogenes," Batten said. "What did he do with himself? Well, the world knows he sat around buck nekkid in an old wooden tub, just watching and waiting for something to happen. Well, one day along came Alexander the Great, the ruler of the whole world, and he said: 'Old man, whatever you ask for is yours.' The oldtimer peeped over the top of his barrel and all he said was 'Just move over a hair. You're blocking the light.' Now, that might have passed for wisdom in Ancient Times. But I ask you—do we want a poor old man in the worn out, cast-off tub of the New Deal, a modern day Diogenes, representing the interests of This Progressive State in Our Nation's Capital?"

"You will remember," Parker said, "you will remember the story out of *Aesop's Fables* about the jackass that put on the skin of a lion and thought he could be the king of the beasts. You will remember what happened to the poor ass. He didn't fool anybody. No matter what he looked like, his voice betrayed him. Now, my Opponent may think that he is able to put on a suit of clothes, *with long pants,* and pretend that he is a Senator of These United States of America. He may think so. But he's not fooling anybody. Everytime he opens his mouth he whinnies and brays and we know him for what he is."

* * *

"The Old Man's halo has slipped. He's been wearing it for twenty years and everybody thought it was real gold. Well, it fell off his head this time, and it turns out to be Fool's Gold and it's rolling in the gutter where it belongs."

"When little boys run out of things to say and do in school, they chew up paper and throw spitballs. My Opponent, long since at a loss for significant words and action, is busy chewing up the dollar bills of his misguided supporters, and hurling them like spitballs into the Face of the Voting Public. We know what needs to be done. He needs a spanking on his bottom. He needs to be made to stand in the corner for a while."

* * *

"You people play a rough game out here in the provinces," Vivian Blanch said.

"It ain't no game, m'am," Benjamin replied. "And we just started. We haven't even squared off good yet."

* * *

Buttons and bumper strips for cars and gimmicks of all kinds flourished, popped out and disappeared like a heat rash. Billboards roared the candidates' names, enlarged their smiles to colossal size. There were advertisements in the papers, on the radios, on television. There were rallies and receptions. There were fish-fries and barbecues and teas and cocktail parties and late, late hurried meetings in smoke-fogged hotel rooms.

And along with all this the work went on, too, in the old way, the way of ceaseless dawn to midnight stumping.

* * *

The campaign of Judge Joseph Royle was of a different nature. Mike followed his father's campaign carefully in the papers and was left wondering what the Judge was up to. In contrast to his own experience with Senator Parker, as blurred as a sped-up newsreel, the Judge's activity seemed casual, in slow motion. There were no antics and very little fanfare. If he *had* a pattern of action it seemed to be to come along a few days behind either Batten or Parker, after the dust had settled and the last handshake was as cold as a print in concrete, to make one or two talks, avoiding, it seemed, all the histrionics Mike knew he was capable of, even pruning his language of the colorful local idiom he could call on if he wanted to, refusing to engage Batten or Parker on any given point, ignoring them really, content to spell out with neutral gravity, his own point of view. Maybe, Mike thought, it was because he knew he was old and tired and was saving himself. Maybe, on the other hand, it was a gaunt, quixotic gesture designed to shame them all.

"I hear he's sold most of the pigs and butchered the rest," Jojo told him. "That's a new twist for you. Well, you can bet your boots he'll never be a senator, but it looks like he's going to have a smokehouse full of cured ham to chew on when it's all over. Which is more than Batten or Parker will have. What will be the next development? Look for Daddy to put on a toga and sandals any day now."

They met once head on, Senator Parker and his entourage hastily leaving a hotel, ten precious minutes behind schedule, already late for a luncheon address, and Judge Royle and his stiff retired Army officer and his young lawyer coming in.

"Why don't you all join me for lunch?" the Judge said.

"Another time, Judge," Senator Parker said, seeming suddenly relaxed, as unhurried as if time were pennies. "I'm already late for some speechmaking."

"I'll hold you to it."

"You're making the rest of us look like monkeys, Judge," Benjamin said.

"Ben," the Judge said in a stage whisper, "that's the whole idea."

Everybody laughed and the two groups moved on and Mike found himself face to face with his father. Judge Royle smiled and put out his hand.

"Hello, son, you look kind of tired."

Mike shook hands with him. "I *am* tired," he said. "You're looking well."

"It all depends on the pace," Judge Royle said, "your pace and your point of view."

As they stood there for a moment with their hands clasped,

looking at each other, a flash camera bathed them with a quick bright light. The Judge flushed and whirled around, snatching his hand free of Mike's.

"Godamn you!" he shouted at the photographer. "You ask me before you take *my* picture."

* * * * * *

Before dawn each day Mike was working. The hotel desk would call him and he'd groan, slip on his bathrobe and go into the Senator's bedroom and wake him. The Senator would sit up quickly, glance at the wrist watch on the bedside table, sigh and get up. They rose and dressed and shaved (the first of several shaves and changes). They would drive to some all-night diner or early coffee shop. There the Senator would climb out of the car, stretch bone and sinew, pat his hair in place and fix his lips in a smile that would last the rest of the day as if it had been painted on. He would enter the place briskly, shaking hands with all the customers, the waitresses, the astonished cooks and dishwashers in the kitchen.

"My name is Allen Parker," he'd say. "And I sure hope you'll remember to vote for me in September."

Meanwhile it was Mike's duty to follow just behind him, passing out cards or match boxes with Parker's picture on them or chewing gum or whatever else they happened to have to give away. Then he ordered breakfast for the Senator: fruit juice, a soft boiled egg, and coffee. At the table Parker dabbled with his breakfast, poked at the egg with a spoon, sipped his coffee, and made a show out of reading the morning paper.

"Hee! Hee! Ho! Did you see this one, Mike?" In a stage voice now as he pointed to a weary cartoon depicting him, once again, as Rip Van Winkle. "What won't they think of next?"

He read through the paper (having been briefed on its contents already as they drove to breakfast) reacting audibly and dramatically to this piece of news and that. Sometimes reading the funnies, too, with laughter or with intense concern for the fate of ageless Orphan Annie or keen-minded, hawk-faced Dick Tracy or that intrepid product of The Air Age, Steve Canyon.

Finishing his coffee, he smacked his lips, lit a cigarette, folded his paper, rose, and shook hands all around once again, leaving Mike to pay the check and hurry after him.

They drove to the railroad station. At the depot other cars were waiting for them, some of the local workers and a car containing Vivian Blanch, a photographer and any reporters she could interest. The Senator made a brief talk to a handful of workers somebody had assembled for him. He spoke of his consistent support of labor. The photographer arranged a picture with Parker hanging in peril on the side of a locomotive to shake hands with the engineer.

Half an hour later they were in front of the bank building in the center of town. A few people off to work in offices gathered around him to hear him say a few words on the subject of business, the necessity of maintaining a free economy, untrammelled by excessive Federal restriction.

With his entourage hurrying behind him he set off shaking hands. Up one side of the street and down the other went Senator Parker, smiling, greeting everyone he passed, brightly pleased by being recognized or by an amiable response, undaunted by any outspoken Batten partisans he might encounter ("More power to you, sir. Vote as you please, but be sure and vote."), unruffled by the ignorant or indifferent who said: "Excuse me, I didn't catch the name." Or: "But I ain't going to *be* here on election day. I just got drafted." Or: "Leave me alone, I already belong to *one* church."

In the car, without ceasing to smile and wave to passers-by, he managed a long sigh, and, looking at his watch, noticed they were five minutes late already, told Mike for God's sake to keep track of the time.

To the mayor's office at the City Hall. The mayor, a staunch supporter of Batten, refused to be photographed with the Senator, but graciously accepted a box of his favorite Cuban cigars and exchanged trout fishing stories with Parker.

To midmorning coffee with a group of doctors at the Medical Center where he agreed with them that socialized medicine was not the Answer.

To a dairy farm where he drank a glass of buttermilk, took

off his coat and rolled up his sleeves to be photographed while milking a cow who didn't need to be milked. Smile didn't waver though the cow's tail switched in his eyes and the cow kicked the bucket halfway across the barn.

Listening to the owner of the farm rage against the margarine industry, he narrowly missed stepping into a fresh, steaming pile of cowdung.

Back to the hotel. A shave and a change of shirt and tie. Hasty phone call to Benjamin who was one town, one step ahead of him, working out a schedule for the next day. Called his office in Washington. Talked to a disgruntled County Chairman who thought the Senator was supposed to be in *his* county today and had arranged a picnic for the women voters.

"I'm sorry there's been a mistake," Parker told him. "Convey my apologies and blessings to the good ladies. And, Joe, you can have my share of the fried chicken."

Made a note to give Ben hell about *that*.

Mike and Vivian Blanch meanwhile were reading through a stack of the morning's papers, circling items the Senator might want to read or know about with a red grease pencil.

Promised a Real Estate Man by telephone that he certainly would look into the possibility of re-opening the local air base which had been closed since the end of the Second World War.

Gratefully thanked an Orange Grower for a two hundred dollar campaign contribution. Guaranteed him that he'd do everything in his power to protect Florida citrus growers against the expanding Californians and Texans.

Arrived, ten minutes behind now, beaming and apologetic, for luncheon with the Democratic Ladies. Wished his wife could be there today to meet them too. Told a few lighthearted stories about the quirks and vicissitudes of Washington social life. Praised them for their free, independent and vigorous interest in public affairs. Agreed with one lady, a mother, that Selective Service ought to be curtailed, if not discontinued entirely, as soon as it was feasible. Promised another to work for more government support for culture and the arts. Picked at a plate of chicken and rice. Stirred up his fruit salad and sipped coffee.

From there to the hospital. Was photographed presenting a donation toward the new Charity Ward and Clinic. Speaking to a group of convalescent patients, he seemed to favor some kind of national health insurance, agreed that some kind of Federal aid to local institutions was a real necessity these days, considering the expenses of doctors, modern medicines and hospitalization.

Attended a gathering of Negro community leaders in the auditorium of the Booker T. Washington High School. Looked forward to progress all along the line in race relations, increasing equity and equality. Promised to put pressure on local officials to fulfill their promise of a Negro Youth Center. Diverted the discussion from race to the pressing peripheral problem of juvenile delinquency in general.

Stopped at the American Legion Hall. Donned an overseas cap and inspected an honor guard of boyscouts. Was photographed shaking hands with the local Commander. Agreed with him that the only way to keep the Peace was through Strength. Promised to fight cuts in military appropriations.

Back to the hotel, slowly up the main street waving and smiling. Checked out. On the road at seventy miles an hour to the outskirts of the next town on the schedule. Arrived at the main street just after five o'clock. Forty-five minutes of vigorous handshaking.

Changed his shirt and washed his face in the Men's Room of a filling station.

To a reception at the Country Club. Sipped a paper cup of fruit punch (dry county) and talked to a line of people:

. . . assured a Jewish merchant that the security of the State of Israel was a basic plank in a sound foreign policy.

. . . agreed with a Greek grocer that we ought to recognize the rights of self-determination everywhere.

. . . said yes to a lady famed in the community for the beauty of her azaleas, yes there ought to be a National Azalea Week.

. . . agreed with an elderly gentleman with a pearl-topped cane that equality for the Negro mustn't be pushed too fast, yes they certainly had come a long way in a short time.

. . . nodded with a business man who said labor ought to clean house.

. . . promised a young man to find out whatever happened to his application for officer's training in the Navy.

. . . assured a lady that he would look into the matter of why her niece's husband was put in the Military Stockade at Fort Jackson, South Carolina.

Supper.

Fried chicken with the Methodist Men's Bible Class. Said his favorite passages in the Bible *these* days were in the Gospel According to Saint Mark. So many miracles in Mark. He could use one now. Everyone laughed and he said grace.

To the TV station. Put on makeup and was interviewed by a local announcer for ten minutes. Managed to say that TV seemed to be bringing the family back to the home and the living room again.

To the hotel. Showered, shaved and changed. Phones ringing. Benjamin walked in. Shrugged about their chances in this county.

Delivered a forty-five minute speech (written by Mike) to the members of the local bar association. Young lawyer heckled him about his apparently pro-Russian sentiments during the Second World War. "Young man, we have made mistakes," he said. "But I suggest you read the history of those times with care. At least we were making history. If my guess is right, you were still making poopoo in your diapers." Young man was very red in the face, but the older members of the bar laughed and he sat down sputtering.

Back to the hotel. Drinks. (Smuggled in by bellboy from bootlegger's around the corner.) Gathered his whole staff. Reviewed the day spent critically. Particularly disturbed by lax and sloppy timing. Planned the next one.

After midnight the Senator retired to his bathroom and sat on the toilet reading the newspaper stories that had been circled in grease pencil for him. Cursed and chortled behind the closed door.

* * *

Benjamin was talking on the phone. Vivian Blanch was studying the day's photographs and making up a press release. Mike was writing a speech. It was two a.m.

"Do you like fried chicken?" Benjamin asked him.

"I can take it or leave it," Mike said.

"I remember one time I ate fifty-seven consecutive fried chicken dinners in one campaign."

"That must be the record," Mike said without looking away from his typing.

"I doubt it. But it sure is a lot of fowl."

"Somebody told me John Batten was allergic to chicken," Mike said.

"Wouldn't that be a shame if it was true?" Benjamin said. "A man in politics who don't like fried chicken is up shit creek without a paddle."

"Gentlemen, *please* . . ." Vivian Blanch said.

* * * * * * *

One hot still July night Mike woke from a troubled dream and saw the Senator standing alone by the window of his room. His cigarette glowed in the dark. Mike sat up and turned on the bedside lamp.

"Do you need something, sir?"

Senator Parker blinked in the sudden light. He was wearing only his undershorts. Age made his big-boned, workman's body seem somehow frail. He shook his head.

"Sorry I woke you up," he said. "I couldn't get to sleep, and Alice is a very light sleeper. I just thought I'd come in here and stand and think awhile."

"Would you like a sleeping pill?"

"No," he said. "I'd just as soon stay awake now. When you get to my age you don't really need as much sleep as you used to."

"Feel like talking?"

"You better try and get some sleep, son. We've got a big day tomorrow."

Mike got out of bed and put on his bathrobe. He poured out some whiskey in two glasses, gave one to the Senator, and sat down in an arm chair. Senator Parker sat on the edge of Mike's bed.

"Well, how do you like the game?" Senator Parker began.

But the question was rhetorical. He sipped his drink and talked, and Mike sat and listened to him.

Remarking casually how the old routine of a political campaign must appear in the eyes of a neophyte led the Senator by a light leap back to the subject of his own youth, to the world then and how it had dawned on his consciousness. He had been a curious mixture, he said, compounded of equal parts of innocence and experience. Never really a child, his earliest memories were of the portioning of his time and energy and hope like an adult toward a future goal, an unlikely one, his mother's proud and lonely, possessive dream of freeing him from the rigid circumstances of illegitimacy, of poverty and of the hard and narrow county where they lived. In short, saving him from his inheritance. It wasn't that he had been equally possessed by her dream and its concomitant fury, but merely that he had had to share it. There was no other in that house. As a little boy he had been compelled to watch her grow old before her time. He saw her almost rejoicing in pure weariness for him, and this early knowledge of the extent of her self-deprivation and his impossible debt to her made him ashamed and serious beyond his years.

They achieved what she wanted between them. He went away to college, and she must have sighed from the depths of her soul and thought it was finished. Let thy servant now depart in peace. But the sense of shame was firm in him, had hardened into guilt by then. It was inevitable (to him, at least) that he would have to come back to the place of their mutual trial and prove himself there, thus in some way to repay her. How could she have known or understood that? In her mind the struggle should have ended when her gangling, ugly, bastard son in his ready-made Sears and Roebuck suit, carrying his cheap tin suitcases like twin pails full of milk, boarded a north-bound train, adequately instructed against making friends or playing cards with strangers on his journey, told to be sure to brush his teeth and say his prayers every night, presented with an edition of Gibbon's *Decline and Fall* which she hoped would teach him something about prose style and vanity, if not history, kissed and shooed aboard the car, leaving her, a small thin worn woman standing in the bright sun on the otherwise empty station platform long after the train had huffed and puffed and disappeared into the pine woods beyond, even the little music of its bell gone forever, tearless, utterly still and composed at this, the astonishing moment of her triumph.

It had been a terrible scene for both of them when he came home for good to practice law there. He was able now, in rambling after-midnight talk, to gloss swiftly over that moment, but the scar of it was visible. Somehow, in the confusion of innocence, he had come to imagine all her sacrifice for him as an act of love. So it was, he guessed now, but he had no way of knowing then, even dimly suspecting how many parts of hate and bitterness and despair and brooding thought compound together to make one small part of love. And all of this knowledge had come to him at once, not slowly like wisdom through its gradual process of wounds and healing, nor like the cuddled folly of old men still sending out their wishes like doves, most disappearing, but always some returning with olive branches in their beaks. Her stored-up rage and despair was hurled into his astounded face. Truth charged him like a wild boar, gored him, and drained away his energy like lifeblood.

So he opened a law office, and there he sat and studied the shine of his shoes on the desk and read his name, backwards from the inside, on the frosted glass. And he read the law books his mother had bought him and he dealt with the trivial, immemorial questions of the land and property, of discord and petty crime, as they arose and sometimes the clients came to him. And she, having lived long enough to have the taste of triumph turn bitter on her tongue, having spat it all out, vomited up the sickness of herself and cursed her son and the world and God once and for all, she could now resume her self-denying pattern of survival, this time in penance, out of her own guilt and shame. Paid his bills when he couldn't. Spoiled him. Ate beans and hominy grits so that he could have red meat on his plate. Made old and worn and shabby things do so that he could wear a crisp white shirt and a good suit when and if he went to the County Courthouse. Heaped ashes on her head so that he could smile. They were right back where they had started, mother and son, with this essential difference, that now each of them had tasted of the fruit of the knowledge of good and evil.

Their lives together were a strange embrace. They were like grotesque lovers so urgent was their dependence on each other, and it might have continued that way always, until she died anyway, and left him behind to wither away at the roots, another unsuccessful smalltown lawyer, probably a drunkard, and in the end maybe a suicide. It is an old story.

"If it had been another time and another place, that might have been the long and the short of it. But it was a particular place and just one time in history. And what a time! You might say, if you were a poet or something, that the whole world had tasted of the forbidden fruit. We had cursed God and flung ourselves against barbwire, but in spite of ourselves we survived, and we had tasted it. We were drunk on it, just like John Milton's Adam and Eve, drunk for a while, joyous and delirious in despair. That's your so-called 'roaring twenties' for you. But it didn't last long. We fell asleep out of pure boredom and woke up grayfaced with hunger and care and sprang at each other's throats. The world was wrung out, squeezed dry as a bone. It was revolution everywhere. Of course, you don't remember, but go back, look at the pictures. Study their faces. You'll find it hard to believe with your mind, but the pit of your stomach, your knotty guts will tell you. After all you were *alive* then."

It had come to him like a calling. He had gone forth like some bumpkin saint, like Bunyan's Mr. Goodman, like the heavyfooted knight of the kitchen. He had run for the legislature. He had felt it like a calling and couldn't have cared less what people might think of him or how the professional politicians laughed at the idea of an ugly, penniless, inexperienced young man standing up to talk against them to the people of the county. The thing was that he was on fire. He caught their fancy. He was wildly naïve, wanted a new, clean and better world for them, and he said so. They listened, and the politicians stopped laughing. He was dangerous. He was preaching the death of them, their requiem. In the end, just before the election, they even tried to kill him. That was the first thing, the natural thing they would have thought of in those days. One evening a carload of toughs, hired toughs from another county, came to his house. He came out shooting, killed all four of them before they could even get out of the car. But he was magically blessed in those days. The incident never passed beyond the desk of the coroner. "Good riddance," the old man said to him and crumpled the paper with their names on it and threw it in the wastebasket. There isn't even a record of it, Parker said. Just four blank tombstones in the cemetery. That act sealed in blood his county's debt to him. He was easily elected and he went on not long afterwards to catch the fancy of the State and become a Senator.

"Now," he said, "as it happens I see the whole thing differently. On a sleepless night, without a stitch of illusion between me and the truth, I begin to think it wasn't a calling at all. It was self-deception. Nothing but a wild gesture to free myself. Or whatever it is you do with yourself. Bury yourself probably, and hope to rise again. You *become* something. But you know, boy, you're still haunted by the ghost of what you were. At my age you dream a lot and I often dream over that whole time again. I dream of the time that car pulled up with a shriek in front of our house—an unpainted shack called a house. I look out of the window past the chinaberry tree that grew in front, and I see their faces pressed against the car windows. We exchange a long look through glass. Then I have the pistol in my hands and I'm running out of the front door and down the steps toward them shooting. I see the driver sag over the steering wheel and the man next to him pitch over too. The two in the back seat have rifles and can't raise them to shoot. The windows are rolled up. I see one of them start to struggle with the door handle. He's sweating, a study in pure uncomplicated concentration. The door handle is jammed and his friend leans across to help him and then both of them are dead on the floor of the back seat. I see every bit of it in slow motion even though it couldn't have taken more than the few split seconds it took me to pull the trigger six times while I was running toward them. Then I go back in the house. I come back in with the hot gun still in my hand and I see my mother kneeling on the floor and crying. And I laugh. I feel like singing and dancing. Oh, I suffer because of it, boy. I've never raised my hand in violence again to any man. But what could I do? They were going to kill me. I had never seen them before and they'd never seen me I guess except to have me pointed out to them. They were going to kill me for money. I killed them instead. It was a bad time, a very bad time."

Senator Parker lay back on Mike's bed. His glass was empty and Mike got the bottle and sloshed some whiskey into it. The Senator held the glass limply. He looked at the ceiling and talked.

The truth is that the rest of it, all of the harvesting of fruits, had been a long anti-climax. He worked. He married well. That is he married a beautiful woman with a fine name who gave him her love and no children. His mother died, but much too late to be any less of a burden to him by dying. He had his public career and his private life. Slowly the times changed around him, and he changed, too, became a good politician, no longer inspired, but now anyway able to make up in calculation, shrewdness and experience what he lacked in inspiration. And now he was able to do his job, to *be* a Senator more efficiently than ever before. Lacking a son of his own, he had found one in John Batten. He had created him, made him what he was, polished and refined him. Then, at the last moment, like a temperamental artist, he had feared Batten, made up his mind to doublecross the man and, if he could, to crush him.

"Of course it's completely foolish," he said. "If I beat him out this time, he's still the man who's bound to have my seat in the end. My reason, the one I gave you and believed in, that Batten had accepted the support of my political enemies, the very same people who've been fighting me for years, seemed valid enough. *Seems* valid enough. But scratch a little deeper. Who trained him for the hurly burly world of politics? Who deprived him of the chance to have any illusions to start with? He was originally sophisticated. How could he fall into sin? What else could I have expected? And why should I envy and distrust him because he had been spared the very things I was at pains to spare him from? Scratch a little deeper and you come to a chaos of questions, no answers. Meanwhile you have to go on living.

"Besides, he's as much the creature of the times as anything else. The times *have* changed. Maybe that's what hurt me most— the realization that time has pulled the rug out from under me. So, I'm back at the old job, selling myself in pieces like an old whore, selling out to get myself elected. And what do you think about this? What *you* think doesn't matter. Not a damn bit. Because it's new to you doesn't make it new. The world's old, boy, old. The thing is you have to get elected whatever you believe in. It's that simple. That's the way it's done."

Senator Parker sighed. He finished his drink and shut his eyes, lay still on the bed like a drowned man. He let the glass roll out of his hand and fall softly onto the rug. Then he stood up and stretched.

"What the hell's the good of talking or thinking about it?" he said. "Get yourself dressed. It's time to go to work."

And Mike looked and saw that the light of day had broken while the Senator was talking. It was morning.

The Senator went through that day with industry and dispatch, just as he had done the day before and would the day after.

He never again referred to the night he couldn't sleep.

* * * * * * *

Alice Parker was a shy woman. She was pretty, dressed well, and given the slight aesthetic distance of a public platform from a crowd, she was a decorative asset to the Senator's campaign. In the past that is all she had been called on to do, to *appear* from time to time as Senator Parker's wife. Mrs. John Batten, on the other hand, was a very blonde, athletic young woman and the mother of three very blonde children. From the start of this campaign she and her children had been much photographed, symbols of domestic felicity. She and the children often appeared with Batten in public.

It was Vivian Blanch who worried about this most. She insisted that Alice Parker was going to have to be used in some way to counteract the effect of the Batten family. Alice Parker could always go one step further. She could not only appear as the Senator's dutiful wife, smiling beside him, but she could do a little active campaigning herself.

"I don't know about that," Senator Parker said. "She doesn't have any idea what it would be like. She's been a little sheltered, you know."

"It won't be hard for her," Vivian said. "I'll coach her along, and she'll do fine."

"It's not as simple as that. It isn't as if Alice *knew* anything, even vaguely, about politics . . ."

"I say we better leave well enough alone," Benjamin said.

"You people!" Vivian Blanch exclaimed. "You make a positive *mystique* out of your backwoods elections. Let me tell you something. It isn't any different here than anywhere else. Maybe a little cruder, that's all. You can sell anything to the public. If we had time enough and money enough we could win the election with a talking dog."

Senator Parker couldn't have been very much pleased with that notion, but Vivian Blanch was persistent and persuasive. Finally Parker consented to give it a try, *if* Alice Parker was willing. Benjamin shrugged, washing his hands of the matter. Alice Parker was interested, agreed, and Vivian Blanch set about preparing her for a baptism of fire.

* * *

"I think some of the Southern women must have been raised under glass," Vivian told Mike. "Why do you do it?"

"Don't blame me," he said. "It's the custom of the country."

"Just like the Chinese binding their women's feet."

"We eat rice and worship our ancestors too."

"I think it's because the men are afraid that the women might possibly find out what a mess you've made out of everything. It's a fascinating experience for me, though. It's sort of like trying to teach a monkey to use a knife and fork."

"There you go," Mike said. "Now you're catching on. We have to draw the line somewhere."

* * *

Alice Parker was armed. Vivian inspected her ample wardrobe and selected the clothes that would do, what Alice Parker cheerfully called her "political costumes." She was briefed and carefully rehearsed. As an initiation Vivian arranged for her to make a little talk to a woman's club in a town that was a Batten stronghold. The club had recently been visited by John Batten himself and his family.

At the last moment something prevented Vivian Blanch from going along on the expedition. Mike was asked to drive Alice Parker to this appointment.

"I *do* hope I can remember everything she told me."

"Don't you worry about it," Mike told her.

"These career women, like Miss Blanch, are fascinating, but they frighten me. They *know* so much. They can *do* so many things."

"All you have to do is stand up there and smile at them. They'll be completely charmed."

Alice Parker managed without great difficulty to deliver her prepared talk. Even her obvious nervousness was becoming, Mike decided, standing alone, the only man in the room, looking over a bright and amazing crop of hats at the Senator's lady on the little stage. He felt at once pleased and relieved for her.

It was the questioning period that gave her trouble. Faced with serious questions from the floor, she floundered, stumbled hopelessly.

"Mrs. Parker, what is *your* view on the integration problem?"

"Excuse me." (She smiled vainly to conceal her embarrassment.) "Would you mind repeating the question?"

"What do you think about the mixing of the races?"

"Oh, I really wouldn't know," she said. "When I was a little girl we always had a houseful of nigra help. I think, I guess, I agree with it."

"I see. What you mean is we *all* ought to have a houseful of nigra help?"

The ladies tittered.

"Well, yes. I mean it's an experience. I don't know what I would have done without Mammy Nancy. You see, my mother was kind of sickly and . . ."

"Thank you, Mrs. Parker."

She was asked if she had met Mrs. Batten yet.

"No, not yet," she said. "But I feel like I know her. I mean I see her picture in the paper almost every day."

"May I ask what your impressions are?"

"Well, she seems like a pretty little thing, and the children are as cute as can be. Of course the times have changed. In my day *nice* young ladies didn't bleach their hair."

It was all very painful, but at last the chairwoman rose and thanked Mrs. Parker and tea was served. She did very well, Mike thought, in the familiar territory of a ladies' tea. She never stopped smiling.

Once they were driving back, however, she broke into tears.

"It was so awful," she said. "I didn't know they were going to ask questions like that. I hated it. I hated every minute of it. I didn't know it was going to be like that."

"You did fine," Mike said. "Just fine."

"No, I didn't. Don't lie to me. I know how I did. I'm just a booby, but at least I know when I'm being a booby. Poor Allen! I'd rather go naked than do that again."

When Mike told her the story, Vivian Blanch laughed. She thought it was hilarious.

"Maybe we'll try that next time," she said. "Alice Parker in the nude could swing more votes than all three men put together."

But Alice Parker did no more campaigning on her own.

* * * * * * *

By the middle of August, with a little less than a month left before election day, it was obvious that Senator Parker was getting very tired. It had been a hot, dry, dusty summer, and he was setting a pace for himself that would have exhausted any man in any weather. Some way he had managed to keep going, on nerves and guts maybe, or out of desperation and commitment. But it began to show. His famous smile was a wan parody of itself. His temper was quick. He was fussy and difficult with his workers and his staff, and then he was numb, almost as if he had been drugged. At this point Benjamin ordered him to take a rest. Benjamin knew that nothing much could be lost by a brief interval of silence. The absence of clatter and campfires in the enemy camp can be as effective tactically as any number of sorties and smoky advances.

Senator Parker was too tired to argue with him. He and Alice Parker flew off in a private plane for a few days in the Bahamas.

The whole thing was handled with discretion and, as far as they knew, no possibility of a leak to the newspapers.

Benjamin wanted Mike to take some time off as well.

"No point in hanging around the hotel over the weekend," he told him. "I can handle anything that will come up. Go somewhere and forget about it and have yourself a good time."

"What do you think about the Senator?"

Benjamin shrugged. "He's pooped. When somebody is worn out, you tell them to take a rest."

"No predictions?"

"If he's alive and sane on election day, he's a winner," Benjamin said. "That is, as long as we can keep going like we have been. You never know, though."

"You wouldn't care to quote odds?"

He grinned at Mike. "I never gamble on politics," he said. "Go! Get out of here! I need a couple of days to collect my wits."

* * *

"They say they have wonderful beaches in Florida," Vivian said.

"So they say."

"I haven't seen one all summer, not in a bathing suit anyway."

"Looks like I'm elected," Mike said.

"Looks like it," she said. "You could do worse."

At that moment Mike was pleased. For the hectic past six weeks of the campaign they had been working closely together, and he had discovered, mildly amazed, that she was easy enough to work with and, it seemed, extremely capable. She handled the problems of press coverage so well that even Benjamin had to admit that Parker's whim was paying off. Vivian and Mike had been together a good deal, working late into the night and early into the morning, occasionally stealing a few minutes to have coffee or a drink together, never really alone for long and never, of course, mentioning even obliquely that first evening in Miami when she was so drunk and lashed out at him in the muttering dark. Mike's feelings about her were confused, but he was lonely, and with a little time on his hands he was delighted to have a chance to disguise and share his loneliness for a while.

For all her various affectations, physical, intellectual, even moral if the chameleon-like adaptation to any moral climate and light can be called affectation, Vivian Blanch was an attractive woman. She wasn't beautiful, if by beauty one meant some irreducible core, a structure like a hard bony skeleton that can shape an outer form, or some inner source of light that brims over in excess and suffuses least and most parts with a portion of its splendor. Stripped and scrubbed and placed on a neutral judgment block, she wasn't likely to have caused a gasp of breath, a tingling of the skin, a prickling of hair on the back of the neck, or any other of the conventional thoughtless responses to Beauty's alien challenge and satisfaction. Paradoxically all her style, all her endeavor seemed designed to avoid just such a disclosure; yet at the same time every gesture implied that judgment above all other things was what she most desired. Inwardly she must have lived in a curious hall of mirrors, some flattering, a few grotesque beyond bearing and none of them true, a kind of cave or echo chamber out of which she cast her name like Noah's dove, hoping always that it would return transformed into a bright-feathered exotic improbable bird from one of God's never-never climates, fearing lest it should come back in the shape of a blind, furred bat, whistling itself home through angles and precipices. Outwardly she was all jerky motion and activity like a woundup toy. She was in flight, ran away into the dense woods, always allowing, however, a swift glimpse of the direction she had taken, leaving behind bits and pieces of torn clothing, a wisp of hair on brush or briar as if to say: *Here I am! Stop me!* She might have been an uneasy novitiate, one of the uncommitted of Diana's band. Reality was for her, indeed, a perpetual striptease, a dance of innumerable veils. Therefore appearance was all.

Or so she seemed to Mike Royle.

Mike, who was so much of the time tossed on the horned duplicity of contradictory emotions, was fascinated and repelled. On the one hand he could clearly see her for what he thought she was—ruthless, without scruple or compassion or even the softening gained from adherence to conventions of good manners, in the end dedicated to herself alone, wielding her sex like a keen-edged weapon, not to be trusted, not to be believed. At the same time he could feel a pang of pity for her, seeing briefly through the veils that layered her like the underwear of Victorian ladies, seeing a hurt, bewildered, restless child within, and recognizing that her abandon and bravado, even her cruelty (as for example, her cruel joke on Alice Parker) were only toys, costume jewelry. But he could never judge her purely. He had himself to contend with and one part of himself that was enchanted, spelled, lured like a clumsy moth to its lucid pyre. One part of him, that needy voice, wanted exactly the image that Vivian Blanch had created for herself to be true, the whole truth and nothing but the truth. Another part of equal power warned him that this desire was just another self-delusion bound to lead to a bed of nails, a crown of thorns. Still another bitter voice that was his laughed at him and said that this, to suffer for his folly, was what he really wanted most. It would serve him right. Shattered into a multitude of warring selves, he was too tired, lazy, lethargic, and he despaired of finding the energy to stoop over and begin to pick up the pieces.

* * *

There was a shack on the East Coast, perched in the dunes on a thin spit of land, that once had belonged to the Singletrees. It was far enough removed from the sprawled and gaudy confusion of the tourist towns to be picturesque and inaccessible enough to be private. It had been a camp for cards and fishing for Anthony Singletree, and it had passed into the hands of Judge Royle. Years ago they had all gone there, and it had seemed a lively place then with the whole family there at one time and a succession of Singletrees coming and going. Beds, or more usually pallets unrolled on the floor, had to be shared with transient cousins. There had been the wild and happy (in a child's eyes) chaos of mealtimes, a picnic atmosphere, a shrill circus of dogs and cats, of cousins and uncles and aunts. Even Anthony Singletree had visited there once, Mike remembered, an old man then, to be dressed by women, clad in white flannel and an ascot and a visored yachting cap, to be led and helped slowly down the twisty path through the dunes to the edge of the beach, to be enthroned in a folding deck chair, shaded by a huge toadstool of an umbrella and left to watch the flash and scamper of his shrill grandchildren playing in the surf, to stare with dimming eyes toward the faint, far blue line where sea and sky meet.

The cabin hadn't been used much since then, not since Mike was a little boy.

There had been one time, though. Mike took Elaine there on their honeymoon. It had been less than satisfactory for that occasion. Both of them got badly sunburned at once. They were tormented by hordes of mosquitoes and sandflies. The car broke down, and there they were miles from the nearest filling station or mechanic. Mike had had to walk those miles in a blazing sun because there was no phone. Things, aged by salt air and dust, crumpled at their touch, fell apart. One damn crisis after another added to the troubles of that already awkward, fumbling time. Later on he and Elaine could laugh about it. It became a story in his repertoire. "Tell them about our glorious honeymoon, Mike," she'd say, and he'd sigh and make a face and tell the story in grotesque detail. It always produced laughter. Still, it remained in Mike's mind a place of loss. It was strange to him that he wanted to go there with Vivian Blanch.

Nowadays Jojo had the key and used the place from time to time. Mike drove them first to Jojo's motel to pick up the key.

Jojo was tickled at the whole idea.

"You're not going to like it," he told Vivian. "The place is falling to pieces, the roof leaks, snakes crawl in through the cracks in the floor . . ."

"It sounds perfect," she said. "After a dreary succession of hotel rooms and motel rooms, there's no place like home, be it ever so humble . . ."

"What's wrong with motels?"

She shrugged. *"Chacun à son goût."*

Jojo giggled. "I know what that means: Know thyself and all that jazz."

When they left Jojo plucked a wax rose from a bouquet he had on his dresser and gave it to her.

"It looks almost real."

"It's better than a real one," he said. "No thorns. Never withers. Bloom unfading. And all the odor it has is imaginary. You can make it smell any way you want to."

"It's too bad they don't make wax people too."

"Oh, they do. People are making them all the time," he said. "I'm just saving up to buy one."

"What kind of a wax person do you want?"

"You tell me first."

"I'd like to have a large wax image of my last husband around to stick pins in."

"That's the difference between us," Jojo said. "All I want is an exact, perfect copy of myself at twenty. The boy I left behind me."

"Lord save me from that," she said.

As they drove away from the motel, Vivian sniffed at her wax rose.

"I think your brother is cute."

"He's a mess," Mike said. "He's a good guy, but he's a mess."

"Anybody can be a mess," she said. "*Everybody* is a mess. But he's got style. He makes an art out of being a mess. He makes it look easy."

"It isn't," Mike said. "He has to work at it."

* * *

He drove to the Coast over back roads, winding, mirage-haunted currents of old asphalt streaming through farm land, scrubby ranch country, pine woods and cypress hammocks, crossing over rickety plank bridges here and there where fishers in wide-brimmed straw hats, slouched over long cane poles slowly turned blank faces to watch them pass. Nearing the Coast they turned onto a trail of dirt and shells, a washboard that jarred them to the teeth until he found the right speed for it. There the trail meandered through a dense green jungle of palmetto, spanish bayonet, an occasional wild and sour orange tree or a century plant pushing up its slender, tapered, lyre-topped column into the sky like Jack's beanstalk. The light sparkled on the road, glinted off the crushed sea shells and dazzled their eyes.

"I didn't know there were any hills in this part of Florida."

"What's that?" Mike said.

"Over there," she said, pointing. "Now, that's a hill if I ever saw one."

"That's a burial mound. An old Indian burial mound."
"What Indians?"
"God knows."
"Can we stop and see?"

Mike found a little patch of shade beneath a ragged palm and parked the car.

"There's a path that goes all the way to the top," he said. "But it's pretty steep and overgrown. Are you scared of snakes?"

"Sometimes," she said. "I don't think I'm afraid of anything right now."

They got out of the car and started to climb the steep mound. The path wound all around it in a slow circle to the top, and he went ahead of her picking the way. They climbed, troubled by the thick spiny growth of brush, slapping at persistent mosquitoes and buzzing blue flies, and sweating every step of the way until at last they came to the cleared top, stood high above the hidden bones and artifacts. The clean seabreeze met them there. They stood and could see behind them the inlet, a gray serpentine track, hemmed by thick green, with the tide moving slowly in it like an easy-going river. And on the other side of the spit of land they saw the dunes, tufted, scraggly with seawheat, the white beach and then the Atlantic Ocean with long blue rollers coming in, each a neat and level line like an ironed crease, approaching the shore, rising and rising until the shuddering moment when they broke and tossed ashore a glittering waste of foam. A slim line of pelicans flew just above the dunes in graceful unison like a crew of oarsmen in a racing shell.

Standing beside him, animated with pleasure, flushed from the effort of the climb, her hair lightly fondled by the breeze, her full skirt blowing free about her slim, muscled legs, smiling and enjoying it, she was good to look at.

"I like this," she said. "I'm glad we came."

"The whole coast must have looked like this once," he said. "I guess this is the way the Spaniards saw it."

"Have you been up here often?"

"Not since I was a kid," he said.

And he told her about the times they had played on this mound and how mysterious, marvelous with mystery it had been to play in a place you *knew* was ghosted, you knew was packed with the bones of people who had lived and died hundreds of years probably before Columbus set his sails in the wrong direction for Asia. It had been like a haunted house for them then. Once he and Jojo and one of his Singletree cousins (It might have been poor Angus. He couldn't remember.) had spent the night on top hoping to see the ghosts of the Indians. They had been very quiet and patient in the starlit dark. The mosquitoes had eaten them alive, but they hadn't made a sound or even moved to scratch. Jojo had slipped away from them somehow in the dark, and when he came thrashing and shouting toward them, Mike and his cousin jumped up and ran stumbling headlong down, scared out of their wits and would have run all the way back to the cabin if they hadn't heard Jojo laughing his heart out on top of the mound behind them. The strange thing was that after that they never really believed it was haunted again.

"It's hard to imagine you as a boy."

"Oh, I was one all right."

She laughed and seized his arm and pointed to the ocean. The line of pelicans had broken up and they were fishing now, singly, farther out behind the breakers. They rose and hovered on nothing a moment, poised an instant in strict repose, then fell in a twisting dive, splashed brightly and bobbed up at once to sit a while, their white heads at that distance making them look like fat women in bathing caps, floating.

For no reason at all Vivian Blanch turned to him and kissed him, then she ran away down the path. When he caught her, he kissed her again, and they walked down the path together, hand in hand.

"I bet that was the first time that's ever happened," she said.

"What happened?"

"I bet that's the first time you've ever kissed anybody on top of a grave."

* * *

They drove along the trail, coming after a while to a cluster of raw, paintless shacks at a place where the island was narrow. There was a little fishing camp with a dock on casual stilts in the inlet. A couple of shabby shrimp boats were tied to the dock, their thin masts and rigs outlined against the windblown sky. Clouds raced behind them, gambolled like freed beasts. A few rowboats rocked and bobbed in the slight motion of the tide. In this settlement there were a few crazy houses, a grocery store with a gas pump in front, one of the old-fashioned pumps with a bubble of colored gasoline at the top, and nearer to the lapping water of the inlet there was a cafe on stilts. As they drove into the clearing a small boy chasing a yellow mongrel pup ran across the road in front of them in a scurry of dust. Then everything was very still in the early afternoon sun.

Mike parked the car in front of the cafe and they climbed the steps and went inside. They stood in the doorway for a moment, sun-struck, blind in the half dark. A fan on the counter circled the air around them. Flies buzzed and there were long rolls of fly-paper hanging from the naked cross beams overhead, richly burdened with captured flies. Mike and Vivian sat down at a crude table. A hulking shadow, a huge, dark, bearded man in a sweatstained undershirt served them cold bottles of beer and boiled shrimp in a bowl. He sat behind the counter reading.

"Is anything running these days?" Mike asked him.

He sat down his comic book and laughed.

"Ain't nothing running," he said. "Plenty shrimp a week or so ago, but now you can't even gig flounder. If anything was running, you think I'd be sitting *here?*"

He snorted and read his comic book.

"You know something," Mike said. "He doesn't care who gets elected. He don't care if school keeps or not."

"Neither do I," she said. "What do they call this place?"

"I don't think it's even got a name. It isn't on the map," he said. "These people just live here and fish. They don't even let the County Sheriff come around."

The cold beer turned their heads after the long hot drive. They felt good, lighthearted, foolish. They played the antiquated juke box in the corner ("Mind if we play some music?" He, without lowering his book: "Suit yourself, it's your nickle. It don't make me no never mind."), danced, Vivian shedding her shoes, and laughed. Finally, bellies drum-taut with beer, they left arm in arm, walked across to the grocery store and bought wildly, cans and cans and bottles, enough food for a week or two, and staggered with their load back to the car, dumped it helter skelter in the back seat.

"I don't know why we bought all this," she said. "I didn't even bring a toothbrush with me."

"Let's stay forever," he said. "Neither did I."

They drove on with their groceries bouncing on the back seat and falling until they came to the cabin. Mike opened the door and they threw everything on the floor. A bottle of catsup broke; cans rolled away out of sight. They scattered their clothes behind them as they undressed and put on their bathing suits and raced down the path to the beach. All the rest of the afternoon in a daze of pleasure they swam in the cool water, sunbathed, built elaborate sandcastles, and lying on their backs, watched the wide-winged pelicans soar overhead.

When the sun went down behind them in a red blaze, a brass-band sunset, and the wind off the water turned cool, they went back to the cabin. Outside the back door there was a crude shower, a plywood cubicle with a metal drum that collected rain water on top. Mike stood outside smoking, waiting while she showered and hummed to herself.

"Is there any soap?"

"I'll look and see," he said.

He found a bar of soap inside and came back, held it discretely through a crack in the shower door. When she took it, she seized his wrist and pulled him into the shower. In a blurred naked moment they were wrestling together, soapslick and wild, crying out wordless, stumbling on the wet latticeboard floor. But when he grasped for her to embrace her she slipped out of his hands, laughing, and ran away to the cabin door, clutching a towel around her. He finished his shower alone, and when he came inside he found she was dressed.

"I didn't *mean* anything by that," she said. "I just felt gay and good like a child."

They sat on the front steps watching the first stars appear. They passed a bottle of bourbon back and forth, feeling it go down warm and spread slowly inside like an inner blush. Mike was feeling good. All of a sudden he felt like singing. He opened some of the cans and they ate with their fingers. After a while he lit a kerosene lamp, and looking at her just then in that soft yellow-orange shadowy glow, he thought that she was a beautiful woman and that he wanted her if he ever wanted any woman.

She wanted to talk. She talked about life and love and finally about sex.

"It's never been right for me," she said. "I mean really right. You've got to understand what I mean. It isn't that it was ever *un*pleasant. It's always fun. But it never *meant* anything. It never really meant what it could, what I know it can . . ."

She said she knew there was only one good and true knowledge in this world and that was the flood of pure knowing of a man and a woman together at the moment of climax; that utter mutual sundering surrender of the self was truth.

But the strange thing after all this talk was that when at last he undressed her and took her to bed with him, though it began in a happy, sweaty, groaning nakedness, when they were finished, spent, she laughed and cried, buried her face in a pillow and shuddered like someone suffering from chills and fever.

Later she sat up, clutching the sheet across her breasts, and asked him for a cigarette.

"I hate it," she said. "I hate for you to see me like this. I can be good, really I can."

She puffed on her cigarette.

"Do you know?" she said. "I really wanted to do that, to make love to you. But do you know what I had to do to let myself go and enjoy it?"

She turned her face from him so she wouldn't have to look while she spoke.

"Let me tell you the truth. I had to imagine you were the dirty man with the beard, the one in the cafe. I had to pretend we were on top of the mound, the one we climbed today. I had to imagine I was being raped. What do you think about that? What do you think of me now?"

"I don't think anything," he said. "I don't know what to think."

✱ ✱ ✱

In the morning light they were shy, sullen, guilty, newly strangers to each other though they tried to hide it. Even trying not to show it failed. Every false affectionate gesture became by exaggeration and in the light of day a kind of arrogance. Their casual nakedness seemed brazen. Without either of them saying anything about it they knew they wouldn't spend another night together in the cabin. Mike buried the remains of their supper in the sand, half-empty cans and opened bottles, they swam once more, and started the long hot way back. For a while they talked eagerly about anything, fencing off the subject of themselves, but soon the humming routine of the drive spared them even that, silenced them, and they were left alone with their thoughts.

Mike was thinking about his marriage, *that* failure. They had failed each other, though for a time since the divorce he had been able to content himself with the idea that she was the one who had failed him. He had a good case for rationalization. She was an only child and fatherless since she was a baby because of a divorce. Spoiled then, and raised by women in that intense, special vacuum the only child lives in. Then, too, she was from New England and different enough to find his ways and assumptions a little strange. And in the mirror of her eyes he had felt compelled to justify not only himself, but also his whole region, its past, its faults and follies as well as its virtues. It had been for Elaine that he went to work in the law firm in the first place, so that they could live near enough to her family for regular visits and close enough to her familiar country so that she would feel at ease, at home. That gesture had been ruined, faulted at the outset by his insistence that a real sacrifice was involved. Was it really so? He knew all the time that he really wanted to be away from his home and his family, the place and its past. Like many a Southerner he loved and hated his history just as he loved and hated himself. And, practically, the job with the firm involved no sacrifice. He made a good salary, and he couldn't admit that he'd been unhappy with his work to begin with. It had been, indeed, what he wanted, its burden of monotony had been satisfactory, empty of meaning or significance to him, simply a blank of his time sold at a reasonable price. Nevertheless he had convinced himself that it was all a sacrifice for her, and, of course, he had found a variety of ways of communicating this feeling to her

—But we don't *have* to stay here, she used to say. Go where you want to. Do what you please. Dig ditches for a living. Catch rare butterflies. But if you stay here, or whatever you do, don't insist that you're doing it because of me.

—Here we go! he would exclaim. The "whither thou goest" pose. Spare me that one please. Can't you just be honest with yourself or me just once?

—Can't you?

Of course, he guessed, the true battleground, the real wrestling for identity and knowledge had been the bed. But it was a simple story. There had been gains and losses, good times and bad, and none of them so cosmic as to cause the stars to throw down their bright spears and weep for pity. It was possible now in one kind of light to see it all as comic, this simple act of two animals, male and female, coupling together in the hushed dark and imagining that by some process of self-transcendence they were able to raise their squandered energy to the power of pretentious mystery, by tricky thinking able to imagine that the little squee-squaw of their bed springs was a matter of earth-trembling importance. But it wasn't entirely helpful to lean on the comic view like a crutch or a cane for long.

The truth of the matter (he was thinking) is that when we come together, grapple in love, we aren't really ever naked at all, but fully clothed still, clad in fine-spun, tough-fibered secrets, armored by the scar tissues of private wounds, and much, maybe all of it, beyond the possibility of telling, beyond all words and gestures. Flesh cries out to flesh: *I want to tell you who I am, who I really am.* But when the body speaks its hurried, whispered moment, it's like a prisoner at visiting time speaking bare words through a wire mesh, overseen by grim and silent guards (gods).

It was a pity, all of it. He wished that love, an illumination or a gift, had been possible for them. He wondered how two people alone and in love could so litter a small stage with the corpses of themselves.

* * *

They pulled up in front of the hotel. Mike started to get out and and open the door for Vivian. She took hold of his arm, dug into the flesh with sharp nails.

"What is it?" she said. "What is the thing I lack?"

He looked at her. Her lips were trembling, her eyes were imploring. He looked the other way out of the window at the barbered hotel lawn.

"You're not so special," he said. "I guess it's what we all lack."

"In a word?"

"In a word—simplicity."

She let go of his arm. As he opened the door for her, she rubbed her eyes with the back of her hand. But she stepped out and swept through the revolving door smiling.

* * * * * * * *

The large glossy photograph lay on the desk. It lay there on the blotter amid chaotic constellations of keys and small change, in which the Senator's twin silver cufflinks shone like stars of the first magnitude, and a taut system of coffee cups in static revolution around a single ash tray, abundantly overflowing. It was late at night, and, squint-eyed from weariness, they were all there, grouped in a slovenly tableau around the desk. Senator Allen Parker, L. J. Benjamin, Vivian Blanch, and Mike Royle stood in a half circle around the picture, aghast, at the moment too tired for words, like mourners around the body of some dear friend.

It wasn't the first thing of its kind to come to their attention. There had been others all along, furtive, even libelous pamphlets, cartoons, insinuations, innuendoes, assertions, attacks on the Senator's character, ancestry, history, sex life, religion etc. And none of these, of course, were connected in any way with John Batten. In fact as soon as Vivian Blanch had prevailed upon the Senator to make news out of these items, Batten had loudly disowned them, denounced them and said to the press and the public that he would "flatly refuse this kind of ignorant and misguided support." He had risen to the defense of his opponent magnanimously.

But the question before them now was of a somewhat different nature.

Mike looked at them: Parker in suspenders and rolled-up shirt-sleeves, even after his few days rest looking worn out, changed under the steady pressure of the campaign, dark bruise-colored circles under his eyes, the print of lines in his face deepened, his face thinner, the posture of his body slumping; Benjamin invariably weary and rumpled, his lips as always compressed as if to keep back a swarm of curses, and quieter now and seeming for the first time to Mike fragile, his shrug as ready but less facile, as if he carried on his thin, stooped shoulders these days an invisible, unshakable weight; and Vivian Blanch, glossy and cared for in her suit, bright and hard and glazed as if refined, finished in the self-consuming kiln of pure activity, any activity, as they were fading she was blooming, but with the brittle perfect glitter of a glass flower, ever more destructible. And himself. A glance in the mirror showed that he needed a haircut (hadn't had time), his suit was spotty and needed pressing (ditto), that his eyes were red-rimmed, granular-lidded, bloodshot. A quick look at his hands clenching and unclenching along the seam of his trousers revealed the tiny shake, the dance of nerves, and the tan stain of too much tobacco on his fingers.

In the slick, two-toned, rectangular world of the photograph Senator Parker smiled broadly, happily for always, as if caught in an overflow of spontaneous delight. He stood in the center of a circle of well-dressed, smiling Negroes, and he was fixed in the act of leaning forward deferentially to shake the hand of a slim bespectacled Negro whose grin equalled the Senator's in intensity. It could have been any number of things: a chance meeting of old friends, of colleagues, a moment of celebration or even the settling of a pact or conspiracy. A text accompanying the picture identified the Negroes in the picture as a group of local leaders for the NAACP and the man who was shaking hands with Parker as a prominent figure in that organization in the state. The photograph had a caption: SENATOR PARKER AMONG FRIENDS.

Over the past week since the Senator had returned from the Bahamas John Batten had been firing away brisk salvos on the subject of integration, on the dangers of a too-rapid breakup of the ingrained pattern of segregation, on the malice and vehemence of Northern pressure. He associated Senator Parker with that pressure, reminding his hearers again and again that Parker had once voted in favor of a national FEPC bill. Now came the photograph with its angry semi-literate text, mailed out to thousands of homes and offices throughout the state.

Senator Parker seemed to be deeply troubled.

"How the hell was I supposed to know that guy was some kind of a big shot in the NAACP?" he said. "He just walked up to me and we shook hands and somebody snapped a picture."

"Forget it," Benjamin said. "Let's forget about it."

"I never thought Johnny would do something like this."

"He probably don't even know about the picture yet. It's just a shot in the dark."

"I don't know," Parker said. "We've been dancing all around the issue without saying or doing anything about it. I think maybe he got in some good licks this time."

"For Christ's sake! This ain't Arkansas," Benjamin said. "Who's been talking to you anyway? You're the Senator. You shake the hand of anybody you feel like."

"I don't know, Ben. I just don't know. I feel like this election is slipping right out of my hands."

The two men stared at each other for a moment, entranced, like rival hypnotists. Senator Parker looked away.

"You're tired," Benjamin said. "Take a pill and go to sleep and forget it."

Vivian Blanch lit a cigarette. "How much do you figure the Negro vote will count this time?"

"Zero," Benjamin said. "Next to nothing except in Duval County."

She merely smiled. She smiled at him and raised her chin and blew a little spurt of smoke in the air above their heads. Benjamin looked puzzled.

"So what?"

"So," she said, "you might say that the Negro vote is a very expendable item."

"You might," he said, "if you wanted to put it that way."

"I'm not putting it any way. I'm just asking. And you don't think this thing, this kind of thing" (she gestured with a slack, languid hand at the flat shiny photograph on the desk) "is going to hurt?"

"I don't see how," he said.

"Oh, maybe a little bit," he went on after a pause. "But my experience is, if you slow down and stop and pay attention to something like this it always ends up hurting you a lot worse."

"I don't agree with you at all, not at all," she said softly. "The whole trouble with this hick campaign from the very beginning has been the absence of anything to fight over. It's just been a big side show . . ."

"What about the godamn international situation?"

"You don't have to be sarcastic," she said.

"Calm down, Ben, and let's hear what she's got to say."

"It looks like you already *heard* what she's got to say."

"What's your idea, Vivian?"

"Very, very simple," she said. "We just whip out ye old Confederate flag, holler 'grampa was a drummer boy' and start whistling 'Dixie.'"

"I expect you'll want the Senator to take lessons on the steel guitar while you're at it."

"Ben, I asked you once . . ."

"Allen, if you do this now, if you come running out in the open now with a whole lot of *excuse-me-pleases*, you're finished. You'll spend the little time that's left in this campaign just poking your head out of a hole in the ground so he can take pot shots at you."

Senator Parker looked pained.

"It comes as a kind of shock to me that you *care* about issues."

"I don't give a damn for issues, m'am," Benjamin said. "All I care about is votes. If eating peanuts gets votes, I say we stuff Parker full of them. If cannibalism gets you elected, I say we throw somebody on the skillet. But if the Senator comes out hollering about white supremacy just because of a measly picture, he's not going to get any votes. He's just going to look like a godamn fool."

"This time I don't know," Parker said. "I think you might be wrong this time."

"Take your time," Benjamin said. "Let's don't do anything. Let it sit for a while and then see how we feel."

"Tomorrow is going to be one day too late," Vivian said. "If we make up our minds right here and now and get out a statement we can still make all the morning papers."

"The hell with the morning papers."

"Ben, if you're not going to co-operate . . ."

"All right," Benjamin said. "It was bound to come to this point sooner or later. Now then, Senator, you've got to go one way or the other. Me or the high-priced lady."

Parker looked at the floor. "I'm afraid she's right on this one," he said.

Benjamin walked to the window and turned his back to them. He stood looking outside. He had picked up his hat off the dresser and he twirled it in his hands. Then he put it on his head.

"So long, Senator Parker," he said. "I wish you a lot of luck."

"You can't run out on me now!"

He touched the brim of his hat in brief salute and walked straight for the door, not looking left or right, not looking at any of them.

"That's just what I'm doing," he said and he shut the door behind him.

Senator Parker slumped into an arm chair. He sprawled there, loose-limbed, with his great crude hands covering his face.

"All right," he said, speaking through his fingers. "Vivian, you draft a statement and let's get it out."

After she had left the room he sat very still for a while, breathing deeply like a man asleep, his hands still hiding his face. When he took them off it was as if he were wiping away his whole face or tearing off a mask, but he had, it seemed, recovered his composure. He grinned at Mike.

"How about you?" he said. "You haven't said a word all evening."

"It was up to you," Mike said.

The Senator jumped to his feet and grabbed Mike's shoulders in his hands, gripped him hard.

"What *good* are you?" he said. "What kind of an answer is that? Are you for me or against me?"

Mike looked him in the eyes and took hold of Parker's wrists and removed his hands from his shoulders. It was a slow thing, like arm wrestling, abstract almost, for neither of them moved another muscle, but Mike took his hands and forced them away from him. He was surprised that he was stronger than the Senator.

"I'm for you," Mike said. "But you have to make up your mind all by yourself."

Senator Parker's eyes brimmed with quick tears and he turned away.

"Don't I know it?" he said.

* * * * * * *

The press release that Vivian Blanch drafted for the papers was moderate enough. It did not commit Parker one way or the other on the touchy issue; it simply denied the implications of the photograph and of Batten's corollary verbal picture of the Senator as an integrationist and an Enemy of the South. It pointed out that the Senator's Southern heritage was firmly rooted, native born.

Still, it appeared that Benjamin was probably right and that later on they were all going to be able to say that in Parker's first hasty reaction to the photograph was the unmistakable odor of weakness, effluvium of despair.

All teeth and claws now, entirely on the offensive John Batten ripped and tore at the scarecrow effigy of the Senator.

* * *

"What *is* this? What is this we are witnessing? For the first time in his long, long career my opponent is saying: 'Behold me! I am a Southerner Trueblue.' No more does he lay claim to be a New Dealer, a Liberal, a Friend of Labor and an Enemy of Big Business. Now he is saying for the first time ever *I am one of you.* The thing is, do we believe him? Can we believe him when he changes his views with every change in the wind? Because the chameleon crawls up and squats on a leaf, does that make it green?"

"My young opponent has declared himself to be the Defender of the Southland, the self-appointed Custodian of Customs and Traditions. Apparently he came to the knowledge by growing up in a large city in fat years, times of plenty and harvest. I came from the country, the heart of the land, and I grew up in the lean years, the ones you remember with a wince. I come from the dirt and dust of this state and I'm not ashamed of it. I have eaten my peck of Florida dirt and I have earned the right to speak of it. He has yet to taste anything but dust. His words are nothing but sound and fury, a crackling of thorns under the pot, a lot of smoke and no flame and not enough heat to warm a baby's bottle."

* * *

"I see where my opponent has assumed yet another pose. He ought to go on the stage. He ought to have his name in lights and we could all go and see him in the movies. He started out this campaign as the Distinguished Elder Statesman. Nowadays I read that he's just a Country Boy, barefoot and gawking, a Poorman's Lincoln. He talks of dirt. He says he has the right. I agree. He knows all about dirt. His hands are dirty from the mud he's been slinging. It isn't Florida dirt that's under his fingernails. It's plain old Politics Dirt, dirty politics. He has one hope. He hopes that his longwinded rhetoric will be dust in our eyes to conceal the truth that he's nothing but a tired, old man."

"It is true that I am tired. My opponent says it and of course it must be true. But, by God, I have the right to be good and tired. I have worked long and hard for this state. I feel the good tiredness of accomplishment. And tired or not I will continue to work and work harder than he will ever be able to if you will honor me once again with your confidence."

* * *

"*Confidence?* Confidence is what he asks for. Does he deserve it? We know him, indeed we know him now. He is Confidence itself, the original Confidence Man. He has doublecrossed all his friends. First he doublecrossed the State when he hobnobbed with his buddies in the N-Double A-C-P. That would be bad enough. But when he was caught at his doubledealing, he turned right around and doublecrossed *them*. *I know you not*, he said. This man, this man for whom no vows or friendships or promises or obligations or loyalties of any kind are sacred, has the audacity to ask seriously that the rational intelligent voters of this state put their interests in his hands. He's not asking for confidence. He's really talking about Faith, Blind Faith, the blind leading the blind into the ditch."

"I ask the voting public simply to look at the facts. I ask the public simply to measure, to weigh my record against John Batten's promises. I'm sure that you'll see the choice before you is obvious. And I hope, I sincerely hope you will return me to my post and my duties in Washington by an overwhelming majority."

* * *

They were having coffee in a drugstore. It was hot and still and the overhead fans were laden with the job of stirring the lukewarm air. Vivian Blanch set down her cup hard, spilling a little and started to giggle.

"What's the matter?" Mike said, irritated, his own nerves taut.

"Excuse me, I was just thinking," she said. "I was just thinking that now I know how Pandora felt when she opened that silly box."

* * *

All this in a few days. And then there were three of them talking. Judge Royle thundered into lonely prominence. Suddenly he had begun, as if inspired, a serious campaign. He was urgently speechmaking and handshaking. He ridiculed his opponents.

"This is an ugly spectacle," he said. "My two opponents are trying to outdo each other in personal malice. They are carrying on like little snotnosed boys at recess. And both of them seem intent on proving that each one is more oblivious to the interests of a quarter of the people of this State, our Negro population. It ill behooves two grown men of public stature, one a paid lawmaker, the other a young and successful lawyer, to flaunt their folly, like a washline of dirty and patched clothes, in the public's face."

* * *

His original supporters vanished like dry leaves in the wind. The retired Colonel, the banker, the business man, the young bugeyed lawyer disappeared from the scene and sight as if they'd dropped through trap doors with a little puff of smoke. And he was all alone. He was all alone with the indubitable knowledge that he had been used exactly as his son had said, the proof positive. But with Jay to drive him and with a sudden sourceless surge of energy he was making a real fight.

The strange thing was that as fast as he lost his original support he was acquiring other strength. The newspapers gave him friendly space. Editorially he was praised for the dignity of his stance. "Judge Royle doesn't stand a chance," an editor wrote. "And our guess is that he knows this better than any of us. What it appears to be that we are seeing is that rare thing, a *moral* campaign. He is teaching us all a lesson in how it should be done."

The Governor came out publically in support of him, spoke for him.

* * *

Jojo thought all of this was very funny.

"A moral crusade, my ass," he told Mike. "He just saw a chance to make some noise and he's doing it. He must be tickled pink. The Governor sticks his nose in just because he knows it can't do the other two any harm and it can't help Daddy and it *may* help him if he wants to run for Senator the next time around. The papers give him a plug because it makes it easier for them to live with their consciences—they're really on the side of the ineffectual angels. Everybody's having their cake and eating it too. Especially him. He couldn't ask for more ample proof, better evidence, that he's living in a world entirely populated by fools and knaves."

* * *

Meanwhile, with Benjamin gone (he sent a picture postcard of a fat-thighed dancer in Havana) the creaky machinery he had rigged for Senator Parker was running down, falling apart. The job of repair or at least slowing down the disintegration was too much for Senator Parker. He cajoled and coaxed, threatened and bluffed and bribed, pleaded and promised, but though he was managing from hour to hour to keep the machine going (at least it *seemed* to be functioning), he was starting to feel, he told Mike, like old Macbeth at the end of the play, alone in a draughty castle, a wind-haunted spacious place, waiting for the end to come to him with not even anyone to answer his summons when he called. His own voice seemed to echo back at him in the grinning reassurance of others.

Election day in early September, now a scant two weeks away seemed a breathless, dizzying distance.

But Mike Royle found himself inspired by the chaos. Somehow, swiftly and without even being aware of it when it had happened, he had lost the weight of himself. He was now a creature to be bathed and shaved and fed and dressed and pushed forward like a stumbling beast on chains, prodded from one encounter and activity to the next. Abstract, inflexible fury kept him working on long after his energy was spent. Like his father, he imagined, he was burning himself up with a dedicated, irrational abandon. He was lightheaded, lighthearted and careless; strangely for the first time he could remember, he felt, at the pitch of his involvement, wholly irresponsible. It gave him a sense of power. He felt like an invisible man.

But there came the day when all this airy gusto fled him and he was left limp and shapeless as a pricked balloon.

Parker sent him racing up to West Florida ("I'm just too tired to do it myself. Do the best you can. Just do what you can for me.") to bolster up sagging loyalties, to shore up if he could the crazy edifice of confidence. He spent a long and fruitless day. He was young; he wasn't Senator Parker; he could be told the truth.

"It ain't that I'm not *for* Allen. It ain't that I don't *want* him to win," the fat gentleman of the string tie told him. "But you know as well as I do, he's through. Let's face it. Now, a man in my position, what do I have to gain by going down with the ship, so to speak? I ain't the captain."

Mike came in the later afternoon to his hotel room, threw himself on the bed and closed his eyes and let the squandered day whirl past in his consciousness like a dream of dancing. In his dazed weariness he heard the phone ringing. Still with his eyes closed, he rolled over on his side and groped for it.

"I've been trying to get in touch with you all day," Mary Ann said.

"Is anything wrong?"

"You better come home right away," she said. "Daddy is dead."

* * * * * * *

For Mary Ann it had been a day of doctors. After they brought him home in the ambulance at night, he seemed to be resting easy, and they said they thought everything was probably going to be all right. But another attack came early in the morning, a bad one, and they arrived again soon after. They came up the walk stepping over and through the wide pools of first shade, quickly, but noiselessly, on cat feet, each with his little black bag, each with the unsmiling but unworried concern they learn to wear like a badge. There were whispering voices at the foot of the stairs and in the upstairs hall. The door to his room kept opening and closing with a click. All that morning and part of the afternoon he was still alive, and then—it must have been around three or maybe three-thirty—she was just going down stairs to ask Charity to make a pot of tea. She heard one high loud shriek, the first unmuffled, indecorous sound of the day, her mother crying out, and she knew Judge Royle was dead.

She stopped for a moment, stood there gripping the banister and listened to that lone cry, the only naked cry of grief she had ever heard, echo pure and sudden in the house. She knew she must go right ahead, and she went through the dining room and opened the kitchen door. Charity looked up from where she was sitting at the table with her Bible already open and her finger stabbed emphatically into the heart of the text. There was nothing written on Charity's face, no sign of any emotion, but tears like single raindrops swelled in her eyes and splashed on the thin pages.

"Would you put the kettle on for tea?"

"Yessum."

She returned, mounting the stairs slowly, aware that she must save, conserve her energy, catching a glimpse of her unchanged profile in the long, narrow hall mirror at the foot of the stairs. One of the doctors, the eldest, met her at the landing.

"We've given your mother a little something to quiet her nerves," he said. "She's lying down now. She ought to sleep a while."

"Fine."

"There'll be a number of things you'll have to do," he said. "If I can be of any help . . ."

"That's very kind of you to offer. But I can manage."

"I *did* take the liberty of calling the undertaker."

"Thank you," she said.

"Are you sure now?" he said. "I mean I'll be glad to stay right here with you until someone can come."

"I'll manage perfectly," she said.

Then after a little while they all filed out of the house as quietly as they had come, declining in courteous whispers her offer of a cup of tea. When they were gone she went into the dining room, alone at the big table, a pen and a fresh blank pad beside her, listing the names of the people she must call and the things, in strict chronological order, that must be done. Charity came in with tea and the silver service.

"Would you bring me a slice of lemon?" Mary Ann said, glancing up from her task.

"Ain't that a shame? After all this time I can't even remember you always takes lemon with your tea."

And Charity began to sob out loud, her whole body shaking.

"Never mind, Charity. You just go and sit down and rest yourself awhile. Everything's going to be all right."

It was lucky, Mary Ann thought, it was lucky that somebody in this family, *somebody* in the whole household, had enough self-control to cope with an emergency. Suppose she allowed *herself* the pleasure of unmasked emotion, let herself shriek or sob?

Even her father—and just then she could picture him perfectly still for the first and last time on his deathbed, lying large-boned and strangely tranquil in the expensive pale silk pajamas he had always loved; his huge, horny, calloused feet, would they be naked or decently covered?—never could meet a crisis with passive composure or cool logic. He always had to act, to *do* something. A creature of moods, the whole spectrum of male moods, he had been for as long as she could remember racked by sudden enthusiasms, quick, inexplicable rages, depressions, even sometimes moments of undiluted sentimentality. Unlike his sons, *she* had seen him in tears. Always he had stirred her admiration as no other man had or could. And in the years since his health had failed he had aroused in her the desire to shelter and protect him, like some mythical frail old king who had been a mighty warrior, against any more of the rude wounds of this world. But respect? The best thing, after all, that she possessed was her self-respect, her sense of discipline that didn't permit her the license of a variable temperament.

In an hour she had called everyone who ought to be notified right away, checked off their names neatly on her list one by one. The undertaker had called her, saying that he would come for the body, as is customary, after dark, as soon as it was good and dark. The Episcopal minister also phoned to say he'd be along as soon as he was able. She had been upstairs and seen her mother sleeping, her drugged pretty face as calm as a doll's against the pillow. She paused with her hand tight on the doorknob to her father's room, wondering if she ought to go in and look at him. She decided against it. Surely the doctors would have left the scene in impeccable repair. Still, it was a strange empty kind of feeling to stand just outside the thin door and not to hear his heavy breathing. Death, after all, was not just going to sleep. At last she released the doorknob and went downstairs to the kitchen again. She found Charity rolling dough for biscuits. It hadn't, any of it, been as difficult as it might have been.

"I guess you better see to the boys' rooms."

"Does Mr. Mike know yet?"

"I haven't been able to reach him yet, but I will."

"Is Jojo coming?"

"Yes," she said. "He's going to try to get down here early this evening."

"That's good."

"I just hope he comes here sober. I hope he's got sense enough not to come drunk."

"Oh, Miss Mary Ann, Jojo wouldn't do anything like that."

"Let's hope not." Mary Ann smiled tolerantly.

Whatever Jojo had done, might do, was and would be all right. World without end. He could let himself go, drift from one ill-fated, ill-conceived venture to another until, stripped of talent and confidence, he found himself at last a glib disc-jockey with an all-night jazz show. Reduced of everything but his mellow disembodied voice that charmed his listeners with idle talk and with absurd and bountiful promises of the miraculous virtues of breakfast foods and appliances, of hair-straightener and skin tint. Now even his looks were gone. She remembered that when she was a girl she had been in awe and envy of his natural beauty. But gradually someway over a few years everything about him had softened and weakened, like a wax doll left too near a flame. But in spite of everything to the dying day of all of them Jojo could do no wrong. Even the gonorrhea had been an accident and (how astonished, ashamed she had been!) her mother met her adolescent bafflement, her tears of shame and disappointment with no sympathy at all, with only a slight, wise smile.

—After all, Mary Ann, your brother is a grown man. These things happen. But there's no use thinking about them or *discussing* them.

—What if they happened to *me?*

—Hush up, child. You get the strangest notions.

These things happen. But they had not happened to her, neither the chance to curse and leave them all for good, and of course to live on foolishly, nor, for that matter, the occasion or the risk of contracting what her mother would have euphemistically called in Jojo's case " a social disease." Above all she was to be made into a lady. Still, she thought, the whole texture of our entangled lives is threaded with bright ironies. Given time a witness will discover them. Given time they will be revealed. If Jojo had melted into fat and self-pity, his early promise and his early beauty vanishing like a long sigh, *she* had come through the fires of her ordeal, of her hungers and discontent, with a smooth, glazed finish. Naked and painted with gilt she could have stood on a pedestal and passed for a statue of Diana the Huntress. Let Jojo be gnawed to pieces. She had been bruised and kneaded and molded into the self-possession and beauty she now had. And she was sure that she wasn't likely to be wounded much by anything now.

Just then the doorbell rang softly as the first of the guests and callers from town, dressed up and wearing long faces, arrived.

The late afternoon and the early evening weren't easy. For one thing there was a sudden, tumultuous summer thunder shower. It flashed brightly among the tossed oaks, the palms like green wild tethered horses, and the rain pelted the stricken flower bushes. It gave a curiously theatrical quality to the otherwise stiff and conventional gathering of mourners as they stood in the living room, the dining room, the hall, and a few in the library, muted and subdued by their wooden formal gestures of sympathy. Outside the lightning flared in vivid tines, and as the thunder exploded instantly after, it seemed as if they were really sharing something, as if they were all huddled together against the indifferent storm. But the shower and the drama of thunder and lightning ceased as abruptly as it had begun, and the late sun came again, rinsed now. The world outside the windows of the house took on a fleeting, submarine softness.

Nancy Royle came downstairs in a black dress, her pale face composed, to be comforted by women. The men stood about in stiff, checked postures, holding on tight to their hats, as grave, as clumsy, Mary Ann thought, suppressing a desire to laugh at her observation, as young boys at dancing class. The young Reverend Fishback finally arrived and tried to establish the proper tone of cheerful acceptance mingled with sympathy. Weren't we all *Christians*, after all? Later on there was supper, and a few friends of the family and the young minister sat around the table to eat and to be served by Charity whose sobs had weakened to sniffles. Afterwards the minister waited until the undertaker came (who might as well have been a thief in the night, it was so quickly, so quietly done). Nancy Royle took another pill and went to bed, leaving Mary Ann to shoo out the minister and the last of the others despite their protested willingness to stay with her. She told Charity just to leave everything and go on home. She wanted more than anything to be alone and quiet.

She walked through the library and unlocked the door to her father's study. She picked up the first book at hand, a paperback mystery, and she sat down in the swivel chair behind the desk to read it. He loved them. *Had* loved them, rather. She would have to be careful to keep the right tense from now on. His would be the past and the past perfect. Hers? Well, the present and the past. The future would have to take care of itself. Here was this one that he had been reading, dogeared just a few pages before the final revelation of guilt and innocence, the final and conclusive denouement. She began reading where he had left off, compelled to finish the story for him, even though she found herself wondering as she read along how in the world he had ever managed to exercise patience enough to get this far. Through the cracked door into the library, over the top of the book she could see the grand piano, black and shiny, its top raised like a great wing, its keyboard like a clown's smile. *That* had been one of his pleasures too, just to sit and hear her play. Not one of hers. She had weathered her early stormy scenes and the grim specter of his insistence that she practice. She had outlived the tears and self-pity until eventually she had been able to please him, playing with perfect dispassion whatever he might want to hear, and playing tolerably well too while the little metronome, tense in its wooden cage, ticked and tocked. All that was going to be hard to forget. It was hard to forgive him that. But there was neither cause nor occasion for forgiveness any more. She needn't ever play that piano again. Or she could if she wanted to. It was a remarkable thing to realize that now she was free to choose whether she wanted to play or not.

Half-dozing over the open book she heard the heavy brass knocker pound against the front door. That was something she had overlooked. There would have to be black crepe or something on the door knocker. Wasn't that what one was supposed to do? Or was that vulgar or something? And that, of course, knocking on the front door instead of ringing the doorbell, would be Jojo.

"Hello there," he said, taking her in his arms (he *had* been drinking, but only a little to fortify himself, she guessed). "How are you holding up?"

"I'm all right. Everything's under control, but I'm glad you could get here."

"Mama?"

"She's all right, Jojo. She's asleep now."

"Have you got any coffee? I'm half dead. Wouldn't you know it. I had a blow-out up the road."

"Come in the kitchen and I'll make a pot," she said. "Charity's gone home."

They sat drinking coffee, Mary Ann answering his vague, uneasy questions and studying him as she would have a stranger, and Jojo looking as always to her, a little troubled and removed, not really aware of what had happened yet. It would dawn on him at the funeral. With music and flowers and prayers he'd realize that his father was, indeed, dead, and he'd probably break down and cry like a child. Well, let him. She'd cross that bridge when she got to it. One thing at a time.

"Things are getting a little better at the station," Jojo was saying. "I've cut way down on my drinking and so forth. The manager's starting to talk about a promotion already."

"Do you really like it?"

"What?"

"Your work."

"Oh, it's all right. Everybody knows announcing is for the birds. But if you can get above the peon level, get into planning or producing or something, it can be a good deal. If I can just get that promotion, I'm just liable to settle down and try and be somebody. (He giggled) I might even get married or something."

"Do you know?" she said. "This is the first time in years and years we've had a chance to sit down and talk together. Isn't that too bad?"

"We used to talk together a lot. I'll never forget when you

were a little kid I used to have to come in your room and tell you a story before you'd go to sleep."

"Isn't that the strangest thing? I'd forgotten all about that."

Now she remembered those nights and his voice, rich and bodiless even then, coming from the close dark with improbable plotless tales of giants and witches and godmothers and wonderful transformations, stories that meandered along like lazy streams until she finally drifted into sleep. She remembered too when Jojo came home from his first semester in college in the North. Bright he had seemed then, touched with all the mystery of things, like a character out of a fairy tale himself, shining with possibilities. On his first night home she had asked him to repeat the old ritual (though of course she was very grown up by then), to tell her a story and talk her into sleep as he'd done when she was a child. He didn't make up a fairy tale. Instead he told her about the snow which he had seen for the first time in his life, its unspeakable whiteness, its chill profusion, the fantastic architecture it created in one falling, how the marvelous snow fell silently everywhere to change everything under the dome of the sky. He told her about the snowman they had made in front of his dorm first thing in the morning and how it had lasted a long time, slowly melting but still recognizable as a work of art, the image of a man, after the rest of the snow was gone and the familiar shape of the old world had reappeared unchanged. For some reason, she couldn't imagine why now, the single ghostly image of a snowman standing, melting slowly away in teardrops while the snow around him, substance of and like himself, vanished, broke up into gray crusts and patches and islands and puddles until he was at last all alone, left on the lawn like a dying beast out of another time, far from his native element, like a fish gasping the cruel air on dry land, that solitary image had touched her to the quick with a sense of ineffable sadness. She remembered (amused and a little ashamed now) that she had wept after Jojo had tiptoed out of her room thinking that she had fallen asleep.

"I've never seen snow."

"What's that?"

"It just struck me," she said. "Here I am. I've been all over, to

Paris and everywhere, and I've just never happened to see snow, not anywhere except in pictures."

"So what?" Jojo said laughing. "You can't have everything. That's what happens when your home is in Florida."

"I'd like to see the snow sometime. I'd really like to see snow falling in the air."

"Well, maybe you will one of these days," he said yawning. "I guess I'd better turn in. I'm beat."

She rinsed out their cups in the sink and then walked with him to the foot of the stairs.

"Aren't you coming too?"

"In a little while," she said. "I'll wait up until Mike gets here."

Impulsively he clasped her hands in his, his sad weak mouth trembling, his eyes suddenly bright with tears.

"It's hard to realize," he said. "I just can't believe he's dead."

"Goodnight, Jojo."

Halfway up the stairs he stopped.

"Mary Ann," he said, not looking back at her. "Do you know anything about the will?"

"Nothing," she said. "I don't know a thing about it."

Jojo shrugged and continued to mount the stairs.

She had done everything she could do. Now there was only waiting. And waiting was her strength. She was used to it. She opened the front door and went outside into the warm night air, seeing through the gnarled oak limbs, the tangled Spanish moss hanging loose like the hair of women grieving and tormented, the clear stars and a young moon as thin as the edge of a knife. After a shower the air was so sweet with summer's richness and decay. If she tore off her clothes with clawing fingers and ran, ran, ran, over the still-wet, jeweled points of the grass, under the shapes of the powerful oaks, under the wheeling clockwork sky, who would ever see her fleeing, fleeting whiteness except God? Would God care?

She heard the sound of a car turning in the gravel drive, and she was running toward it. She ran into the glare of the headlights and the car stopped suddenly and she saw the inside light go on as Mike, tall and tired, jumped out and came running toward her. She threw herself into his arms.

"Oh, Mike, Mike, Mike," she heard herself saying. "Daddy is dead. My daddy is dead and they didn't cover up his feet and I don't know what to do."

"Hush, baby," he said. "Don't you worry. Everything's going to be all right."

* * *

After she had cried she calmed down and was able to tell him how it had happened. Saturday morning the Judge had gone, alone except for Jay who was driving him, to swing through Volusia County and spend a long hot day of campaigning. Late in the afternoon he made a speech in Deland. It was during the speech, right in the middle of it, that he had collapsed. They took him to the hospital, but then he had seemed all right and they let him come home, as he insisted, in an ambulance.

"I knew this was going to happen sometime," Mary Ann said. "He was just too old for it. Why did he have to do it to himself?"

They walked slowly, arm in arm to the house. She looked sick, fragile and sick and much older to him.

"You better try and get some rest," he said.

"I don't know if I can sleep. I just don't think I can."

"Take one of those pills they left for Mother."

"I don't want to have to do that."

"Go on," he said. "You've got to get some rest."

She nodded and went slowly up the stairs to bed.

He sniffed the air. There were flowers already in vases around the house, florist's flowers, the sweet conventional smell of all our occasions and ceremonies, of our births and our weddings and our funerals. (Strange how they all smelled alike.) It gave the house a kind of strangeness. He couldn't remember another time when the rooms of this house had been so thick with the odor of slowly dying flowers.

He went back to his father's study where he was surprised to find the door open and the light burning. It was hot in there and he turned on the fan. He sat down behind the desk and picked up the telephone and called Senator Parker.

Parker sounded dazed and tired. He tried to picture him, to separate a physical image from the voice, and the image that he created was old, sleepless, numb. This was going to hurt Allen Parker. The news had probably already cut him deeply.

"I'm sorry, Mike, real sorry," he said. "My God, it's a shame."

"Yes, it is a damn shame."

"I'll definitely be in Oakland for the funeral. Lord, I didn't expect anything like this to happen. It makes me sick."

"I'm afraid I expected it. It was bound to happen," Mike said. "Do you think Batten will show up for the funeral?"

"Oh, I don't know. I wouldn't know about that," Parker said. Then after a pause: "Maybe so. Yes, I guess maybe so."

Mike was in some way disappointed. He had hoped, he had expected (what had he really expected?) more from Allen Parker than a sense of shock and dazed sympathy. What troubled him wasn't Parker's reaction, but his own expectations when he made the call. Why should he expect anything from Parker? What answer did Parker have to give him? Parker had more than enough troubles of his own. With or without Judge Royle as an opponent, Senator Parker was fighting a losing war now, retreating and withdrawing all along the line. The chances were that this would do him harm, if anything. By dying Judge Royle could very well have cut much more into his vote than if he had lived to the bitter resolution of the campaign. Then there was the fact that the two men were about the same age. It would remind the voters that Parker was an old man. And it would remind Parker of that fact too, in case he might have managed for a moment to conceal it from himself, if not forget it. And Batten, John Batten who had smiled and lied to him and denied knowing anything about it at the beginning. How would he feel now? Pliable and bouncy as Fortune's ball, he'd be at once aware of all the implications. He would have to be pleased. And he'd be there at the funeral to be photographed, solicitous, deeply mourning. He'd be the very model of a good young man grieving for the fallen hero.

Mike got up and went into the kitchen. He poured himself a long drink. He swore he'd kill John Batten if he came to the funeral and acted like that.

* * * * * * *

"Children," Nancy Royle said. "We've all failed each other, and that's the sad truth of it. We could have been a family. We could and should have been bound to each other by love and understanding. And when you can look back on all of it, it looks like it would have been so easy, the simple thing to do. But none of us—and I'll include your father in this judgment—none of us knew himself. So how could we know and love each other? We let our private ghosts get the best of us. Instead of making offerings and sacrifices of love, we laid our wreaths to dark gods."

They were sitting together at the dining room table waiting for Jay to come in the rented limousine and drive them to the funeral. Charity had made coffee for them, and the silver service, freshly polished, gleamed against the dark surface of the wood. They were all in black, and Nancy Royle, her pale face veiled, poured for them and talked. Mike, Jojo, and Mary Ann facing her were spent and empty. It seemed to Mike that they were grouped together like the survivors of a shipwreck or some other common disaster. The victims were tired beyond talking. And so they sat in silence and sipped their coffee and listened to her. She alone seemed really alive at that moment. It was as if the death of her husband had awakened her from a long and dusty sleep, had broken the spell of a chill dream.

"I won't pretend to know what secret feelings may be gnawing away at you all. It's too late for that kind of understanding, though at least I know that as your mother I *should* know. I just want to tell you a little about myself and my feelings. That much I'm able to do."

She had been the youngest daughter, the youngest child of the Singletrees, the last in a large family. Anthony Singletree had been too young for much more than a brief and casual baptism of fire at the tag end of the War Between the States, the war that killed his father and left his brother in another way a victim. Not physically wounded, in fact untouched except for the soldier's universal burden of unbearable weariness, Richard Singletree had returned carrying in his head, in his thoughts and dreams, a hive of terrible, tumultuous images, and most persistently and vividly, like the scar of a brand, the moment of his father's death in action.

He had seen it and ever after he might as well have been a cripple.

That left the younger brother the sole surviving heir, and heir to everything that was gone, a land lost, a world turned upside down, and he was faced with the truth, or anyway took it to be the plain truth that all of that, the things that might or possibly should have been his proper heritage had been a false dream, a sand castle that the first wave of the rising tide had washed away clean without a trace of its spurious magnificence. And that early —still no more than a boy really, he learned or decided that money, not land and the dubious prestige of having owned it and fought for it and lost it, money was at once the key and the god of the new kingdom. Money was the whole armor of the new man.

He too, strangely enough just as Judge Royle had, began a struggle with great difficulty to educate himself for a new role. He won a scholarship from a college in the North and went there with no more possessions in the world than the suit of clothes on his back and his luggage packed with bricks and old books wrapped in paper to give it a decent weight. There was the story (all three of them knew it already) of how he spent a night in a hotel on the way to the college, far from friends and family, and a child fell into the fountain there and he jumped into the water and pulled out the child. Then he had to sit for hours in his room by the slight coal fire drying his clothes and listening to the music and the voices from the ballroom below because he would not borrow anything from a yankee or admit to anyone that he wasn't a gentleman of means.

Well then, a gentleman of means is what he became, the rich man, the distinguished lawyer. He chose for a wife a beautiful woman whom he saw one time singing in the choir of a little country church while he was riding the circuit. She gave him eight children and died after giving birth to the last of them.

"I came along late and last," she told them. "I'm telling you all this not because you may not already know it and have heard about it until you're weary of the whole subject. The thing is, certain things bear retelling. We never act alone on an empty stage. From time to time we ought to be reminded of all the crowd of ghosts in the space around us.

"And already by then the world was changing. They had done something, my father's generation. Leaving his brother Richard to muse on his wounds and nurse them, he had said to himself 'This is the way the world is. I take it for better or for worse.' Money was the new god all right, but at the end they found out it couldn't be their private god, enshrined in domestic security like a trophy in a gentleman's club."

A new generation had come to life and later to power after them, one that hadn't walked through the same desert or made the same choices and renunciations, one that had never had anything much to lose or regret or try to regain, stronger and tougher, more durable and enduring, not in the least weakened by sentiment and perfectly capable of propitiating the same god and winning the same favors. Anthony Singletree, always a gambler, always the child of fortune, felt himself slowly being transformed into fortune's fool. The same code which had helped him before now inhibited him. The sweet fruit he had tasted left a bitter smart on his tongue. And late in life with his youngest daughter now a young woman but still unmarried he lost everything. (She, of course, knew nothing of this at the time.) It was one of his typical gestures that he took all the cash he had left for a pleasure trip. He took his daughter by ship from Jacksonville to New York for a season of shopping and the theater, a gracious leisurely expensive trip in those days, worthy of the man who had often chartered whole Pullman cars to take his friends duck hunting or to the horse races. What a gamble it had been, she realized now. How calmly and gracefully he had taken the risk.

As it happened on the boat there was a young lawyer, Joseph Royle, enjoying *his* first fruits of modest success, not the last wine of an old harvest. He was intelligent, quick-witted, good-humored, handsome in a rude and powerful way, and he was entirely different from any man she had ever known. She was fascinated. In her innocence she loved his struggle. In wonder she listened for the first time to a man all of whose thoughts were of the future. And she loved him, the strangeness and the strength of him. In New York he saw them often, dined with them, went to the theater and concerts with them, and talked for hours, happy and easy with a great man in his profession, one who must have seemed to him to be tailored in radiance, the image of all his desire and effort, worthy of all the admiration he could offer.

What a disillusionment it must have been in a single climactic scene between the two men when Joseph Royle, after the fashion of the times, asked Anthony Singletree for his daughter in marriage. And he found that behind a careful fencing of oblique words she was simply for sale. He found that he had been duped and deluded by his own wishes, that this gracious, always soft-spoken, fine example of the "gentleman" was a false creation, partly his own, a lure of his own hungers. He must have learned too, sensed anyway, the contempt which Anthony Singletree reserved for him and his whole kind, would keep for him whether or not he was willing to pay the price for a wife with a good name and respectability. However, partly in love ("And I think we did love each other then," she told them.), partly the victim of the sheer momentum of his own ambitions, and maybe too partly out of his own inborn contempt (For, regardless of what the old man might think of him, *his* was still the magic power to break the spell. Even in humiliation he still shamed Anthony Singletree.), for whatever reasons, he accepted the bargain, knowing all that it meant, never even guessing all that it would mean.

After a conventional interval they were married in her house in Jacksonville. And they were even happy for a while.

"We are so many different things at once, so many parts," she said. "Only once in a while and not for long is love one of them. We were married and I could have loved him then. God knows marriage is the occasion for it if there ever is one. But, you see, for my part there was plenty of mischief and motive in disguise too. I suppose, now that I can see it as it was, there was a great need in me to find a man completely different from my father. I was a motherless child. I would show him and find myself. I guess, too, deep down there was even a silly notion, like something out of the romantic fiction of the time, of some kind of abasement or self-sacrifice, as if I had to pay for being myself. And all this was united with a young woman's typical inflated idea of her own beauty and worth. And, as your father used to say, all of these things put together were, one way or another, vanity.

"My God!" she cried out. "How we are all victims of our own folly!"

The three of them sat perfectly still listening to her, waiting for her to continue. Pained and tearless, she sighed and went on talking.

They had tried, she surmised, both of them had tried and failed themselves and each other. By a thousand covert signs and signals she never let him forget that she could never really forgive him for anything, and he for his part never asked for forgiveness or to forget. And then there were the children and finally his career, his public life, and gradually over years the pattern of their lives became inflexible, not uncomfortable, just inflexible, to be broken by the death of one of them if it was to be broken at all.

"Children," she said to them, "I want you to try and see these things as they are. Try to see your father as he was, a strong man, in many ways a good and admirable man. But narrow too, and often vain and petty and even cruel, and crippled by pride long before some men crippled him with their fists. A hurt man. And all of us hurt him one way or another; all of us let ourselves be hurt by him. I ought to weep for him, to weep for us all, but the truth is it's too late for that now. Let us simply try to be a little bit less foolish and to love one another."

There was a soft crackle on the gravel drive outside, and looking up Mike saw the black rented limousine come to a stop by the front steps.

III. END: ACTOR

And another of his disciples said unto him, Lord, suffer me first to go and bury my father.

MATTHEW 8:21

The Reverend Hobart Fishback was a very young man, recently ordained and so fresh from the Seminary in Virginia that some of its pallor and fire lingered undiminished in his cheeks like a blush. His eyes could still brim with tears of light when he preached a favorite text. He liked to preach the "hard sayings," Christ the incomparable, incomprehensible Avenger, Christ the maker of parables so edged and tough they resisted fracturing or, if broken at all, revealed nothing for the soul, wren-like, to gather and make a pretty nest with, but instead, harsh shards and fragments, cruxes, secrets beyond the power of the easy-going reason. Not peace but a sword. Heaven having many mansions, but high-walled and on top of that wall, like the ragged teeth of a yawning shark, the forbidding glitter of broken glass.

The little Chapel of St. Luke was his first parish, a small mission surrounded by a jungle of fundamentalists and overawed by the great brick buildings of other liberal and moderate protestant sects. His congregation was small, a few members of old families who had his faith by birthright, thin shadows at the Early Service advancing slowly on tiptoes to the hushed mystery of the Holy Communion. And he had discovered, sadly for one so young, that all his preaching, far from thundering against and shattering the windows of his church, far from stirring up a clamor of controversy and doubt, far from bringing the Bishop from Orlando down to chastise him, fell as quietly as offering coins into the velvet-bottomed silver plates passed by palsied ushers. Their faith in the old God, God the Nineteenth Century Gentleman, was deep-rooted and not so easily shaken by the wind of a young man's preaching if it had already survived all their losses and a century of perplexity and terror. He found that his calling would have to be that of a spiritual physician and comforter, and he lacked the brute singlemindedness to be a good surgeon of the soul. He could *preach*, until his tongue was wrinkled as a fig, the doctrine of the merciful swift scalpel, the burning cauterization, but in practice, at a moment of spiritual crisis, he could only listen patiently and in the end offer a warm young sympathetic hand, a shy bouquet of moral platitudes.

He never had known Judge Royle. The Judge had stopped attending his wife's church or any other church probably about the time that Hobart Fishback was christened. He knew Nancy Royle, who came regularly to his services, brought flowers from her garden for the altar and sometimes managed to bring along her skeptical unmarried daughter. Nancy Royle was (in his eyes) an energetic, even a dedicated woman and clearly a soul not to be too much troubled about. For how could he have imagined her lonely room and her books and her music and the inner thunder of her headaches? How could he have guessed the extent of ironic sacrifice implied by her flowers, bright against his altar cloth? There she was in the front pew for the mourning family, in widow's black, under control, resigned and—who knows?—joyful in acceptance. Next to her sat the daughter, her face suddenly alive with the lines of her age that he hadn't noticed before. Then the two men, the brothers. The older one fattish and balding, yet still shaggy-haired, mustachioed, soft- and white-faced (color of a trout's underbelly), dissipated and maybe ruined, yet comical too as he sat there beside his lean sister with his round child-man's face all awry with stunned emotion like a face made out of soft dough, a cookie man waiting for his turn in the oven; blubbering, dabbing at his eyes with a handkerchief and, from time to time, blowing his nose with a definitive noise something like a barking seal. Then the younger son, made out of different stuff it seemed, all in flat crude planes like a one-eyed Jack, a face handsome but uncommunicative that might have been burning with bitterness or just as well the weary look of utter indifference, a spiritual giant sloth. Then the two Negroes, the old woman—how old? God knows—and her son, dignified, their faces like carved ebony, primitive masks revealing nothing except that they took the occasion seriously. They always come, the Negroes, for weddings and christenings and funerals and always with the same expression, dignity, reserve, reticence, like strangers, foreigners in an honored and unlikely place, a museum for instance. They sat with the white families, yet still the sudden inexplicable blackness of them disturbed (he would have said *surprised*) him whenever he entered the chapel in his robes to conduct a service and saw them. Where did they *really* come from? Where did they go afterwards? What was the shape and color of their souls? In what peaceable kingdom would black and white like lion and lamb lie down together? (A flippant Seminary joke flashed through his mind. A Spaceman lands from a flying saucer. He has seen God. Is asked to describe Him. "Well," he begins, "first of all She's black . . .") Often when he drove through Black Bottom, going or coming from one white part of the town to another, to call on his parishioners, the sick, the troubled, the bedevilled and perplexed, the dying or new-born, he was left in awe and wonder, baffled by the squalid, persistent vigor of alien lives, the soft secrecy of overheard voices, a sourceless laugh, a song, some loud shouting, a sad or noble or corrupted face seized from among those passed by and to be pondered on long afterwards. They might as well, in all glare of honesty, have been brutes, beasts that is, creatures whose blood moved to other tunes. But were we not all God's creatures, God's strange brutes? Where did the tunes and wild songs of the blood begin? On Judgment Day would all the spilled blood of the world run together in one great river, an Amazon, a Mississippi or a Nile, to become one hymn of praise? Would all the tired tongues flutter in one joyous prayer?

Behind them in the next pews there was an odd mingling. A few hard-faced country people, the Judge's relatives most likely, in stiff, cheap, go-to-meeting clothes. Mixed among them were others of a type more familiar to him, Nancy Royle's family he surmised, who could have been among his parishioners had they happened to live there, pale faces of an older family whose blood was thinning, whose nerves were each generation turned and tuned more tautly, fretted music; but now at ease in these surroundings and with this service, at home in their own church. And cropping out among the known faces of his own congregation there were others, the public faces he was seeing in flesh for the first time. There was the well-known, embattled Senator, more rudely made, uglier than he had let himself imagine, and wearing now the numb shocked look of a somnambulist abruptly awakened on a precipice. His wife was beside him, very pretty, weeping quietly. Not far from him the young bland serious face from many photographs, unlined, subdued, the kind of look his young acolytes might wear if their parents had come to church to see them serve. His wife, though solemn and unsmiling, was blonde and healthy and altogether simply good as a peach, as a ripe apple on a bough. Behind them the Governor, youngish, curly black ram's hair, handsome and bulky. Had arrived minutes before in an air-conditioned Cadillac with the sirens of the State Police whining ahead of him. Prepare me a way. Make straight the highway. And there were others, many others, judges and lawyers, old and young, the Mayor of the town, legislators, a Congressman, a few Sheriffs, an Army officer splendid in a dress blue uniform.

He had never seen his chapel so full before, and all of it was hemmed, fenced in place by an enormous fantasy of floral decorations, a gaudy explosion of perfect flowers from some wild, grotesque, imagined garden. And outside the chapel there were all the others who couldn't get in, standing. Women, men with hats in their hands, country people, Negroes, Jews, the town's Armenian family, policemen, workers who had left their jobs for a few minutes, a butcher in a blood-stained apron, a grocer, a roadworker leaning on a shovel. For as a judge, if not as a man, he had with strict impersonality touched their lives to the quick. Whether they came out of love or respect or long-harbored bitterness, they somehow honored him by being there. The crowd spread all the way out into the street and across, stood on the sidewalk and on the lawns of houses opposite. He could see them framed in the sunny space of the open doors.

And he was greatly tempted. What a time, a once-in-a-lifetime, to preach the gospel! What a time to tug at the very roots of his being and, God willing, summon up a holy eloquence to save them all from themselves! Let him speak the truth over a corpse. But, of course, he reflected, it wasn't the *right* time. He had nothing more than duty to do. He had just to conduct an ancient and formal service in an expeditious manner. Anyone could have done it, but he was chosen. Had he opened his mouth and let the Word spring from his lips like a snowy dove, they would have risen up in righteous indignation against him, sprung from wooden lassitude and shouted him down.

The organist (a little old woman who earned her bread by giving piano lessons to one generation after the next, most of whom progressed to the ability of being able to play "The Skater's Waltz" with both hands before discovering that after all music wasn't to be the consuming passion of their lives and left her to grow old and mousy and to initiate still others into that much knowledge of music's mysteries and delights), this lady let the solemn music she had been playing—as if solemn were synonymous with bittersweet—fade away in a hushed chord.

"The Lord be with you," the Reverend Hobart Fishback heard himself saying.

"And with thy spirit."

"Let us pray."

* * *

When the service was over the congregation stood and waited for the family to leave the church. The Royles came up the aisle, Mike and his mother first, then Jojo with Mary Ann. Once they reached the doors and stood for a moment at the top of the steps, the crowd outside moved back and away from the doors to give a wide path for them. It was a sudden giving way like a field of grain struck by a gust of wind.

It was then that Mary Ann began to weep. She bowed her head and dug her fingernails into Jojo's arms.

"Help me, help me," she whispered. "I'm going to faint."

Jojo put his arm around her waist and then she relaxed, sagged against him as he led her to the waiting car.

* * *

It was a raw deep rectangular cut of dark earth against the suave green of the grass. Even the false grass, the undertaker's carpet made to look like rich grass and pulled up tight to the very lip of the grave, even the awning with its rows of folding chairs underneath for the family, couldn't disguise or subdue the simple darkness of the grave. The earth was black. The neatness of it, carefully smoothed sides, exact, knife-edged corners, couldn't convert the brute fact of earth into anything else. The mute efficiency of the undertaker was a vain gesture. Shovels make holes in the ground, and Mike Royle had the notion, at once amusing and vexing, that if he slipped away from the graveside ceremony, wandered nearby among the white stones, behind some tree or bush he'd ambush a couple of men, sweaty and shirtless in the hot bright sun, smoking, talking and joking together, leaning on their shovels and waiting to finish what they had started. It was an enraging picture. But suppose it *did* happen? Suppose he had confronted the gravediggers? All that he could do was to offer them a coin. What was there to think or say about it? Nothing, he knew. Just that men, shirtless, sweaty, indifferent men with shovels, clowns, dig our holes and fill them up and have the last word always.

The hearse was waiting by the time they got out of the car. The real pallbearers had swiftly removed the coffin (Men with muscles. Dead weight is heavy.) and placed it on a contraption with rollers so that the gentlemen pallbearers could roll it without strain across a space of grass to the edge of the grave. The grave had been rigged over with a webbed netting, and an apparatus was set up alongside, a kind of elevator so that when the time came the coffin could be lowered with a becoming dignity, slow and level.

Mike led his mother to a chair beneath the awning. She was all right, strong at his touch, and since she had given Mary Ann a pill in the car, Mary Ann seemed calm enough on Jojo's arm. They took their places and waited as the rest of the cars arrived, a slow procession winding through the cemetery, headlights burning in broad daylight. In a tree nearby a mockingbird sang a few notes and then was quiet. There was the quick noise of a squirrel, a brittle scuttling of claws against the rough back of an oak. The earth in the open grave and the grass had a sweet, lonesome deepwoods smell. Mike looked down at the polished toes of his shoes and saw a small, fat worm, pinkish and earth-flecked, crawling among the white roots of the grass, a good fishing worm. Very slowly he raised one foot and covered the worm and crushed it to a pulp with his weight. Then he was aware of the minister thumbing through the Book of Common Prayer and clearing his throat to begin the service.

"Senator Parker doesn't look well," Nancy Royle whispered. "Ask him to come and take a chair with us in the shade."

The Senator was standing hatless in the sun. His face was red and sweaty, his eyes bloodshot. His legs gave a little at the knees. Mike started to lead him to a chair, but Parker resisted, pulled away from Mike's hand.

"No, no, no," he said. "I'm all right. I'm fine."

"Come along, please, sir."

And he relaxed and let Mike find a chair for himself and his wife. Mike brushed past John Batten and thought (would he dare?) Batten grinned at him. At what? At Parker staggered with shock or at himself having to help the man along?

The service began, following the prayerbook to the letter. Reverend Fishback might as well have been an auctioneer for the impersonal sing-song rhythm he spoke the text of old words.

That was all right, Mike thought. That was the way it ought to be. In all our significant moments we can only at best fall back on the minted clichés, out of self-defense, if we are going to depend on articulate speech at all. The only true language we were capable of at these moments was made up of visceral groans and snarls and sighs. So we gathered together and opened a book and read the words, spun prayer wheels, clicked beads, anything at all to keep our fidgeting fingers from tearing out hair by the roots, from plucking eyeballs out of sockets. The Judge would have liked that notion, and he had probably spoken the ritual words of the law in much the same way when he sentenced a prisoner or passed judgment. Only God was going to be able to say something in Judgment. Only God wouldn't be at a loss for words when the time came.

The service was soon over. The undertaker's deft machine dropped the coffin into its appointed place, so quickly, so quietly it was astonishing. It fitted its new home like a coin in a slot. Reverend Fishback scattered some earth on the shiny, expensive, (wormproof?) brassknobbed box. The family filed by, each of them armed with a small silver shovel (the property of the undertaker) to toss some dirt into the grave. Nancy Royle stopped, bowed her head in silent prayer, then passed on. Mike and Mary Ann were next. Jojo walked to the edge of the grave. He stood there looking down. Then he threw the shovel away over his shoulder. End over end it sailed in a crazy half-circle and fell and glittered in the grass. In a fury he pushed the undertaker's admonitory arms aside and scooped up handfuls of dirt, clods of earth and sod, and hurled them at the coffin. He was laughing. He dropped to his knees by the grave laughing and crying together and digging up great chunks of earth and throwing them into the hole.

Mike came running back and put his arms around him and lifted him to his feet.

"Godamn it! Leave me alone, leave me alone!"

They wrestled together almost falling into the grave while the aghast crowd, shamed, looked away. Mike slapped him across the face. Jojo blinked and stopped fighting.

"Come on, Jojo, it's time to go home."

Jojo hung his head.

"All right," he said finally. "All right. I guess I'm ready to go now."

* * *

Through the car windows Mike could see the others filing by the open grave now, the Governor, Parker, John Batten. Flashbulbs winked as each man stopped and stood, head bowed, mourning for posterity. Then the spot was out of sight. As they drove toward the entrance of the cemetery he saw out of the corner of his eye two Negroes with shovels coming across a little space of tombstones in the direction of his father's grave. One of them saw him looking at them and raised a battered hat.

For some reason Mike winked at him and felt better about that anyway even though his heart sagged in its net of veins like a rock in a sling and he was possessed by nameless furies.

* * * * * * *

The hardware store he went to was in a little country town, a crossroads place not far from Oakland. It was ranch country around there, and the store was rich with the good clean oiled smell of new leather, of saddles and bridles and boots and heavy shoes, of harness and feed bags. Against the natural darkness of the great piled room and the somber elegance of the leathergoods there was the keen shine of new tools, of chains and bright rolls of wire and screening not yet tested by weather. There were weapons, too, shotguns and rifles and pistols of all makes and kinds. It was a strange thing to have grown up in this part of the world and never to have owned a weapon. Houses were full of them, gun racks and closets were little arsenals; and a boy's progress toward manhood could be measured by his swift skipping from bee-bee gun to twenty-two, to four-ten shotgun, to, finally and young even then, a heavy thirty caliber deer rifle or a double-barrel twelve gauge shotgun. The Judge's refusal to tolerate firearms in his house was as nearly unique as it was inexplicable. Maybe he had made that rule because he didn't trust himself, knowing better than anyone else the power of his angers and whims, to have within reach a dangerous logical extension of himself in the form of a weapon he could kill with and with as little effort as it took to strike a match. Maybe it was because he was too arrogant to think he needed one. Whatever the true reason, he had it with him now, folded with himself in the little plot of ground that was his for perpetuity. When Mike had gone hunting as a boy he had always had to borrow a gun from a friend, a cast-off or second best. Now anyway he was going to own one for a while. He was even teased by the notion of buying a very expensive one, a worthy instrument, but he coldly decided that would be pure extravagance.

He spent the better part of an hour sitting on a low stool behind the counter and looking through a wooden crate of secondhand pistols. There were big heavy revolvers, Army .45 automatics, a lone black Italian Beretta somebody had probably brought home from the war as a souvenir, thirty-eights, long, slender-barrelled target pistols, fancy ones with handles of pearl or chrome or ivory, and even a tiny nickelplated one made to fit a lady's handbag. He studied them, holding them in his hand, sighting at nothing, feeling the weight and shape, and wondering who had owned each of them, who had carried this one and for what reason, who had cared for this one like a religious relic, whose carelessness and the sweat of whose fear or rage had given a coat of irremediable corrosion to this grip or that trigger and housing. Most of them probably had no stories to go along with them, but a few *must* have. It gave him a sense of belonging to a kind of club, the faceless, anonymous fraternity of the anguished and absurd.

In the end he settled for a squat, well-blued, snub-barrelled thirty-two caliber revolver that would fit easily into a goodsize pocket or could be stuffed under his belt without bulging his coat.

"You can't hit nothing beyond about ten feet with a thing like that," the clerk told him. "Course it makes a hell of a noise if that's what you want."

"It suits me," Mike said. "I'm not planning to use it for anything fancy."

He signed for it in the storekeeper's register with his right name, paid for it, bought a small box of bullets, loaded it and stuffed it into his coat pocket. Then he drove back to Oakland. All the way back the engine hummed, the tires sang on the road. He drove along fast and let the known countryside, the regimented telephone poles whip past him. The flat fenced fields were jerked behind. Cattle, Santa Gertrudis and white Brahmas glanced up and went on grazing. He wasn't even angry, he guessed. He thought he was possessed by a passionate lucidity that was beyond all emotion and entirely premeditated.

* * *

He hadn't planned on trouble finding John Batten. It was evening by the time he was back in Oakland. The streetlights were on and already yellow patches and squares of light cast from the windows of houses grappled with the growing darkness. At the hotel the desk clerk told him that Mr. Batten had gone out earlier with his stenographer to work on a speech. He didn't know where he had gone. Mrs. Batten and the children (He didn't want to be reminded of them now!) were having supper in the hotel dining room.

Mike took the elevator to the floor where Batten had his suite of rooms. He tiptoed down the quiet corridor (Mike Royle, the secret agent; Mike Royle the private eye) listening. In one room light spilled over the open transom and he could hear some men, probably the newspaper men, playing cards, killing time. He could picture them, grouped around the card table in various stages of undress, the bottle and the glasses, the overstuffed ashtrays, the smoke filtering through the lampshades, the wisecracks and at once the boredom and intensity of the game.

He came to Batten's room, tried the door, opened it and stepped quickly inside. A Negro bellboy was bent over a pair of Batten's shoes, shining them up. He looked up and seemed to wince away from Mike's look, concentrating on his work.

"Where's Mr. Batten?"

"I don't know, sir."

"You didn't see him go out?"

"No, sir."

The bellboy was absorbed in his work. Sweat shone on his face. Mike guessed he was lying. He fumbled in his pocket one-handed and came up with a fifty-cent piece. He tossed it across the room. It fell on the soft rug just in front of the toes of the shoes. The bellboy still didn't look up. His shoerag stopped dancing and he stared at the coin, his hands hanging slack. Then one hand groped for it and settled over the coin like a fat spider.

"He gone out some place," the bellboy said. "I went and got him a fifth of whiskey and he gone somewhere."

"Where?"

Still without looking the bellboy shrugged his shoulders. Mike decided to show him the pistol. He started to reach into his coat pocket for it, but there it was already in his right hand, squat and heavy and threatening. It must have been there in his hand since he opened the door and came into the room. He laughed out loud.

"I don't want to cause no kind of trouble," the bellboy said. "I'm a married man myself."

"There's going to be some trouble if you don't tell me where he is."

219

"I didn't have nothing to do with it. I just told him where he could take the lady—the Colonial. He asked me. I didn't suggest a thing."

Mike shut the door behind him and ran down the hall. It was going to take a while, a little while, before the bellboy worked up his nerve and decided that he'd have to tell somebody. He nodded affably to the desk clerk, walked through the lobby, and, once outside, drove off in a hurry.

* * *

The Colonial Motel is an expensive curiosity, a single make-believe Colonial mansion, an office with a false front, with white slender columns and a low, wide porch, flanked by scaled-down cabins, each a miniature imitation of the original, like playhouses for children. A small colored boy in some kind of a costume was perched on the gate post and blew a posthorn when Mike turned into the driveway. They probably even had a cottonheaded old Uncle Tom of a Negro in a tailcoat to greet you at the office and tote your bags, suh, but Mike didn't wait to find out. He saw Batten's car and parked alongside. He left the lights on and the engine running and the front door swinging loose on its hinges like a broken wing.

He banged open the door and flicked on a light. The woman—a flash of flesh, of wide, horrified eyes, of dark loose hair, seen like a running deer through the leaves—snatched the bedspread to cover herself and backed into a corner. He noticed her dimpled knees, soft and round as cherub faces, knocking together. John Batten had whirled around in a red-faced fury, but when he saw Mike, he slumped and his face went soft and the color of potter's clay.

"Working on the final draft?"

Batten shrugged and the color came back in his face.

"At least give me a chance to put on my pants."

He got up and pulled on his trousers and turned his back to Mike to look at the girl. She was biting the back of her hand now to keep from screaming.

"Lucille," Batten said. "You go in the bathroom and sit down on the pot and stay there. Understand me?"

She nodded her head, but she didn't move from the corner.

"You go in there and don't make a sound." He seized her arm and led her around the bed and to the bathroom door. "Count to a hundred to yourself before you make a noise."

He shut the door behind her and turned around to face Mike. They heard her start to whimper like a well-trained pet wanting to be let out.

Batten lit a cigarette. His hands shook, but his face was controlled now. In awful recognition Mike realized that he had already done more than enough, that here he was and he wasn't going to do a thing.

"It doesn't suit you, Mike," Batten said. "I mean it. You shouldn't come busting into bedrooms at night waving a gun around . . ."

"Any more than you . . ."

". . . than I ought to be here in the first place pawing over my poor stenographer. The thing is there are times when it seems like you just can't help yourself. Here you are—you feel like you've got to kill somebody. Me, I guess. And I . . . Well, I guess maybe this is another way of killing somebody or myself. I mean . . ."

". . . perfectly pointless, fruitless, stupid mechanical sex. A bottle of whiskey, a cheap bedroom in an expensive motel. An empty-headed, or anyway, let's say, a vulgar, uninteresting woman. A little twitch or heave or shudder and you close your eyes and maybe when you open them up again you won't be there anymore. Maybe you'll find you've just vanished in a puff of smoke."

"Except you never do. You open your eyes and you're still there," Batten said. "Give me a little more credit than you have been. We're a lot more alike than you think."

"I know that," Mike said. "The real thing is you *lied* to me. You lied to me and made a fool out of me and in the end you killed him."

"No, I didn't lie to you. Believe me, I can swear to that. It *was* a lie all right, but I didn't know I was lying. We—I know it now and I can't pretend it isn't *we*—used him and we dropped him and he died."

"There have been about enough lies in this whole business."

"Lies compounded on lies," Batten said. "Only I didn't know I was lying then."

"How do you feel now that you know?"

"Up to my ears in shit, if that's what you mean. We all are. All we can do is whisper together 'Don't make waves.' Oh, I know just where I am. And you must know something about it too. How clean are your hands? Do you really want my blood on them? Maybe you don't know yet what it feels like to have blood on your hands."

Mike felt the pistol wilting in his hands. It drooped as if the metal were melting. It might as well have been made out of chocolate candy.

"Did you know when I came in here that I wasn't going to do anything? That I wasn't going to be able to shoot you?"

Batten grinned weakly.

"No," he said. "I hoped. I knew you might, but I *hoped*."

Then they heard the siren and the sound of a car turning fast into the gravel parking lot of the motel. Batten grabbed the pistol out of Mike's hand and opened the door of the bathroom.

"Lucille, put this in the toilet and sit on it."

"I'm already up to ninety-three."

"Good, do what I told you and start over."

The police, with pistols drawn, found the two men quietly drinking together.

"Damn nigger must have been into my bourbon," Batten told them. "Mr. Royle's a good friend of mine."

They laughed and put their guns back in their holsters. They eyed the puddle of female clothing by the bed and the light under the bathroom door. They winked and touched their caps in salute and left.

The two men, pale and shaken, stared at each other.

"I ought to thank you," Mike said. "I must have been out of my head or something."

"We're all crazy," Batten said. "It's all crazy. Just look at me."

"You've got guts. I may hate your guts, but you've got them all right."

Batten shook his head.

"I could say the same thing about you and it wouldn't be true either. Do you really know the first thing I thought of when you busted in here? For one terrible second I thought it was newspaper men or my wife or God knows who with a camera. I was almost happy when I saw it was just a *pistol* in your hands. That's how bad it is. We're in a hell of a fix, that's all, a terrible crazy situation. Maybe when it's all over and done with we can start thinking about it and make some sense out of it. If there *is* any sense to it."

"Think about it in Washington."

"I imagine I will," he said. "I guess I'll have some time to think about it."

Batten turned on the radio by the bed and the room filled with dance music.

"Did you see her *knees?*" Mike said, beginning to laugh. "Did you see those fat little knees shaking?"

Batten pounded his fist on the bathroom door.

"All right, Lucille, you can come out now. Come on out and have a drink with a friend of mine."

* * *

When he left, leaving the two of them half-drunk, playing gin rummy (Batten joked feebly that he guessed his gun wouldn't go off either now) and listening to the late music, he found that somebody had turned off his lights and the engine and closed the car door for him. It was a dirty shame that people always had to come along and pick up behind you.

Well, he had been a damn fool. That was clear enough. But how was he going to be able to explain to himself, rationalize the clarity, what he had grotesquely conceived of as "passionate lucidity" with which he had acted? Batten, with pants down literally, had whirled around and must have seen at once, at a glance the reflection of his own folly in Mike. It was just as if Mike had been standing there with his pants down too, two different men mirroring each other in naked absurdity at the moment when by all rights, in *justice*, some sort of climax should have been achieved. Batten's sex had wilted like a flag in the rain. Mike Royle's pistol turned to wax, went limp in his hand.

223

No wonder Lucille backed into the farthest corner (clutching a cheap bedspread modestly around herself and biting her edgewise palm—a gesture she'd surely learned from the movies or anyway the illustrations accompanying the stories in confession magazines; she *couldn't* have been responsible for the trembling of her dimpled knees) no wonder the poor woman had been scared half out of her wits.

Well, they had been saved from further folly, or maybe they had managed to save each other. Afterwards they had drunk and laughed together, talked recklessly like three people thrilled by a single fever. ("You people in politics are wild," she said. "Real wild!") And now he was alone and back where he started again. He seemed to be on a wheel, on wheels. (It was curious to think how much of his time was spent just driving, the servant of four spinning wheels, hither and yon.) Except that now his whole body rebelled against strenuous and specific misuse. Roused to commit a murder, veins and muscles and bones and glands had joined together and sung pure activity like a choir. Stopped short he was all taut and trembling (O, irresponsible knees!). And it would be more or less like that for John Batten too. Mike Royle was left feeling bad, boundlessly foolish, with nothing but more time wasted and nothing but one, his first and only gun (Would they remember it? Would they find it? Or would some anonymous maid cleaning up the mess in the cabin behind them find it floating, somnolent and mysterious like a horny submarine beast, at the bottom of the toilet bowl?) forgotten and lost.

Better to have wept and carried on like Jojo.
Better to have taken a pill like Mary Ann.
Better to have gnashed his teeth to a fine white powder.

* * * * * *

The house was a checkerboard of lights. Light from the windows fell, sprawled and settled in pools on the dark grass. Here and there the heavy, muscular limbs of the liveoaks were fiercely silhouetted. Of course it would be all lit up. There would be a crowd of relatives there for the night, cousins and uncles and aunts. There would have been a long noisy supper with everyone trying to talk at once. For after a funeral or a wedding it was a curious fact how every tongue wagged as if with pure relief. And there would have been a good deal of drinking, and by now the men would be separate, gathered in the library and the old ghosts would have been summoned up and the ashes of the old stories, the tall tales, would have been blown and fanned hopefully for one more flame to warm their hands by. He could have gone inside.—Where in the world have you been?—I have something I wanted to take care of. I was going to kill John Batten.—What?—Well, he'd have to say, not really, you see. It was just that I knew I had to do something. The time had come for me to *do* something and I thought that was it. But it turned out it wasn't.—Oh, of course. Well, now, what are you drinking?

Mike walked around the house in the darkness, just beyond the border of splashed light, seeing the shapes of people, his blood kin, pass to and fro by the windows, hearing the sound of familiar voices without hearing a word they were saying. He walked down the lawn in back, stopping for a moment in open treeless space to breathe the night air and to look up at the far bowl of stars, whatever they told us really just a dark bowl overhead riddled like a sieve to admit some glimmer of inscrutable light. Then he went on down the slope to the pig pen. It was empty now of everything but the smell. *That* would stay a while. He put a foot in the first rung of the fence and leaned over the top rail breathing the dungy odor. He could close his eyes and conjure up a vision, not just of the pigs that his father had made a hobby of here, but a ghostly multitude of swine stretching and swarming across all time and space into dim, brutal, unrecorded history, and all coming forward, advancing bulky shapes on dainty feet, naked snouts designed for sniffing at, rooting for sustenance in the mud and garbage and waste of the whole world. He thought for a moment of Jesus Christ and the madmen who had asked to be saved. And Christ had cast their tormenting demons into a herd of swine. The poor pigs took on the burden of human filth and madness. If he even started to think of counting those pigs he could conjure up, like sheep, he could have fallen asleep on his feet.

"It's kind of too bad he decided to get rid of them."

Mike twisted around and saw that Jay was standing in the dark behind him, against the lights of the house no more than a tall shadow.

"They left behind a little token of remembrance anyway," Mike said.

"I expect you'll keep smelling them for a while if that's what you mean."

"I think it's a good thing, Jay. I think all of us ought to come down here once a day, first thing in the morning, and close our eyes and take a big deep whiff to start the day off right."

Jay came and stood beside him leaning over the fence.

"That's crap and you know it," Jay said. "A pig can't help smelling the way he does. He's just made that way."

"That's just what the Judge would have said."

"He'd be right, too. That's just the way it is. The Judge, he was nobody's fool."

"Nobody but his own."

They swung down from the fence together and walked away from the empty pig pen and along the dark lawn. The night grass was faintly sweet now.

"Jay, I want a drink in the worst way. I want to go somewhere and get good and drunk. Will you go with me?"

"All right," Jay said. "I'm game if you are."

* * *

Mike bought a bottle at a liquor store, and they drove out into the country, into the woods, parked under the pine trees off the road and sat in the front seat passing the bottle back and forth and talking. The death, the funeral in which each of them had played an allotted part, the warm whiskey and the lonesome quiet of the woodsweet night made it easy for them to talk. They were able to shed some of the accidents and attitudes of years. Their masks, Jay's of the cautious, happy-go-lucky, grinning archetypal servant, Mike's of the tolerant, guarded son of the master, fell away as they tried mutually to recapture a lost childhood of at least some shared experience, evoking from the vague, dreamed time a realm of dares taken or declined, treehouses made and climbed, fights against others and each other, all the wild forsaken country where for a little while imagination wrestled with reality with equal strength. There had *been* once imaginary nations and wars and kings and queens. There had been real haunted houses and hermits who shied rocks and curses at them when the children had appeared to ambush and tease. There had been a kind of brotherhood. But even so, as they talked, exchanging anecdotes of that past, they knew that all was discolored and distorted by nostalgia and that after the novelty of rediscovery and the joy of a moment's unmasking had passed, their separate thoughts were bound to take bitter command.

It gave an edge of excitement at first, but sooner or later they had to talk around the subject of what had happened to them both since then. Slowly like a misty veil, time isolated them. They got drunk and thick-tongued and belligerent in self-defense.

"The trouble with you-all, the whole bunch of you," Jay said, "is you never really *knew* the Judge. I knew something about him. He was like a father to me in a way. I had a real black father who was like a stranger to me. Well, the Judge was kind of my *white* father. I knew him better than all of you put together. He was tough, a very tough man, but a good man too."

"I could say the same damn thing," Mike said. "I could make the same kind of a claim. I could say that Charity was a lot more of a Mother to me than she was to any of you."

"That might even be true in a way. But whose fault is it?"

"How the hell do I know whose fault it is? How am I supposed to know who's to blame?"

"The trouble with you people, you *white* people, is you think too much. You think about yourselves too much. You think so much you stop being anything except sorry for yourselves. You think so much you make me sick at my stomach. The Judge, by God, he wasn't like that. He was more like a black man."

"The trouble with you people, you *niggers*, is . . ."

"Don't tell me," Jay said. "You don't have to tell me about being a nigger. I know and I can show you."

They finished off the bottle and threw it away among the dark trees. They switched places and Jay started the car and drove it away deeper into the country.

Jay said he wanted him to see some places, some of the country honkytonks, windowless shacks in the woods, lit by candles and kerosene lamps, lost places where the poor country Negroes came to drink themselves into a sodden stupor. The beast in his lair. What a life! What a beast's life! Jay kept telling him. Work hard all day in the broiling sun. Sweat rivers. Come after dark to these places—"Moonlite Klub," "Bucket of Blood," "Sweet Josephine's" —to sit down on cheap benches or patched-up, strung-and-wired-together chairs (always being broken to pieces), to drink bootleg, moonshine whiskey with a taste like raw gasoline or maybe cheap wine, to play a beatup juke box so loud the glasses and bottles rattled on the table and your head throbbed, to sit and sulk or drink or to get up and dance to the music in a sweaty frenzy until you fell down, to fight if you had a chance with knife blades and razors and broken bottles and pistols, to maybe drag a drunk woman (and she more than likely with the crabs and carrying a dose of clap or the syph) out in the trees or the bushes and lay her dazed and dreamy on the hard ground and she'd raise her knees and howl like a cat in heat for you, to stagger home in the first gray light without a penny left in your pocket to buy even groceries with to a houseful of hungry children and pets and a wife who either suffered in silence or nagged you to death, to stick your whole head in an ice-cold bucket of well water and shake yourself dry like a dog, to feed the mule and go to work as the sun came up, feeding the avaricious earth with your sweat drop by stinking drop.

"Don't you think I'd rather be a white man? Don't you think I'd like to be at least *like* a white man?"

And the night blurred out of focus for them, a montage of surprised, hard looks ("Let 'em look, the godamn brutes," Jay said. "But let one of them *say* something to us or make a move and I'll be cutting black meat off of bones."), a crazed succession of noises and the flat tasteless burn of cheap liquor and the close bitter-sweet smell of Negro sweat, and both of them vomiting outside behind trees and driving on to the next place until finally it seemed like they were the last two human souls awake in the whole world, driving aimlessly along sandy deep-rutted roads, at last just coming to a dead stop as the darkness weakened, faded, turned to dirty gray and the dawn was coming on.

They climbed out of the car and fought each other. Caught

in the still-burning headlights, they cast gigantic shadows of themselves. Drunk and clumsy, but strong, they hit and were hit and knocked down and got back up again, bloody and dirty, until out of sheer exhaustion they fell to wrestling on the ground rolling over and over in the dirt of the road and, spent, they lay side by side on the ground breathing hard.

Jay started to laugh. He propped himself up on his elbows and laughed through his bloody lips.

"I ain't *never* going to get drunk with white folks again."

"Christ what a night!" Mike said. "Who would ever believe it?"

He wiped at his hurt face with a handkerchief.

"Jay, you're a godamn mess. You look like hell."

"You don't look such a much yourself."

They struggled to their feet and, sobered, solemnly shook hands in the light of the headlights. They heard a rooster crowing, and they went off arm in arm down the road in that direction to find some water and see if they could clean up a little.

* * *

By the time they reached town and he let Jay off in Black Bottom, it was all over between them. They were sober and hurting and their separate inhibitions gripped and pinched like a vise. There wasn't anything else either one of them could say or do. They shook hands and said so long.

* * * * * * *

"What in the world happened to you?" Vivian Blanch said.

"I had a kind of a fight."

"So it seems. Maybe you better pick on somebody your own size next time."

"Oh, I'm all right," Mike said. "You ought to see the other guy."

She touched the bruises on his cheekbones with her fingers. When he winced and blinked at her touch her eyes lit as if he'd given her some wonderful surprise, a gift or a little bouquet of flowers.

* * *

Senator Allen Parker was busy talking to a man with one arm, a big burly man named McWhirter. He offered a warm strong calloused handshake and his condolences, and he went on talking to the Senator. In a moment Vivian entered with a photographer and they staged and posed some shots of Parker and the one-armed man smiling and shaking hands.

Mike smoked and sat in a chair and waited until McWhirter had left.

"Do you happen to know who that man is?"

"Elroy P. McWhirter," Vivian said. "Five feet eleven, one hundred and ninety-five pounds, red hair, eyes hazel. Age forty-seven. Occupation: construction worker, heavy machinery. Married, two children. Religion: Primitive Baptist—I believe that's the footwashing kind isn't it? Brilliant war record, paratrooper in 82nd Division. Distinguished Service Cross. No convictions other than minor traffic violations. Lost his left arm in an industrial accident, 1950. Here photographed congratulating the Senator on his firm stand against school integration."

"I mean do you know who he *is?*"

Vivian smiled. Senator Parker sighed.

"Mike, we are aware that rumor has it McWhirter is a member of a secret fraternal organization, the Ku Klux Klan, if that's what you're talking about."

"That's what I'm talking about," Mike said. "And it's a little more than rumor and he's a little more than just a member in good standing."

"I can give you the facts, the record," Vivian said. "If you want to swap suppositions . . ."

"Suppositions my ass! Do you two people have any idea what a picture like that in the papers may mean?"

"I can shake *anybody's* hand," the Senator said.

"Can you? I seem to remember another occasion and another photograph . . ."

"Mike, leave him alone. Can't you see how tired he is?"

"I don't care how tired he is or you are or I am. I can't go along with this. In plain cracker language, Senator, it just won't cut it for me anymore."

The Senator was very tired. His face was sad and weary and watery-eyed, pitiable and comic like a small dog begging.

"Vivian," he said, "would you please call downstairs and order some hot coffee. I'm about to go to sleep on my feet."

Then he turned back to Mike Royle.

"What's come over you, son? I'm sorry about your loss. I liked your father, admired him, but . . ."

"My father hasn't got anything to do with this. I'm speaking up for myself."

"One by one they lose heart, I ought to say the *guts* for it. And they sneak out on me. First Batten, then Benjamin, then . . ."

"Nobody's *sneaking* out on you. You've got it wrong. But I have a right to protest, I mean it. I *protest* against your stooping to use a man like McWhirter in the hope of grubbing a miserable handful of votes you don't really want anyway."

"I hadn't noticed the air ringing with your protests before this," Vivian said from the phone table. "Since when the big moral take?"

"Let's leave morals out of it," Mike said. "I'll admit that line of argument must sound funny coming from me. Let's just say it's impractical. We have less than a week until election day. It won't do you any good at all and it's likely to do you some harm."

"All right, Mike," Parker said. "What's your moral argument?"

"You know what I mean."

"No, I'm not sure that I do," he said. "I'll be the judge of practicality. You just give me the ethics this time."

"Those guys, McWhirter and his bedsheet boys, are the *real* enemy, bedrock underneath the dirt. They hate you and everything that you've stood for. You hate them. They're underground now. Back when you started out, when my daddy started, they were riding high. You had to knock their heads together and fight your way through them or get killed. They damn near killed my daddy. Now the morals are real simple. It seems to me that nothing, not even the wild hair of a chance that you might muster a few more votes and beat John Batten at the polls, is worth throwing away thirty years for."

"I am *not* throwing anything away. You have to get yourself elected. *You have to get elected.* That's all there is to it."

"Is it worth getting elected if you have to shit all over yourself to do it?"

Parker's face clouded with anger. He lunged at Mike, but Vivian Blanch stepped blithely between them.

"Gentlemen, your coffee is served."

The door opened and a deferential bellboy wheeled a tray into the room.

* * *

Over coffee they calmed down. They were able to argue about it. Parker pooh-poohed the idea that anything was seriously implied or signified by a photograph of himself shaking the hand of Elroy McWhirter.

"It doesn't mean a thing," he said. "It can't possibly be misconstrued as any kind of endorsement of McWhirter by *me*."

"You really believe that?"

"I'll bet my life on it."

"All right," Mike said at last. "You're the boss."

They had just a few very difficult days ahead and then it would be all over. Why not finish the job? Why not work together and see what could be done? A public opinion poll showed that Batten had a good lead in most of the big counties, but the survey had been made before the death of Judge Royle. Now it would be hard to predict how things might go.

"Sometimes I feel like I'm playing a card game on his coffin."

"I know how you must feel," Parker said. "But one thing about the Judge, he was a realist."

"I don't know about that," Mike said. "I wish I believed it."

At any rate they would have to give everything they had, all energy, all time to these last few days. Parker and Vivian had drawn up a fierce schedule of public appearances, speeches, TV and radio spots. They planned to finish it all up in Oakland with a speech on the afternoon before election day. They would ride out the storms of that day in the hotel there.

"Why Oakland?"

"Well," Parker said. "That's where we started out and I guess that's where it ought to end."

Strangely Parker seemed to gain in color and strength and energy again just thinking about all of himself that he had to squander in such a short time. Maybe it was a subtle form of emotional inebriation, the wild bubble dances that fill the brains of desert hermits when their guts are most shrunken and flesh is most corrupted. Maybe it was just the coffee. But he looked recovered, even glowing.

One thing, though. Just one small item. Would Mike agree to fill the gap for the Senator and make one speech for him? It wasn't really a big thing but there had been a promise. A long time ago, long before the campaign, he had agreed to make a talk at a small Negro college up near St. Augustine, just an evening auditorium address, non-political, for the opening of the school session. He had made a promise and he wanted to keep it. But, well, it just didn't look like he'd have time now to fulfill it. And it might be a little awkward for everybody right at the tail end of a rough campaign.

"Okay, I'll do that," Mike said. "What am I supposed to talk about?"

"Talk about anything. Talk about whatsoever things are true and beautiful and of good report."

"Talk about anything," Vivian said, "except race relations, segregation, politics . . ."

"And Justice."

Parker set down his coffee cup hard in the saucer spilling a little. He looked at Mike.

"You understand I just don't have the heart to go up there and talk to them right now, don't you?"

"I'll do it for you," Mike said. "They tell me I haven't got *any* heart."

* * *

As he was walking out of the hotel lobby Mike met Alice Parker who had just succeeded in negotiating the revolving doors with both arms full of packages. She was a little out of breath and marvelously groomed.

"Mrs. Parker, you're as pretty as a picture."

"That's how come I'm late," she said. "I've been to the beauty parlor. Do you think Allen will be furious?"

"What about?"

"*These!*" She rattled the leaning tower of packages in her arms. "I found the nicest little shop downtown."

"No, m'am," Mike said. "I don't think those packages are going to worry him at all."

* * *

When he got home he found the telegram waiting for him on the flat newel post at the foot of the stairs.

SHOCKED AND DEEPLY SORRY TO HEAR OF JUDGE ROYLE'S DEATH. PLEASE ACCEPT MY DEEPEST SYMPATHY.
ELAINE

That was so like her in so many ways. Conventionally formal; reticent. She never had been able to accept the Southern notion of family, that by marriage she had to assume a whole new family of blood kin as elaborate as a graph, not so much a family tree as a root structure, twisted and complex. Judge Royle had always been "my husband's father." Perhaps in the end that had saved her, enabled her to resist the tug, pull, clutch of those roots.

He read it and folded it up and stuck it in a pocket. He went upstairs to his mother's room. She was resting, asleep maybe, lying on the chaise longue. The venetian blinds were partly drawn. Light filtered through the angled slats and cast a series of barred, slender shadows across her body and the room. Dust danced in that light. The hi-fi was playing softly. She lay there in her black dress, small and pretty, like an expensive doll.

When he closed the door to behind him and it clicked she opened her eyes.

"I'm glad you're back. Where have you been?"

"The world goes on," he said. "I've been out in it and it's still there."

"Well, you're here now," she said, smiling, sitting up, propping a pillow behind her head. "There's something I ought to talk to you about."

"What's that?"

"Mary Ann. It's very hard on her. She was so close to him and it's hard now. I was thinking that maybe a trip would be the right thing for her."

"A trip? Where would she go?"

"Well, to tell you the truth, I've already talked to her about it. We talked it over this morning. I think she'd like to go to Rome for a while."

"By all means," Mike said. "She ought to go then."

"There *is* one problem. The thing is about the estate."

"Is there going to be any trouble about the will?"

"There isn't any will, Mike."

"How about that?"

It was strange that the Judge, schooled as a lawyer and with long and complex experience for years on the bench, handling the intricate details and problems of estates, often as judge required to trouble with the estates of those people who had died and left what they couldn't take with them in a tangled gnarl of contention, curious that he had never bothered himself with making his own will. Folly any lawyer would have called it, but if it was folly it must have been reasoned, meditated folly. What had he intended? To leave them embroiled with the law and its problems, to impress upon them by indifference his memory in a way that the simple giving of himself in his various things of this world could never have done? Or was it, maybe, contrived simply to wash his hands of the matter and to leave them at the last his finest gesture of contempt for the world? It was foolish and funny and enigmatic. And it was a gesture in character.

"It will be a while before we can touch anything," Nancy Royle went on. "And then I have no idea, I mean I'm not really sure . . ."

"I've got a little money in a savings account," he said. "She's welcome to it. When will she want to go?"

"Very soon I imagine. Just as soon as she can get her passport and her passage and all."

"All right, I'll take care of it," Mike said. "What about Jojo?"

"Lord, I don't know. I just don't know what's ever going to become of that boy," she said. "Do you know, Mike, it's the strangest thing."

"What's that?"

"I've been just lying here all afternoon waiting for the headache to start. I've been waiting and it just won't come. I haven't had any pain in my head since your father died. It makes me feel terrible. You don't know how bad it makes me feel to have those pains go away like that."

She began to cry and he gave her his handkerchief and sat down beside her taking her in his arms.

* * *

Charity clucked her tongue when she saw his face. She touched his cuts and bruises with dark gentle fingers.

"You boys!" she said. "You and Jay both been out and got yourselves in a whole lot of mischief."

"We didn't have any trouble at all," Mike said. "We just got drunk and roughhoused a little."

"Children! That's what you are, a couple of great big overgrown children. When you two going to decide to grow up?"

"I wish we were," he said. "But I'm afraid we aren't children any more even if we act like it sometimes."

"You surely have been acting like it."

"It isn't liable to happen again," Mike said. "Do we have anything to eat in the house?"

Charity laughed.

"Now that's a silly question," she said. "You know just as well as I do, a house that has a wedding or a funeral has always got an icebox cram full of good things to eat."

He followed her into the kitchen.

* * * * * * *

"Perhaps you'd like something a little—uh—more fortifying than a cup of coffee," the President whispered by his ear, just touching the point of his bent elbow.

"Thanks," Mike said. "That might be good."

He was standing in the room, holding his coffee cup and saucer and making the requisite smalltalk with some of the faculty and their wives. The room—booklined walls, carpeted floors, respectable prints, leather chairs and ash tray stands, tables laden with recent issues of magazines—might have been any faculty club anywhere in the country. It was homely, yet at the same time as severely impersonal and uniform as some kind of waiting room. Like most faculty clubs it didn't convey a sense of being much used. The books looked good, but decorative and unread; the ash trays were so clean to start with that there was a real moment of hesitating to violate them with ashes and crumpled, stubbed cigarette butts. The leather chairs were stiff and forbidding as colonels, though the material seemed to cry for an oldness, a solid familiarity that ought to be expressed in good worn places, in cracks, in moon-shaped sunken circles made by many a comfortable buttocks. It seemed, then, just as it should have and very much like a museum piece, a model room to be inspected but not inhabited. The faculty men were professional and professorial, some of the older ones in dark, conservative suits, even a few with vests and watch chains, some of the younger members of the faculty in the universal uniform of gray flannel trousers, sports jackets, loafers, and all cleaned, all creased and cared for, very neat. The wives were maybe a little too dressy, but elegant in good hats, jewelry, fashionable and (he guessed) expensive cocktail dresses. Mike felt out of place in his already rumpled suit, his daysoiled shirt, and he was painfully aware of his healing cuts and bruises.

Alone among this group of cultivated Negroes, of a type that he had never known, who spoke and dressed as well or better than their white counterparts, he felt like an uninvited guest who has strayed in, to be received with formal and decent hospitality, at a masquerade party. It was a little like witnessing a dead serious minstrel show.

But his uneasiness was more basic. The room, the scene, the people there were even more startling seen in and against the context of the place. He had seen the college for the first time at twilight when he had turned into the driveway past the feathery, paint-peeling, tilting sign. He had seen the hunched cluster of brick buildings, old and small with here and there the jagged grin of a broken window pane, the wide and shaggy lawn, and it had confirmed his expectations. It had seemed like a poor parody of the conventional, calendar-picture façade of the small liberal arts college. He had sensed poverty and struggle and gradual decay, the decay of ambition, of high aspirations, of original intentions. (Turning into the driveway just then he had recalled the story of one of his friends who had visited a Negro college in Atlanta. Walking behind a coed in a sweater and skirt, a young man in an athletic sweater. Overheard: "Honey, is you did your Greek yet?") It had been what he expected it to be, at once an object of patronizing amusement and mildly sentimental guilt. But what he had failed to do was to people the place. (What had he to people it with? Jay? Charity? The poor country Negroes in the honkytonks?) He hadn't anticipated the faculty and their wives, turned out for his inspection in incongruous splendor maybe, but curiously not involved at all in his vague created world of realized or evanescent impressions. They were clearly involved, engaged in their present task of teaching and at this moment of entertaining a white stranger. They didn't see themselves or the expense of their energy as absurd. In the room talking with them, though the talk was as conventional and stylized as if it had been printed in a phrase book, he sensed, felt, knew the energy, the sense of dedication and even their slightly disguised hostility toward him. It was as if by a simple act of self-transcendence they were fully cognizant of his first impressions, of their context and of themselves seen from his point of view, and maybe even of his baffled unease. He could feel their contempt for his faulty judgment and even share it.

This moment of transcendence left him feeling naked and hollow as if his whole soul had deserted him in a single breath, leaving behind a rudimentary, stuffed scarecrow of a man. Consciousness, fine or crude, was one thing, one particular kind of burden and anguish. You were able to corrupt it or cultivate it, letting time and space and the world splash over you, formless as a breaking wave. But what happened when the world and time and space were peopled? Only God had known the world unpeopled. What happened when you suddenly became aware of the forms that you thought of as parts of your own consciousness, shadows, pasteboard cutouts to be arranged and changed and shifted in various combinations, summoned or dismissed, aware of each of these forms as equally conscious, equally aware, dangerous or loving, and saw yourself as just the pasteboard figure to another pair of eyes? It was one thing to wave a pistol at a man in what must have been a dream or to trade blows with another in a drunken outburst. But what happened, what did it mean when you thought of these things as involving human souls?

It made his hand tremble holding the saucer. It made the cup rattle like bones in the wind.

It made the President of the college—a suave exemplar of his metier, all his difficulties and triumphs increased, all his successes intensified by the brute process of natural selection in an alien hostile environment—offer him something a little stronger to drink.

* * *

The President led him into a little kitchenette adjoining the room, a cell of immaculate porcelain tile and finish and waxed linoleum. He let the door swing to behind him and he opened a cupboard, fumbled behind some crockery and produced a bottle of whiskey. He poured some in two glasses and apologized because somebody had forgotten to plug in the icebox and there wasn't any ice.

"You'll understand naturally there's a wee bit of resentment, maybe disappointment would be the right word for it, that the Senator himself isn't able to be here."

"It's too bad," Mike said. "But maybe it's just as well. The Senator's pretty worn out. It's been a rough and tumble time for him."

"I can imagine that."

Mike took a long swallow of his drink and felt better. It helped. But you could get to depending on the stuff too much. Better watch it. Still he made no more than polite objection when the President poured another shot in his glass.

"Of course *we* understand, the faculty I mean, we understand how these things are."

"Naturally."

"But the students are young and eager and inexperienced and so—*impractical*. They may be, shall we say, a little more demonstrative."

"You mean they may make it plain that the second team isn't good enough."

"Not exactly. It's just that they're a little disappointed and I want to be sure that you understand . . ."

"I'd feel the same way myself."

"I wonder, Mr. Royle, how you'd like to handle the business of questions after your talk. We can do it any way you want to: no questions at all, questions submitted in writing, direct questioning from the floor . . ."

"Let them ask anything they want to."

At least he could do that much even if it meant figuratively being torn to shreds, skull cracked open and spilling out dry sawdust for all to see.

The President looked at his gold pocket watch.

"It's about that time," he said. "Shall we start down to the auditorium?"

* * *

He was introduced and stood up to a polite patter of applause. He took his place behind the little speaker's table with its pitcher and glasses, and he looked out into a room full of dark young faces. Of course this kind of thing was done all the time. For convocations, commencements, assemblies and other occasions the Negro colleges often asked some white man or other to come and make a talk. Anthony Singletree had done it in his day. Judge Royle had done it. And now it was his turn. The motive of the colleges and schools was involved with the politics of survival, the insurance of interest and good will of at least some of the leading members of the white community, patronage or protection or however you wanted to put it. For the faculty and the administration it must have been a necessary evil. For the students it must have been at best a bore, at worst another subtle humiliation, part of *their* education for survival.

Education was, in fact, the topic he had picked for his talk. It was, he guessed, one of the easiest things in the world to talk about. Almost like the weather. The thing to do was to stand up and throw several colored balls in the air at once, to keep them moving, rising and falling, now you see it—now you don't; and if you were careful not to drop any of them, at the end you could have and show them all safe in the palms of your hands. You could smile and sit down. Nobody hurt. Nothing risked, nothing lost, nothing gained. He had planned to play in the abstract with several notions about education: formal learning and learning by experience, depth versus breadth, knowledge and/or wisdom, contemplation or activity. He intended to end with a brisk flourish and flag-waving about the virtues of public education in a democratic society. It couldn't have been more abstract in conception, bloodless as a turnip or a stone. But once he began to speak, following his notes, he felt the structure and the subject slipping out of his grip. Somewhere early in his notes he had made a passing reference to Telemachus in search of his father. "Re: Classical Ideal. Education by example and experience." When he came to this note his mind stumbled like someone in a dark, but well-known room tripping over furniture. He felt for an instant passionately involved in that mythical search, the boy with Wisdom to point the way and his untrained wits to save him; the wily old warrior lost on his long dream of a voyage, outwitting all in the end, calling himself Nobody to the illiterate, but always Somebody and always headed for his true home as surely and inevitably as a compass needle finds its own charmed magnetic promised land.

And he talked a little too long and too much about the *Odyssey*, wondering even as he spoke why, after years, that idea had popped into his mind in the first place and why he seemed to care about it here and now. Finally he managed to right himself and he was able to bear down hard on his planned platitudes and was able to finish on time and with at least the rhetorical appearance of order and coherence.

His audience with good manners clapped again, and he drank a glass of water while the President asked if there were any questions.

The first two or three things he was asked were vague and harmless and polite. His answers were the same. He kept studying his audience as he listened and answered, waiting for the first real sortie, and when at last a tall thin boy rose with his hand in the air and there was an almost imperceptible shifting of weight, a slight difference in the breathing of the whole group— he could really *feel* their expectation—he allowed himself to smile. At that moment he could understand some of the inherent pleasure of it, the Judge's, John Batten's, Parker's, the politician's pleasure and version of pure theatrical joy. You moved alone like the quick fox ahead of an indiscriminate blurred mass of barking hounds, depending on your wit and agility to escape their teeth. Caught or cornered, as the Judge had been literally years before, as Parker was finding himself in a sense that was symbolic, but no less real, you turned if you could and you became another kind of beast, a wild boar maybe, savage, ruthless, indifferent, intent only on survival, ready to gore and gut yourself to open air again. No wonder there weren't any morals in it when the game was as lonely and as furious as a hunt.

"Sir, you've been talking this evening all about education . . ."

"I *hope* that's what I've been talking about. I always know where I am when I start, but after the first sentence it's like a merry-go-round. Round and round she goes and where she stops nobody knows."

A counterpunch. A little nervous laughter. The young man shrugged it off and began again.

"I've been sitting here wondering how all this applies in real life."

"You mean how's *my* education getting along?"

His antagonist, undaunted, thrust home.

"What's your view on the segregation of the schools?"

So there it was, and there couldn't be much more backing up. He wondered what kind of rabbit out of what kind of hat Parker would have pulled in this place, under these circumstances.

"I'm here on behalf of Senator Parker," he said. "I think his position is pretty clear."

"Very clear."

There was a good laugh at that and a kind of leaning forward in chairs, an intensification of interest. Mike heard a couple of half-stifled chuckles in the row of faculty chairs close behind him.

"As I was saying," he went on, "Senator Parker's *record* shows that . . ."

"We know about Senator Parker's views, sir. I was wondering about *your* views."

"As you know," Mike said, "when I'm working for the Senator I have to speak for him."

"It's too bad he can't be here to speak for himself."

All the students laughed. Mike had to grin. He had lost ground in a great big hurry. He knew without glancing over his shoulder that the politic President was already poised on the edge of his chair, ready to rise and call the assembly over and done with at the least signal. He knew, too, that he would have to give that signal. The President wasn't going to make a move to save him now unless he asked for it. He wasn't going to.

"It sure is," Mike said, wiping his brow emphatically with a handkerchief, though he was as sweatless as a bone.

"We were wondering, sir, if you *had* a view of your own."

"You know, that's the first time in a long time anybody's asked me that. I'm glad you asked me. It's flattering. You get so used to selling other people's ideas that you sometimes forget you've got any of your own."

"And what are your ideas?"

"All right," Mike said. "I don't see any reporters here. I don't see John Batten or Allen Parker either. Just us. In the family so to speak. All right, I'll tell you what I think. I don't think there can *be* any real education, formal or otherwise, any real knowledge and no wisdom, so long as our two groups of people are living in the same time and the same place and with some of the same history, but are separated, segregated from each other if you will, by a kind of barbwire of mutual distrust, prejudice, bigotry, mythology, guilt and what have you. I say it is mutual and I say, too, we have got to share the *responsibility* of our own peculiar society equally and together. Chew on that a while."

He received a scattering of applause.

"If that's how you really feel, how do you happen to be working for the election of Senator Parker?"

"Because, young man, you and I aren't candidates for the Senate. Nobody is voting for us. You have got to make a choice and my choice was Senator Parker."

"And you're willing to compromise . . ."

"I *have* to compromise. Let me say this. Let me tell you about one of the things I've learned by being mixed up in this campaign. Politics, the business of getting yourself elected, is false and phony as a two-headed nickel. Government is, or can be anyway, something else again. I still believe that when this charade is over with Senator Parker will return to his true position, to what he really thinks. Let's don't put all the blame on the politicians. We—you and I included—put the spotlight on them and demand a show. If they have to lose most of their dignity to get our votes, it's at least partly our fault. Any more questions?"

When it was all over the President thanked him for his patience and candor. Some of the faculty came up to shake hands with him and wish him well, and then he went outside alone in the dark to find his car and drive home.

He felt bad, not because he had been a failure at the job he was supposed to do, but because, even though he had said what he guessed he meant, in the end it had been just another kind of performance. He guessed it was that way with all politicians. After a while even the truth seemed counterfeit. No matter how naked or honest you got, you still felt dressed up like the emperor in the fairy tale. Though he had said what he guessed he meant it turned out to be just another christening of lies on his head. He wasn't working for Parker, loyal to Parker because he was the best man. Maybe he had been the best man, but God knows what he was now. There wasn't, or didn't seem to be, much choice involved. He was loyal to Allen Parker because he wasn't basking on a beach in Pago Pago. How would that sound? It didn't seem likely that he would ever be able to stop telling lies to other people. They wanted to be lied to. It didn't seem likely that he wouldn't enjoy himself while he was lying. It didn't seem likely that he would ever stop fooling himself.

He fumbled with the key to unlock the door.

"Sir . . ."

He turned and saw a young man standing behind him, a boy with a college jacket on and the numerals of his class, impossibly remote (Lord, have we come that far already?) on it.

"Sir, we've been reading the *Odyssey* in class and, well sir,

I was very interested in that part of your talk. I liked that the best."

"Thanks," Mike said. "Did you finish it up?"

"No, sir, we haven't got to the end yet."

"Finish it up. By all means finish it," Mike said. "It has a happy ending."

* * *

Old father, he thought, wily old warrior, how you'd laugh at me now! How you'd laugh in my face!

* * * * * * *

The morning paper headlined the story.

During the early evening the Negro, a middle-aged history and civics teacher at the local high school, had been kidnapped from his home by a carload of white men. He had been taken into the woods, stripped, beaten and thrown in a ditch by the side of the road. He had been found half-dead and taken to the hospital. His condition was called critical. Police said he was unable to identify any of his assailants. They had been wearing masks. He thought one of them might have been a one-armed man.

It wasn't known why he had been singled out and attacked. It was suggested that possibly it was connected with the election. The man had been outspoken in urging the Negroes to turn out and vote on election day.

There was a photograph of the victim, a slight, light-skinned man with glasses, wearing a mild smile.

* * *

Senator Parker was in a state of shock.

As soon as Mike saw the story in the paper he went to the Osceola Hotel to see him. In the lobby workmen in overalls were putting up streamers and bunting for Parker's election day headquarters. Posters of him in various poses, smiling and looking much younger, were going up. Mike watched two men on a stepladder struggling with a huge photograph. It tipped and slipped and troubled them, and they cursed it. But the smile on the picture never faded. Not a hair was mussed. It looked like it would have winked if it could.

In the suite a chamber orchestra of telephones rang. Vivian Blanch, busy with the phones, entangled in a net of black wires, motioned Mike toward the bedroom.

"See what you can do. You talk to him," she said, cupping her palm over a speaker.

Senator Parker lay flat on his back in the bed with a blanket pulled up to his chin, as stiff as a wooden Indian. Alice Parker was fluttering ineffectually around him straightening the blanket, wiping his brow with a wet washcloth.

"Get up," Mike said. "You can't just lay there."

The Senator turned his head slowly to look at Mike, a sad and stricken gaze like a wounded deer. He shook his head.

"You've still got a few things you've got to do," Mike said. "Like making a speech."

"I can't," he said hoarsely. "I'm all through. Call them up and cancel the whole thing. I'm not going anywhere."

Mike jerked the blankets off him. The Senator lay there in his pajamas, perfectly still.

"Godamn it, you can't get off the hook that easy. Get up! Get your ass out of that bed!"

Alice Parker gasped and began to cry. Mike steered her toward the door.

"Go order some coffee for him. Get some hot coffee up here right away."

She left the room, her face averted from the scene, a lace handkerchief held to her nose.

"What I really need is a drink."

Mike found a bottle and held it to his lips. He sat up a little and took a long swallow. He licked his lips and sat up all the way, rubbed his face hard with his hands.

"I never even dreamed anything like this," he said. "I called McWhirter and he just laughed at me. He laughed and said he didn't know anything about it."

"What did you *think* was going to happen? Did you think all your boy McWhirter wanted was a pretty glossy picture of himself shaking hands with The Great Man? Something to put on his mantlepiece and show his friends?"

"I don't know what to do."

"You've got a lot of things you've got to do," Mike said. "One of them is to pull yourself together the best you can and go out there this afternoon and tell the truth. Eat crow. Eat dirt. But tell the truth for once."

"I can't make that speech. I haven't got the nerve any more."

"Take a pill, take a shot. Do anything you want to, but you've got to make that speech."

"Believe me, I didn't want anybody to get hurt in this campaign."

"Well, that one laying in the hospital, he's hurting pretty bad right now."

"I'm so tired. I'm so damn tired."

"We're all tired."

The Senator rolled over on his stomach and covered his head with a pillow. His body shook, not with tears or sobbing, but with dry heaves of shame and weariness. Mike went into the bathroom and turned on the shower. He came back and took the Senator's bathrobe out of the closet. He removed the pillow and gently lifted the man to his feet, helped him to slip his arms into the sleeves of the bathrobe.

"Go in there and take a shower. In a few minutes we'll have some coffee for you."

He pushed him into the bathroom and shut the door. He lit a cigarette and waited outside the door until he heard the shower curtain slide open and shut again on its metal rod. He heard the water splashing, and after a moment the Senator began to hum a little tune to himself.

* * * * * *

The afternoon was hot and bright and breezeless. Sun came through the west windows of the suite and fell like a spotlight on the Senator where he stood in front of the mirror tying his necktie. His clothes were freshly pressed, his shirt was crisp and starched, his shoes gleamed. His hair was trimmed and he had been shaved—they had the hotel barber come up to the room. After that ritual treatment of shaving and hot towels and lotion his face had acquired a glow that might have passed for ruddy health.

"Hand me my cufflinks, will you, Mike."

Mike picked the two silver cufflinks, the masks of the drama, off the bureau and Parker slipped them into his cuffs. His fingers trembled a little.

"You look splendid," Vivian Blanch said, cracking the door into the bedroom. "There seems to be a mayor out here waiting to take you down to the park."

"Tell him to come on in."

Parker slipped his arms into the coat Mike was holding for him, looked one more time in the mirror, stern-faced, for a final assurance or a blessing, and whirled smiling just in time to shake hands with Joe Beardsley as he came in the room. Beardsley was a fat man and already the heat was working on him, wrinkling and rumpling his suit.

"Joe, I'll make a deal with you," Parker said. "You think up a couple of nice things to say about me in your introduction and the first thing I'll do is take my coat off."

Beardsley chuckled. "Done," he said. "I'm roasting alive."

"You ought to float a bond and get the whole town air-conditioned."

"Thought about it," Beardsley said. "Trouble is it might bring a whole lot of tourists down here in the summer time."

"What's wrong with that?"

"Why if *that* happened we'd all get rich. We'd be finished."

"You'd just have to change your politics, Joe. You might even have to turn Republican."

"God forbid."

Parker ushered the Mayor back into the living room of the suite. Mike fell in behind them. They started for the door, but Mayor Beardsley paused.

"Won't Mrs. Parker be coming with us?"

"No," Parker said. "She's got a bad headache and I told her she could skip this one."

* * *

248

They had just about finished decorating the lobby. Bunting and streamers and flags—the American, the State Flag, the Confederate—were up. The picture posters grinned from all around the room. And against one wall they had rigged a large blackboard with all of the counties of the state listed on it and blank columns to record the vote when it began to come in. There was a switchboard and a plywood counter crowded with telephones waiting in dark and delicate poise to ring and ring with news tomorrow.

When the elevator opened and the three men stepped out, the handful of Parker's local workers, already on duty, applauded. He shook hands with them and murmured thanks. Flashbulbs popped and glared. There were some reporters near the front door, and now they swept forward in a pack, pressing close around the Senator, pencils and pads busy, moving with him as he headed for the door. All but one. Lean, gray, cynical, his mouth pursed as if to spit, Atkins slouched against the wall and watched.

Senator Parker spotted him and grinned.

"You don't want to miss this one, Atkins. I guarantee a story for you."

"I don't doubt it," Atkins said without moving. "I'd say it's about time."

Senator Parker stopped in his tracks and guffawed.

"Good old Atkins, the poor man's Jeremiah," he said. "How did you get to be the conscience of this state? Who picked you?"

"Nobody," Atkins said. "Like a damn fool I volunteered."

And then they were outside and settling themselves in the back seat of the car.

* * *

The Mayor finished his introduction and stepped aside. Senator Parker rose from his chair and nodded, a kind of bow, to the Mayor. He slipped off his coat, laid it across the chair, and he stepped forward on the flag-draped platform. Mike, watching him from behind, from the back row of chairs on the platform, could picture his pose from the crowd's point of view, where in clotted shirtsleeves and summer dresses the little field of faces white and black were close-pressed and tilted up and toward the speaker's platform like a bunch of wild flowers in a breeze. But there wasn't any breeze, and Senator Parker began his speech with a casual, off-hand joke about the weather in Oakland and the climate of Hell. His voice crackled over the loudspeaker and the crowd laughed. He pushed back from the rostrum and its microphones and laughed too.

Mike could see his back, high and framed by the faces of the crowd, his white shirt loose around his rawboned frame, like a huge blister, his head tossed back to laugh. Yet without difficulty he could imagine the changes that were taking place in Allen Parker's expression as the crowd laughed. His mouth would be tightening and turning down. The high angle of his cheekbones, the soft hound's eyes, the thicket of unruly hair, the ruddy, splotched complexion would become no longer clownish and familiar, but, in a wink of time, the rude composite pieces of a tragic mask. The crowd's laughter dwindled, and the Senator moved closer to the bright microphones and their tangled net of dark wires and started to talk in the soft harsh voice all of them had heard before, all of them knew.

His words were lost. The public address system whistled and fogged with static. Joe Beardsley, the fat, fussy, grinning, kindly man, the easy-going smalltown politician, jumped from his chair and stepped up beside the Senator to fiddle with the microphones, bending to twist a set of dials and for a split second passing his bulk between Senator Parker and the crowd, eclipsing him. As he was leaning over two shots sounded, whip cracks in succession followed by the smell of burnt gunpowder. Mike saw it happen with a painful slowness, the thick slowmotion of a dreamed event. All in an unmeasurable fraction of time a young Negro standing in the crowd had calmly raised a pistol (the light danced off the barrel) and fired twice quickly before a hand struck full force across his arm and the pistol fell away to the ground. And the people standing nearby scattered back and away as if it were a live thing freed from a cage, as if somebody had loosed a snake among them.

Mayor Beardsley sat down hard, jarring the whole platform, rattling the water pitcher and the glasses. He fell sideways against and off of the arrested rigid body of the Senator, and he fell sitting like a great soft teddy bear, like a stuffed animal, dropped.

By the time Mike got to the front of the platform, running and pushing from his chair in back, the Senator was kneeling beside Beardsley, and the Mayor's soft full moon of a face was wrinkled in a spasm of pain and pure astonishment. Beardsley was shaking his head and mumbling something to himself. Mike knelt and put his arm around the Mayor, yelled at the Senator to move, to get back and out of the way, but his voice was lost in the noise that came from the crowd now, a noise like rough surf.

Where they had sprung back, recoiled in one reflex, the crowd rushed forward again, poured into the tense void they had created. In the center the young Negro stood, limp, his head bowed, like a man praying on his feet. They overwhelmed him with a fury of fists and feet and flailing arms. And he collapsed under the sudden weight of them. But a policeman, a big man in his creased and tailored immaculate blue, short-sleeved uniform, black boots and leather belt glassy from care, charged into the middle of the ragged vortex. His whistle shrieked high above their rage, and his pistol caught the light like a drawn, naked blade. They stepped back again. The policeman seized the Negro, now sprawled in the trampled dirt, the crushed grass, lax as a drowned man, hoisted his sagging body in the crook of his arm and dragged him clear, still blowing on his whistle, still waving his pistol like a knife. He moved along slowly, dragging the man with him, made it across the park to one of the police cars parked along the curb. The crowd fell back, aghast and silent as he passed through them. He threw the body of the Negro into the back seat, hopped in the front seat, started the car and swirled off and away and out of reach in a wide u-turn, the siren screaming, the tires making a high-pitched squeal, the red light on top pulsing like an opened artery. Only with the noise of the siren and the engine and the tires, the swift motion of the car, did the crowd's fury find a voice again.

And then there was another siren, more distant but growing louder, coming toward them, a white ambulance coming from the hospital.

The Mayor was sitting up. Mike and the Senator held him in their arms just below the speaker's stand and its cluster of microphones that were still wheezing and coughing with static. Beardsley's face had softened into a mask of dismay, a look like a man who has seen a monster in his mirror. His white shirt (he'd grinned foolishly and taken off his coat when the Senator did) clung to his body, soaked through with blood. They couldn't stop or even check the bleeding, and blood, warm, thick, sticky, lay around him in a pool. Mike and the Senator were splashed and flecked with it.

The siren coming toward them got very loud, stopped suddenly with a rich sound like a phonograph record running down, and then Mike heard the doors open and shut and the heavy sound of running. He turned his head and looked directly into the eyes of the Senator. They were so unseeing they might as well have been made of glass or the button eyes of a doll.

"I think that was meant for me."

"Maybe so."

"Why? Why would somebody do a thing like that?"

Mike started to say something, but both of them were gripped and pushed aside by the hands of the ambulance driver and his assistant, two men in white breathing hard. They put the Mayor on the stretcher. He lay back easy and closed his eyes. They picked up the stretcher and might even have started to run with it if a doctor who had worked his way up from the crowd hadn't grabbed the driver's arm.

"Take your time, boy," he said. "He's gone now."

* * *

When Senator Parker started to stand up, his legs jellied and failed him. He threw his arm around Mike's shoulders, staggered and leaned heavily against him. His breath came short and hard. Mike led him away from the stand and got a police car to take him back to the hotel right away. They helped Parker into the back seat. He lay down on the seat, his face drawn, drained, colorless, his lips turning bluish. He was shivering. He shut his eyes, and they drove away in a hurry to the rear entrance of the Osceola Hotel. (He couldn't be led through the decorated lobby in a state of physical shock, looking like the very image of Death.) They went up in the service elevator, and they helped the Senator into an unoccupied room, covered him up with blankets. The policeman took off his visored cap and sat down in an easy chair to watch over Parker while Mike went to find Vivian Blanch.

Whatever she felt, she showed no sign or tremor of surprise when she saw Mike and he told her what had happened. She lifted a phone off the hook and called a doctor. She told the switchboard operator that everything was all right and to keep on putting all calls through to her. She told Mike Alice Parker was still sleeping. She'd take care of *that* problem when the time came. She intended to keep the people downstairs and the reporters pacified and pretty much in the dark.

"You'll have to tell the papers something."

"Don't worry," she said. "I can handle all that."

Mike lit a cigarette for her. She took a deep puff and smiled and stretched like a large, comfortable cat.

"I like excitement," she said. "It's good for me."

"Where do we go from here?"

"I don't know. I really wouldn't know," she said. "One thing for sure. The odds are against Washington, D.C."

* * *

The policeman played with his cap. His heavy revolver lay on the table beside his chair. He'd flip his cap by the visor in a little somersault and it would fall right side up in his lap.

Treated and drugged the Senator lay sound asleep under a pile of blankets. He looked a little better now. Sweat glistened on his face.

"Jesus," the cop said. "He sure takes things hard. You'd think it was *him* that got shot."

"It damn near was."

"Too bad poor old Joe Beardsley had to get it."

"Are you going to be able to stay here a while and look after the Senator?"

"Surely," the cop said. "I'm just as glad to be right here in this room."

"Why's that?"

"Well, you know," the cop said, grinning, "that fellow McWhirter's going to stir up a regular hornet's nest. There's going to be a plenty of trouble around here. I'm a Klansman myself, but I don't let it interfere with the line of duty so to speak."

"How about that Lieutenant, the one in the park?"

"Who, Rogers? Man, he don't belong to nothing. He's all by hiself."

"What's he going to do?"

"God knows, I don't. All I know is along about tonight there's going to be some hell in Oakland. When it comes, I'd just as soon be sitting right here."

* * *

Most of the people in the park had gone by the time Mike got back to pick up the Senator's coat. There were two little clusters of the morbidly curious. One group had gathered around the spot of the trampled grass where the Negro had stood and fallen. There wasn't much to see except a space of ground a little larger than a man where the grass had been crushed flat. They just stood looking at it. Another group was on the speaker's platform looking at the splashed spot where the Mayor had died. A few small black flies sang and buzzed around it. A man in coveralls was vainly trying to get the people to move off of the platform so he could start removing the microphones and wires and speakers of the public address system.

"Come on, come on now," he kept saying. "Ain't you folks never seen any blood before?"

* * * * * * *

It was twilight by the time Mike got to the County Jail. He had driven there through quiet streets. The stores were already shut up tight. Cars weren't moving. It was like midnight on the main street. The town had withdrawn on itself, front doors were closed, few lights were burning, and the children who should have been shrill at just this hour, playing with the frantic abandon of the last moments of the light before whistles and shouts summoned them home to supper, were absent.

He was startled when the streetlights suddenly flashed on, bright and lonely and incongruous along the hushed, empty blocks.

The County Jail was an old two-story brick building at the edge of the town overlooking the Dump. There all the garbage and waste of the town was hauled and burned up. As Mike parked the car and got out, he could see the whole desolate area, decently inaccessible from the homes and buildings and property of those who depended on it, still smouldering. Wisps of smoke were veiled dancers above the ashes. On the far side of the Dump an old woman was poking around with a short stick to salvage something. (In a flash he remembered her story. Widow of a banker who shot himself when the Florida Boom collapsed on itself like a circus tent coming down, she lived alone in a ramshackle three-story house, once a mansion, not far from the Dump. Ever since her husband had killed himself she had done this, prowled in the Dump, wandered the streets at night investigating ash cans, garbage cans, trash piles, dragging a child's red wagon behind her, looking for something. Her porch and yard were littered with broken and cast-away things, shoes and books and umbrellas and old clothes and worn out machinery and letters and bottle and cans and boxes. Children hooted at her when they found her by daylight on the streets. Hadn't he and Jay and the others done it once, too, shied rotten oranges at her? But by and large the town left her alone to do what she wanted with herself, seeing her husband had been a respectable man and that she did no real harm.) The smell of the Dump was bad, but he guessed it was like any other odor in the world, you could get used to it.

The lights were on in the jailhouse. From the upper story where all the windows were barred he could hear the sound of voices and somebody playing a tune on a harmonica. He heard a big voice laugh out loud and clear. He opened the front door and went inside. There was a bare waiting room with a raised desk. A small bald wizened monkey of a man, jailcolored, the Turnkey probably, sat at the raised desk reading a comic book, spellbound. He looked over the top of it and saw Mike and raised the book again and went on reading.

Mike walked past the desk and down a long narrow hall, stone floor smelling of disinfectant, to a room with *Visitors* on the frosted glass of the door.

"I wondered how long it would take you to get here," Atkins said when Mike opened the door. "Come on in. I was getting kind of lonesome."

* * *

"The nigger's dead," Atkins said, picking up his cards spread out in a game of solitaire, shuffling the deck.

"Which one?"

"The one in the hospital. The one that got kidnapped."

"That's bad," Mike said.

"It just makes it even. They ought to call it quits, tie score, and let everybody go home."

"How about the boy from the park?"

"Oh, he's *here*," Atkins said. "He's a real celebrity. He's got a corner cell all to himself upstairs. He's pretty beat up, but he ate a good supper and asked me for a pack of cigarettes."

"They ought to get him out of the county."

"Sure. I expect they'll get around to it. But not tonight."

"How come?"

"Lieutenant Rogers wants to keep him here overnight. He *could* get him out, but he won't. It's getting pretty complicated. As soon as people get involved it starts getting complicated."

The young Negro from the park was, it turned out, the son of the high school teacher who had just died in the hospital. He hadn't heard the news yet. (Mike's hands trembled when Atkins told him this.) He hadn't even known until they told him that he had shot and killed the wrong man. He laughed when they told him. (What else could he do?) And now, patched up, sitting on the cot in his cell, he could smoke and wait for whatever happened to him. He didn't seem to care much what that would be. He told Atkins he was just sorry they hadn't done it right there in the park. He figured it was just a reprieve, a stay of execution, any way you looked at it. And so he ate a good supper and asked for a pack of cigarettes.

"He's a bright kid and I doubt he's a day over twenty," Atkins said. "It's a damn shame."

"You think they'll come and take him?"

"Depends," Atkins said. "Depends on a lot of things. Something's bound to happen all right. It's going to happen tonight and right here. All we can do is wait and see."

Atkins produced a pint of whiskey from his coat pocket. He took a swallow and offered it to Mike. Then he shuffled his deck of cards.

"Tell you what," he said. "We better play a game and talk along a while. You got to do something. It's been so long since I spent a night in jail I'd forgotten all about what a drag it is."

* * *

The two men pulled a chair between them to serve as a card table. They sat on either side of it in identical straight chairs: the lean, gray, aging, ageless newsman, in his shirtsleeves with the cuffs rolled back around his wrists, wearing his hat pulled down over his eyes to shield against the harsh glare of the lone bright overhead bulb, cigarette dangling at an angle from his lips and the ash growing and curling like a gray caterpillar until it would finally fall away altogether to be replaced by a fresh white cigarette, the single raw shaft of smoke rising and causing one eye to squint in a fixed wink, his thin neck shrivelled, corded and veined, a turkey gobbler's neck inside the opened collar from which a cheap necktie dangled like a long loose weary tongue; and as his hands (small and slightboned and nervous as bird wings) shuffled and dealt and caressed the cards he might have been in another time and place and costume a caricature, a typecast actor playing the image of an oldtime Mississippi riverboat gambler; and facing him the younger man, he himself like a playing card man, something dealt out from the same deck, all angles, some of the hard crudely whittled quality of his father's bloodline etched into his face, a face that might have passed for the mask of bitter endurance (like the newsman's) at a first glance, at a second might just as likely have been read as veneer, lacquer, protective armor of coloration of a deeply troubled boy-man, he in a sweatsoaked summer suit and hatless, his largeboned, square-fingered hands uneasy with the thin cards; the one, the older one, having seen too much and learned enough so as not to be likely to be wounded again any more than a skeleton hanging on a hook in the classroom can suffer; the other, the younger, still seeing and learning, still able and likely to suffer and to make other people suffer, skipping from folly to folly with as yet, though perilous, no more than stubbed toes and cracked shins to show for it, wincing from wounds real and imaginary, and beginning the long, slow painful process of being able to distinguish the one kind from the other.

Above them prisoners stirred in their tight cells or slept. Above them the young Negro waiting to die sat on his laced canvas cot and dangled his feet and smoked, all alone with himself. Between them and the world in darkness outside, at the raised desk the Turnkey sat and read his comic book.

The light glared off the bare whitewashed walls, the disinfected, rugless, cold stone floor. And they could still smell the Dump out there where the waste and rubbish of the town was taken in isolation to be converted, transformed into simple ash. It probably took some getting used to.

They played with the limp cards, passed the pint bottle back and forth from time to time. And they talked. Loosened, abstracted, alone, like two men marooned on a desert island, two men in the heart of a cave, they talked to each other and at moments like one man, hermit or prisoner, in a cell alone talking to himself.

* * *

Atkins: You think I'm a hard old bastard, I guess. Hard? That's nonsense. What am I supposed to do? Weep for the boy upstairs because he lost his head and murdered a man? Weep for poor old, fat old Joe Beardsley because he happened to step right in the line of fire at the wrong time? Or the history teacher, or your daddy, or poor old Allen Parker fumbling around in his hotel like a blind old ghost sucking wind? For every manjack of of them? My ass, boy! My aching ass! Pity is one thing. Pity and compassion, even sometimes understanding, I can offer. But by God I'm not interested in sentiment. I'm not planning to put myself in anybody else's shoes. Mine don't fit too good either and one fine day some unlucky undertaker is going to have to clip my cruddy toenails just like everybody else's. Ever notice how a dead man's feet are the most comical, pitiful thing about him? When it comes to sentiment I've had a belly full. All I care about is the brute plain naked present fact.

Mike: Which proves my point. You call yourself simplified. You're cut off. You've amputated history, imagination, feelings, responsibility, even charity, just to say that you're simplified. All you are is *reduced*. A pair of eyes and ears, an ugly broken nose, five senses and they're getting a little older and vaguer and a little less reliable every day for you . . .

Atkins: . . . and don't you forget what goes with the receiving instruments—a roller of good graph paper (memory), a little needle, a lot of finely adjusted busy humming tubes and machinery that goes clickety-clack . . .

Mike: . . . and is always breaking down and making mistakes and going crazy just the same as the mind that hasn't got a particle of all that machinery in it, that's just a hollow cave full of voices.

Atkins: Wait a minute! I was talking about brute plain naked present fact. And here you are bringing in imagination, history, feelings, voices, etc. Let's take one—imagination. Corruption! The imagination must be the most corrupt and corruptible thing under the sun, unless you want to include the human heart—and they're siamese twins anyway. The difference, one of the differences, between you and me is you have to *create* your own bestiary of facts and then believe in them. An act of faith. Faith and corruption!

Mike: Didn't Adam . . . ?

Atkins: . . . Named them. Didn't make them.

Mike: You're acting on faith too. You have to act as if the thing you see, the thing you've got a grip on, the thing you're wrestling with like Jacob's angel, the thing you call a brute fact is really and truly there.

Atkins: You kick a stone to see if it's really there and you'll bust your foot to chalk. Take your man Parker. Take Imagination and History together. Take the story he must have told you by this time (He even told me, a *newspaper* man for God's sake, years and years ago) about the time he killed four men who came to his house to kill him. Let me give you a historical fact, buddy-buddy. It never happened. *It didn't happen to him.* Something a little like it *did* happen in the very same county just before Allen Parker was born. Not to him. He wasn't alive yet, let alone running for public office. Man tried to defend himself from some hired killers and was shot down on the front steps of his own house. Now, along into this world comes Allen Parker and for some reason this story means something to him, fascinates him. (Maybe that man who was running— as it happens for County Sheriff—maybe he was Parker's real daddy. Who knows? Maybe Parker thinks there's a fine chance that the man *might* have been his daddy. Maybe Parker's crazy old bitter mother told him so.) Anyway, he gradually takes it over, appropriates it while he's still a little boy, turns his imagination loose on history and away it goes like a runaway horse. He converts it. And now when he's all tired out to the bone or sick or drunk out of his mind, he dreams about it and wakes up believing it and he might just as well have done it.

Mike: Well, God knows there's enough violence around here to make that sense of guilt real enough.

Atkins: Violence? Let's be honest, please. We've just witnessed a real dose of it and it may not be over and done with yet. Violence is a fact. It happens every day everywhere under the sun. What about the violence of cities, the whole redeyed, anonymous, faceless mass of clenched fists and bared teeth from Portland, Maine, all the way South as far as Norfolk? We've got our own brand here. Our violence, our heritage of violent action, is just the ghost of the rural age we lived in so long. Death pangs! But don't you ever forget that all of us, here and elsewhere, ain't nothing but hairy cavemen dressed up in clothes. Oh, we get refined with time. We have long since learned to torture, kill, maim with a word, a look, a raised eyebrow or even a kiss. We live on the violence we do each other the way moss feeds on air. (Sometimes I think that one of the things that was in the breath that God breathed into Adam's dust was an element of pure, terrible, godlike violence.) But let's try and be honest. Let's don't heap up *imaginary* corpses too.

Mike: Which only goes to prove my point in a backhanded way. Parker's guilt, real or imaginary, is as natural as the air he breathes. It's given. It doesn't make any difference whether he really did it or not.

Atkins: That's nothing but luxury, man, letting yourself go around shivering with guilt and feeling bad about a lot of things—*not things undone*—but things you didn't do.

Mike: Who looks at a woman with lust in his eye, who kills his brother in his heart . . .

Atkins: . . . True! Nothing truer. We are all guilty. We are all monsters. But godamn it, that don't mean let's start *acting* like monsters, admit it and join hands and dance the monster dance together. I say like the law, man's law, I say sure as we're all guilty and hell-bound (If there isn't a brute fact of hell there ought to be.) and bound to be judged, hangman and magistrate and turnkey, right alongside and unsegregated from your rapist, your arsonist, your Jack-the-ripper, I say with the law that meanwhile until that Judgment Day I'm interested in doings, not imaginings. Lord knows, the doings, the things really done and undone, are bad enough. If there wasn't a brute fact of God, we'd have to make one just because we've got to have Somebody who's *entitled* to weep for all of us.

Mike: There's another side to it. The doings are bad enough, you say. Well then, how else and where else can the world, the dirty world, be scrubbed clean, purified, renewed, except in the human heart? The heart's that nigger washerwoman that you secretly long to be. Where are those wonderful stacks of clean laundry? You can't do a thing with your brute facts. You can't do anything with those stones that bust your foot except to stop going around kicking them. In the right kind of a dream, with a good imagination, I can kick boulders like footballs.

Atkins: Yet I say to you, I insist that that same heart, imagination, call it what you want to (We haven't got a name for it. Too bad Adam didn't think to give names to the parts of himself.), that heart is much more likely in my limited experience to corrupt utterly than it is to purify. If you call it purification, it's giving that name to an action like that stinking Dump out there. Acres of ashes. Everything turned into ashes. Just more corruption.

Mike: And I say that Dump out there is where all *your* so-called Brute Facts end up anyway. They all turn into ashes, pure and simple.

Atkins: *Your* History. Take Pompeii. There's a pile of ashes for you. What's underneath? They got down to the bottom and discovered the amazing fact that people ate and and slept and excreted and kept pets and had dirty pictures on the whorehouse walls.

Mike: That Dump out there is the best garden you people will ever be able to make out of your world.

Atkins: My ass! My aching ass! That there is a dump. A garden is something you got to plant and cultivate and weed and sweat over and even pray over. A garden is a garden and a dump is . . .

Mike: . . . Let me ask you one thing. You know the parable of the four sowers?

Atkins: All right. Maybe I am the seed that falls among the thorns. Whoever said it was anything except thorns? Truth is thorny. When Truth came down and walked among us they gave Truth a crown of thorns. It was the right kind of a crown. Let me ask you one while we're at it. You remember the parable of the good Samaritan?

Mike: And who, Lord, *is* my neighbor? I guess every lawyer knows that one. The Last Word on the legal profession.

Atkins: Right you are. But which one are you in the story?—Don't interrupt me!—You people, you imaginary people swimming along in your imaginary stream, floating on it or drowning in it, you identify yourselves every time either with the hypocrites who went rolling by the man in the ditch. (And you feel pretty bad about having to leave him there.) Or, if you're in the right kind of a mood to fox yourselves and get all the grapes, you may just identify yourself with the good old good Samaritan. Point is both ways are wrong. The point is you're missing the point. The one you're *supposed* to recognize and identify with is the poor beat-up naked bastard lying in the ditch. That's who we are. That's the poor nigger history teacher. He is a plain brute naked fact. You can't make him up or wish him away. He's hurting. He's there.

Mike: A point for you. But you pragmatists fail . . .

Atkins: I ain't no pragmatist. No teacup philosopher with white hair. I'm just simply what I have to call a realist.

Mike: That must make me a *romantic* then.

Atkins: Don't like the word a damn bit. Never did. But it will have to do.

Mike: Let it do. The thing is what are we going to do?

Atkins: You must mean you. I know what I'm up to. I'm just sweating out a story. Whatever happens, in the morning I'll write it up and move on to the next one which will probably be a description of Allen Parker losing the election.

Mike: And what about this one? What are you going to make out of it?

Atkins: Now that's a good way to put it. I make the claim to be passionately concerned with the fact. But when it comes to making a *story* out of it, to making *news* out of it, I have to play on the Nero-fiddle of imagination as much as the next man.

Mike: What good's your knowledge, such as it is, if you can't tell anybody about it? Here you are, making your living, sweating and earning your bread by collecting and communicating to people what ought to be not much more than the pared down brute facts . . .

Atkins: . . . Ah! There you are. If I told, if I wrote down things the way they really are I'd be out of a job. Who would believe me? And what purpose would it serve anyway?

Mike: I'm afraid I don't follow you now.

Atkins: Give me half a chance without interrupting and I'll show you. The trouble begins with people, the people who read the papers. They aren't interested in naked facts. They just want more fuel for the imagination, grist for the mill, mash for the still. More confirmation of their own hopeful guesses. They are not interested in causes or motives or even, truly, in results. Just give us the action, buddy, and we'll do the rest.

Mike: And rightly so. And you, if you're being true to yourself, shouldn't be mucking up news with causes and motives and results either.

Atkins: Wrong! That's where you're dead wrong. A cause or a motive is as much a fact as anything else. Action without it is nothing but gibberish, news in Swahili and Urdu, meaningless jive. Results are the same. Let me offer you one example from old Atkins' interior index card file. A little parable, if you will. This Lieutenant Rogers of the Police Department. He came tearing in there right in the middle of that crowd today with his gun waving and his whistle blowing and he saved a boy's life. It was a brave thing to do. I mean a mob's reflexive reaction, and a mob not created by slow attrition, but by a moment of terrible action, turned from a group of passive listeners and onlookers into a mob, it's a dangerous thing. One mistake, say if Rogers had slipped or fallen or if he had pulled the trigger instead of using his pistol like it was a knife or a club or a baton, he might have been killed right along with the boy he was trying to get out of there in one piece. Am I right or wrong?

Mike: I'd say it was brave. And he didn't have time to weigh results or to think about anything. He just reacted and did what he had to do. I have to admire him for it.

Atkins: Right. He just *did*. But *why* did he do it and *how* did he manage to get away with it?

Mike: That belongs to the realm of the imagination if anything could . . .

Atkins: . . . No, no, no. Scratch a little deeper. There are some facts that shouldn't be ignored. They help to explain some raggedy odds and ends like why he insists on keeping that boy here tonight instead of getting him out of the county where he could be sure to be safe and stand trial and die legally. Not the whole story, but some of it. Did you notice the man at all? Did you pay attention to him? A perfect fitting, clean and creased, tailored uniform, boots and belts spitshined. Must have taken hours to get them that way. Rogers is, as it happens, an ex-Marine. Which doesn't—God and Harry Truman know—classify him one way or the other. But let's say it kind of went to his head. He's imperial. Gung-ho. A martinet. But besides that this Lieutenant Rogers happens to be a sadist and a misanthrope combined. I guess that's the best way to describe it, two different terms out of two different groping, rudimentary, pseudo-scientific ways of describing the factual mysteries of a man's mind. Sadist? Well, cruel as can be anyway. He beat one prisoner to death right here in this jailhouse a few years ago. They couldn't prove a thing on him. And I got a good idea that he works them over now whenever he has a mind to—beatings, castor oil, a little fire, etc. He likes to call little boys over to his police-car, little niggerhicks and whitetrash that are too lowly to be able to do anything about it. When they poke their heads through the window, he'll roll it up quick. And while they're scared half out of their wits, choking and blue in the face and bugeyed, he can pinch and pick their noses and pull on their ears and their hair and and make believe he's going to burn them with cigarettes. *Ad nauseum. Ad infinitum.* No real harm. Just a little fun.

Mike: What you're trying to say is that the fact of heroism . . .

Atkins: . . . No! I'm not saying anything about the facts of heroism or bravery or courage in general. Just merely giving some of the little half-facts that shroud this single action. My mind doesn't work in big general rules like that except to tell me that things aren't always what they seem.

Mike: Okay, go on.

Atkins: Oh, I won't go deep into it, not into *your* area of speculation. I'll just say this. For a number of reasons Lieutenant Rogers hates his fellow man. He is entirely contemptuous of his fellow man and godamns his eyes. Does he care about the nigger? Hell no! If anything weakness brings out his contempt more. Proves his point to himself. Like the cartoon says, "People are no damn good." Does he really care about his Duty? His past record wouldn't prove it, unless you call being the best *dressed* policeman doing your duty. Well, what does he care about? About showing mankind, people in general, what a bunch of damn contemptible puny fools they are and how inordinately superior he is. He sees a man down, attacked by a mob. He doesn't think; he doesn't have to. He charges right in there. That mob is his private dragon. So he does the brave thing and the right thing. It looks to be bravery, heroism, duty or whatever you want to call it. Now, let's just suppose I wrote up this Rogers from A to Zed, told as much as I know about his past and built a fairly tight case to show that his actions were about as meaningful as when the bell rings and one of Pavlov's dogs starts to drool; that his actions are motivated by an unspeakable self-esteem and by the earnest desire to insult and frustrate and humiliate the greatest number of people he can in one lifetime? Who would care? Who would want to know?

Mike: So how are you going to write it up?

Atkins: The action, buddy, just the action. I'll show him for a hero and so will all the other papers and he may even get his picture in *Time* or *Life* or somewhere. And in the end he may be so pleased with this image of himself that he'll start to live up to it. He might even make a fine Police Chief one of these days, if he can imagine himself right into the job.

Mike: My father always used to say that a shyster lawyer often makes a pretty good judge.

Atkins: Let's get off the subject. When you get to examining the facts of Virtue, it makes you want to puke. I can stand poking around with the vices. What always turns my stomach is when I find out a virtue is just a vice in disguise.

Mike: All right, your point of view is pretty clear. But what I'd like to know is how you ever expect to get any joy out of your life?

Atkins: Joy? Oh, sonny boy, my aching ass! Joy is for you

folks, the joyriders. I ain't looking for it. Joy is something for the birds, I mean literally, and the fish and the trees and the stones. Let's try another human word —*happy*. I can be happy once in a while. I've had such a steady diet of poison in my time that it even tastes good to me once in a while. Sometimes I actually start to like it. That's when I start to worry. Puts me in mind of a friend of mine. Had some kind of trouble with his prostate gland. Had to go to the doctor once a day and get it massaged. Very painful and disagreeable. But he bore up. Took it like a man. Then one day I ran into him on the street. He was white-faced and trembling all over, wild-eyed.—What's wrong with you, I said.—Atkins, he said, I'm starting to like it. *I'm starting to like it!*

Mike: That's fine. That's well and good for your humor and your pose. But I'm living in a different world . . .

Atkins: . . . And in just five minutes you'll be working around to ask me what I would do if I was living in your world.

Mike: I might. I might be working around to something like that.

Atkins: Then we'd be right back where we started, wouldn't we, with the shoes that don't fit?

Mike: Just about.

Atkins: Deal the cards, boy. I ain't your daddy.

* * *

A little before midnight the curious vigil, the lazy card game and wandering talk ended abruptly.

Loud noises, the slamming of the front door, then the sound of shouts and scuffling roused them from their thoughts and lethargy. They dumped over the chairs, cards scattering across the floor, and ran down the hall toward the main entrance.

There stood Lieutenant Rogers in front of the raised desk with four dishevelled, handcuffed prisoners. One of them was the one-armed man McWhirter. Strangely, standing side by side, the two men, Rogers and McWhirter, looked much alike. They were big, powerful, bulky men, of the same height and size, brute sensual faces brooding like the busts of certain Roman emperors. But McWhirter with a hook for a left arm and with rage and frustration kindling his cheeks and eyes was a grotesque, distorted mirror image of the still immaculate policeman with his close-cropped cannonball of a head and his face entirely ruled by one bright smile of triumph. By the time Mike and Atkins got there whatever the yelling and scuffling had been about was all over. The four prisoners were lined up in a straight row meekly before the desk. One of them, a boy really, held a bloody handkerchief to his nose.

"What's the charge?" Atkins asked McWhirter.

"Dog if I know. Ask *him*."

"Disturbing the peace. Inciting to riot with a clear and present danger. Resisting an officer of the law," Rogers said. "By tomorrow it's just liable to be kidnapping and first degree murder. They're flying some FBI men down."

"Sheriff ain't going to appreciate this worth a damn," McWhirter said.

"Sheriff's home, sound asleep in bed," Rogers said. "By the time he knows anything about this, you all will be done through breakfast, such as it is, and scratching the bug bites. Lock 'em up."

The wizened Turnkey finished filling out a yellow form, stuck it in a wire box stacked with similar forms, and opened a drawer. He produced a heavy ring of keys.

"Follow me," he said. "And walk quiet. Everybody's asleep up there."

"*Everybody?*" Rogers said.

"Yeah. Your boy's been sleeping like a lamb since about nine or nine-thirty."

"Don't that beat all," Rogers said.

McWhirter kept looking at Mike.

"I knew I knew you from somewhere," he said. "You go and tell that Senator of yours to get out of bed and get us out of here."

"He wouldn't lift a finger for you now."

McWhirter hawked and spat on the floor, and the four men

sullenly followed the Turnkey down the hall. Rogers walked behind them. They could hear all of them going up the stairwell one at a time.

After a while Rogers came back. He took off his hat and put his pistol belt on the desk. He lit a cigarette, looked at the Turnkey's comic book, crumbled it up and threw it in the wastebasket.

"Think you can make it stick?" Atkins said.

"Doubt it," Rogers said. "There aren't any witnesses and the Sheriff, he's one of them Klan boys. I doubt the government men will turn up much."

"How did you get them?"

Rogers smiled. "Well," he said, "it didn't take much figuring to know this bunch would be getting together somewhere after dark. The thing was to locate them. So I cruised around the places and finally got hold of them in the back of this garage out on 17."

"Have any trouble?"

He held up one arm. The shirtsleeve flapped loose from the shoulder down.

"This McWhirter took a swipe with his hook and near about nailed me. So I grabbed him and the first three guys I could get cuffs on and hurtled them out. There won't be no trouble now. The town is crawling with State Troopers and I got these four by the short hair."

"What you going to do next?"

"Reckon I'll sit up just to be sure," he said. "Tomorrow's election day and I'll run the nigger over to Orange County."

"What about you?"

"I ain't scared, if that's what you mean. Not of *them*. I wish they would try and tangle with me."

"It's a pretty big day for you."

"How's that?"

"I mean a whole lot has happened around here."

"You might say so."

"How do you feel about it all? About what you've done?"

"Mister, are you asking all these questions for real? For the papers?"

"That's right."

Lieutenant Rogers grinned like a boy and ran his hand over his hair.

"You tell 'em I said it was easy," he said. "It was easy, that's all."

Atkins walked outside with Mike. They stood in front of the jail in the dark smelling the foul odor of the Dump. Up in one of the cells on the second floor someone cried out in his sleep.

"Ride me downtown with you," Atkins said. "I might just as well send in a story before I lose my job."

The town asleep with no lights burning now except the lonesome streetlights looked peaceful and calm. You could imagine, Mike thought, that behind all those front doors and facades, behind those windows there was only tranquil sleeping and dreaming. If you were a perfect stranger driving through the town at that moment nothing could have suggested to you the reality of sensational violence that had erupted and bathed the town like a dirty fountain that day. You would just imagine them all sleeping and dreaming, and if you had a curious or bitter frame of mind you might be thinking a little of the sad and sordid dreamworld they rooted in like pigs, like the old widow woman with her red wagon and her stick at the Dump hunting for something, searching for something that must be there after all. But you could hardly even dream up the brute fact of the blood that had been spilled that day.

They drew near the lighted Telephone Office.

"I'll get out here," Atkins said.

Mike stopped the car.

"How do you get along without a car?"

Atkins laughed. "I can always get a ride."

He got out and started across the street toward the patch of light. Halfway across he turned around and came back, leaned on the front window.

"Enjoyed talking to you," he said. "Don't take me *too* serious, though. If I really believed everything I said, I reckon I'd cut my throat and go out with a double barrel grin.

"Just one more thing," he went on. "When I took that boy a pack of cigarettes he asked me for one more thing."

"What was that?"

"He wanted to know the name of a good lawyer. You're a lawyer ain't you?"

"I used to be."

"Think it over."

Atkins touched the brim of his hat in salute and turned away toward the lights of the office and the business of his story.

* * *

At the hotel Mike couldn't locate either Senator Parker or Vivian Blanch. The volunteer switchboard operator in the lobby headquarters was very upset.

"All kinds of people, the Governor and everybody, have been trying to get in touch with the Senator and I can't tell them a thing."

"Don't worry about it," Mike said. "I'm sure everything's all right. He just slipped off somewhere to get a good night's rest."

* * *

He must have tried a dozen or more motels along the highway before he came to the Wigwam Motel. As soon as he saw it he knew it would be the place and he would find them there. Of all the motels around Oakland, curious self-contained gardens of delight designed to meet the needs of shadowy transients who came by dark and left at dawn, the Wigwam was the most unusual. It was a circle of enormous steel and concrete "teepees," very authentic in appearance, painted in a gaudy camouflage to look as if they were made of hides and blankets, and built around a continually glowing artificial campfire, a whole cord of wood decoratively stacked and lit by red light bulbs variously concealed and interspersed. Everything had been scaled as if for a world of giants, the huge teepees, the enormous campfire, and it was with a shock like Gulliver's that you noticed the tiny doorways to the teepees weren't designed for the convenience of pets or pigmy creatures, but big enough for a man. There were animals, elk, moose, wolves and buffalo, in stone and bronze, grazing on the crisp turf. Well behind the motel, he remembered, there was a kind of little zoo, wire fence enclosures for alligators, armadillos and a few small white-tailed deer, mangy- and sad-looking, who stared with wide wet luminous eyes from their shitstrewn arena. (The "teepees" were windowless. Sealed up and air-conditioned, they were secure against the noise of the night highway or the odors of animals.)

Jojo had always admired the place.—If I *had* to live in Oakland, he used to say, it would have to be there. It's got the *Tahiti* beat to hell.

And, of course, it would have been Vivian Blanch who would be doing the picking and choosing tonight, with the ruined Senator no more than a staggering zombie on her arm. Doubtless, she would have been charmed by the absurdity of this place.

The office was identical with the other teepees except for a lurid neon sign over the door that kept blinking a bloodred *No Vacancy* and an antique cigarstore Indian, freshly painted, who stood guard. Mike rang a doorbell that played some kind of a tune ("Indian Love Call?") on chimes inside until finally a short, squat, redeyed, baldheaded, gimpy man came to the door. He was wearing a woman's pink dressing gown with a limp, frayed fur collar. He was furious. Couldn't Mike read? There wasn't no vacancies, and no he couldn't have a look at the register. But—mirabilis!—money, wampum, key universal to gates and gardens and bedrooms and temples and tombs, magic potion for shrinking or growing to gigantic proportion, for thinning and fattening, for beauty or youth in the eye of the beholder, sweetened his disposition, transformed his suspicious middle-of-the-night glare into a slight, sly, conspiratorial smile. There in Cabin #9 were "Robert and Elizabeth B. Browning/69 Fur St./Elbow, Illinois." And there, of course, was nobody else's extravagant feminine calligraphy but Vivian's. A little more sweetening and a vague allusion to the FBI permitted Mike Royle to disturb the slumber of the guests in Cabin #9.

"I was sound asleep all night long," the man in the dressing gown said.

Vivian greeted him, wrapped in a bath towel designed for giants, one finger to her lips to signal hush. He stepped inside the door and a blast of hot air struck him.

"The thermostat," she whispered, giggling. "We turned it all the way up."

"How come you picked this place?"

"He's part Indian, you know."

She turned on a small hooded table lamp by the door. In the dim light he could see the Senator crudely sprawled, naked as God made him, on the bed. Passed out cold. One limp arm was wide-flung, the hand touching the floor. A broken glass and a puddle of spilled whiskey lay just beyond his fingers' reach. He had been sick in his sleep. The pillow and the sheets on his side of the bed were vomit-stained. Sweat crawled along his body and he was breathing deeply. Perched on his head, absurd and small, was a child's feathered headdress, part of the conventional costume of an Indian chief.

"Where the hell did the feathers come from?"

"They give them to you," she said. "They're kind of cute. Allen wanted to buy a tomtom too, but they wouldn't let him."

"Vivian, do you have any idea how crazy this is?"

She bristled.

"He's finished, washed up, all through," she said. "What else was there to do with him? He'll be all right now."

"Sure, a good solid dose of oblivion is just what the doctor ordered. Why don't we get together around the campfire and join hands and sing songs and have a happy ending?"

"Don't you pity him even a little?"

"Not a damn bit."

"He was a great man, Mike. Doesn't it make you want to cry?"

"You've got it all wrong, doll. This isn't how a tragedy ends up—King Lear dead drunk, dreaming that he's a cave man."

"You said it before. You haven't got any heart. That's the whole trouble with you."

"If having a heart means sniffing out other people's weakness and going for it like a shark after blood, you can have it. You can have my share."

"What about *me*? Don't you feel anything at *all* about me?"

"I pity you," he said. "I'm really sorry for you. But that isn't what you want to hear."

Only when he was outside again and alone in the dark did he realize that *she* was cold sober. Her inebriation, like Eve's, like Circe's, was built in.

* * *

On the way home State Troopers stopped him twice. Their tan cars nuzzled forward lightless out of dark concealed places without a sound, forced him to the curb. A Trooper in a wide-brimmed hat, pistol drawn, came to the window and put a flashlight in his face while he identified himself. The Governor must have rushed them there as soon as the news of the incident reached him. Somebody besides the policeman Rogers hadn't been paralyzed, lamed into total inactivity.

He decided to park his car in the garage. As he turned in his headlights caught a clump of dark faces and bodies and white eyes, like a piece of group sculpture, crouched and shrinking into a corner of the garage. He opened the door and jumped out. From the corner, in the lights Jay rose from his hunched position and walked toward him.

"What's the trouble, Jay?"

"We thought it would be safer here."

Mike saw that Jay had a pistol jammed into his belt.

"Why didn't you go on inside the house?"

Jay shrugged. A shrug like that was worse than a blow by a fist.

"All right," Mike said. "I'll take you on home now. There isn't going to be any trouble. It's all over now. For the time being anyway."

Jay and his wife and their two small dazed sleepy sons came and got in the back seat. Charity led her blind granddaughter and they climbed in the front seat beside him. (How very seldom he had driven with a Negro in the front seat!) No one said a word. He backed the car out of the garage and drove slowly across town toward Black Bottom.

He was stopped once again by the State Troopers.

"It's all right officer," he said. "I'm just taking these people home."

The lights were all out in Black Bottom too. But in those low flat acres of mostly unpainted shacks interlaced with narrow dirt roads and rutted trails he sensed that there was little sleeping or dreaming. Dogs barked. He could feel that the late lights of his car stirred restless bodies in the darkness of the rooms, brought anxious faces to the shaded windows, tightened fingers around whatever weapons were handy, placed the mother's body between the flesh of the child and the world outside.

And what could be said? Whatever his feelings were or would be he was wearing the uniform, the coloring of the enemy, by birth. It was like coming under a flag of truce into the enemy camp. The hush around him was tense and alien and hostile. He might even have been afraid or angry if he hadn't been so ashamed.

* * *

There was a letter from Jojo waiting for him in his bedroom.

"I think I've found what I've been looking for," Jojo wrote. "It seems like a good deal. A little risky, but, then, I've always been bluffing when it comes to taking chances. What I mean is I'm not risking much if I'm just risking *myself*.

"I can't tell you much about it. The job will take me South of the Border. If you don't hear a word from me or read anything in the papers by Christmas, please go up to the *Tahiti* and collect my different things. (Every time I move on from one place to another I always end up leaving a little trail of stuff behind me.) The rent is paid up through the year, so it's okay.

"There isn't much. Some books and records. A damn fine collection of pornography. You'll laugh at this, but the thing I'm really worried about is my poems. You didn't know I wrote poems, did you? Well, anyway, they're in the second bureau drawer underneath some underwear.

"Take care of everything, will you, Mike? You're the only one left to do it. And don't worry. If all goes well I'll pull up in front of the house one of these days with a brand new Rolls Royce (Loudest noise is the godamn clock. It keeps ticking all the time.) with a built-in redhead."

"Don't tell anybody else about this.

"Love to Everybody. And Love Everybody. I hope you can

still be wild and crazy and beautiful by the time you're my age."

Mike lay on the bed and looked at the ceiling. He halfway wished that the cockroach would come and crawl across the plaster. As it was the ceiling was blank and bare and still as a polar wasteland.

* * * * * * *

Dawn came with a fine, driving rain. It had turned cooler and the sky was shaggy and low, wind-whipped. Mike looked out of his window at the thrashing oak leaves, darker and richer for being wet. The gray moss was like the beards of drowned patriarchs. The clipped grass was flooded.

Out in the country the roads would be turning into paste. That was going to cut to pieces even Parker's dim, elusive hope that the country people would rally behind his name, would rise up and come from the woods and farms and ranches, the sawmills and turpentine camps and crossroads places, trudging along the shoulders of the roads, riding in beatup clay-spattered cars and pickup trucks and horse- and mule-drawn highwheeled wagons once more, one more time in his favor, swarming, like an endless line of refugees, like the irrational migration of a secret and barbaric people. If he had allowed himself any hopes at all during the past few weeks (And which of us, Mike thought, isn't fallible enough to be lured to the bitter end by dreams and mirages?), any sort of logic stringing together his turns and counterturns, alliances and betrayals, that single image must have been it—a dream of a sunny election day dominated by interminable dusty lines of these people, the mythical enduring yeoman backbone and viscera, heart and guts, of the South, coming steadily on in tides to the public buildings where flags were flying, shivering and flapping in a light breeze, and remembering him as one of their own who had come through and done some service, pulling the lever in the hardwon, brief curtained privacy of the polling booth, his name being recorded again and again until he would be carried along by the sheer momentum of their accumulated will-power and faith, swept floating on a tidal wave of applause and approval to become again, harbored among the tranquil white neo-classical stones of the capital, the articulate voice of his region, the right representative of his place and time.

It was a false, drunken hope for the middle of this century. Most of the people he imagined were ghosts. Even their children and grandchildren weren't of the land anymore. Our country towns were withering away as the great cities grew. These, the yeomen he believed in, had vanished, consigned now to museums and history books (already in leather in Anthony Singletree's day). And the nation, and of it this State, swarmed with the movements of a new and restless people, rootless and possessed anyway by different follies than the old. He was just as likely to wake this morning and discover that he had been made an Indian chief, Chief of the Sioux Nation, by virtue of his dime-store headdress, as he was to witness himself being re-elected to the United States Senate.

Still, he was all too human. He was very likely to be stricken to the quick when he woke to a day of gray driving rain.

And you could say this about John Batten. He was new and young. At least he was young enough to have youth's shine of possibility around him like a magic cloak, though already it must have seemed to him a mocking luster like the remnants of original fire that haunted the fallen angels.

* * *

Mike got in the car and drove away without breakfast. He drove out of town, North and West, along the highway without any thoughts of where he might be going, driving fast, watching the smooth, rain-glossed black ribbon of asphalt succumb to the glory of his speed, staring through the *swish-swish* of the windshield wipers swinging back and forth across the wet glass with a steady metronomic rhythm. Soon he was in the open country and saw vacant fields, farmhouses. They would all be huddling inside today, probably in the kitchen close to the stove.

He drove with a kind of fury, seventy, eighty miles an hour on the rainslick lonely highways, leaving the roadside farms, the crossroads with stores and filling stations, the brief towns whose trees were soaked and shiny with rain, in a swift glazed blur behind him. Finally he turned off the paved roads altogether, drove on muddy, rutted trails into the silent heart of the country. Now there were a few ranches, an occasional poor farm, a country church with its little plot of cemetery alongside, and once he passed by a clearing where there was a ruined sawmill, the shed fallen, its great, circular, toothed blade broken, rusty, warped.

And then he came to the place and came to himself and knew where he had come and why he had come there. It was a lopsided paintless shack, a crude brick chimney leaning and falling away from it, a sagging porch, a rusty pump without a handle, the trunk of a dead tree. He parked the car by the ditch and looked at the place for a while through the rolled-up window.

So he had come here. It occurred to him then that he hadn't, not since the funeral, been back to the cemetery to look at his father's grave. Had they really filled it in and packed the earth tight and smooth with their shovels and sodded it and carpeted it with fresh green grass? Was there a headstone and what did it say? Who would there be to go there now, with Jojo off to another misguided adventure, a "risky" one, and Mary Ann soon to be off to search for herself among the fountains and the old stones of Rome? Nancy Royle would go there from time to time with offerings of fresh-cut flowers. It was right that he should be the one to come *here*.

He climbed out of the car and shut the door behind him. He turned up his collar and struggled up the mud-slippery bank of the ditch, picked his way through running rivulets and soft mud to the front of the house. He stood outside a moment listening to the rain patter on the rusty roof. He could see clear through the doorless frame in back, through the shack and across the whole length of weed-thick field and beyond that to the edge of the woods, the pine trees and then the pine giving way to the cypress of lower ground.

Then he went inside.

It might have been a sound, the least subtle creak of an old board or just the sense of the slightest movement, or it might have been the odor, a sickly smell or just the sense of an alien warmth in the room, but he knew as soon as he was inside that someone, not just an animal, but a human animal, was in there with him. He turned his head slowly to look in a dark corner of the room, and as his head moved he heard just a little flick, then saw the glint of a switchblade in the shadow. A man rose out of that shadow, bent over, crouched.

He was foul and filthy and bearded. He wore the ragged khaki remains of the uniform of a prisoner from the State Road Camp. He might have been young or old, black or white. He rose from the shadowy corner in a bent crouch and eased forward with the knife held sidearm slightly in front of him. He made a sound like the low growl of a dog guarding a bone, and he lunged.

Mike jumped, sidestepping, and both of them whirled, reversed now with Mike's back to the dark corner. He thought he could see against the matted beard, the filthy face, black or white, the grin of bared teeth. He came at him again and this time Mike went for the arm that held the knife, stepped aside, grabbed for it just above the wrist, caught it and wrestled the man to the floor. Over and over they rolled, wrestling, the rain from the holes in the roof falling on them. Mike was too strong for him; *that* was a quick flare of pure joy, but the man was weak from hunger or fear or fatigue or all. Once Mike had made him drop the knife free, he kicked and pushed himself to his feet and snatched the knife off the floor. The man gave up then, knelt on the floor with his head bowed, panting.

"Get up."

He got up and looked at Mike and waited. He was a small, sick, tired man. His eyes were white with fear. He smelled of sweat and excrement. They stood and looked at each other. The man rubbed his eyes with the back of his sleeve as if he could wipe them away.

"What are you going to do with me now?"

"Nothing," Mike said. "Nothing at all. I'm ready to call it quits."

He dropped the knife to the floor and turned his back on the man's whine and walked back to his car. He got in and started it, doodlebugged with wheels spinning in the mud to turn it around, and headed back the way he had come.

* * *

A few miles down the road he came on a posse from the State Road Camp working the woods with trusties and bloodhounds. The hats, raincapes and rifles of the guards glistened. He waved at them and drove right by.

* * * * * * *

He ate supper at home with his mother and Mary Ann. He took a long, leisurely hot shower, shaved, changed his clothes and came down into the dining room to have supper with them by candlelight. If either of them were aware of the world beyond the confines of the driveway and the sheltering oaks, they made no mention of it. The major problem considered was whether or not the dining room table was too big for them these days.

"I really think I'll have to get the centerpiece out," Nancy Royle concluded. "Otherwise it's going to be just too lonely for words around here."

Charity served them coffee in the living room. Mary Ann began to talk excitedly about her trip to Rome. She had collected books and folders and maps and she spread them out on the floor and lay prone among them pointing out this and that famous and storied place that she would soon be seeing. She was eager and animated, but there was nothing of the little girl about her any more. She seemed, which was closer to the truth, like a schoolteacher on the verge of the holidays.

"I envy you," he said. "You'll have a fine time."

"Why don't you come too?"

"I'd like to," he said. "But in a way I've already had my vacation. I'm going to have to go to work one of these days."

"But Rome, Mike, it's Rome. What kind of things can keep you *here*?"

He smiled at her and looked at his watch.

"We have an election today among other things."

She looked startled.

"Isn't that strange," she said. "Do you know I'd forgotten all about that. I seem to have forgotten about everything."

* * *

The hotel lobby masquerading as a campaign headquarters was forlorn. Smoke had settled in the room like a ground mist, veiling and muting the garish bunting and streamers and the gas balloons clustered at the ceiling, obscuring the smiling picture posters of the Senator, blurring them anyway so that the pictures looked out of focus. A grayhaired lady, precarious on a stepladder, was patiently recording the news of Parker's defeat, county by county, on the blackboard as the phones rang one after the other and together in improbably swift, furious succession, bearing their bad news with the alacrity of Job's messengers. At the bar there was a little group of men, weary remnants of the band of captains he had last seen gathered together in Miami. Some of the wives were in evening dresses, looking just now sadly overdressed for the occasion. One of the men was amusing the others around the bar by trying to shinny up a pillar and pop balloons.

Senator Parker wasn't there. Mike stopped to ask the switchboard operator.

"Has the Senator been around?"

"He was in here just before supper," she said. "He wasn't feeling very well."

"Miss Blanch?"

"She checked out of the hotel this afternoon."

"For good?"

"She had all her luggage with her."

Mike stepped back to look at the blackboard. The chalked numbers were changing so fast they seemed to be dancing. The phones rang in fugal counterpoint.

"Put me a call through to John Batten," he said. "I'll be over at the bar."

"Well, well, look who's here for the finish."

Hunched over the bar, nursing a tall drink without benefit of ice cube or branch water to dilute its flavor or weaken its dark honey color, deeply suntanned beneath a bleached boater and looking not an ounce heavier than a mop handle, L. J. Benjamin had seen him coming across the room in the mirror. He turned around and shook hands with Mike.

"Criminal always comes back to the scene of the crime," Benjamin said.

"How was Havana?"

"Same as always. Poor man's Sodom and Gomorrah. And I feel like the poor old pillar of salt. You people sure made one big mess out of things."

"I'd say so. We made a mess."

"What are you fixing to do next?"

Across the room the switchboard operator was waving one hand wildly, calling his name, trying to catch his eye. He took a drink and watched her in the mirror.

"When you break something," Mike said, "somebody's got to stoop over and start to pick up the pieces. I'm fixing to start trying to clean up a little behind myself."

"That's better than nothing," Benjamin said. "A whole lot better than nothing at all."

He heard John Batten's voice and behind it the laughter and loud voices of a crowd and the sound of music playing.

"John, this is Mike Royle. I'm calling from Senator Parker to concede. Yes, that's right. Sure, go ahead and put a stenographer on and we'll make a statement out of it."

He heard the telephone bang against a table. He heard somebody start to yell and then the applause began. He stood listening to the music and applause and waiting for the stenographer to come to the phone.

EPILOGUE

EPILOGUE

WHEN the young man entered the hotel room, the Senator and his wife were having breakfast in bed. In their bathrobes, propped up by fat pillows, fresh from a good night's sleep, with the tray—a wheeled rectangle of white linen and plates masked with silver covers—between their twin beds they looked like a perfect advertisement of the happy middleaged couple on vacation. Sun streamed into the room from a bright rinsed sky. The curtains swayed with a light cool breeze.

"Well, you did all right by me," the Senator said. "I've just been reading the statement in the papers. I couldn't have done any better myself."

"And what are you going to do now, sir?"

"Me? Why, I guess I'll finish my breakfast and take a bath and call the barber to come up and give me a trim and a shave. I'll put on my good suit and a great big grin and go downstairs and show these folks what a Good Loser is supposed to look like."

"I didn't quite mean that."

"Well, you know how it is. It's a setback, but I'm not really through. There's a lot of life in the old bones yet, and there's always the Governor's mansion in Tallahassee."

"I've always loved that beautiful old house," the Senator's wife said, and the two men grinned at once.

"What about you? You've had a lot of good experience. You could probably have a career in politics."

"I'm afraid I'm not suited to it," the young man said. "I'll be around here for a while though. There are a lot of loose ends."

"Are you really going to defend that nigger when he stands trial?"

"If he wants me."

"A lot of people are going to misunderstand that. You'll make yourself a lot of enemies."

"I guess so."

"What would the Judge have said?"

"I'm not asking myself that question. I'll make a fair guess, though. Under the circumstances I expect he might approve."

When he left them he went down on the elevator and walked out of the lobby. Workmen were taking down the bunting and the balloons and stacking the picture posters face down. The mob of telephones was disconnected, silent as statues. The desk clerk was busy with his pigeonholes. The potted palms looked as sickly as ever, but, after all, they were still there.

He walked through the front door without looking back and stood on the sidewalk for a moment waiting until his eyes got used to the hard bright light.

Voices of the South

Hamilton Basso
  The View from Pompey's Head
Richard Bausch
  Real Presence
  Take Me Back
Robert Bausch
  On the Way Home
Doris Betts
  The Astronomer and Other Stories
  The Gentle Insurrection and Other Stories
Sheila Bosworth
  Almost Innocent
  Slow Poison
David Bottoms
  Easter Weekend
Erskine Caldwell
  Poor Fool
Fred Chappell
  The Gaudy Place
  The Inkling
  It Is Time, Lord
Kelly Cherry
  Augusta Played
Vicki Covington
  Bird of Paradise
Ellen Douglas
  A Family's Affairs
  A Lifetime Burning
  The Rock Cried Out
  Where the Dreams Cross
Percival Everett
  Cutting Lisa
  Suder
Peter Feibleman
  The Daughters of Necessity
  A Place Without Twilight
George Garrett
  An Evening Performance
  Do, Lord, Remember Me
  The Finished Man
Marianne Gingher
  Bobby Rex's Greatest Hit
Shirley Ann Grau
  The House on Coliseum Street
  The Keepers of the House
Barry Hannah
  The Tennis Handsome
Donald Hays
  The Dixie Association
William Humphrey
  Home from the Hill
  The Ordways
Mac Hyman
  No Time For Sergeants
Madison Jones
  A Cry of Absence
Nancy Lemann
  Lives of the Saints
  Sportsman's Paradise
Beverly Lowry
  Come Back, Lolly Ray
Willie Morris
  The Last of the Southern Girls
Louis D. Rubin, Jr.
  The Golden Weather
Evelyn Scott
  The Wave
Lee Smith
  The Last Day the Dogbushes Bloomed
Elizabeth Spencer
  The Salt Line
  This Crooked Way
  The Voice at the Back Door
Max Steele
  Debby
Walter Sullivan
  The Long, Long Love
Allen Tate
  The Fathers
Peter Taylor
  The Widows of Thornton
Robert Penn Warren
  Band of Angels
  Brother to Dragons
  World Enough and Time
Walter White
  Flight
James Wilcox
  North Gladiola
Joan Williams
  The Morning and the Evening
  The Wintering
Thomas Wolfe
  The Hills Beyond
  The Web and the Rock